Humphrey's Great-Great-Great Book of Stories

Betty G. Birney worked at Disneyland for many years, has written several children's television shows and is the author of over twenty-five books, including the bestselling *The World According to Humphrey*, which won the Richard and Judy Children's Book Club, *Friendship According to Humphrey*, *Trouble According to Humphrey*, *Surprises According to Humphrey* and *More Adventures According to Humphrey*. Her work has won many awards, including an Emmy and three Humanitas Prizes. She lives in America with her husband.

Humphrey's Great-Great-Great Book of Stories

Betty G. Birney

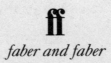

faber and faber

This omnibus first published by
Faber and Faber Limited in 2010
Bloomsbury House, 74–77 Great Russell Street,
London, WC1B 3DA

Typeset by Faber and Faber
Printed in England by CPI Bookmarque, Croydon

A CIP record for this book
is available from the British Library

ISBN 978–0–571–25594–8

2 4 6 8 10 9 7 5 3

Contents

'ö'

'ö'

Contents

👣

👣

Spring has Sprung

Monday mornings are different from other mornings.

That's just one of many things I've learned in the months I've lived in Room 26 of Longfellow School.

For one thing, on Mondays, I'm usually tired from a weekend spent visiting the home of one of my classmates. That's the BEST-BEST-BEST part of my job as classroom hamster.

My friends are also quieter than usual on Mondays. It takes them at least a half a day to get back up to speed after their weekends away from school.

Don't-Complain-Mandy Payne complains more than usual on Monday. Today she complained that it was too hot. Our teacher, Mrs Brisbane, opened a window.

Sit-Still-Seth Stevenson jitters in his seat more

on Monday mornings. But he tries to sit still – he really does.

And even Lower-Your-Voice-A.J., who can rattle the walls with his loud voice, is quieter on Monday mornings. It's weird.

Mrs Brisbane, however, is always up to speed, and she likes to get Monday mornings rolling with something interesting.

'Class, in case you hadn't noticed, spring has sprung!' Mrs Brisbane announced one Monday.

I don't know about the other students, but I'd certainly noticed that the March rains had stopped and everything had changed. The world, which had been drippy and dreary, was now bright green. The trees, the grass – just about everything outside – matched the colour of my goofy green neighbour, Og the Frog, who lives in a tank next to my cage.

For some reason, all that green made me feel like springing up onto my bridge ladder, which goes across my big cage.

Mrs Brisbane kept talking. 'And today, I have a special spring surprise for you!'

Surprise? Surprises are fun, like birthday presents. But surprises can be not-so-fun, like unexpected storms with LOUD-LOUD-LOUD thunder that can hurt the ears of small, sensitive creatures like me. Just thinking about thunder made me bobble, then wobble. I tried to catch my balance, but tumbled off my ladder with a loud 'Thump!' Luckily, I landed in a pile of soft bedding (and not in my poo corner), but still, I was very surprised and quite startled.

My neighbour Og was startled, too, I suppose, because he let out a large 'BOING!' which is the strange twanging sound that green frogs, like him, usually make.

'What's going on over here?' Mrs Brisbane walked towards the table by the window where Og and I live.

'Humphrey fell! I saw him!' a voice called out. Even though I couldn't see who was talking from underneath all that bedding, I knew it was Raise-Your-Hand-Heidi Hopper, because no matter how many times she'd been told, Heidi never remembered to raise her hand.

'Hands, please, Heidi,' Mrs Brisbane reminded her.

I poked my head out of the bedding and saw her looking down at me. 'Are you all right, Humphrey?'

'I'm not hurt,' I explained. 'But I am a bit shaken up.'

As usual, all that came out was 'SQUEAK-SQUEAK-SQUEAK.'

'He certainly sounds fine,' said Mrs Brisbane. 'Now, back to our surprise.'

I stood up to give her my full attention.

'I've been working you pretty hard on our pre-test exercises,' she continued.

That was certainly true. We had tests from time to time in Room 26. But there were *bigger* tests coming and Mrs Brisbane wanted to make sure her students did well. There were maths exercises and reading exercises and her favourite: the dictionary exercise. Every day, she had a list of words for us to look up in the dictionary. Then we were supposed to write sentences using the words correctly.

There was just one problem: everyone in class had a dictionary except me! This was very annoying to me, because I try to keep up with my friends. Finally, I came up with a solution and made my own dictionary by writing words and definitions in the tiny notebook I keep hidden in my cage. Ms Mac, the wonderful supply teacher who brought me to Room 26, gave it to me. (She also gave me a broken heart when she left to teach in faraway Brazil. I still think about Ms Mac a lot.)

Now Mrs Brisbane was smiling broadly. 'This morning, we're taking a break from exercises to decorate the room.'

My classmates cheered.

'What did she say?' Pay-Attention-Art Patel asked Lower-Your-Voice-A.J.

'No test exercises!' A.J. bellowed loudly.

That got Stop-Giggling-Gail Morgenstern chuckling and her best friend, Heidi, joined in.

Mrs Brisbane shushed everyone. 'Settle down now. The theme of the day is Spring into Numbers. Now, let's get to work!'

None of us knew what she was talking about, but soon, all my friends were busy with paper, paint, markers, cotton wool, string and wire. How I wished I could get my paws on some of those things!

While Mrs Brisbane explained that the students were supposed to hide maths problems in their flower, tree and kite projects, I scurried to my wheel for a little exercise. Spring made me feel frisky and full of life! I spun faster and faster until the whole room was a blur. And then the break bell rang.

My classmates dropped their markers and construction paper and raced towards the door. Wait-For-The-Bell-Garth Tugwell was the first one out, as usual.

For some reason, the bell surprised me, maybe because it sounded a little softer than normal. I think it surprised Mrs Brisbane, too, because she glanced at the clock and shouted, 'Children! Come back here!' She raced to the door and called the students back. 'It's not break yet.'

I could hear them objecting.

'It was the bell!' A.J. bellowed.

'We'll miss break!' Mandy protested.

But Mrs Brisbane was firm. Once my friends were back in the room, she pointed to the clock. 'See? It's not time yet.' She checked her watch. 'Not for another half an hour.'

'But the bell rang!' Heidi argued.

'Raise-Your-Hand-Heidi,' Mrs Brisbane said, just as she's said hundreds of times before. 'Would someone like to tell me what just happened?' Mrs Brisbane's eagle eyes stared out at the classroom.

'April Fool!' a voice called out.

'I-Heard-That-Kirk Chen,' the teacher said. 'It was you, wasn't it?'

Kirk was the class comic, but he'd been better lately about playing practical jokes during school hours.

'I'm sorry, Mrs Brisbane,' Kirk answered. 'But it's April the first. April Fools' Day! You're supposed to play jokes on people.'

Mrs Brisbane asked him to explain what he did.

'Last week, I made a recording of the break bell.' He held up a TINY-TINY-TINY tape recorder. 'I just played it a little ahead of time.'

Mrs Brisbane shook her head. 'Kirk, I don't know what I'm going to do with you.'

'I didn't hurt anybody,' Kirk protested.

'No, but –'

Mrs Brisbane didn't finish, because all of a sudden the loudest sound I've ever heard rattled my furry little ears. It was much louder than the buzzers and bells that sound at morning, break, lunchtime or at the end of the day. It was louder than the loudest voice A.J. ever used. It wasn't a ringing or a buzzing – it was an ear-splitting BEEP-BEEP-BEEP without stopping.

'Help!' I squeaked, plummeting off my wheel and somersaulting through my bedding. It's never a good idea to stop spinning too quickly.

'Fire drill!' Heidi called out. She didn't raise her hand but this time Mrs Brisbane didn't scold her.

The beeps kept blaring. Couldn't someone turn them off?

'Boys and girls, it *is* the fire alarm,' Mrs Brisbane shouted. 'Leave everything on your desks. Line up row by row and we'll calmly walk out to the playground.'

'BOING-BOING!' Og sounded worried.

We hadn't had a fire drill since Og came to our classroom. No wonder he was alarmed. I quickly explained that a fire drill is a time for students to practise how to act if there's a fire. My friends knew just what to do. They put down their pencils, scissors and papers, stood up and began to form lines.

'Stay calm,' Mrs Brisbane said. I don't know how *anyone* could stay calm with that noise. 'They didn't tell me about a fire drill, so this one could be a real alarm.'

I was impressed with how orderly the students were, except for Miranda Golden, who was usually one of the best-behaved students in class. She left the line and hurried to my cage. 'Come on, Humphrey, I'll look out for you.'

Good old Miranda. I think of her as Golden Miranda, because she is an almost perfect person. And her hair is as golden as my fur.

Then Garth and A.J. broke ranks and raced over to Og. Each of them took one end of his tank to carry him.

'Children! Stop!' Mrs Brisbane shouted. 'Leave Og and Humphrey here. You must leave everything in the classroom!'

'But if it's a real fire, we can't leave them here!' Miranda protested. I do love that girl.

'Yeah, that would be awful!' A.J. agreed.

Mrs Brisbane bit her lip and looked out into the corridor. 'It's probably a surprise drill, but all right. Hurry along. And keep that tank level, please!'

I didn't know if there was a fire or not, but it felt like we were having an earthquake, because as Miranda carried my cage, I was slipping and sliding. Thank goodness for that nice soft bedding!

As my cage lurched down the corridor, I saw us head towards a side door. This was a surprise because I'd only been in and out of the school through the main entrance before. Suddenly, I felt fresh spring air on my fur and there was BRIGHT-BRIGHT-BRIGHT light in my eyes. I couldn't smell any smoke, and best of all, the awful beeping stopped.

'It's okay, Humphrey,' Miranda told me. 'We're out on the playground.'

The playground? The playground! The place where my classmates went every day, but where I had never been before. I took a chance and stood up to look around. I saw swings, a slide, a tall something-or-other with rings hanging down from it. It was almost as cool as my cage, with its wheel, ladders and tree branches.

And there were students and teachers from other classes standing around. There was Small-Paul Fletcher, who was in Mrs Loomis's class, but came into Room 26 for maths every morning. He didn't look so small compared to the other students in his class.

Wow, I'd never seen that tall teacher with the bright red hair. Or the teacher who looked a bit like Father Christmas. They were all talking and laughing, so I knew it was just a practice fire after all. I was still taking it all in when – SCREECH! – the loudest whistle on earth blasted very near my cage.

'Mrs Brisbane!' a voice bellowed.

A shadow fell over my cage. I looked up and saw that the large object casting the shadow was actually a woman. A woman holding a whistle.

'You should know by now that nothing should be taken from the classroom. Nothing!' Her voice was almost as loud as her whistle, but a lot deeper.

'I know, Mrs Wright, but the children had a point. If this was a real fire, they would want to save their pets.'

'Unacceptable!' the woman called Mrs Wright declared. I braced myself in case she blew her whistle again.

'He's a living creature! A living thing!' said Miranda. Did I mention how much I love that girl?

Then I heard a familiar voice. 'What's going on here?'

'A serious breach of the rules,' Mrs Wright roared. 'Nothing must leave the classrooms except the students. Nothing!'

'And the teacher!' I added. I was a little afraid of this woman, but still, someone had to squeak up for Mrs Brisbane.

I saw Mr Morales's face smiling down at me. He's the head and also the Most Important Person at Longfellow School. As usual, he was wearing an interesting tie. This one had fluffy white clouds on a blue background.

'You mean Humphrey? And Og?' he asked.

'They're not things, Mr Morales. They're living creatures,' Miranda protested.

'And they're part of our class,' added Garth.

'Yeah!' A.J. bellowed and this time Mrs Brisbane didn't tell him to lower his voice.

Mrs Wright waved a paper in Mr Morales's face, which was RUDE-RUDE-RUDE!

'There are rules, and as Supervisor of Emergency Services, I must strongly protest,' she said. 'I'm sorry, but Mrs Brisbane has chosen to ignore the rules!'

Those were fighting words. Because nobody I knew followed the rules better than Mrs Brisbane. At least if they were good rules.

'Look, the children have a point,' she said, in a nice, soft voice (unlike Mrs Wright's loud, unpleasant voice). 'You can't expect them to leave behind their beloved pets.'

'It's up to us to enforce the rules.' Mrs Wright fingered her whistle but thank goodness, she didn't blow on it.

'Well . . .' said Mr Morales.

'If I had argued with them, it would have slowed us down,' Mrs Brisbane explained. 'That's not good in a fire.'

'BOING!' Goodness, I was surprised to hear Og squeak up, but I was glad he was on our side.

Then I heard a brand-new voice. 'That went well,' a man's voice said.

Mrs Wright shook her head. 'Not entirely. We'll have to try again before the end of the year.'

The person behind the new voice came into view. He was wearing a big shiny yellow jacket and big yellow trousers. And on his head was a COOL-COOL-COOL black hat with a big brim.

'Hi, everybody,' he said, smiling. 'I'm Jeff Herman from the fire station.'

'Did you bring the fire engine?' Garth asked.

'It's out front. You guys did a good job with the fire drill today.'

Mrs Wright shook her head. 'I'm afraid these children did not. They took the time to bring this rat and this frog outside. Strictly against the rules.'

A rat! You would think that a person who teaches in a school could tell the difference between an ordinary rat and a handsome golden hamster like me!

Firefighter Jeff pushed his hat back on his head. 'If there's a real fire, you shouldn't stop to get your pets. Your job is to get out safely. Don't go back in for anything. But tell the firefighters your pet is inside. We rescue pets from fires all the time.'

He bent down and looked me right in the eye. 'Especially nice little hamsters like this guy.'

At least one clever person could tell a hamster from a rat!

'But the best thing to learn is how to prevent a fire from happening,' he continued. 'I'll tell you about that when I visit your class later.'

WOW-WOW-WOW! A real live firefighter was coming to Room 26! Now, *that's* the kind of surprise I like.

DICTIONARY: a book giving the meanings of very cool words, how to say them and where those words came from. (Question: is the word 'dictionary' in the dictionary?)
Humphrey's Dictionary of Wonderful Words

2

Stop, Drop and More Surprises

Kirk had to stay in during afternoon break and write a letter of apology on the blackboard.

Even though she pretended to be annoyed, I don't think Mrs Brisbane thought his prank was that bad. After all, it was very clever of him to think of recording the bell.

True to his word, Jeff Herman visited our classroom late in the day. He showed us pictures of very cool fire engines with noisy sirens, and he told us not to play with matches (which I've never done). Then he told us something very important: if your clothes ever catch fire, you should remember three things.

'Who knows what those three things are?' he asked.

Seth and Garth raised their hands right away but before anyone called on them, Heidi blurted out, 'Stop, drop and roll!'

'Raise-Your-Hand-Heidi Hopper, *please*!' Mrs Brisbane sounded really annoyed. 'Sorry, Mr Herman,' she told the firefighter.

He just smiled and explained that if your or a friend's clothes ever catch fire, you should stop, drop to the floor and roll. That will put out the fire. Then came the fun part. He made us all practise. My friends stood by their desks (and I stood in my cage) and shouted, 'Stop! Drop! Roll!' Then we'd drop to the ground and roll on the floor. I was luckier than my friends because I have such soft bedding on the bottom of my cage. I think even Og must have practised because I heard splashing coming from his cage.

Jeff Herman gave the students stickers that said 'Stop-Drop-Roll' and suddenly, school was over for the day. Everybody was smiling and happy except for Mrs Brisbane. She frowned as she stopped Heidi on her way out of class.

'Heidi, it's bad enough when you won't raise your hand in class, but when we have a guest and you speak out like that, it's rude and embarrassing.'

Heidi looked up at Mrs Brisbane with big sad eyes. 'I'm sorry,' she said. 'I forgot.'

'You remember to come to school and you remember to do your homework, I'm happy to say. Why can't you remember to raise your hand?'

'I suppose it's a bad habit,' Heidi explained.

Mrs Brisbane sighed loudly. 'I'd better call your parents in. Again.'

The Hoppers had already been in twice this school year and both times they said Heidi was well behaved at home. They promised to talk to her about her disruptive behaviour. Each time, Heidi was quiet for a day or two after the meeting, but she'd always gone back to blurting things out.

Mrs Brisbane dismissed Heidi so she could catch her bus. Then she slowly walked over to the table where Og and I live.

'Fellows,' she said, 'if there's one thing I want to accomplish by the end of the school year, it's getting Heidi Hopper to raise her hand.'

'If anyone can do it, you can!' I shouted, but of course all she heard was SQUEAK-SQUEAK-SQUEAK. That's the problem with being a classroom hamster. I can read, I can write and I can help my friends. But it's hard for me to make myself understood.

'Sometimes I wish I had a magic wand to wave all my students' problems away,' she said. Then she stared right at me. 'Come to think of it, Humphrey, you're not too good about raising your paw, either. See you boys tomorrow.'

After she left, I thought about what Mrs Brisbane had said. 'You know, Og, I understand Heidi's problem. I do forget to raise my paw before

squeaking up in class. Of course, I wouldn't get called on anyway. But Heidi could, and she's a clever girl. She should be able to learn.'

'BOING!' I'd finally decided that the odd sound Og made was his way of agreeing with me.

'And Mrs Brisbane knows so many things, like how to get Speak-Up-Sayeh to speak up, and how to get Pay-Attention-Art to pay more attention. Surely she can find a way to help Heidi!'

Og apparently didn't have any opinion on the subject, so I crawled into my sleeping hut to think things over.

⚬

SQUEAK-SQUEAK-SQUEAK. The sound woke me from my doze, and this time I wasn't the one squeaking. It was Aldo, coming in to clean the room. His trolley needed a little bit of oil to stop that noise.

I peeped out from my sleeping hut. The lights came on, temporarily blinding me, but I heard Aldo's familiar voice.

'*¡Buenas noches, señores! ¿Como estás?*'

The voice sounded like Aldo's, but for the first time ever, I couldn't understand a word he was saying. It reminded me of the weekend I spent at Sayeh's house, when I couldn't understand her family. It took me a while to realize that they were speaking another language. But Aldo had

always spoken English until tonight.

'Aldo? Is that you?' I squeaked.

My eyes got used to the light and I could see that the person in the room actually was Aldo. He stopped and looked up at the clock. *'Son las siete y medio.'*

'Huh?' I squeaked.

Og let out an alarming 'BOING!' I suppose he was surprised to hear Aldo's strange new way of speaking, too.

Aldo looked puzzled. 'Or is it *media*? I always forget.' He set to work, moving the desks, sweeping the floor, dusting the desks, all the while muttering strange words, like *'Me llama Aldo. ¿Como está usted? ¿Donde está el . . . ? ¿Donde está la* – oh, mamma mia, those *el*s and *la*s – *¿Donde está la escuela?'*

He swept more and more furiously.

'Tengo un lápiz. El tiene un lápiz. Tienen . . . tienen . . . lápices.'

'Og, can you understand what he's saying?' I called over to my green, goggle-eyed friend.

'BOING-BOING!' he twanged back.

Yeah, he was just as puzzled as I was.

Aldo put the desks back in place, then pulled up a chair close to my cage and took out his lunch bag. He tore a little piece of lettuce from his sandwich and poked it through the bars of my cage. 'Here, *muchacho.'*

'Thanks!' I squeaked.

'I don't know the word for lettuce.' Aldo sounded discouraged.

What on earth was my friend talking about? The word for 'lettuce' is 'lettuce', isn't it?

Aldo ate in silence, then suddenly stood up. 'Well, gotta go, *amigos*,' he said, opening the blinds.

I remembered that Mr Morales called me *amigo*, too.

'*Hasta luego!*'

'Whatever,' I squeaked back in total confusion.

Soon, Aldo was gone, the lights were out and the room was bathed in the silvery glow of the street-light coming through the open blinds. I could hear Og swimming in his tank but I didn't pay much attention.

I was too busy thinking about Aldo and wondering what on earth was wrong with him. He and I had always understood each other pretty well . . . until tonight.

Night is a funny time. It's the time when most of us hamsters are the most active. And it's the time when most humans are sleepy. It's a good time for thinking, but sometimes thinking can turn to worrying, at least for me.

I wasn't just worried because I couldn't understand Aldo. I was also worried about what would happen if the fire alarm started beeping at night.

Who would carry Og and me outside? At least I knew how to STOP-DROP-ROLL, thanks to that nice firefighter Jeff.

Then I remembered my lock-that-doesn't-lock. While it appeared to be locked to humans, I could open it and come and go as I pleased. So, in case of a fire, I could escape if I had to. That was a relief. But what about Og? Then I remembered that he had popped the top off his tank a few times before. Somehow, I knew that Og and I would scurry, hurry and hop our way to safety.

Once I worked that out, I felt a LOT-LOT-LOT better and the next thing I knew, the morning bell was ringing and another day of school was about to begin.

> SURPRISE: Something totally unexpected and unplanned for. A surprise can be good, like a postcard from Ms Mac. Or a surprise can be bad, like Ms Mac moving to Brazil. A surprise can be good and bad, like a shiny balloon (a good thing) that suddenly pops and scares you (a bad thing).
>
> *Humphrey's Dictionary of Wonderful Words*

Hamster on a Roll

I learned a lot about human behaviour during my first seven months in Room 26. I had already worked out a lot about what makes people tick. Humans can be funny, sad, happy and angry . . . all in one day! But the one person I can't quite understand is Mrs Brisbane. Just when I think I understand her, she does something she's never ever done before.

For instance, every single morning she comes into the classroom, puts her books on her desk and her handbag in the desk drawer, checks her hair in the mirror, then walks towards the window and says, 'Good morning, guys. Here's hoping for another great day!'

I always tell her that I'm sure it will be unsqueakably great and Og sometimes answers with his goofy 'BOING!'

But on Tuesday, for the first time all year, she came into the room, dumped her books on the desk, put her handbag in the drawer and slammed it shut. Then she walked over to the noticeboard and stared at the cut-outs of the planets that were up there. 'I wonder how many noticeboards I've put up and taken down over the years?' she asked.

I hoped she wasn't asking me because I didn't have an exact answer. I did know that Mrs Brisbane had been teaching for many years, so the answer would be LOTS-LOTS-LOTS.

She shook her head and began taking down the cut-out picture of planets with interesting names like Neptune, Jupiter and Saturn.

Then there was Mars, which is an angry-looking red colour, with spots on it that look like big scary eyes, especially at night. I wasn't sorry to see that picture go.

The noticeboard was empty by the time the students started streaming in. For months, they'd come in bundled up in coats and boots, hats and gloves. Now they had on light jackets and sweaters and it didn't take long for them to hang their things in the cloakroom and hurry to their seats.

I-Heard-That-Kirk Chen came bounding into the room with a big smile on his face.

'Mrs Brisbane, I'm sorry about yesterday. To

make up for it, I have a surprise for Humphrey. Can I give it to him now?' he asked.

A surprise for *me*? That got my whiskers wiggling.

And it started Gail giggling. 'What is it?' she said. 'Let me see!'

Soon, the other students were gathered around Kirk, begging him to let them see the surprise.

'Okay, Kirk. What is it?' asked Mrs Brisbane. Her arms were folded and she had a suspicious look on her face. After all, Kirk had done a few things that would make any teacher unhappy. Once, he put a cushion on Richie's chair that made a VERY-VERY-VERY rude noise when Richie sat on it. He called it a 'whoopee cushion'. My friends laughed so hard (including Richie), they all wanted a chance to sit on it, but Mrs Brisbane took it away and made Kirk sit in the cloakroom for a while.

This time, Mrs Brisbane held out her hand. 'Let me see it, Kirk,' she said. Dear me, she really didn't trust him.

Kirk reached into his backpack and pulled out something I couldn't see. All of my friends went 'Ooh' and 'Aah,' which made my heart thump faster and faster.

'Can you see it, Og?' I squeaked to my tablemate.

There was no answer.

'It's a hamster ball. We can put Humphrey inside and he can roll around the classroom. See, there are air holes in it. It's good exercise,' Kirk explained. 'Can we try it?'

The thought of rolling around the classroom during the day was so exciting, I climbed up on my ladder to get a closer look.

Mrs Brisbane held the clear yellow ball in her hand. 'Well,' she said, 'I suppose it would be nice for Humphrey. But we have to be careful that we don't step on him or that he doesn't roll somewhere dangerous.'

My friends all cheered and I joined in. Og started splashing, so I knew he approved.

'*And* we can't let this interfere with our school work. Testing is coming up, you know,' Mrs Brisbane said with a frown.

Kirk had already opened my cage.

'Don't hurt him,' said Golden Miranda, who's always looking out for me.

Kirk placed me in the ball, then snapped the top shut.

'Make sure it's closed tightly, please,' Speak-Up-Sayeh said softly. She was shy, but she always looked out for me, too.

It was a bit weird being enclosed in a round object. Since it was yellow plastic, the world looked yellow to me and Miranda was more golden than ever. I checked to see that there were holes in the plastic. YES-YES-YES! I wouldn't have trouble breathing.

'Careful now,' warned Mrs Brisbane as Kirk set the ball on the floor at the front of the classroom.

My fellow students crouched down to watch.

'Go on, Humphrey Dumpty,' said A.J. 'Make the ball go.'

Let me tell you, it's very strange to be inside a ball. For one thing, there's nothing flat to stand on, like a floor. So even standing still, the ball felt wobbly.

'Run, Humphrey,' said Seth. 'Get it moving!'

I hesitated for a little bit, but when I heard Og go 'BOING!' I knew I had to move.

I went slowly at first, just moving my paws along at a slow jog. My friends moved back to give me room to roll down the centre aisle.

'Go, Humphrey, go!' said Kirk.

I jogged a little faster.

'Go, Humphrey, go!' the other students chanted. 'Go, go, go!'

I liked the encouragement and I liked the feeling of going fast, so I began to run. It was like spinning my wheel, only this time I was actually going some-where!

Many times before, I'd scurried across the floor of the classroom, but never when the other students were there. As I zoomed down the aisle between the tables and chairs, my friends followed behind me.

The bell rang, which meant school had begun, but once I got rolling, I didn't know how to stop. As much fun as the hamster ball was, it was SCARY-SCARY-SCARY, too, because I couldn't control where I was going.

I heard Mrs Brisbane say, 'Class, we need to begin our work!' But I was on a roll, heading right for – eek! – the wall!

Someone gasped. I think it was Miranda. 'He'll crash!' she said. 'Stop him!'

I tried to slow down but it was too late. The ball bounced off the wall and shot back towards the aisle. I was now upside-down, and before I could get back on my feet, I came to a stop that was so sudden, I did a double flip inside the ball. I looked up and saw a large foot in a sensible black shoe.

It was Mrs Brisbane's foot.

'Class, I want you all in your seats. Take out a sheet of paper for the dictionary exercise. I'll take attendance while you get started.'

I was catching my breath when she leaned down over me. 'And you, young man, will settle down.'

When Mrs Brisbane talks like that, nobody argues with her, especially not a small golden hamster enclosed in a ball. Once she removed her foot, I cautiously headed back down the centre aisle between the desks.

Mrs Brisbane kept a close eye on me while my friends took the test. Usually, I took the test along with them, writing the answers in my notebook. But I was enjoying my freedom a little too much for that. I kept on jogging up and down the centre aisle, but now I was careful to slow to a stop before hitting a wall. That way, I just tapped it, rolled backward, then turned my body inside the ball and jogged towards the opposite wall again.

My friends wrote quietly while Mrs Brisbane gave out the words. I tried not to make too much noise as I sailed past Don't-Complain-Mandy Payne's shiny red shoes, Pay-Attention-Art's black basketball boots and Garth's scuffed white trainers. Sit-Still-Seth's feet TAP-TAP-TAPPED as he wrote.

I don't know how many times I went back and forth but it was getting a little boring. If only I could turn the thing! After the test papers were collected, Mrs Brisbane said it was time to finish the Spring into Numbers project. I think my friends forgot about me while they cut and pasted, coloured and stapled their papers.

By break time, Room 26 looked completely different. The noticeboard was covered with cut-outs of flowers, rabbits and robins – but they all had maths problems on them. Plus and minus numbers, multiplying and dividing numbers peeked out from the leaves of the blossoms and ran up and down the rabbit ears and robin wings.

Tabitha and Richie made clouds in all kinds of shapes – even triangles and squares. Gail and Sayeh tacked a row of colourful flowers all around the blackboard. There was a pattern to the colours and it took me a while to work it out. Garth and A.J. made a huge kite with a LONG-LONG-LONG tail that had a LONG-LONG-LONG problem on it.

I began to jog with joy. Spring was bright! Spring was happy! Spring was fun!

While Mrs Brisbane helped hang the kite, I suddenly hit the leg of Seth's desk and veered off towards the door, which was open to let in the spring breeze.

I sailed out of Room 26 and not one of my friends noticed.

'HELP-HELP-HELP!' I squeaked. In the distance, I heard Og's 'BOING!' but everything was completely silent in the corridor. As I rolled out of Room 26, towards the side door, I wondered if I'd end up on the playground again. I frantically tried to guide the ball away from the door, but it wouldn't turn quickly enough.

Luckily, the door was closed tightly so I bounced off it. I was heading towards another door. It was FAR-FAR-FAR away, past a long row of classroom doors. Suddenly, I wished Aldo hadn't polished the floor quite so well. I also wished the hamster ball had brakes. The best I could do to slow it down was to stop moving my legs.

What an unsqueakably dangerous situation for a small hamster! At least my cage had that lock-that-doesn't-lock. But there was no way for me to get out of the ball.

'Goodbye, Room 26!' I squeaked.

Suddenly I heard a piercingly loud noise. (Hamsters are very sensitive creatures and we don't appreciate loud noises.)

'Stop right there,' a voice firmly ordered me. The ball stopped abruptly and this time I did a triple flip. But I recognized the voice . . . and the shrill sound. It was Mrs Wright and her whistle. She was standing right in front of me with one of her huge white puffy shoes resting on top of the ball.

Just for fun, I suppose, she blew her whistle again.

'Mrs Brisbane!' she bellowed.

Mrs Brisbane rushed out into the corridor and hurried towards us. 'What's wrong, Mrs Wright?'

That sounded funny, but I wasn't in the mood to laugh. I was afraid Mrs Wright might blow her whistle again.

'I just happened to be coming down the corridor when I found your *rat* out here!'

'For goodness' sake!' Mrs Brisbane leaned down

and picked up the ball. 'How did you get out here?'

'You created a very dangerous situation,' said Mrs Wright. 'Someone could trip over him and get hurt.'

'Well, no one did,' said Mrs Brisbane. 'Don't worry, it won't happen again.'

Mrs Wright sniffed loudly. 'Still, I must report this to Mr Morales.'

'Do whatever you think you should.' Mrs Brisbane sounded a little snippy and I was GLAD-GLAD-GLAD. 'Come on, Humphrey.'

My classmates gathered at the door, waiting for my return.

'Back in your seats,' Mrs Brisbane told them. 'And you, Humphrey, are going back in your cage.'

I was so happy to be back in my cage, I took a long drink of water, then headed straight for my sleeping hut and a nice long doze.

> WHISTLE: A shiny device which, when someone blows it, makes an ear-splitting sound that can seriously hurt the delicate ears of small creatures like hamsters. Use whistles sparingly, if at all. (Some humans can whistle without a device, but hamsters never can.)
> Humphrey's Dictionary of
> Wonderful Words

4

Spring Fever

'Wait-For-The-Bell-Garth.'

Mrs Brisbane's words jolted me from my nap.

Garth always jumped out of his chair just before the bell rang for break, lunch or the end of the day. When Mrs Brisbane reminded him, he sat back down again until the bell actually rang.

'Now you may go, class,' Mrs Brisbane said.

Once the room was empty, she shuffled the papers on her desk. Then the door opened and in came Mr Morales.

'Got a second, Sue?' he asked.

'Of course,' Mrs Brisbane greeted him. 'What can I do for you?'

'Ruth Wright put in a complaint. It's about . . .'

Mrs Brisbane finished his sentence. '. . . Humphrey.'

The head smiled. 'Yeah. Just try and keep him in the classroom.'

'I intend to,' said Mrs Brisbane.

'Don't worry,' Mr Morales chuckled. 'She also complained about the squeaky door in the cafeteria, some fingerprints on the trophy case and the fact that the clocks are running thirty seconds slow.'

'Well, she teaches PE. I guess rules are very important to her.'

Mr Morales strolled over to my cage. 'So Humphrey had a little adventure today? Maybe he has spring fever,' he said.

'I think the whole class does,' Mrs Brisbane answered. 'It happens every year. The weather turns nice and the class gets silly.'

The head leaned in close to my cage. 'Well, no more silliness from you, Humphrey. You stay put.'

'I will try because that Mrs Wright is MEAN-MEAN-MEAN!' I squeaked.

Mr Morales chuckled. 'Oh, don't let it bother you, Humphrey. Mrs Wright likes to complain.'

Then he turned back to Mrs Brisbane. 'Don't forget, deadline's coming up, Sue.'

'Sorry, I forgot. I'll write myself a note.'

Mr Morales smiled. 'Great.'

The bell rang again and the head excused himself. In seconds, my classmates came racing back into the room, pink-cheeked, out of breath and smiling. At least most of them were smiling.

'Good game, Tabby,' Seth told Tabitha. 'We almost won.'

'Yeah, we would have if it wasn't for you-know-who,' she answered.

Then she glanced at Garth, who was right behind her. He definitely wasn't smiling.

'Take your seats, children,' said Mrs Brisbane. 'Get out your social studies books and turn to page 112.'

Sometimes being a classroom hamster is like being a detective. You hear little bits of conversation and try to work out what's going on. Like, what was that about Mrs Brisbane forgetting something Mr Morales wanted? She never forgets anything! And why did Tabitha say 'you-know-who' instead of Garth's name? And why wasn't Garth happy, like everybody else?

I was sorting out my thoughts when something even more puzzling happened.

Instead of reading his social studies book, Garth was writing something in big letters on a piece of paper but I couldn't see what he wrote.

He kept the paper on his desk and read the book, but he stopped to look at the paper once in a while. Then he wrote another word next to it.

I climbed up my ladder to see if I could get a better look at it.

'Og?' I squeaked softly. 'Can you see what Garth wrote on that paper?'

I heard some gentle splashing but no answer.

Mrs Brisbane started writing questions on the board, and soon my friends were busily writing the answers. This went on until the lunch bell rang.

My classmates all got up and headed for the door. Garth pushed forward, clutching the paper in his hand. He paused near A.J.'s desk and dropped the paper in front of his friend, then hurried towards the door. A.J. stared at the piece of paper, crumbled it into a ball and dropped it on the floor. (Oh dear, Aldo wouldn't like that!)

When Mrs Brisbane got ready to leave for lunch, she spotted the paper on the floor, picked it up and smoothed it out. She frowned when she read it, then put it on *her* desk and left the room.

'Something is unsqueakably wrong between Garth and A.J.,' I told Og. 'I've got to know what that paper says!'

It's a LONG-LONG-LONG way from the table where Og and I live to Mrs Brisbane's desk and it's a perilous journey, but once I'm curious about something, I can't get it out of my furry hamster head.

'Keep a look-out, Oggy, okay?' I told my friend. 'I'm going over there.'

He answered with a reassuring 'BOING!'

I pushed on the lock-that-doesn't-lock and the door swung open. I took a deep breath, and as I had done before, grabbed onto the leg of the table and slid down so fast, I could feel the breeze ruffling my fur.

I zigzagged across the room, happy to be outside the ball, since I didn't have to worry about bouncing off tables or chairs. I quickly reached Mrs Brisbane's desk at the opposite side of the room. I can't tell you how unsqueakably tall it looks from a hamster's point of view.

Between the chair legs were two horizontal wooden bars. I reached UP-UP-UP, grabbed the lowest bar and slowly pulled myself up.

'Are you watching the clock, Og?' I squeaked.

'BOING!' Og answered.

Grabbing the next bar, I used all my strength to pull myself up. I was getting tired, but knowing that lunch didn't last very long, I wrapped my legs around the chair leg and slowly inched my way up to the seat of the chair.

I sat on the chair seat for a few seconds, trying to catch my breath. I was still a long way from the desktop and that piece of paper. Above my head, there was a desk drawer with a handle on it. I had to leap up to grab hold of it – oooh, cold and slippery – and then I reached up for the edge of the desk and pulled myself up again, finally flinging my whole body onto the surface of the desk.

I lay there on my stomach, muscles quivering from all that work. It's a good thing I work out every day on my wheel and my ladder. It helps strengthen my arms. Or my legs. Or whatever.

'BOING-BOING!' said Og and I didn't need to look at the clock to know I needed to hurry things along. I sat up and saw the piece of paper laid out neatly before me. Of course, to my small eyes the letters were huge – I had to squint and strain to finally make out what it said:

DIRTY RAT

That was it? I'd come all this way and put myself in great danger to read the words 'dirty rat'? I had no idea what Garth was getting at, although I knew that being called a rat, which sometimes happens to me, is not supposed to be a compliment.

Og began splashing wildly. I glanced up at the clock and OH-OH-OH, I barely had time to get back!

I had to take the quickest (though not the safest) route back, so I slid down the side of the desk, landed on the floor with a large thump, raced across the room and grabbed onto the cord of the blinds, which I always used for swinging myself back up to the table.

'BOING-BOING-BOING-BOING!' Og sounded like the fire alarm, but all I could think about was getting back to my cage on time. I heard the bell ring as I skittered across the table and swung the cage door shut behind me.

Every muscle in my small body ached.

'BOING!' Og twanged.

'The paper . . . says . . . "dirty rat",' I told him, panting from all my effort. 'But don't . . . ask me why.'

All that work and I still didn't know what was going on!

My classmates began to trickle in from lunch. As usual, Miranda was with her best friend Sayeh, and other best friends were together: Heidi and Gail, Seth and Tabitha, A.J. and – whoa! It was very unusual to see A.J. without Garth.

A.J. slid into his seat first. When Garth sat down, A.J. leaned over. I strained my small furry ears to hear. 'What was that about? That "dirty rat" thing?'

Garth glared at A.J. 'Friends don't pick their best friends last. Rats do.'

'You're my friend,' A.J. protested. 'You're just not very good at sport.'

'Like I need you to remind me,' muttered Garth.

Right then, Mrs Brisbane started to talk about seeds sprouting, and there was no chance to learn more about the trouble between Garth and A.J.

'Wait-After-Class-Garth,' Mrs Brisbane said when the bell rang at the end of the day.

'Og, did you hear that?' I asked. 'She didn't say Wait-For-The-Bell-Garth. She said Wait-After-Class-Garth.'

Og splashed a bit, but I'm pretty sure he heard, too.

The room emptied quickly and soon Garth was alone with Mrs Brisbane.

Being kept in after class is never a good thing, at least in my experience. And in my months in Room 26, a number of my friends had been kept after school.

Mrs Brisbane went to her desk and picked up the crumpled paper. 'Did you write this, Garth?'

Garth shrugged his shoulders.

'It looks like your writing,' the teacher continued.

'I was just messing around,' answered Garth.

'I found it under A.J.'s desk,' Mrs Brisbane explained. 'I thought the two of you were friends.'

'We're not friends.' Garth wrinkled his nose. 'Not any more.'

Mrs Brisbane sat down and looked thoughtful. 'Would you tell me what happened?'

'I've got to catch my bus,' Garth answered, looking towards the door.

'Think about it and we'll talk tomorrow.' Mrs Brisbane folded up the piece of paper and dropped it in her handbag. 'I'll just hold onto this.'

Garth raced out of the door without looking back. Mrs Brisbane stayed sitting in the chair. She stared at the student tables, the noticeboard, the blackboard. She looked at the room as if she'd never seen it before.

After a while, she picked up her books and her handbag and came over to adjust the blinds. 'I hope you two can get along for the rest of the night,' she told Og and me.

'We'll TRY-TRY-TRY!' I assured her, and I meant it.

Og didn't say anything, but I don't think he was annoyed at me or anything like that.

Maybe he just had spring fever.

RAT: A perfectly nice rodent with a bad reputation. Some rats even make nice pets. There are rats of all shapes and sizes, but when one human calls another human a rat, it's never meant as a compliment.

Humphrey's Dictionary of Wonderful Words

Surprise from Outer Space

I don't know if I had spring fever, but I did have aching muscles following my adventure that afternoon. Besides that, I had a funny feeling in my tummy after I read the note that said 'dirty rat'.

I ate a good helping of Nutri-Nibbles, but my stomach still felt weird.

Later, Og and I were both in a somewhat dreamy state when the door opened, the lights came on and I heard a familiar squeaking sound.

'It's Aldo!' I rushed to the front of my cage to greet my friend. I was hoping he would be a little easier to understand than he had been the night before.

'BOING!' Og sounded quite alarmed and I could see why.

There was Aldo's trolley, piled high with his broom, his mop and pail, lots of spray bottles and cloths and rubbish bags to be filled.

And there was someone pushing the trolley, just as Aldo did every night during the week.

But that person was NOT-NOT-NOT Aldo!

'Eeek!' I squeaked.

The person with the trolley was much shorter than Aldo. The person had no moustache and had longer hair, pulled back in a ponytail. The person had on a red sweatshirt and grey trousers and black trainers.

That person was definitely a girl. Or a woman. A female, anyway. And there was something strange about the way she moved. She tugged at her ear, snapped her fingers and swung her arms in an odd rhythm. Still, she straightened the desks, swept the floor, then mopped it (which Aldo didn't do every night). She even dusted the shelf where Og and I live, but she didn't seem to notice we were there.

'How do you do?' I squeaked up as politely as possible. 'Could you please tell me, WHAT DID YOU DO WITH ALDO?'

Og seemed quite upset as he hopped up and down, up and down, repeating one 'BOING' after another.

The person who was cleaning didn't even seem to notice. As she swept closer to my cage, I saw there was a device attached to her ear!

'Og,' I said nervously, 'I saw a film at Seth's house once about an alien from another planet, and that alien acted very strangely. A bit like this person.'

Og stopped hopping and started listening.

'You don't think she could be one of *them*?' I asked. 'Because in that movie, the space aliens captured a human and took him to their planet. I mean, you don't think that happened to Aldo, do you?'

Og stayed very quiet. In the film, the space alien had wires in his head, too.

I was sorry I'd seen that movie, because it made me think scary thoughts.

'See that thing in her ear? She could be getting signals from the mother ship.' I tried not to become hysterical. 'That's what they called it in the film – the mother ship.'

Finally, the person, who had done a very nice cleaning job for a creature from outer space, wheeled the trolley out of the door. She turned off the lights (without opening the blinds the way Aldo always did) and left Room 26.

The room was quiet, except for the TICK-TICK-TICK of the clock, which seemed to be louder than usual.

Suddenly, the lights came back on. The person walked back in without the cleaning trolley. She came over to my cage and reached into her pocket.

'A ray gun, Og! The space aliens in the movie had ray guns so they could capture the Earthlings!' I squeaked.

She pulled out a small carrot and shoved it between the bars of my cage. Then she left again, turning out the lights so we were plunged into darkness.

'Eeek!' I squeaked. When my eyes adjusted to the dark, I stared at the little carrot. 'I don't suppose that's really a ray gun,' I said. 'But it could be an alien carrot.'

'BOING!' Og agreed.

It was nice of the creature to give me a carrot, but I have to admit I didn't touch it. Not all night long. You can't be too sure about aliens, you know.

And I still had no idea what had happened to my good friend Aldo.

·ö·

The world looked normal again in the light of day, and the morning went along like any morning in Room 26, except for the fact that Garth and A.J. were both very quiet. In fact, they never even looked at each other.

Then came time for break.

While Mrs Brisbane wrote word problems on the board, I spun on my wheel, knowing my friends were out exercising on the playground.

Suddenly, the door swung open and in walked Mrs Wright, pulling Garth along with her. He looked very unhappy.

'Mrs Brisbane, you'll have to do something about this boy!' the PE teacher announced.

Mrs Brisbane was truly surprised. 'Garth? What happened?'

'You know our students are required to get a certain amount of physical activity at break every day,' said Mrs Wright. 'But I found this young man hiding behind the building when he was supposed to be playing ball. *Strictly* against the rules.'

'Were you hiding, Garth?' Mrs Brisbane asked.

'Sort of,' he mumbled.

Mrs Brisbane told Mrs Wright that she'd take care of the situation.

'What will you do?' the PE teacher asked, fingering her whistle.

'That's between Garth and me.' There was ice in Mrs Brisbane's voice. 'Thank you, Mrs Wright.'

Mrs Wright left, thank goodness, and Mrs Brisbane asked Garth to sit down. She sat down next to him.

'Why weren't you playing ball with your friends?' she asked.

'Don't have any,' said Garth. His face was squinched up like he was going to cry.

'Of course you do, Garth,' Mrs Brisbane insisted. 'You have lots of friends.'

Garth shook his head. 'Not any more.'

Mrs Brisbane spoke very softly. 'Please tell me what happened.'

'I'm lousy at softball and when they choose teams, I always get picked last.' Garth's voice quavered. 'Yesterday, A.J. was the team captain and got to pick his players and he picked me last, even though I'm his best friend. I mean, I *was* his best friend. He even picked Sayeh before me and she's not very good either. Then Tabitha told Seth they lost because of me. So I decided not to play any more.'

He sniffled and Mrs Brisbane handed him a tissue.

'I'm sure that hurt a lot. It always hurt me when I got picked last. I wasn't very good at sport,' she confided.

'But you're a *girl*,' Garth told her. 'Girls don't have to be good.'

Mrs Brisbane smiled a little. 'I understand that Tabitha is the best player in the class and she's a girl.'

'Yeah, but still, it's different being a boy.' Garth sighed. 'A.J. would probably pick Humphrey ahead of me.'

Well, yes, he might. I'm very popular with my friends. I don't how you play softball, but I have to admit, I was good at hamster ball.

Garth and Mrs Brisbane sat in silence for a while until I just couldn't stand it any longer.

'I think A.J. was MEAN-MEAN-MEAN not to pick Garth,' I blurted out.

'It sounds like Humphrey has something to say on the subject,' said the teacher.

Garth didn't even smile.

'Tell you what,' she continued. 'You and A.J. bring your lunches in here today and we'll talk.'

'He'll think I told on him!' Garth protested.

'I'll make sure he doesn't,' Mrs Brisbane assured him. 'But I can't make him choose you first.'

'Even if he'd picked me third or fourth, it would have been okay,' said Garth. 'Just not *last*.'

Mrs Brisbane glanced at the clock and said that break was almost over. She asked him to feed Og some of his yucky crickets, something Garth likes to do.

I headed for my sleeping hut to think about what I'd just heard. I didn't know a thing about softball. I'd never been chosen for a team, either. But I knew one thing: I wouldn't want to be picked last, especially by my best friend.

˙ȯ˙

Lunchtime rolled around and Mrs Brisbane told Garth and A.J. to bring their lunches to the class-room. This was a surprising thing that had never happened before, like being in a hamster ball or having Aldo captured by aliens.

A.J. brought his lunch from home in a bright-blue bag. Garth carried his in on a tray and it smelled yummy. Mrs Brisbane took a container of yoghurt and a spoon out of her bag.

But no one, not even Mrs Brisbane, ate a bite.

'A.J., Mrs Wright said that you picked a very good softball team yesterday,' she began.

'Yes, ma'am,' said A.J. loudly.

'But she was surprised that you didn't pick Garth until last.'

A.J. stared down at the untouched sandwich in front of him.

'I was surprised, too,' the teacher continued. 'Since you're such good friends.'

'Yes, ma'am,' said A.J. 'It's just that Garth's not the best player. And I think when you're choosing a team, you've got to pick the best players. Don't you?'

'I suppose so,' said Mrs Brisbane. 'How do you feel about that, Garth?'

Garth squirmed in his chair. 'It wouldn't have hurt him to pick me. I ended up on the team anyway.'

'So it made you feel bad to be picked last?' Mrs Brisbane asked.

'Yes.' Garth looked miserable. So did A.J.

'Somebody's got to be picked last,' said A.J. 'The rest of the team would have been annoyed if I picked you before somebody like Richie or Kirk.'

'I never thought of that,' said Mrs Brisbane, stirring the yoghurt with her spoon.

'Well, now *I'm* annoyed, because it feels really awful to be picked last,' said Garth. His cheeks were flaming red.

'I should think it does,' Mrs Brisbane agreed.

As far as I could see, the conversation was going nowhere. Back and forth, back and forth. Mrs Brisbane agreed with both of them, but neither boy changed his mind. Not one bit.

'I imagine A.J. is sorry you felt bad,' said Mrs Brisbane. 'Right?'

'Well . . . yeah.' A.J. didn't sound totally convinced but at least he agreed.

'And I'll bet Garth realizes what a hard decision it was for you, A.J.,' she added. 'Right, Garth?'

'Yeah . . .'

Garth sounded like he had more to say, but Mrs Brisbane didn't let him. 'Good. Then you two can play ball together and be friends as well. After all, softball is only a game. It shouldn't be important enough to break up a friendship. Agreed?'

The boys nodded. They didn't have much choice.

Mrs Brisbane wasn't quite finished. 'Then at the next break, you'll play ball, won't you, Garth?'

Garth groaned. 'I'll just strike out and then everybody will be annoyed at me.'

'You don't keep your eye on the ball,' A.J. blurted out.

'I do too,' Garth snapped back. 'I keep my eye on it as it sails past my bat.'

Mrs Brisbane glanced at the clock. 'Eat your lunches now. You've got to keep your strength up for the next game.'

She sounded very cheery, but Garth and A.J. looked about as un-cheery as two people could be. They ate their lunches in silence until I couldn't stand it any more.

'For goodness' sake, make up!' I squeaked.

Mrs Brisbane craned her neck to look at me. 'I didn't know you were so interested in sport, Humphrey,' she said. The boys finally smiled a little.

I don't know much about sport but I do know about Garth and A.J. And if Mrs Brisbane couldn't get them to be friends again, I suppose I'd have to.

It's just that I didn't have a single idea about how I'd do it.

> ALIEN: Somebody – or something – from another land or even another planet. Aliens can be any shape, size, colour . . . but they usually want to take you to their leader.
> *Humphrey's Dictionary of Wonderful Words*

The Space Alien Squeaks

Later that afternoon, when it was time for break again, Mrs Brisbane asked Garth to stay inside.

He looked pretty miserable because I guess he thought he was in trouble again. But once the other students had left, Mrs Brisbane told Garth he could read or erase the blackboard for her or work on his homework.

'You're not in trouble, Garth,' she explained. 'I just thought you'd like a change from break, just for today.'

He clearly did, because that was the cleanest blackboard I've ever seen.

Once school was out, I didn't have much time to worry about Garth and A.J. I had creatures from outer space on my mind.

'Og, I've been thinking about that alien movie I saw at Seth's house,' I told my neighbour. 'They talked a funny language. Like they said "*roka mata*" instead of "hello". And "*oobo trill*" instead of "goodbye". They could understand each other but no humans could understand them.'

'BOING!' Og sounded truly alarmed.

'I was thinking – that night Aldo talked so strangely, maybe he'd already been taken over by space aliens.'

'BOING-BOING!' Og replied.

'But the alien – or whoever she was – didn't say a word last night. Maybe she will, if she comes back tonight.'

I was feeling shivery and quivery just thinking that a creature from another planet might return to Room 26.

The clock loudly ticked off the minutes as the room grew darker.

'It won't be long now, Oggy,' I squeaked.

Og splashed around in the water. How I wish he could really talk so I could understand him!

Then I heard it: the SQUEAK-SQUEAK-SQUEAKING of the cleaning trolley. My heart skipped a beat. Maybe Aldo would be back! I'd be so happy to see him, I wouldn't care what came out of his mouth.

The lights came on and the trolley rolled into the

room. It took my eyes a few seconds to get used to the bright light. When I did, I saw who was pushing the trolley. It was the creature from the night before, only this time she had a hood over her head. I couldn't see if the device was attached to her ear or not.

As she went about her work, I wondered why space aliens would come to earth to clean Room 26. And I wondered what this creature had done to Aldo. Just thinking about my missing friend made me angry. What was her evil plan? Suddenly, I wasn't scared any more.

'PLEASE-PLEASE-PLEASE tell us what you did with Aldo!' I demanded.

Either the aliens on the mother ship told her to ignore me or she didn't hear me. She just kept on sweeping.

Suddenly, there was a loud sound – not exactly music but not exactly a ringing either. It sounded like the music of another planet.

The mother ship was calling!

The alien cleaner reached up and touched her ear. The music stopped.

'Hi. Yeah, it's me. I'm cleaning.'

WHAT-WHAT-WHAT was going on? First she has Aldo saying things I don't understand, and now *she* speaks English.

'I'm finished with the programme. Yeah, I don't

take off for Spurling till summer.' She hesitated, then laughed. 'Don't worry. It'll be a while before I'm performing surgery on people. Listen, I'll ring you later. Bye.'

She touched her ear again. Then she pulled a tiny piece of cauliflower out of her pocket. She walked to my cage and dropped the cauliflower between the bars.

'Here,' she said.

Without another word, she pushed the trolley through the door, turned out the lights and was gone.

It took me a few seconds before I could squeak at all. 'Og?' I said. 'Did you see that? She can talk to the mother ship through her ear. And she's taking off for Spurling. Ever hear of that planet?'

'BOING!' he answered, but it wasn't much help.

Spurling had not been one of the planets on our noticeboard, but I remembered that Mrs Brisbane had said there were other solar systems. Maybe this strange creature was from one that was FAR-FAR-FAR away.

But that wasn't what made me feel shivery and quivery. 'Did you hear her say she'll be performing surgery on *people*?'

'BOING-BOING-BOING-BOING!' Og was clearly alarmed. So was I.

'Maybe that's why she captured Aldo,' I said. My

heart was pounding. 'Some kind of experiment. Thank goodness she said it won't be for a while.'

Og's response was a huge splash as he dived into his tank.

I stared at the piece of cauliflower. It's usually one of my favourite crunchy vegetables, but just to be on the safe side I hid it down in the corner of my bedding, with the alien carrot.

I was relieved to see that they didn't glow in the dark.

It was unusually dark in the room that night, since the creature didn't open the blinds the way Aldo always did. Surprisingly, I dozed off. But I didn't have a very restful night because of my dream.

I'm sure most humans would be surprised to learn that I dream when I sleep. Humans seem surprised at everything I do. 'Look, he's spinning that wheel,' they'll say. Or 'Ooh, he's washing his face!' (That isn't even accurate as I don't exactly use soap and water.)

They'd be even more surprised at the things they *don't* see me doing, like escaping from my cage and helping my friends solve their problems. Or writing in my notebook, which is something most hamsters don't do.

But they'd be *flabbergasted* (now that's a word for my dictionary) by my dreams.

Especially the one I had that night.

There I was, standing next to a space ship that looked a lot like Aldo's cleaning trolley. It was parked in front of Longfellow School and I was surrounded by creatures that looked exactly like green, glowing carrots!

'Take us to your leader,' one of them commanded me.

I was very confused because I couldn't decide whether to take them to Mrs Brisbane, who is certainly my leader in Room 26, or Mr Morales, who is the leader of the whole of Longfellow School.

The alien carrots moved in closer.

'Take us to your leader,' they began to chant. 'Leader, leader, leader!'

'*Oobo trill*,' I said, remembering that those words meant 'goodbye' in the movie I'd seen.

Then I took off running across the car park with the alien carrot-people following close on my heels.

'Og, help me!' I called out. 'Oggy!'

Suddenly, I saw my green goggle-eyed friend gliding towards me, riding the top of his tank (the TOP-THAT-POPS) like a skateboard.

'SCREEE!' he shouted.

I hopped onto the back of the speeding top and we zipped across the car park, leaving the space beings far behind.

When I woke up, I sleepily squeaked, 'Thanks, Og,' before I dozed off again – and this time I didn't dream at all.

The next day, I was busy worrying about how it feels to be picked last for a team, and about space aliens whisking Aldo off to the mother ship (wherever that was).

Somehow, I had to let people know what had happened to Aldo. His wife Maria would be worried, as well as his nephew Richie Rinaldi, who was a student in Room 26. I watched Richie carefully in class, but he seemed just the same as ever. Maybe he didn't know his uncle was missing yet. Still, on Thursday morning, I woke up with a Plan.

It's very important to have a Plan when you want to accomplish something important, like saving a friend from beings from outer space.

I got my idea while watching my classmates finish off the noticeboard. Mrs Brisbane brought out a big pile of shiny cut-out letters. She used them to spell out S-P-R-I-N-G. There were a lot of extra letters left over, neatly stacked on the floor right under the noticeboard.

When Mrs Brisbane and the students left for lunch, I made my move.

'Og, I have an idea, but I don't have time to

explain it. Will you watch the clock for me?'

'BOING-BOING!' Og twanged.

If there was one thing that frog was good for, it was for keeping watch when I was out of my cage. More than once he had warned me when I was running out of time.

I flung open the cage door (thank goodness for that lock-that-doesn't-lock), glided across the table and slid down the leg.

Once I was on the floor, I had a clear shot between the desks and wasted no time in getting to the letters.

But once I was up close, I realized that they were MUCH-MUCH-MUCH bigger than I had expected. Probably five times bigger than I am, maybe more.

Still, when I have a Plan, I don't let anything stand in my way.

'Watch the time, Oggy!' I called out.

Og assured me with a giant 'BOING!'

I stared up at the tall stack of letters. This was going to be a test of strength . . . and a test of my spelling!

When I first had the idea, I'd thought of spelling out something like this:

HELP! ALDO HAS BEEN CAPTURED BY SPACE ALIENS!

But with such big letters and so little time, I quickly changed my plan of attack. First, I had to get the letters on the ground, so I backed away, then ran forward at top speed.

'Hee-yah!' I closed my eyes as I hit the stack of letters, sending them scattering in all directions.

'BOING!' warned Og.

I glanced up at the big clock. Og was right. I didn't have a lot of time left, so I quickly went to work. Let me tell you, it's not easy to read those tall letters when you're a small hamster and they're lying flat on the ground. I stood on my tippy toes so I could get a better look.

Luckily, there were several As to choose from. I picked a red one and pulled it out onto the floor. The L was a little more difficult. It was upside-down, which means it looked like a 7. I turned it around and dragged it to the spot next to the A. The I and E were easy.

'BOING-BOING!' Og twanged loudly.

Oh dear. A glance at the clock told me time was passing a little faster than I expected. I turned back and searched for the next letter.

There were plenty of Zs but no Ns in sight. I'm afraid it took me a while to realize that a Z turned on its side looks like an N. And vice versa.

A-L-I-E-N. Not quite right yet, I decided.

'BOING-BOING-BOING!' Og warned.

'Okay, Og. I'm almost finished!' I assured him.

One more letter to go. I didn't want a B. A-L-I-E-N-B would be confusing. I didn't want a C or a V or a W.

'BOING-BOING-BOING-BOING-BOING!'

I didn't dare look at the clock.

'Where are you?' I asked. Just then I saw it.

'Good old S,' I said, pulling the letter into place. A-L-I-E-N-S.

It wasn't a full explanation but it was the best I could do.

'I'm coming back, Og!' I alerted my friend.

I raced across the floor, leaped up to grab the cord of the blinds and madly started it swinging.

'SCREEEEE!' That was Og's most serious warning. As soon as I was almost level with the table, I let go of the cord and slid across the table, landing with a thud right at the door to my cage.

The door to Room 26 opened and I heard the familiar sounds of my friends chatting away as they came into the classroom.

'Take your seats,' Mrs Brisbane told them.

I was at great risk of being discovered as I darted into my cage and pulled the door behind me. Luckily, no one was watching.

'Thanks, Oggy,' I told my neighbour.

All I heard was splashing.

'What on earth . . . ?'

Mrs Brisbane stared down at the letters on the floor. 'Kirk, is this more of your work?'

'Huh?' It wasn't one of Kirk's funniest lines.

'Never mind,' said Mrs Brisbane. 'But remember, April Fools' Day is over now.'

'I didn't do it,' Kirk protested.

'LOOK-LOOK-LOOK!' I squeaked. No one noticed. I glanced at Richie. If only he understood his uncle was in danger. 'Richie, look!'

Richie paid no attention. He was busy scribbling in his notebook.

Mrs Brisbane gathered the letters, stacked them up again and put them on her desk.

All that work for nothing! I was out of breath, out of luck and, for once, out of ideas. So I did the only thing a small hamster can do: I took a nap. After all, I'd need to be alert if aliens from outer space invaded Room 26.

At the end of the day, Mrs Brisbane asked, 'Now, who will be taking Humphrey home this weekend?'

'Me!' a voice called out.

It was Heidi Hopper, of course.

Mrs Brisbane shook her head. 'You didn't raise your hand, Heidi. I think maybe you need another week to work on that. Now, who else would like Humphrey?'

Several hands waved in the air. Over the months,

I'd gone home at least once with all my fellow students and they had all invited me back again.

'Garth, is it all right with your parents?' she asked.

'Yes, ma'am. They signed the paper.' He pulled a crumpled piece of paper out of his pocket and held it up. Mrs Brisbane walked to his desk and looked at it.

'All right, then. Humphrey is going to the Tugwells' house tomorrow,' she announced.

I felt sorry for Heidi, who looked so disappointed.

Garth, on the other hand, looked happy for the first time all week.

> DREAM: Like a surprise, a dream can be good or bad. Dreams are pictures you see in your head while you are asleep. Day-dreams, which unlike other dreams happen when you're awake, can be very nice, but teachers don't like them.
>
> Humphrey's Dictionary of Wonderful Words

7

Surprise Attack

That night, after dark, the being from outer space returned to clean Room 26. As nervous as I was about Aldo's disappearance, I was glad that she'd said she couldn't operate on anyone for a while. She wasn't going to take off for the planet Spurling until summer, so I had a little time to save my friend.

Still, when she came up to my cage with a piece of broccoli, I just had to squeak up. 'Release Aldo right away! And go back to where you came from.'

'Gosh, you're a feisty little thing,' she said.

That was a first. She was talking to *me*. 'You're so cute, I'd like to take you home with me.'

'BOING!' That was Og's reaction.

My reaction was to quiver and shiver, just thinking of being taken to the far-off planet of Spurling, home of the alien carrots.

'BOING-BOING-BOING!' Og twanged.

The creature giggled and then pushed the trolley out of the room and turned out the lights.

The room was dead silent for a few seconds. Maybe longer. At last, I stopped twitching long enough to squeak. 'Og, she wants to capture us!'

Og splashed briskly.

'We can't let her do it!'

He splashed a whole lot more.

I was relieved to be going home with Garth for the weekend. But my friend Og usually stayed in Room 26 for the weekend, since he could go longer without eating than I could. I wouldn't rest easily, knowing Og might be going to outer space while I was having a grand old time with Garth.

ᵒᵒ

'Morning, Sue. Got something for me?' Mr Morales was all smiles when he came into Room 26 on Friday morning. His tie had little kites with red tails trailing down.

'Oh, sorry. I forgot again,' Mrs Brisbane replied.

The head's smile quickly faded. 'Is there a problem, Sue?'

'No, I just forgot. I'll bring it on Monday,' Mrs Brisbane declared.

Mr Morales looked a little worried and I didn't blame him. Mrs Brisbane had NEVER-NEVER-NEVER forgotten anything before. Goodness, if she could forget something important that Mr Morales wanted, she could forget something *else* important, like helping my friends and me learn our vocabulary words!

I was worried about my teacher, and there was more to worry about. Garth and A.J. still weren't acting like old friends. In fact, Garth went to great lengths to avoid A.J., which wasn't easy because their desks were very close.

At the end of the day, A.J. tapped Garth on the shoulder. 'You taking Humphrey on the bus?' he asked.

'No, my mum's picking us up,' Garth replied.

'Can I have a lift?' A.J. was at least trying to be friendly.

'No way. We have to stop somewhere on the way home.' Garth turned his back on A.J. and came over to my cage. I could tell his feelings were still hurt.

He gathered up my cage, food and even the new hamster ball. While he did, I had a last-minute message for Og.

'I wish you were going with me, Og! I hope you'll still be here when I get back!' I squeaked.

'BOING-BOING!' he twanged at the top of his voice.

I wondered if there were any frogs – or hamsters – on the planet Spurling.

'Farewell, froggy friend!' were my parting words.

I'd had several adventures on the bus with A.J. and Garth, but on that day, Garth's mother picked us up in a very tall car. Garth's brother Andy was in the back seat.

'Ham!' Andy shouted. I didn't mind. He was little and didn't know the difference between a hamster and a ham yet.

The ride home was smooth, nothing like the bumpy bus. Strangely enough, we didn't make a stop, like Garth told A.J. Instead, we went straight home.

Once I was settled on the living-room table, I heard an odd twanging noise that reminded me a lot of Og. Could my friend have come along after all?

'BOING!' went the sound. Then 'BLING-BLING.' That didn't sound like Og at all.

Garth came into the room carrying a large stringed instrument. He ran his fingers over the strings and out came the sounds. 'BLING-BLANG-BLING!'

It sounded quite nice.

'How do you like my guitar?' Garth asked.

'It's unsqueakably wonderful!' I replied. I was just sorry all that came out was SQUEAK-SQUEAK-SQUEAK!

'I've been taking lessons,' Garth told me. 'Want to hear a song?'

'Of course.'

He strummed those strings and played a great version of 'Twinkle Twinkle Little Star'. I only heard two mistakes, and they were small ones.

'Bravo!' I squeaked when he was finished.

'Did you like it?' asked Garth. 'Here's one called "Down in the Valley".'

He played it from start to finish, without any mistakes at all that I could hear.

'Bravo!' I shouted again.

My classmates constantly surprise me with their talents. Tabitha and Seth know so much about sport, Sayeh sings beautifully and Art can draw. And ever since his birthday party, where a magician performed, Richie's been doing magic tricks. I could never work out how he did them.

Now Garth was playing the guitar. I only wished our other friends in Room 26 could have heard him.

When his fingers got tired, Garth decided to clean out my cage. He was very surprised to find the carrot and cauliflower at the bottom of my cage. 'Hey, Humphrey, are you on a diet?' he asked me.

'Be careful,' I warned him. 'They're from the planet Spurling. They may not be safe!'

Luckily, he threw them in the rubbish and examined my food bowl. It was empty, so he knew I'd been eating something.

'I suppose you were just full,' said Garth. 'But I'd better watch what you eat this weekend.'

I could guarantee him I'd eat just about anything, as long as it was from the planet Earth!

That night, I was more awake than usual. Yes, I'm nocturnal, which means I feel a little livelier at night than during the day. But what kept me awake that night was the thought of Og. I could almost picture him boarding the space ship and taking off for Spurling.

I hoped they understood frog language there.

'It's a beautiful day! We should all go outside,' Garth's mum announced the next morning.

She was right. The Tugwells' garden was a carpet of green grass with red and yellow flowers blooming around the sides. Two-lips, Garth's mother called them.

Garth put my cage on a table on the patio. Garth's dad pushed Andy on a swing at the end of the garden, while Garth's mum dug around in the soil, planting seeds.

'Come on, Humphrey, you need some exercise,' Garth said as he gently took me out of my cage. 'Let's try your hamster ball.'

I would have preferred to run freely in the grass – just like my wild ancestors once did – but at least I had the chance to roll *on* it. The grass looked brighter and greener from inside the yellow plastic.

'Watch him go,' Garth said. His mum, dad and brother gathered around. The sound was a little muffled, but I could hear them laughing.

It was harder to make the ball move on the grass than it had been on the smooth floors of Longfellow School. The ground wasn't even, and once in a while I'd hit a bump and veer off in an unexpected direction. But I didn't mind because it was fun to explore the garden on my own.

Garth's mum went back to planting seeds and his dad helped her.

'Want to roll!' Andy insisted, so Garth showed Andy how to do a somersault. Then Garth helped Andy get his legs over his head and roll across the lawn.

'Roll, Ham!' Andy called to me. 'Roll!'

So I rolled some more until I hit a hill. It wasn't a big hill, but it was enough of a slope for my ball to pick up speed. Faster. And faster. And a little bit faster.

It was fun! It was exciting!

It was also SCARY-SCARY-SCARY! I stopped walking but the ball kept rolling. I knew that cars slow down when humans step on the brakes.

Unfortunately, hamster balls don't have brakes, so I tried to flatten myself on my tummy, pushing down hard with my paws, hoping that would help slow the ball down.

It didn't. The ball rolled and rolled and rolled some more until it finally came to a stop near some bushes at the back of the garden. Whew.

The ball may have stopped but my head was still spinning. I was tired and a little thirsty, but at least I was safe inside the plastic.

It was nice in the shade. Dark, leafy and quiet. A little too quiet.

I could hear Garth and Andy laughing, but they sounded very far away. And they didn't sound like they were looking for me. I realized that if they didn't miss me, I'd never be able to roll the ball back UP the hill.

I sat there in the ball, catching my breath and hoping to come up with a Plan. I was distracted, however, when a long dark shadow fell over the ball.

I looked up and was shocked to see two beady eyes, a number of huge teeth and some horrible long whiskers, hovering directly over my head!

I recognized the face. It was – oh no – a cat!

'Eeek!' I squeaked.

The face moved in closer to the ball. A long pink tongue poked out from the sharp white teeth.

I might have fainted, but I didn't dare risk it. I needed to stay calm to deal with this crisis, but 'Eeek!' I squealed again. I didn't mean to. It just slipped out.

A huge paw dropped down on top of the ball. BOOM! – I fell flat on my back. Funny how I'd worried all night about Og's safety and here *I* was the one in great danger! (Well, that wasn't so funny after all.)

The cat leaned in closer and opened his mouth wider to show off his pointed teeth, just in case I missed them the first time. He took his paw off the top of the ball. Whew! Maybe he was losing interest.

But no, the next thing he did was lie on the ground with the ball – and me – between his front paws. Then he began a charming little game. He batted the ball from one paw to another, which made me feel like I was in a game I saw at Kirk's house. Pinball, they call it. BOP-BOP-BOP the ball spun from side to side – I spun, too. One second I was upside-down, then I was right side up, and I also slid from side to side. This might have been the cat's idea of a fun game but it wasn't mine, because I was pretty sure I wasn't going to be the winner.

While I was being tossed around, I started wondering how easy it would be for the cat to open the ball and get at me. My cage, after all, has a lock-that-doesn't-lock. What if this hamster ball had a catch-that-doesn't-catch? The catch was . . . I'd be caught!

'Sweetums! Where are you, Sweetums? Time for din-din!' I heard a voice call in the distance. The cat's head suddenly jerked to one side. So this must be the Sweetums who was being called. While he was distracted, I hurled myself against one side of the ball, which then rolled down under a bush.

'Sweetums, Mummy wants her baby girl to come home! Din-din!' the voice called out again.

Oops. Sweetums was a girl. A downright mean one, too.

Sweetums poked her head under the bush and batted at me with her paw. Luckily, the ball was wedged against a branch.

'SWEE-TUMS!' The voice was more insistent. 'Yummy din-din!'

I suppose Sweetums decided that din-din in the dish was more of a sure thing than a hamster in the bush, and she trotted away, leaping over the fence and into the garden behind the Tugwells' house.

I was relieved but I was also a little lonely. And a little thirsty, too.

I suddenly thought that after Sweetums finished her din-din, she might come back to the Tugwells' garden for dessert. Namely me!

Speaking of the Tugwells, where *were* they? They seemed as far away as the planet Spurling.

> CAT: Like dogs, cats are extremely dangerous creatures with sharp teeth, gleaming eyes, pointed claws and an appetite for small, cuter animals such as hamsters. If a cat gets hold of a hamster, it can lead to a catastrophe, which I don't even want to think about.
> *Humphrey's Dictionary of Wonderful Words*

The Hunt Continues

The Tugwells were looking for me. They just weren't looking hard enough.

I could hear them in the distance, calling my name and arguing among themselves.

'How could you take your eyes off him?'

'I've looked everywhere!'

'Have you checked those bushes?'

'Of course!'

'We have to find him before dark!'

'Maybe we need some help.'

'Help find Ham!'

I tried to move my ball, but it wouldn't budge. I was stuck.

It was quiet for a while, which made me a little nervous, but I tried to stay very still and rest. I tried not to think about water . . . or Sweetums.

I woke up when I heard big footsteps clomping

through the grass.

Voices called out, 'Humphrey! Hum-phrey!'

And one voice was so loud it was unmistakable, saying 'Humphrey, tell us where you are!'

It had to be A.J.

'I'm HERE-HERE-HERE!' I squeaked as loudly as a hamster can.

I don't think anyone heard me because the voices kept calling.

'Humphrey! Humphrey! Humphrey!'

'HERE-HERE-HERE!'

For some reason, we weren't making any progress.

It was quiet again, and then I heard more foot-steps, thudding through the grass.

'Look over there,' a small voice whispered.

'I'm here!' I squeaked.

'How about those bushes?' a second voice asked.

'OVER HERE!' I yelled.

Then I heard it. 'MEEOW!'

I made the mistake of looking up.

Sweetums was poised on top of the fence, staring down at me. Din-din was over. It was time for dessert.

'UNDER THE BUSH!' I yelled at the top of my tiny lungs.

I heard more footsteps crunching on the fresh new grass.

'Down there,' said a voice. 'Ham?'

That, I knew, was Andy.

'I'll crawl under there,' said the other voice.

It seemed like a long time before I saw someone looking right at me. It wasn't Sweetums this time, thank goodness. It was DeeLee, A.J.'s little sister.

'Here's a ball. Oh, it's Humphrey. Come here, sweetie.' DeeLee reached in and grabbed the ball. She was a little rough, but I didn't mind.

'Hi, Humphrey.' She had a big smile on her face. So did I.

'Hi, Ham,' said Andy. I didn't mind being called a ham. I just didn't want to be called 'dessert'.

'Meow!' called Sweetums, obviously jealous of the attention I was getting.

'Hi, pretty kitty,' DeeLee answered.

I cringed at her cat-friendly tone, but I forgave the girl, because she'd saved me.

Carrying the ball (and me), DeeLee raced up into the garden. 'We found him! We found him!' she squealed.

Soon, all of Garth's family and all of A.J.'s family gathered around.

'Well done!' said A.J., hugging his sister.

'Let's get him to his cage,' said Garth's mum. 'He needs food and water.'

She sure got *that* right.

As we all hurried towards the house, I thought about Sweetums and how disappointed she must have been.

Too bad, I thought. I only hoped that Og was as lucky as I was when the aliens came to take him away.

·ö·

I drank and drank and drank. I know my friends drink fruit juice and lemonade but nothing in the whole wide world tastes better than water. Trust me on that.

Mrs Tugwell served the Thomases lemonade and biscuits, and they all laughed and shared stories about me, Garth and A.J.

'When you rang and asked if A.J. could help look for Humphrey, I said, "We're all going",' Mr Thomas said. 'We had to help our little friend.'

'*I* found him!' DeeLee bragged.

And I was GLAD-GLAD-GLAD she had.

While the families talked, Garth and A.J. stayed unusually quiet.

'Why don't you take A.J. to your room?' Garth's mum asked.

'Okay.' Garth didn't sound very enthusiastic. 'Can we take Humphrey along?'

'Yes,' said Garth's mum. 'But be gentle with him. He's been through a lot today.'

This was a very clever woman.

Once we were in Garth's room, the boys got quiet again.

'It wasn't my idea to ring you,' Garth finally said. 'My dad made me.'

'I'm glad he did. My sister found Humphrey, didn't she?' A.J. replied.

'Along with my brother,' Garth snapped back.

They were quiet again. Under ordinary circumstances, I would have spun on my wheel to entertain them, but I was far too weak.

'What's that?' A.J. asked after a while.

'My guitar,' answered Garth.

'Can you play it?'

'Sure.' Garth took the guitar out of its case, fiddled around with the strings then began to play 'Down in the Valley'.

'Hey, you really can play,' said A.J.

'I said I could.' Garth's voice had an edge to it. He started playing another song.

'I wish I could play.' A.J. sounded wistful. 'Can I try it?'

Garth thrust the guitar at A.J. 'Okay.'

A.J. tried to play, but I have to say it sounded AWFUL-AWFUL-AWFUL! We hamsters have sensitive ears, and mine were hurting from the terrible sounds that came out of the guitar when A.J. tried to play.

He stopped abruptly, thank goodness, and handed the guitar back to Garth.

'Here,' he said. 'I'm no good.'

'Nobody's good in the beginning,' said Garth. 'I've been practising for months.'

He started strumming again and it sounded good.

'We're going home, my boy,' A.J.'s mum poked her head round the door. 'Garth's parents said you can stay if you'd like.'

'Okay,' said A.J.

'Okay with you, Garth?' asked Mrs Thomas.

'Yeah,' Garth answered, but he didn't sound as if he meant it.

After A.J.'s mum left, Garth and A.J. were quiet for a while, which wasn't normal for them. They stared at my cage and finally Garth said, 'Maybe Humphrey's ready for another spin.'

My stomach did a somersault at the thought of meeting up with Sweetums again, but this time he put me in the ball and let me roll around his bedroom floor. I was pretty tired of rolling, but the thought of coming face to face with a cat or a dog or some other dangerous creature had me worried. It was time for me to take charge of my hamster ball!

Garth strummed the guitar but I hardly noticed. I already knew how to make wide turns, but now it was time to try sharp turns. I spun my body to the right as fast as my legs would go, but the ball wobbled rather than moving very far.

A.J. laughed. 'Look at Humphrey Dumpty.'

Garth laughed, too. 'He looks a little seasick.'

Once the ball stopped wobbling, I decided to try again. I remembered once seeing some boys on skateboards on the pavement. They could leap up in the air and land, reversing the direction of their boards. I took a deep breath and leaped up, turning my body at the same time. The only thing that happened was that I hit my head on the ball and did a double somersault, which is a pretty good trick, but not what I was aiming for.

Meanwhile, I heard A.J. ask Garth if he could teach him to play the guitar.

'I'll try,' said Garth. He didn't sound too convinced.

As the boys sat side by side on the bed, Garth showed A.J. where to put his fingers and how to strum the strings.

It still sounded terrible, horrible and very, very bad!

'I'm hopeless,' said A.J.

'You could be good.' Garth sounded a little friendlier. 'Try it again.'

I was already trying again. This time I didn't hit my head and I kept my balance as I leaped to the right. And what do you know? The ball made a faster turn to the right. It was still circular, but I felt more in control.

But A.J.'s guitar playing was way *out* of control.

'I give up.' A.J. handed the guitar back to Garth.

Garth picked out a few notes. 'It sounded terrible when I tried in the beginning, too. You just need practice.'

Suddenly, A.J. jumped up and pointed right at me. 'Hey, look at Humphrey! That's so cool!'

What I was doing was pretty cool, if I do say so myself. First, I made a tight left-hand circle. Then I leaped to the right and did a tight right-hand circle.

Garth and A.J. got down on their knees and watched me. 'That's amazing!' A.J. exclaimed. 'How'd he work that out?'

'I think he was practising,' Garth said. 'Now he could be in the hamster ball Olympics!'

'You know what? You could throw the ball better if you practised,' said A.J. 'Don't you ever play catch with your dad?'

'Dad said he's not very good at playing ball,' Garth told him.

'Oh,' said A.J. Then after a while he added, 'Maybe I could practise with you. You could help me with the guitar and I could help you with softball.'

'You really think I could get better?' Garth asked.

'Of course,' said A.J. 'Look at how good Humphrey is at playing ball!'

And I was very good indeed. Sweetums would have a hard time keeping up with me now.

Garth's dad popped his head in the door. 'We're ordering pizza for supper. You like pepperoni?' he asked A.J.

'Yeah!'

'If you want to spend the night, your mum said she'd drop your clothes off,' Mr Tugwell added.

'Okay with you, Garth?' A.J. asked.

'Okay!'

I was glad to hear that Garth answered without a bit of hesitation.

Garth took me out of the hamster ball and put me back in my cage. While the family ate pizza, I took a long nap, and I dreamed about beautiful guitar music instead of space aliens and cats.

∴ö∵

The next afternoon, A.J. talked Garth into coming outside. 'We'll just toss the ball around,' he said.

'I won't be good,' Garth warned him.

'Maybe not, but you'll get better than you are now,' A.J. said. 'Just like the guitar. Or the hamster ball.'

I was happy they left me in the house. Although I had a new technique, I wasn't anxious to come nose to nose with Sweetums again. She might still be looking for dessert.

Even though I was inside, I could still hear Garth and A.J. laughing and shouting in the garden.

'Nice catch,' A.J. said once. 'Well done!'

I spun on my wheel with pure joy. Even without a Plan, I'd managed to help my friends. *That* was the best trick I'd learned all day.

> PRACTICE: Doing the same thing over and over again in order to get better at it (and all I can say is, if you play the guitar the way A.J. does, you'd better practise a lot). Practice always pays off, especially when steering a hamster ball.
>
> *Humphrey's Dictionary of*
> *Wonderful Words*

9

No Surprises

'Well, well, if it isn't Humphrey.' That's what Miss Victoria, the bus driver, said when she picked up Garth and me at the bus stop on Monday morning. 'The best-behaved student on the bus!'

That was NICE-NICE-NICE to hear.

Things went so well between Garth and A.J. over the weekend that they sat next to each other and acted like best friends again.

As the bus approached Longfellow School, my whiskers began twitching and my fur began itching. Would Og be there when I got back? Or had he been whisked away to the faraway planet of Spurling?

I'm happy to say, he was there! Nothing at all had changed in Room 26, thank goodness.

'Greetings, green and faithful friend,' I greeted Og.

'BOING-BOING!' was his response.

Mrs Brisbane walked over to the table by the window where Og and I live. 'Are you guys glad to see each other?' she asked. 'Humphrey, I was afraid Og would miss you over the weekend, so I took him home with me.'

Whew! She saved him from an alien kidnapping and didn't even know it.

'Lucky frog,' I said. 'The Brisbanes don't have a cat.' I told him the whole story about Sweetums.

So there we were, back on the shelf by the window and everything looked completely normal in Room 26. But the events of the past week made me realize how quickly things can change. Fire alarms can jingle-jangle, best friends can become foes and things from outer space can invade.

During the morning break, Mr Morales stuck his head round the door and said, 'Did you bring it?'

'Oh no! I forgot again,' Mrs Brisbane replied.

'Okay. I don't want to nag you. Maybe tomorrow?'

'I'll try,' said Mrs Brisbane and the head moved on.

After he left, Mrs Brisbane said something very surprising: 'It was only a little white lie.' She said it softly to herself but I heard it plainly. A little white lie.

I had no idea what she was talking about, but I'd never heard anything good about a lie. Even more confusing was the fact that Mrs Brisbane would lie at all. She might be sad or even angry, but she was always honest.

I couldn't puzzle over what she had said for long because my friends returned from break. For the first time for a while, Garth came in with a big smile on his face. Tabitha slapped him on the back and said, 'Good catch!' Then A.J. high-fived Garth.

I guess all that practice over the weekend paid off after all and I was GLAD-GLAD-GLAD.

But I didn't feel so happy later in the day. Mrs Brisbane became extremely annoyed when Heidi Hopper blurted out answers – not once, not twice, but three times! (I was a little annoyed with her, too.) If Mrs Brisbane had talked to her parents, it hadn't done any good.

After lunch, Mrs Brisbane announced that we were going to have a surprise guest! That got my brain spinning as fast as my wheel. The surprise guest at Richie's party had been a magician! Or maybe it would be Firefighter Jeff to help us practise Stop-Drop-Roll. (I hoped it would be him.) Just as I was getting excited, I realized that the guest might not be somebody so nice. It could be Mrs Wright and her really loud whistle. Or it could even be a space alien!

I decided to wait in my sleeping hut. A small hamster can't be too careful.

It wasn't long before the mystery was solved and no one was more surprised than Miranda – because the surprise guest turned out to be her father, Mr Golden! I was almost as surprised as she was.

Mrs Brisbane introduced him to the class and said, 'Mr Golden is an accountant. That means he works with numbers all day long. So he volunteered to spend the afternoon helping us with our maths exercises for the exams coming up.'

Mrs Brisbane is perfectly fine at teaching us all about numbers and the things you can do with them, but it was interesting to see how differently he taught from her. He and my friends played a cool quiz game that just happened to use all the maths that would be on the test. Paul, who usually only comes into Room 26 for maths in the morning, joined us for the fun. Even Pay-Attention-Art paid attention and so did I.

I'd had a pretty exciting day and by the time the last bell rang, I was looking forward to a quiet evening and a nice long doze.

Then I remembered the room cleaning. Would Aldo be back? Or would the space alien return? Would she be taking us with her?

I suddenly didn't feel like dozing, not one bit.

'Og? You know what to do?' I asked my friend later that night. It was dark outside and someone would be coming to clean the room any minute.

He splashed around, which I decided meant 'yes.'

I'd used the time wisely since school finished and had come up with a Plan.

I waited, I watched, I wiggled my whiskers.

And then I heard the squeaking of the cleaning trolley.

'Remember,' I told Og, 'if it's Aldo, we yell "Welcome back!" If it's you-know-who, we hide and stay perfectly still.'

As usual, the lights were blinding when they were first switched on, but I made out the silhouette of someone too short to be Aldo. It was HER! I dived down and burrowed under the bedding in my cage, completely covering myself.

Things were quiet from Og's direction so I figured he remembered his part of my scheme, which was to crouch down and hide behind a big rock.

If we both stayed perfectly still, the creature might not notice us and forget all about taking us back to the mother ship.

I could hear her moving chairs around, sweeping, probably dusting, emptying the two waste-paper baskets. I even heard her make that strange, other-worldly sound. Was that music – or vibrating signals from the mother ship?

'Hi,' I heard her say. 'Yeah, still cleaning.'

Then she paused. 'No. Just a few more days. Thursday's the big day for Aldo. Talk later.'

I heard a click. There was more shuffling, then the lights went out and I heard the door close.

She was gone. That was good.

She was moving on soon. That was good, too.

But if Thursday was Aldo's big day, did that mean he was moving on with her? Because that was a VERY-VERY-VERY bad idea.

'DID YOU HEAR THAT?' I asked Og once the coast was clear.

'BOING!' I knew that was a 'yes'.

'Aldo's big day is Thursday,' I told him. 'Does that mean she's taking him to Spurling with her that soon?'

Og didn't answer and I understood. I couldn't answer that question. And I certainly couldn't sleep, not for the rest of the night.

My friends worked hard the rest of the week. In addition to Mr Golden, Sayeh's dad and Tabitha's mum all came in to help the whole class with maths.

While they multiplied and divided, I worried about Aldo and a different problem: Heidi Hopper.

There hadn't been any improvement in her behaviour, but every day she asked Mrs Brisbane if she could PLEASE-PLEASE-PLEASE take me home for the weekend. And every day Mrs Brisbane told her she needed to see some improvement in the hand-raising situation before I could go home with her.

I didn't want Heidi to be disappointed, so I worked on a Plan to help her remember to raise her hand. So far in my notebook I'd written:

A PLAN TO HELP HEIDI
1.

I hadn't thought of one single thing, and I suppose Mrs Brisbane hadn't either.

On Wednesday, tears welled up in Heidi's eyes when Mrs Brisbane told her it wasn't looking good for the weekend.

'I just need a sign that you're trying,' the teacher said. 'Couldn't you raise your hand just once?'

Heidi nodded, but she didn't seem sure she could do it.

Neither was I.

Thinking about Heidi took up a lot of my time during the day, but in the evenings I only had one thing on my mind: the alien. She said Aldo's big day was Thursday. By the time she arrived to clean on Wednesday night, I'd been spinning on my wheel for two hours straight, trying to whirl away my worries.

When she turned on the lights, I dived under my bedding to hide. I'm quite sure Og slipped behind his rock.

I heard the usual sounds of sweeping and waste-paper-basket emptying. Suddenly, there was that strange humming noise. The mother ship was calling!

'Hey, what's happening, Max?' the strange being said in a cheery voice. 'Long time no talk.'

I took a big chance and poked my head out of the bedding.

'Oh, you'll never guess where I am.' The space alien sat in Sayeh's chair and pulled her hood back. Her hair wasn't in a ponytail tonight. It was long and straight.

'Longfellow School! I'm not kidding,' she said. 'I'm cleaning.'

She paused and laughed some more. 'Seriously. I'm helping out my Uncle Aldo.'

Uncle Aldo? Aldo was an *alien's* uncle?

'He cleans here at night and goes to college during the day.' She hesitated. 'Yeah, he wants to be a teacher. But he ran into problems with Spanish. So he's got this huge exam and he's freaked out about it,' she explained. 'He got a tutor to help him study at night. I have this break, so I said I'd help him out.'

'Og?' I asked in a shaky voice. 'Are you getting all this?'

Og dived into the water side of his tank and splashed loudly.

The alien – I mean, Aldo's niece – stopped talking. She adjusted a thing that was hanging on her ear. Maybe she wasn't talking to the mother ship at all. Maybe she was just talking on a phone attached to her ear. What a relief!

'I'm happy to help Uncle Aldo out. He's always been so good to me, taking me to the fair and to bowling, always ready to listen to my problems,' she explained.

Yeah, that sounded like Aldo all right.

'He's the one who encouraged me to apply to medical school at Spurling. Yeah, I start in June.'

She stood up and started to pace around the room as she talked.

'It's really weird to be back at this school. It's the same as when I was here, only different.' She examined the decorations on the noticeboard. 'Everything seems smaller than I remember.' Then she gasped. 'Max, I can't believe it, but this is Mrs Brisbane's class! *I* had Mrs Brisbane! She was awesome! She was my favourite teacher.'

She was staring at a big bunch of cut-out flowers that Mandy had made. It was labelled: 'To Mrs Brisbane.'

'I can't believe I'm in Mrs Brisbane's room,' she repeated. 'She made me believe I could do whatever I set my mind to – even being a doctor.'

She listened for a while and then said, 'Oh my gosh, I'd better get back to work! I'm only halfway done.'

Still talking, she strolled over to my cage, reached into her pocket and pulled out something. I gasped, but then I saw it wasn't a ray gun. It was a piece of broccoli. 'I'm supposed to give the classroom hamster a treat from Uncle Aldo. There's a frog here, too. Uncle Aldo told me to talk to them, but I feel a bit silly doing that. I wish we'd had pets when I was in Mrs Brisbane's class. Anyway, I've got to run. Talk to you later. Bye!' She tapped her ear and stopped talking.

Just when I was beginning to think Aldo's niece was clever, she said she'd feel silly talking to us!

But other than that, I sort of liked her. I wished I knew her name.

Og splashed away. After a while, I decided to eat the broccoli, because Aldo's niece wasn't from outer space after all. Spurling was a place on earth, not some other planet. And the only reason she was going to perform surgery on humans was because – thank goodness – she was going to become a doctor! Best of all, I knew why Aldo hadn't been coming to clean and I was pretty sure he'd be coming back soon.

NIECE: The daughter of your sister or the daughter of your brother, but a niece is always a girl. If Aldo happens to be her uncle, she's not just a niece, she's also nice.

Humphrey's Dictionary of
Wonderful Words

The Return of Mi Amigo

'Heidi, do you know I really like you?' Mrs Brisbane had kept Heidi in during break. I was expecting another lecture about raising her hand and I think Heidi was, too.

'Not really,' said Heidi.

'Well, I do,' the teacher told her. 'You're clever, you're funny and you're a very good student. I enjoy having you in my class.'

Heidi wrinkled her nose. 'Really?'

'Really,' Mrs Brisbane replied. 'I realize that I have never told you that. I've been too busy getting you to raise your hand.'

'Og, are you listening?' I called to my neighbour.

He splashed in the water gently. He was listening all right.

'That's a shame,' the teacher continued. 'I wish I didn't have to spend so much time on that. But I worry that your teacher next year might not get to know what a wonderful student you are, the way I do. I'd like you to break that habit before you move on. Would you like that?'

Heidi nodded her head.

'I think I've made you very unhappy because you haven't been able to take Humphrey home with you. Is that correct?'

Heidi nodded her head again.

Mrs Brisbane smiled her kindest smile. 'I think this weekend you should take him home. As long as you promise to keep on trying to break that habit.'

Heidi's smile was as wide as her face. 'Oh, thank you!' she exclaimed. 'And I will try! I promise.'

Mrs Brisbane smiled, too.

'Then it's all settled. Would you like to give Humphrey some fresh water and tidy up his cage?'

Of course she did.

'Oh Humphrey, I can't wait till tomorrow so you can come home with me!'

I couldn't wait either. But in the meantime, I had a lot to think about. It was Thursday – Aldo's big day, according to his niece.

Would he pass his Spanish exam? Would he come back to clean Room 26 again? There'd been so many surprises in recent days, I was looking forward to things getting back to normal.

It turned out I'd have to wait a lot longer for that to happen.

·ö·

I was spinning on my wheel after school when Mr Morales came into the classroom again.

'Just checking on that contract, Sue,' he told Mrs Brisbane.

Contract? Was *that* what he wanted from her? I stopped spinning and started listening.

Mrs Brisbane sighed and shook her head. 'I haven't been honest with you. I haven't forgotten the contract. But I haven't signed it yet, either.'

Mr Morales looked worried. 'You *are* coming back next year, aren't you?'

Eeek! The thought of Mrs Brisbane not coming back to Room 26 was unsqueakable!

'I can't imagine not teaching next year. But this is my thirtieth year of teaching and I qualify for full retirement.'

Retirement? I panicked. When you retire, you don't go to work any more.

'But you don't have to retire,' the head said.

'No. It's just, well, Bert.'

Bert was Mrs Brisbane's husband and a thoroughly nice human.

'Bert's had a rough year now that he's not working. I want to be there for him,' she continued.

Bert had had a bad year all right. He'd been in an accident and was in a wheelchair, but he could go FAST-FAST-FAST in it and he seemed pretty happy. He spent most of his time in his garage, making things out of wood.

Mr Morales stood up and started pacing around. In fact, he paced right up to the shelf where Og and I live. 'I understand,' he said softly. 'I just can't imagine Longfellow School without you.'

'Neither can I,' Mrs Brisbane agreed.

They were VERY-VERY-VERY quiet and it was time for me to squeak my mind. 'Neither can I!' I said. 'And Bert Brisbane is doing just fine! Better than your students would do without you.'

'BOING!' Og unexpectedly chimed in.

'Thanks for your support, Og,' I thanked him.

Mr Morales chuckled. 'I think your friends Humphrey and Og want you to stay.'

Even Mrs Brisbane had to smile.

'Take your time, Sue,' the head told her. 'I just want you to know which side I'm on.'

I knew he was on the same side as I was. But would our side win?

Mr Morales left, then Mrs Brisbane left. Og and I had plenty of time to think over what we'd heard.

I looked out at Room 26, at the blackboard full of maths problems and the Spring into Numbers noticeboard and tried *not* to think about Mrs Brisbane . . . but how could I help it?

I crawled into my sleeping hut and tried to imagine Room 26 without Mrs Brisbane. It was pretty hard to do. Of course, Mr Morales wouldn't let us students stay alone in the classroom. He'd have to bring in another teacher.

Suddenly, I *could* imagine Room 26 with another teacher and it wasn't a pretty picture, because the teacher I imagined was Mrs Wright. It wilted my whiskers to think of her blowing her whistle at shy Sayeh to get her to speak up. Pay-Attention-Art Patel would be scared silly if he happened to be daydreaming and Mrs Wright blasted her whistle at him.

And my small, sensitive ears would be aching by the end of a whole day with Mrs Wright in charge. Mrs Brisbane knew how to handle my friends' problems without whistles or shouting or being mean. I started to imagine going home with Mrs Wright on a weekend but it was too terrible to consider.

Then I thought of another possibility. What if Mrs Brisbane took me to her house for ever? As much as I enjoy going to the Brisbanes' home, I couldn't stand the thought of not being a classroom hamster any more. I wouldn't get to visit different homes or meet new families at the weekends. And who would help the students of Room 26 with their problems?

I poked my head out of the sleeping hut and loudly squeaked, 'Og, you and I will have to stop her!'

Og took a long, loud, splashy dive into the water of his tank.

He had a lot of wonderful ways to agree with me.

'ö'

I was still trying not to think about Mrs Brisbane when I heard some wheels squeaking down the corridor, towards Room 26.

By now, I was pretty sure that no space ships were landing on the car park. But I wasn't at all sure just who would be pushing that cleaning trolley.

The door swung open and the lights came on. Naturally, I couldn't see anything for a few seconds.

I held my breath and waited. I didn't have to wait long.

'*Buenas noches, señores*,' a voice boomed out. 'You are looking at one very happy *amigo*. An *amigo* who has a bee-plus!'

The voice was definitely Aldo's. But I still couldn't understand everything he said. I knew he was happy. I knew *amigo* meant friend. But why did he have a bee with him? Bees are annoying, noisy insects. And a huge bee-plus would be even more annoying.

My eyes got used to the light – and oh, it was wonderful to see Aldo in his usual work clothes, his lovely moustache bobbing up and down above his smiling lips. He waved a piece of paper in the air.

'A B-plus! I got a B-plus in my Spanish exam.' He walked right up to my cage and waved the paper at me. 'Okay, okay, I usually get As for most of my tests. But this B-plus makes me very happy because I thought I might fail.'

I couldn't imagine Aldo failing at anything. And now I understood that the B he was talking about was a grade, not a buzzy insect.

'Congratulations, Aldo!' I shouted with unsqueak-able happiness.

Og bounced up and down like the goofy frog he is. 'BOING-BOING-BOING-BOING!' he twanged.

'*Gracias, amigos,*' Aldo answered. Then he looked around Room 26. 'Well, the place looks pretty good. My niece Amy did a fine job. *Muy bueno!*'

'She did,' I answered. 'But I thought she was a space alien and I thought she captured you and I was SO-SO-SO worried!'

Aldo laughed heartily, which made his moustache bounce. 'I think you missed me, Humphrey. And you know what, I missed you, too. But if I'm going to teach in a school some day, I needed to pass a foreign language. So I took some time off to study. And it paid off.'

Then Aldo, who has done some very funny things, such as balancing a broom on one finger, did something even funnier. He began to snap his fingers. Humming a catchy tune, he lifted his arms above his head and began dancing between the desks, tapping his feet wildly.

'Go, Aldo!' I shouted.

'¡Olé!' he shouted.

'¡Olé-Olé-Olé!' I chimed in.

I was so happy to have Aldo back, I forgot that Mrs Brisbane might not come back at all.

At least for a minute I forgot.

CONTRACT: A piece of paper that you sign as a promise that you'll do something, like teach in a school or pay your bills. Signing a contract is a very serious thing and you should think carefully before you sign one. (Except for Mrs Brisbane, who should sign that paper without thinking for one more second!)

Humphrey's Dictionary of
Wonderful Words

11

Hoppin' with Heidi

Some things are not surprises at all. Like the fact that as soon as we got into the car after school on Friday, Heidi asked her mother if Gail could come over to spend the night. Heidi and Gail are BEST-BEST-BEST friends and do just about everything together (except once when they had a *bad* argument).

I wasn't surprised when Mrs Hopper said 'yes', either, because she's a very nice mum.

As soon as I was comfortably settled in Heidi's room, Gail arrived with her backpack. It wasn't long before the two girls were giggling.

'Let's dress up!' said Heidi.

'Okay,' said Gail.

Heidi opened a big square box and the girls pulled out all kinds of hats and scarves and jewellery. 'Let's be princesses.'

Gail put on a firefighter's hat. It was just like Jeff

Herman's hat, only this one was red. 'Stop, drop, roll!' she shouted.

So I did. I dropped down in my bedding and rolled over three times. The girls didn't notice.

'No, Gail. Find something fancy,' Heidi said. She had a shiny gold crown on her head.

Gail took off the firefighter's hat and poked around in the box. Soon the girls had on all kinds of lacy, frilly things and sparkly jewellery.

After a while, Heidi took off her crown. 'Let's play a game.'

'Okay,' said Gail. 'Let's play . . .'

'Cards!' Heidi interrupted.

Soon the girls were playing a game where they slapped down playing cards really fast. They were having such a good time, I decided to take a little nap.

I woke up when Heidi said, 'I'm tired of this. Let's do something else.'

'I have an idea,' said Gail.

I never found out what Gail's idea was, because Heidi said, 'Time for smoothies,' and raced out of the room. Gail sighed, but she followed her friend.

The girls returned a while later, with glasses full of something that was bright pink and looked delicious.

'Here, Humphrey. I've brought you a treat,' Heidi said. And what a treat it was: a big, juicy strawberry!

'I've brought a treat, too,' said Gail. She pushed a perfect little raspberry through the bars of my cage.

'THANKS-THANKS-THANKS!' I squeaked, which made both girls giggle.

'How about we draw pictures of Humphrey?' Gail suggested. I thought it was a very fine suggestion.

Heidi shook her head. 'Not now. Let's watch the princess movie.'

'Oh, I've seen that a million times,' Gail said.

Heidi grabbed Gail's arm and pulled her towards the door. 'So have I. It'll be fun!'

The girls were out of the room for quite a while, which gave me time to think. They were having a lot of fun, but I'd noticed something odd. No matter what Gail suggested – or tried to suggest – Heidi interrupted her with her own idea. And they always ended up doing whatever Heidi said. I was sure that Heidi didn't mean to be so bossy. In fact, I don't think she even knew she did it. But I was starting to wish that Gail could get her own way for once.

That's when I came up with a Plan. I do like making Plans, so while I nibbled on the strawberry, I thought about what I could do to help Heidi see what she was doing.

I slipped my notebook out of its hiding place behind the mirror and turned to the page that said:

A PLAN TO HELP HEIDI

1.

And I started to write.

·ö·

Much later that night, my notebook was back in its hiding place and the girls were ready for bed. While they were in the bathroom, brushing their teeth, I opened the lock-that-doesn't-lock, quietly slipped out of my cage and hid under Heidi's desk.

The girls were giggling when they came back in. 'I'll take the top,' said Heidi.

'Okay,' said Gail.

Heidi's bed was very unusual, because it was really two beds, with one stacked on top of the other.

Gail was already climbing into the bottom bed when Heidi said, 'We'd better wish Humphrey good night.'

Heidi leaned over my cage and said, 'Good night, little Humphrey.'

What she saw was an empty cage with an open door.

'Humphrey?' she said in a much louder voice. 'Humphrey, where are you?'

From my vantage point under the desk, I could see the look of panic on her face as she twirled in a circle, searching every corner of the room with her eyes.

Gail leaped up. 'He's not there?'

'No, look,' said Heidi. 'He's out of his cage.'

Gail looked frightened, too. 'But I'm sure the door was closed.'

'I know,' Heidi agreed. 'But he's not there! Oh, if anything happens to Humphrey, I'll never forgive myself!'

Gail looked around the room. 'But he has to be in this room.'

Soon, the girls were crawling around the room on their hands and knees, calling my name. Finally, Gail spotted me. 'There he is,' she told Heidi in a loud whisper.

'Whew,' said Heidi. 'I'll get him.' She crawled over to the desk and reached out to grab me, but I was way ahead of her. I skittered away to a spot I'd picked out under the bed.

Heidi looked pretty frustrated. 'Humphrey! Why did you do that?'

I wanted to squeak up and say, 'To help you,' but I stayed quiet.

Gail closed the door to the room. 'I have an idea.'

Heidi jumped up. 'I'll chase him out into the open and you catch him.' She was already crawling to the bed.

'Come on out, Humphrey,' she said.

She swung her arm under the bed. I came out all right, and dashed under the dresser.

'Humphrey!' Heidi sounded irritated. 'Come here!'

'He's not going to listen to you,' said Gail. 'Listen . . .'

But Heidi didn't listen. 'I'll get a cup and catch him in that. Keep an eye on him.'

She raced out of the room. Gail sighed and stared at me. Heidi was back in a flash with a large plastic cup in her hand. 'You chase him out into the open and I'll put the cup over him.'

We played that game for quite a while. Gail chased me out from under the dresser. Heidi tried hard to put that cup over me, but I was too quick and too clever. Each time she thought she was going to be successful, I changed directions. I felt a little sorry for the girls. After all, it was time for bed. But I was determined to carry out my Plan.

Finally, Heidi stamped her foot. 'This isn't working.'

'No,' said Gail. 'But maybe . . .'

Heidi suddenly brightened up. 'Wait – I know! We're doing it all wrong. We should move really slowly and tiptoe up to him, so he doesn't even notice us and then we'll get him into the cup.'

'I don't know . . .' Gail sounded doubtful.

'Try it.' Heidi was already tiptoeing. 'We can't talk at all.'

It was funny watching the girls tiptoe around the room, trying so hard not to make a sound. To make it even more fun, I came out into the open more, so they'd think they could really catch me. Of course, the second Heidi started to lower the cup over me, I darted across the room and under the desk again.

'Bad Humphrey!' Heidi said. I actually felt like a bad little hamster, but I wasn't giving up on my Plan yet.

Heidi flopped down in a chair. 'I give up. Don't *you* have any ideas?'

'Yes,' said Gail. 'I have a very good idea. Come with me.'

Gail left the room and Heidi followed.

When they came back, without a word Heidi moved my cage to the middle of the room. Gail got down on the floor, opened her closed fist and placed something orange on the floor.

I stared out at the floor, trying to work out what was happening. Then I saw it: a luscious, juicy, beautiful little carrot wiggling and waggling across the floor. I'd never seen a vegetable dance around like that before. I shuddered to think it might be an alien carrot – until I noticed that the carrot was attached to a string!

This was my chance. I was longing to get back to the comfort and safety of my cage. Gail and her carrot gave me the perfect excuse to go back home.

I waited a few seconds before I ventured out from under the desk.

'There he is!' Heidi announced in a rather loud voice.

'Sssh!' Gail reminded her.

I stopped in my tracks, then headed straight for the carrot.

Gail pulled on the string, drawing the carrot closer to my open cage door.

She wiggled the string and I skittered towards the carrot. She drew the string closer to the cage and I dutifully followed.

At last, the carrot was at the cage door. She jerked the string and the carrot crossed over the threshold of the open cage door. I followed it and was back home again at last.

'Close it,' Gail said, but Heidi was ahead of her. Bam! The door closed firmly behind me.

'We did it!' Heidi was hopping up and down. Gail jumped up, too, and the girls hugged.

'I wish you'd thought of that a lot sooner,' Heidi told Gail.

'I did,' said Gail. 'You just wouldn't listen to me.'

Heidi stopped hopping and stared at Gail. 'Yes, I would.'

'I tried about a million times,' Gail explained. It

was an exaggeration, but I understood how she felt.

'Heidi, you're my best friend and I have fun with you,' Gail continued. 'But every time I have an idea, you interrupt me and never give me a chance to talk.'

Gail was following my Plan even better than I expected. It was all up to Heidi now.

'I do?' said Heidi.

'Sometimes,' Gail answered. 'A lot of times.'

'I don't mean to,' Heidi said. 'These ideas just pop into my head and I say them. I'm sorry.'

Gail gave Heidi another hug. 'You're still my best friend.'

'And you're mine,' Heidi agreed.

Mrs Hopper knocked on the door and said it was time for the girls to go to sleep. Soon, they were tucked into their beds and the lights were out.

'Tomorrow, let's practise being rock stars,' Heidi said.

'I have an idea,' said Gail.

I held my breath, waiting for Heidi's response. 'What is it?' she asked.

'We could make up a hamster dance,' Gail suggested.

Heidi was quiet for a few seconds. 'That's a great idea,' she said.

I was so happy that Heidi had listened, I did a little hamster dance of my own.

'Quiet, Humphrey,' said Heidi.
And I was.

BEST FRIEND: A SPECIAL-SPECIAL-
SPECIAL friend that you want to
spend a lot of time with. A true best
friend is someone who will tell you the
truth (gently) and help you solve your
problems. A true best friend isn't
necessarily a human. A hamster can
do the job very well.

Humphrey's Dictionary of
Wonderful Words

Testing, Testing . . .

Any hopes I had that Heidi was cured of her problem vanished quickly once we returned to school on Monday morning. As soon as class started, she blurted out something about how great it was to have me at her house. Okay, she raised her hand in the middle of her sentence, but it was a bit too late.

I had helped to solve Heidi's problem with Gail, but that was only Step One.

Step Two would be to get Heidi to remember to raise her hand in class. And just like Garth, A.J. and me, she needed practice.

But I couldn't do anything to help Heidi for a while because Monday and Tuesday were testing days! For months, my classmates had been preparing for these big tests and now it was time. I wasn't sure what to expect, but I finally found out: tests were very quiet periods when no one was supposed to squeak up at all.

No one did, except Heidi, who managed to say 'Mrs Brisbane?' without raising her hand at least twice a day.

Unfortunately, I wasn't given a copy of the test, so I spent most of the week catching up on my sleep. Or *trying* to catch up. Just as I would begin to doze off, troubling thoughts would creep into my mind and wake me up. Thoughts about Ms Mac. I could still see her huge dark eyes, her bouncy curls and her great big smile. But over time, the picture of her was getting a little fuzzy, which was a bit sad. She was the first teacher who surprised me by going away and I wasn't ready for that to happen again with Mrs Brisbane.

I suppose the contract was just a piece of paper, but I saw it as a SCARY-SCARY-SCARY thing. If Mrs Brisbane didn't sign it, what would happen to me?

Then I thought about Mrs Wright and her whistle. Whenever I pictured her, I would shudder and concentrate on coming up with a Plan to make Mrs Brisbane stay.

The only good news during those days was when break came and Garth and A.J. happily raced outside to play together. Garth didn't think

A.J. was a dirty rat any more and neither did I. Another thing that made me HAPPY-HAPPY-HAPPY was that Aldo was back to his old self: happy, laughing and full of life. I wished I could say 'Gracias' to the person who had helped him study for that test! And I also wished I could ask him more about Amy. I tried, but even Aldo couldn't quite make out my squeaks.

I felt for my friends who worked so hard at their tests. It wasn't easy for Sit-Still-Seth to keep from wiggling or for Pay-Attention-Art to keep his eyes on the paper and not stare out of the window. It wasn't easy for Gail not to giggle, Kirk not to joke or Garth not to watch the clock, waiting for the bell to ring.

Even super students like Golden Miranda and Speak-Up-Sayeh chewed on their pencils and sighed a lot while they stared at their papers.

'Why do we have to take these tests, anyway?' Don't-Complain-Mandy Payne grumbled during a break between tests.

'So you can prove what fabulous students you are,' Mrs Brisbane explained. 'I know you'll make this school proud.'

I knew it, too, but it was still hard to work out how somebody could be graded on filling in little bubbles on paper.

Mrs Brisbane, being a good teacher, made sure

my friends took time to stand and stretch and relax between tests. Those moments made me feel good, until I remembered that she still hadn't signed that contract yet and there was a very good chance she'd never teach again.

But on Tuesday afternoon, just before the bell rang, Mrs Brisbane made an announcement.

'The tests are all over and tomorrow I have a big surprise for you!'

My friends cheered. So did I.

After class, Mrs Brisbane gathered up her handbag and her lunch bag. Before she left, she came over to check on Og and me.

'You know, Humphrey, I was hoping maybe you could cure Heidi of not raising her hand,' she said. 'But if I haven't been able to make a difference all year, how can I expect a little hamster to change her in one weekend?'

I had to squeak up. 'I made a lot of progress,' I told her. 'We just have to get her to practise.'

Mrs Brisbane grinned mischievously. 'Sounds like you have an idea! Well, so do I, and you can help! See you tomorrow.'

She left quickly and I hopped on my wheel and spun with delight. Wednesday couldn't come fast enough for me!

My whiskers wiggled with excitement when the morning bell rang and Mrs Brisbane began class.

'You all worked so hard on your tests, I'm very proud of you,' she announced after the bell rang. 'So today we're going to have some fun!'

My friends cheered and I let out an extra-loud squeak. Even Og let out a joyous 'BOING!'

'Let's just call this Wacky Day. Or how about Wacky Wednesday?'

Stop-Giggling-Gail led a chorus of laughter, and Mrs Brisbane explained the rules for the day. First, she gave her desk to Og and me. That's right: she asked Richie and Seth to move Og and me from our places by the window to the top of her desk. 'I'll let them be in charge today.'

I LIKED-LIKED-LIKED that idea.

Then she asked all the students to change seats. 'Get as far away from your usual seat as possible,' she said.

There was quite a commotion as my friends all raced around to switch seats.

Once they were settled, Mrs Brisbane explained the rest of the rules:

* All students who were right-handed should use their left hands to write or draw.

* All students who were left-handed should use their right hands to write or draw.

* Students should blurt out questions and answers, and should *not* raise their hands. If a student accidentally waved his or her hand, the other students were required to jump up, wiggle their arms and legs, and make monkey sounds.

My classmates loved that idea, especially when Mrs Brisbane let them practise their monkey movements. I joined in.

'Look at Humphrey. He's a monkey, too!' Art shouted. (For once, he was paying attention.) My friends loved it, even Mrs Brisbane.

So far, Wacky Wednesday was great and it got wackier as the day wore on.

First, we had the Wrong-Hand Art Contest. Everybody had to use the hand they didn't usually draw with. I tried it and it was HARD-HARD-HARD.

'My baseball player looks like he's from outer space,' Kirk chuckled.

He was making a joke, but I still didn't like to think about aliens.

To squeak the truth, the drawings all looked pretty strange. Tabitha won the contest because it turns out she can use both paws – I mean hands – equally well!

Then there was the Trivia Bee. This wasn't like

the 'bee' Aldo got in his Spanish test. This was a game with two teams. Guess who Mrs Brisbane asked to pick one of the teams? Garth Tugwell, the boy who hated getting picked last. The other team captain was Miranda Golden.

'You go first, Garth,' Mrs Brisbane told him.

Garth looked out at his classmates. His eyes rested on A.J. and I was sure he was going to pick him first. Instead, he turned to Mrs Brisbane and asked, 'Wouldn't it be fairer just to count off?'

Mrs Brisbane had an amused smile on her face as she nodded. 'I think that would be very fair, Garth.'

So the rest of the students called out alternating numbers: one, two, one, two, one, two. All the 'ones' lined up next to Garth. All the 'twos' lined up next to Miranda. The funny thing was that A.J. ended up in Garth's team after all.

Next, Mrs Brisbane asked funny questions, like 'What country did Dracula live in?'

Garth had no trouble answering that one. 'Transylvania.'

As I recall, Dracula is a vampire with sharp teeth, so I hope I never have to go to Transylvania.

Mrs Brisbane turned to Miranda and asked, 'What does the legend say you'll find at the end of a rainbow?'

Miranda correctly answered, 'A pot of gold.'

And so the Trivia Bee continued. Any person who missed the answer had to sit down. The first one was Pay-Attention-Art. I guess he stopped paying attention again.

The next to miss was Mandy. 'Can't I try again?' she begged.

Mrs Brisbane told her to take her seat, but she said it kindly.

On the second round, Mrs Brisbane asked A.J., 'Which weighs more: a ton of feathers or a ton of bricks?'

A.J. quickly answered, 'Bricks.' I think he knew it was wrong as soon as he said it, but it was too late. He had to take his seat while the teacher explained that a ton of feathers and a ton of bricks weigh exactly the same – a ton. She is a very tricky questioner!

'Did you get that one, Og?' I squeaked.

The loud splash I heard made me think that perhaps he'd thought the same thing as A.J. did.

'Sorry,' I heard A.J. tell Garth as he passed by him.

'No problem,' Garth replied.

My friends in Room 26 are pretty clever and it took a long time before Sayeh and Garth were the only ones left standing.

Mrs Brisbane asked Sayeh how many biscuits are in a 'baker's dozen'.

Sayeh, who is hardly ever wrong, answered, 'Twelve.'

'Sorry, that's wrong,' said Mrs Brisbane. 'Garth, do you know the answer?'

Garth took off his glasses and cleaned them with his shirt. Then he put his glasses back on and said, 'Thirteen.'

'That is correct,' Mrs Brisbane said. 'If you answer the next question correctly, you win. What did Prince Charming have to do to wake up Sleeping Beauty?'

Garth grinned. 'Kiss her!' he answered. Then, making a face, he added, 'Yuck!'

And so Garth and his team were the winners of the Trivia Bee. As much as I love Miranda, this time I was happy Garth won. When Miranda high-fived him with a big smile on her face, I knew she was GLAD-GLAD-GLAD, too.

Late in the afternoon, Mrs Brisbane played a Brain Teaser game with our class. She would ask a trick question that had a trick answer. The person who gave the first correct answer would receive a very cool sticker with a riddle on it.

The first question was: 'Why can't a man living in the USA be buried in Canada?'

Sayeh raised her hand first. This was a good thing, because Sayeh is quiet and sometimes doesn't answer at all. But it was also a bad thing, because according to the rules of the day we weren't supposed to raise our hands.

'Class? Sayeh raised her hand,' Mrs Brisbane said. 'What do we do?'

Kirk was the first one to jump up and my other friends followed. I joined in, too, as we made funny monkey sounds and jumped around. Even Mrs Brisbane tried it. Nobody laughed harder than Sayeh.

Once everyone was seated again, Mrs Brisbane repeated the question. Tabitha, Art, Kirk, Heidi and Sayeh all shouted out, but since A.J. had the loudest voice, he was the one I heard. 'Because he's still alive!' his voice boomed out.

'That's correct,' Mrs Brisbane replied. 'You can't bury a person who's still living.'

The next question was just as tricky: 'If you only had one match and you walked into a room where there was a candle, an oil lamp and a wood-burning stove, which one would you light first?'

Voices shouted out and I couldn't understand any of them. Heidi looked very frustrated as she waved her hand in the air. When they saw her, the other students leaped up and did the monkey imitation. Heidi seemed annoyed. 'I *know* the answer but no one can hear me.'

'The candle!' shouted Mandy.

'No, the match,' said Art.

The match was the correct answer, even though I would have voted for the stove. It turns out that you can't light anything else in the room without lighting the match first!

The same thing happened with the next question and the one after that. Heidi couldn't make herself heard. Finally, she stood up. 'Mrs Brisbane, I don't think it's fair because the winner is always the person who's the loudest!'

Mrs Brisbane bit her lip and looked thoughtful. 'Do you think it would be fairer if people raised their hands?'

Heidi nodded. 'Yes, and you could call on the first person to raise her hand.'

'So you agree that by raising our hands, this game would run in a fair and orderly way?' asked the teacher.

'Yes!' Heidi sounded very sure.

'Then maybe tomorrow when we go back to our usual rules, you can remember to raise your hand. Do you think you can, Heidi?'

Heidi's face turned bright pink. 'Yes,' she said, 'I can.'

Brilliant! Mrs Brisbane had shown Heidi why it's important to raise your hand, she'd made it fun and everyone – including me – had helped. When class ended that day, I was convinced that she was the BEST-BEST-BEST teacher in the whole wide world.

I was also convinced that I'd be unsqueakably sad if she left and didn't come back to Room 26.

WACKY: Crazy, silly, goofy, loony, nutty, wild, and if it's a Wednesday, something that's FUN-FUN-FUN!

Humphrey's Dictionary of Wonderful Words

13

The Big Break

'Og, that was the Wackiest Wednesday ever, wasn't it?' I happily squeaked to Og when we were alone.

'BOING-BOING!' he twanged. I'm sure that meant 'yes'.

'And weren't you HAPPY-HAPPY-HAPPY to see Heidi raise her hand?' I asked him.

All I heard was a huge splash, but it sounded like a happy splash to me.

I was so excited about our amusing day, I jumped on my wheel and spun as fast as I could. When I got tired of that, I spun the wheel the opposite direction for a while. I was tired and happy by the time Aldo came in to clean the room.

'*Hola, amigos*,' he said when he arrived.

I'd thought about it for a while and decided that *hola* meant hello.

'*Hola* right back at you,' I squeaked.

Aldo was cheerier than ever now that his Spanish test was over. He hummed and sang and waltzed his broom across the floor. The nightly show Aldo put on was better than anything I'd seen on television at my friends' houses. When he had finished, he offered me bits of lettuce while he ate his sandwich.

'Well, *amigo*, it's time to say *adios* and move on.' He stood up to arrange his bucket, broom and rags on his cleaning trolley. 'I won't see you for a while. I hope you enjoy your trip, wherever you are going.'

Aldo was saying strange things again! I was so stunned that he was halfway out of the door before I could squeak, 'But I'm not going anywhere!' It was too late for him to hear me. He was gone.

I didn't think I was going anywhere, but Aldo seemed pretty sure.

'The contract!' I told Og. 'If Mrs Brisbane doesn't sign the contract, maybe I'll be going away.'

Og didn't respond. Maybe he was as worried as I was. After all, if I went away, he probably would, too.

As I lay in my sleeping hut that night, I thought about what would happen if Mrs Brisbane didn't come back to Room 26. Maybe I was going to live with the Brisbanes. Maybe I was going back to Pet-O-Rama. Maybe *real* space aliens were coming to take me away. None of those thoughts made me very happy.

At least Aldo had said 'for a while'. I hoped he meant that some day I'd be coming back to Room 26, the place I like best in the world.

The next two days, my friends seemed sillier and more excited than usual while I was much more serious. I think Mrs Brisbane was, too, especially when Mr Morales came in during break to remind her about the contract. 'Think it over next week, Sue,' he told her. 'I know you'll make the right decision.'

The right decision would be for her to come back. Because if she wasn't in Room 26, who would think up things like Wacky Wednesday and work out how to help Heidi, just as she's helped all my friends throughout the year?

On Friday, just before my classmates returned from break, I looked up to see Mrs Wright standing in the doorway. Her silver whistle glittered.

'Mrs Brisbane, I just want to say that Garth Tugwell is participating much more in sport now. And his skills are improving.'

'Oh, I'm so glad,' Mrs Brisbane answered.

'However, two of your students came out to break without jackets or sweaters on. It's exactly 65 degrees outside and the rules say that students must wear jackets or sweaters when the temperature is below 70. I'm sure you'll remember that rule from now on.'

'I don't think it's a very good rule,' Mrs Brisbane answered. 'If the children play hard, they'll get overheated, which is just as bad as being cold.'

Mrs Wright did something strange with her eyebrows, bringing them down low over her eyes. I think that's called a scowl. 'If you don't like the rules, then why don't you make a proposal to change them? That's why the head has a suggestions box outside his office.'

'That's a good idea,' Mrs Brisbane said. 'I think I will!'

The bell rang and Mrs Wright left, thank goodness.

'Grrr!' Mrs Brisbane made a fist and pretended to pound her forehead with it. 'Maybe I wouldn't miss this place so much after all!' she said. I think she was talking to herself, but I heard her say it.

'But we'd miss you!' I squeaked. 'You have to stay!'

Mrs Brisbane swung around to face my side of the room. 'Humphrey, I hope you're not agreeing with that woman.'

'NO-NO-NO!' I assured her.

•ö•

All day long, I kept my eye on Heidi. Once she started to blurt out an answer but I shouted 'Hands please!' and even if she didn't understand my squeaking, she got the message and raised her hand.

When the day was almost over, Mrs Brisbane asked my classmates to clean up their tables and the area around them. 'We'll be gone for a week for the spring holidays,' she said. 'We want to come back to a nice room.'

Spring holidays? Where were *we* going for a whole week?

'Eek!' I squeaked.

Heidi's hand shot up. Goodness me, I was proud. When Mrs Brisbane called on her, she asked, 'Where will Humphrey and Og spend the holiday?'

'Humphrey and Og will be at my house,' the teacher answered. A few kids groaned and she asked what was wrong.

'I wish I could have Humphrey for a whole week,' said Garth.

'Me too,' Miranda agreed.

Knowing that Sweetums could get into Garth's back garden and knowing that Miranda's dangerous dog Clem lived at her house made me VERY-VERY-VERY glad I was going home with Mrs Brisbane.

I knew I'd be safe there and maybe – just maybe – a small hamster with a Plan could convince her to sign that contract and come back to Room 26.

All I needed was that Plan.

'Bert? Are you there?' Mrs Brisbane opened the front door of the house. Bert didn't seem to be around.

'I bet he's in the garage,' she said. She put my cage on the living-room table. 'I'd better bring Og in.'

It was nice to be back at the Brisbanes' house. Next to my cage was a vase of pink and white flowers. Mrs Brisbane always had flowers in her house – real ones. Soon, Og's tank was next to me on the table.

'Nice to be back, eh, Oggy?' I asked my companion.

'BOING!' he twanged.

I do like visiting the Brisbanes, I really do. But the thought of never seeing my friends in Room 26 was still a worry. *If* Mrs Brisbane didn't sign that contract.

Mrs Brisbane left again and when she returned, her husband came in his wheelchair behind her. A smile now replaced the grumpy old frown he had the first time I saw him.

'My two favourite mates!' he exclaimed when he saw us. 'I've missed you.'

'You spend so much time in the garage, you wouldn't know if they were here or not,' Mrs Brisbane said in a teasing way.

'I used to spend my time cooped up in a little box in a big office. I love having that whole garage all to myself,' he said. 'I'll have to show you my latest creation: a three-storey bird box.'

Mr Brisbane liked to make things. The best thing he'd made was my large cage extension, with all kinds of wonderful places to hide, swing and climb.

'I should think you're happy to have a break,' he said to Mrs Brisbane.

'Yes, I am,' she said. 'Especially after today. Ruth Wright complained that I let some children go out without sweaters when it was 18 degrees instead of 20. Is that all school has become: rules about sweaters and fire drills instead of teaching children to learn and grow?'

'It never will be with you around, my dear,' he answered.

'She said I should put my suggestions in the suggestions box. Well, I have a suggestion for her!' Mrs Brisbane was getting pretty heated.

'I suggest you come out and see my bird box,' he said. 'And that afterwards, we order some Chinese food and watch a film.'

Mrs Brisbane gave his cheek a little pinch. 'You're the cleverest man I know,' she said.

Maybe Bert could think of a way to get her to sign the contract.

The next morning, Mrs Brisbane went shopping for new spring clothes. As soon as her car left, Bert came to talk to me.

'Humphrey, I've got to go somewhere and it just occurred to me that it would be a very good idea for you to come along.'

Since I am a hamster in a cage, people hardly ever take me with them when they go out. I've never been to a restaurant, a cinema or a shopping centre. I've never been bowling, skating or camping. Wherever Mr Brisbane was going, I wanted to be with him.

'Let's GO-GO-GO!' I said.

I didn't know where we were GO-GO-GOING but it was fun to be heading out with Mr Brisbane. It took a while for him to get me, his wheelchair and himself into the car, but it was a beautiful day and I was excited to be going somewhere new.

As he was driving, Mr Brisbane said, 'I didn't ask permission to bring you along today, but I'm counting on you to win them over.'

Win them over? When *didn't* I win humans over? I just didn't know which humans he meant. Because if one of them happened to be Mrs

Wright, I'd have to work pretty hard.

Suddenly, the car made a sharp right turn. 'Welcome to Maycrest Manor,' Mr Brisbane said. 'Today we're having a surprise party. And you, Humphrey, are the surprise!'

No one was more surprised than I was.

> BREAK: Another good/bad thing. If you break your arm or a vase, it's a bad thing. But a break at school is like a holiday, and holidays are definitely good things.
>
> *Humphrey's Dictionary of Wonderful Words*

A Day at Maycrest Manor

Before we went inside, Mr Brisbane covered my cage with a cloth. 'Just for a few minutes, my friend,' he told me.

Still, I could peep out just enough to see that Maycrest Manor was a huge building with lots of tall windows, plants and trees. Inside I saw people with sticks and walking frames and wheelchairs, and there were other people in colourful uniforms helping them.

'Hi, Bert,' a friendly voice called out. 'What have you got there?'

'Hi, Joyce. This is today's entertainment,' Mr Brisbane answered.

'Great! You can go straight to the recreation room. We'll bring the people in about five minutes.'

We took a lift, which always makes my tummy feel queasy and uneasy, and then we entered a great big room with chairs and tables all around it. Mr Brisbane wheeled us over to a table in the centre and uncovered my cage.

'The people here are all trying to recover from illnesses and injuries so they can go back home again. I was here for a while last year and they helped me a lot,' Mr Brisbane explained. 'Now I want to help them back. All you have to do is be yourself, Humphrey.' As if I could be anybody else!

Soon, the people in uniform helped the people with sticks and walking frames and wheelchairs to come into the room. They all gathered on chairs facing the table. I looked around. I was used to having giggly, wiggly children around me, but these were tired and serious faces.

'Okay, Bert. They're all here,' the woman called Joyce said.

'Good morning,' said Bert in a cheerier than usual voice. 'I've brought you a visitor today. His name is Humphrey. I know how hard you all work at your exercises every day, so I thought maybe you'd like to watch Humphrey work out.'

There was no reaction, just unsmiling faces staring at me from all sides of the table.

Bert had said that *I* was the entertainment, so I decided to be entertaining. I jumped onto my wheel, just to get things rolling. Then I leaped up onto my tree branch and began to climb. I didn't dare look at the faces around me, but I heard a little commotion. Next, I dropped down onto my bridge ladder and hung from one of the rungs.

Surprise, surprise, I heard chuckles.

'Look at that little fellow!' someone said.

Then I let go and slid down to the floor of my cage. I burrowed into my bedding, and temporarily dropped out of sight of my audience.

'Where did he go?' I heard a voice ask.

'Just watch,' Bert said.

Keeping low to the ground, I tunnelled through the bedding and suddenly popped up on the other side of my cage.

'SURPRISE-SURPRISE-SURPRISE!' I squeaked.

This time people laughed. When I looked at the faces again, many of them were smiling and all of them were leaning in to watch me more closely.

'Of course, Humphrey doesn't always stay in his cage,' Mr Brisbane said. He opened the cage door and put me in my yellow hamster ball. I hadn't even seen him bring it along. 'Sometimes, he likes to go for a walk.'

He gently put me and the ball on the floor. 'Go for it, Humphrey.'

I could see a lot of feet making way for me, so I started walking to propel the ball forward. Since I'd learned how to control my right and left turns,

I decided to zigzag across the room. After a while, I looked back and saw that many of the patients were following me. Some of them were helped by the people in uniform. Some of them were on their own.

'He's over in the corner!' a man in a wheelchair said.

Another man pointed with his stick. 'Look out, here he comes again.'

'If I had one of those contraptions, I could go anywhere,' laughed a woman with a walking frame.

It became a fun game of Follow the Leader and I got to be the leader. It was a lovely afternoon and we all had a good workout. Those serious faces looked a little less serious as my new friends wished me goodbye.

When it was time to leave, Joyce was very pleased. 'Bert, can you pop into my office on the way out?' she asked.

That's how I ended up on Joyce's desk while she talked to Mr Brisbane.

'My goodness, didn't that work well! Humphrey got them moving like nobody else,' she said.

'He did the same for me,' Mr Brisbane said.

Then something amazing happened. Joyce offered Mr Brisbane a job as entertainments manager. He'd work for Joyce, who was too busy to come up with new and interesting projects for the patients. And they'd even pay him!

Bert accepted, but said he'd have to talk it over with his wife. He said he was pretty sure she'd be pleased. So was I.

That evening, I was back on the living-room table when Mr Brisbane told Mrs Brisbane the good news. 'I'd really like to go to work every day,' he said. 'And I'd enjoy that work more than I ever liked my old job. What do you think, Sue?'

Mrs Brisbane looked surprised – no, stunned. Then she burst out laughing.

'What's so funny?' Mr Brisbane asked.

'Oh, Bert, I've been trying to work out how to talk to you about this. I still haven't signed my contract for next year.'

Mr Brisbane looked surprised. 'Why not?'

'This is my thirtieth year,' his wife replied. 'I can retire now.'

'Sue! I'm so sorry I didn't realize,' he said. 'Thirty years! We should have a party or something. Do you want to retire?'

Mrs Brisbane sighed. 'I'd miss Room 26 terribly. I'd miss all the wonderful students, especially Humphrey and Og. On the other hand, maybe it's time for someone else to have a chance. Am I really making a difference any more?'

I had to squeak up. 'YES-YES-YES!' I shouted. 'You make a difference every day!'

'Humphrey seems to think so,' Mr Brisbane said. 'And so do I.'

'If I retired now, I'd be the one at home alone all day.' Mrs Brisbane stood up. 'I'm going to think about it for a few more days.'

What was there to think about? Sometimes Mrs Brisbane could be quite frustrating. Sometimes Mrs Brisbane even made me a bit annoyed. But always, Mrs Brisbane was a really great teacher.

Bert spent the rest of the week making plans for his new job. He asked his wife if he could borrow me at the weekends once in a while.

'My students won't like it,' she said. 'But if you tell them it's for a good cause, they might not complain too much.'

They didn't talk about it again for the rest of the weekend, so I spent many a long night spinning on my wheel and wondering what Mrs Brisbane would decide.

On Monday morning, when Mr Morales looked in during break, Mrs Brisbane handed him the contract.

'I've signed it,' she said.

The head smiled. 'That's a great relief. What did Bert think?'

'Bert's got a job and he can't wait to get out of the house,' she said with a laugh. 'It looks like neither of us is going to retire, at least not this year.'

I was so unsqueakably delighted, my heart went THUMP-THUMP-THUMP. Og was splashing so much, he practically created a tsunami in his tank, so I knew he was as happy as I was.

When my friends returned to the classroom, I watched them take their seats. I thought of how I'd watched Mrs Brisbane help Sayeh and Garth, Art and Heidi, Seth, Tabitha, Mandy and Kirk – everyone in the class. Did they realize what she'd done for them?

I was afraid they didn't. I was GLAD-GLAD-GLAD Mrs Brisbane was coming back. And I felt SAD-SAD-SAD that none of us appreciated her as much as we should.

> REHABILITATION CENTRE: A place where people who have been ill or injured go to rest and exercise so that they can get strong again. This process works best when it involves a handsome, creative hamster.
>
> Humphrey's Dictionary of
> Wonderful Words

15

Suggestions and Surprises

'That's what she said, Og,' I told my froggy friend later that evening. 'She wondered if she really made a difference.'

'BOING-BOING!' He sounded truly alarmed.

'I know!' I answered. 'No matter how much I try to tell her that everyone appreciates her, she doesn't understand.'

'BOING-BOING-BOING!' I was so glad that Og seemed to understand.

'If there was just some way to get all her students together to thank her for all she's done! Goodness me, wouldn't she be surprised?'

Og took a huge dive into his tank and splashed noisily.

I remembered what Mr Brisbane had told me on the way to Maycrest Manor. He said they were having a surprise party and that I was the surprise.

'Og, we should give her a surprise party,' I squeaked excitedly. I could just see it! Og splashed like crazy. He wouldn't have any water left if he kept that up.

But how could a tiny hamster and a small frog manage to throw a party?

'*We* wouldn't have to give the party,' I continued. 'If we could just suggest it to somebody like Aldo, or a parent, or Mr Morales.'

Og was silent. Maybe he was thinking. I was thinking, too. I was thinking that Mrs Wright had said that the head had a suggestions box outside his office. If I could just put a suggestion in that box, maybe he would give a surprise party for Mrs Brisbane.

I quickly told Og my idea. His response was quick. 'BOING-BOING-BOING-BOING-BOING!'

'Great!' I answered. 'All I have to do is write the suggestion and take it down to the office.'

The fact that my tiny writing was hard for humans to read, and the fact that I had no idea which office was the head's did not discourage me one little bit.

Now I had a Plan.

∴

I waited until Aldo had cleaned Room 26 before starting on the note. I neatly chewed a piece of paper from my notebook and took my small pencil. Then, in letters as big as I could make them, I carefully wrote:

Suggest: MRS B.
30 YEARS
SURPRISE PARTY

Then I put the note in my mouth and opened the lock-that-doesn't-lock.

'Wish me luck, Oggy. I'm on my way!' I announced.

'BOING-BOING!' I knew that meant 'good luck'.

I then began the longest and most dangerous journey of my lifetime.

∵ö∵

Of course, the door to Room 26 was shut. Aldo always closed the door and locked it when he left. How stupid of me not to think of it. I'm not one to give up easily, so I examined the bottom of the door and saw that there was a narrow opening beneath the edge of the door. It wasn't much, but hamsters are able to flatten themselves and slip through some very small spaces, so it was worth a try.

Grasping the paper in my teeth, I crouched down close to the floor and slid under the door. I could feel the bottom of the door scraping my back, but I didn't mind because I'd made it!

It was dark out in the corridor and eerily quiet.

Now I faced another obstacle: which way was the head's office? I knew it was near the main entrance, where I'd been carried in so many times. But the cage was always so thumpy and bumpy, it was hard to see where I was going.

I rushed past the side door to the playground – I certainly didn't want to go *there* at night – to the end of the corridor. The only way to go now was left, so I knew I was going in the right direction. There was some low lighting in the corridor, which made it seem even creepier than if it had been completely dark. The doors here looked like other classrooms, except for a small door that had a sign reading 'Caretaker' over it. Aldo has his own room at Longfellow School? You learn something new every day!

I noticed something else: a sound was following me. *Crinkle-crinkle. Crinkle-crinkle.*

I stopped for a second and the sound stopped, too. I crept forward. *Crinkle-crinkle. Crinkle-crinkle.* The sound was back.

I stopped again and looked back over my shoulder. I couldn't see anything: no Aldo, no aliens, nobody at all. When I turned back, the piece of paper I was holding in my teeth brushed against the floor. *Crinkle-crinkle-crinkle-crinkle*. Whew – that was the sound. I was following myself! I reminded myself to tell Og that part of the story when I got back. But first, I had to find the suggestions box.

I hurried down the corridor, glancing at each door. Then I looked straight ahead. There was the main entrance! And next to it, instead of a normal door, there was a big glass window and an even bigger door than all the other rooms. I moved closer and read the sign over the door: 'Headteacher'.

JOY-JOY-JOY! I scurried as fast as I could towards that wonderful door. All I had to do was to drop my note into the suggestions box and race back to Room 26 for my scheme to be a complete success.

Crinkle-crinkle-crinkle-crinkle. I looked up at that big door but there was no box in front of the head's office! Nothing next to it, either. It simply wasn't there. I stood there feeling completely crushed.

And then I looked straight up. There was a large box attached to the door, way above my head. I backed away so that I could read the writing on it: SUGGESTIONS BOX. That was great, but how was I supposed to get up there? I couldn't climb straight up the side of the doorway because it was completely smooth and there was nothing to hang on to. And even though I'm quite an acrobat, I certainly couldn't jump *that* high.

I remembered once when Richie and Seth made little aeroplanes by folding pieces of paper and throwing them. I wished I'd paid more attention. I considered making an aeroplane out of my suggestion, but I couldn't work out how to fly it up to the box.

Just then, I heard the familiar squeaking of Aldo's cleaning trolley. Normally, I was delighted to see my friend, but this time I didn't want him to find me out of my cage. I dropped my suggestion on the floor and darted across the corridor, into the shadows under a drinking fountain.

Aldo whistled a happy song as he pushed his trolley past the drinking fountain. He didn't notice me, thank goodness. But he stopped in front of the head's office and bent down to pick up the piece of paper. My heart sank when I saw him start to toss it into his rubbish bag. But then he stopped and examined it, lifting the note up so he could get more light.

'*Mamma mia*,' he said. 'Thirty years?' He looked puzzled. But instead of throwing the note into the rubbish, he dropped it into the suggestions box. Then he continued down the corridor, turning right at the corner.

I heard another loud noise: THUMP-THUMP-THUMP. But I wasn't scared this time because I knew it was just the pounding of my heart.

I peeped around the corner just in time to see Aldo lock the door marked 'Caretaker'. He didn't have his trolley any more so I guess he was finished for the night. He wore a hat now and he turned right and disappeared from view.

I counted to one hundred. When I was sure the coast was clear, I raced down the corridor, turned right and slid under the door of Room 26.

Once back, I had to swing back up to my table using the cord from the blinds like a trapeze, but I'd done that many times before. As scary as it was, it couldn't compare to what I'd experienced in the corridors of Longfellow School that night.

'BOING-BOING-BOING-BOING!' Og greeted me.

Once I was back in my cage, I took a long drink of water and caught my breath.

It took most of the rest of the night for me to tell Og all that had happened, and for us both to ponder what Aldo thought about that note and whether Mr Morales would even read it.

I spent most of the next day dozing, but once or twice I woke up. I was pleased to see that Heidi Hopper was raising her hand, at least most of the time. When the last bell rang, Mrs Brisbane quietly congratulated her and gave her a riddle sticker.

The rest of the week was QUIET-QUIET-QUIET. After all the testing, and all the silliness, it was nice to be back to a normal classroom, but I was worried. Had Mr Morales got the suggestion? Did he like the idea? And what would he do about it? In my time at Longfellow School, I've noticed that humans can be clever, nice and even important like the head, and still not understand the simplest thing a hamster tries to tell them.

You can have a great idea, you can have a Plan, but sometimes it doesn't work out. Maybe I could think of another way to tell Mrs Brisbane what a great teacher she is, but for now I was fresh out of ideas.

•ö•

Two weeks later, on a Friday afternoon, Mrs Brisbane read aloud to us, which is something she does so well. This was a thumping good story about a pig. I've never seen a pig, but this story made me care about him a great deal. In fact, I was so nervous about what would happen to that pig, I hopped on my wheel for a good fast spin.

Then it happened. That unbelievably loud BEEP-BEEP-BEEP was back and I was so surprised, I tumbled off my wheel into my soft bedding.

'Class, it's the fire bell,' said Mrs Brisbane. She seemed a bit nervous. 'Please form two lines.'

Even though Jeff Herman had said to leave the pets and let the firefighters rescue them, Garth and A.J. took Og's tank, while Miranda gently picked up my cage. Sayeh came forward to help her.

'Children, no!' Mrs Brisbane said.

'Please?' asked Miranda. We were already at the door.

Mrs Brisbane shook her head. 'Oh, go ahead.'

Before I knew it, we were out in the corridor, where all the other classes were lining up. In the distance, I heard the screech of Mrs Wright's whistle.

And then we were outside. It was such a beautiful day! I was hoping there wasn't a real fire, not here or anywhere. But if there was, I was prepared to STOP-DROP-ROLL. As I looked around, I noticed that the playground looked a lot different from the last time we had a fire drill.

For one thing, there was a big shiny fire engine parked near the swings. Sitting on top of the fire engine was our old friend Jeff Herman, smiling broadly. A small stage had been set up with a microphone. Sitting on the stage was none other than Mr Brisbane, in his wheelchair. He was smiling, too. There were all kinds of familiar faces. Was that Aldo? And his wife Maria? Many of my friends' parents were there. And some people who didn't seem to belong there at all, like Joyce from Maycrest Manor and Aldo's niece Amy.

WHAT-WHAT-WHAT was going on? I wondered. And then I saw a banner draped above the stage. It said: MRS BRISBANE APPRECIATION DAY.

I glanced over at my teacher. I've seen Mrs Brisbane look happy, sad, annoyed, tired, puzzled and even discouraged. But I've never seen her look so surprised.

Mr Morales stepped up on stage and tapped the microphone. 'Ladies and gentlemen, students, we are gathered here to honour one of Longfellow School's greatest assets: Mrs Sue Brisbane of Room 26. For thirty years, she's been informing, supporting and inspiring students in our community. And I think it's time that we all said thank you!'

The crowd cheered wildly. 'THANKS-THANKS-THANKS!' I shouted as loudly as my little lungs would let me. I heard an enthusiastic 'BOING-BOING-BOING' behind me.

The head continued. 'As we all know, it's not easy to get Mrs Brisbane out of her classroom, so I want to thank Jeff Herman of the fire brigade for helping us arrange this fire drill as part of our scheme. Thanks, Jeff.'

After more applause, Mrs Brisbane was called up to the stage, where she took a seat next to Mr Brisbane, who just couldn't stop smiling. Then, one by one, people came up to the microphone to thank Mrs Brisbane. Aldo said she'd inspired him to go back to college to be a teacher. Amy said she'd inspired her to become a doctor. Joyce said Mrs Brisbane had realized her son had a hearing problem and had got him help. Other parents thanked her. And then, the students of Room 26 were called up to the stage.

Miranda brought me along and Richie and Kirk brought Og, too. Mrs Wright stood in front of the stage and blew her whistle (of course). Garth started strumming his guitar (where did that come from?). Then my friends began to sing a song that sounded a lot like 'Yankee Doodle Came to Town', but with different words.

> Mrs Brisbane came to school,
> To teach us to be smarter.
> When we tried to mess around,
> She made us work much harder.

> Mrs Brisbane, keep it up,
> You are oh so handy,
> Keep on teaching kids like us,
> And we will all be dandy.

> Mrs Brisbane taught us well,
> Starting in September,
> We have learned so much from her,
> And we will all remember.

Mrs Brisbane, thanks a lot,
We will not forget you,
Don't stop helping kids like us,
For we will never let you.

And then they all shouted, 'Thanks, Mrs Brisbane!'

Mr Brisbane handed his wife a handkerchief and she wiped her eyes. I wished I'd had a handkerchief, too.

Mr Morales came to the microphone again and thanked Mrs Wright. 'It took some clever planning to keep this party and this song a surprise,' he said. 'Mrs Wright taught the children the song during PE. Our classroom volunteers, Mrs Hopper and Mrs Patel, made a lot of phone-calls and our caretaker, Aldo Amato, and his wife helped to organize this day.'

It was nice to think that Mr Morales had made a Plan, too. I always knew he was a very clever human.

Everyone applauded again. But Mr Morales wasn't finished. 'Most of the time, we don't thank our teachers until they retire. I'm so glad we had the chance to thank Mrs Brisbane for *not* retiring. We hope she'll be here another thirty years.'

'At least!' I squeaked, which made Miranda giggle.

'Finally, I can't take credit for thinking of this surprise party,' Mr Morales continued. 'I have to thank the unknown person who left the suggestion in my suggestions box. Thank you, whoever you are.'

'You're welcome,' I squeaked softly.

'So things worked out, Og,' I said that evening when my friend and I were alone.

Og leaped up and dived down into his tank with a gigantic splash. That meant he was happy. So was I.

Sometimes you have to give a Plan a long time to work.

Sometimes things work out differently from what you expected, but they still work out.

Life is full of surprises. And I think that's a VERY-VERY-VERY good thing.

> SUGGESTION: An idea you offer to someone else in order to be helpful. It's a good idea to listen to suggestions, especially if they involve parties and more importantly, if they involve *parties honouring friends you REALLY-REALLY-REALLY* like. If those parties include your favourite humans and nice speeches and some singing, so much the better.
>
> *Humphrey's Dictionary of Wonderful Words*

Humphrey's Top Ten Good Surprises

1 Share something with a friend: like ice cream (or broccoli – yum!) or a great book.
2 Put a note saying something nice about someone on his or her desk. Don't sign it! (And don't use the word 'rat' in the note – NO-NO-NO! Unless you're talking about a pet rat you love. Because pet rats are almost as nice as hamsters.)
3 Throw a surprise party for someone special.
4 Help somebody (like your mum or dad or teacher) without being asked. Now *that's* a nice surprise!
5 Visit someone in hospital or a retirement home. Bring something you can do together, like a puzzle or music to listen to.

6 Offer to read to your younger brothers and sisters. Or offer to play a game with them.

7 Draw a picture of someone you like and give it to that person.

8 Give your dog or cat (or hamster) a good scratching. They'll like it – but be gentle!

9 Smile at someone when they least expect it.

10 Invite a friend over to play with your hamster. FUN-FUN-FUN!

Contents

We Set Sail for the Library

'Guess what *I* did this weekend!' Heidi Hopper blurted out one sunny Monday morning.

As usual, my friends in Room 26 of Longfellow School had come back to class with wonderful stories about what they'd done over the weekend.

'Raise-Your-Hand-Heidi, please,' said Mrs Brisbane. Heidi had been better about speaking out of turn lately, but she still slipped up once in a while. After all, she's only human.

When Heidi raised her hand, Mrs Brisbane asked, 'Okay, what *did* you do this weekend?'

'We went on a hike to a cave and waded through an underground stream,' Heidi proudly explained.

I was so amazed, I almost fell off my wheel. (That's what happens when you stop spinning too quickly.) A cave and an underground stream? Now that was an adventure!

'Sounds like quite an adventure,' Mrs Brisbane agreed. Then she noticed all the other hands waving in the air. 'It looks as if a lot of you had adventures.'

Oh, yes, they had! Lower-Your-Voice-A.J. and Wait-for-the-Bell-Garth had gone for a bicycle ride. Miranda Golden (whom I think of as Golden Miranda because she's an almost perfect human) visited the zoo, where many large and scary animals live. Sit-Still-Seth had gone horse-riding.

'I had Humphrey at *my* house,' I-Heard-That-Kirk Chen proudly announced. 'We had an amazing time. Right, Richie?'

'What?' asked Repeat-It-Please-Richie Rinaldi.

'With Humphrey. At my house,' Kirk repeated.

'Yes!' Richie reached across the aisle and high-fived Kirk.

It was true. I'd had a great weekend at Kirk's. I got to watch TV and listen to people talk. Richie came over, too, but whenever he and Kirk did something FUN-FUN-FUN, like going outside to fly a kite or toss a ball around, they left me behind. I know that small furry creatures don't usually do things like that, but as a classroom hamster who goes home with a different student each weekend, I must admit I sometimes feel a little left out. After all, I'm always ready to help my friends (or even my teacher or headmaster) solve a problem. It would be nice if they let me share in their adventures, too.

Don't get me wrong. People have been very nice to me. But ever since the day I left Pet-O-Rama and came to Room 26, I've been trying to understand human behaviour. It's been interesting . . . but it hasn't been easy.

I'm luckier than Og the Frog, who is the other classroom pet. He doesn't need to be fed as often as I do and usually spends weekends alone in Room 26. He doesn't seem to mind, but then, it's not easy to understand frog behaviour, either.

While I was thinking about my friends' adventures, I lost track of what was happening in class for a moment. Mrs Brisbane was giving us our new vocabulary words for the week and, oh, what words they were! Beautiful words, like *nautical*, *treasure* and *squall*, which Mrs Brisbane said was a violent gust of wind. They were the best vocabulary words I'd heard since I started school back in September, and I quickly jotted them down in the tiny notebook I keep hidden behind the mirror in my cage. Ms Mac, the supply teacher who first brought me to Room 26, gave me the notebook before she moved to far-off Brazil. No one else knew I had it. No one knew that I had learned to read and write, either.

My classmates seemed to enjoy the vocabulary words, too. Kirk, the class clown, shouted out, 'Squall! Squall!' Then he took a deep breath, puffed out his cheeks and loudly blew out all the air like a big gust of wind. Stop-Giggling-Gail Morgenstern giggled, but just about everything made her laugh.

The words reminded me of a pirate movie we watched at Kirk's house. Some of the pirates were SCARY-SCARY-SCARY, but it was exciting to see the big ships with their sails flying in the wind. How I'd love to feel the sea breeze ruffling through my fur! And to hear the pirates saying things like 'Avast, matey' and 'Land ho!' I'm not sure what those things mean, but they sound thrilling!

To top it all off, the pirates were fighting with other pirates over buried treasure. I sometimes hide food to save for the future, but the pirates hid gold and silver and shiny jewels. Buried treasure sounds like the most wonderful thing on earth!

I do manage to have adventures of my own, especially when I escape from my cage. I can easily do that because it has a lock-that-doesn't-lock. It looks firmly closed, but I can jiggle it open, get out of my cage to help my friends and return without anyone knowing it. Most of my exploits have been in houses, apartments or in Room 26, but now that I'd been around humans for a while, I longed for bigger adventures.

Lower-Your-Voice-A.J. must have read my mind. (How does he do that?)

'Mrs Brisbane, can we put Humphrey in his hamster ball?' he yelled out.

'A.J., did I call on you?' Mrs Brisbane asked.

'Sorry,' said A.J., lowering his voice. 'But may we, please?'

Our teacher glanced over at my cage. 'I guess he would like a break from his cage,' she said. Maybe she could read my mind, too.

Although I hadn't had my see-through yellow hamster ball for long, I loved rolling up and down the aisles of Room 26. You can learn a lot from studying the floor of a classroom. You can find out who is messy (Richie, Mandy) or who is twitchy (Seth, Art). You can even find out who is growing the fastest by seeing whose jeans are a little short (Garth, Sayeh).

That day, I rolled up and down the aisles of Room 26 at a relaxing pace. The good thing is, I can go where I want to unless Mrs Brisbane stops me. The bad thing is, it's a little hard to hear inside the ball, especially when I'm daydreaming about adventures. Especially adventures on a boat, in the water, on the –

'Ocean,' Mrs Brisbane said, and I heard her quite clearly.

'In the library,' she added.

Maybe I didn't hear her clearly after all. I knew that oceans were VERY-VERY-VERY large bodies of water. And I knew that the library was a place where my friends went to get books. In truth, I'd never seen an ocean or a library, even though there was one right down the hall. A library, that is. (There was no ocean at Longfellow School, at least as far as I knew.)

As I rolled up the aisle to hear better, I saw Mrs Brisbane look at her watch. There's a big clock on the wall, but Mrs Brisbane still checked her watch a lot.

'It's time to go right now,' she announced.

I wasn't sure whether she was going to the ocean or to the library or maybe both places, but I was sure that I wanted to go, too.

'Mr Fish will be waiting,' she added.

Mr Fish? She *must* have been talking about the ocean. I speeded up my hamster ball, spinning my way right up to Mrs Brisbane's feet.

'Me too! Me too!' I squeaked.

Mrs Brisbane looked down at me. Because my hamster ball is yellow, she looked all yellow, too. Everyone did.

'Not you, Humphrey,' she told me. 'You'll have to go back to your cage.'

There was a loud groan from my classmates. I think every single one of them groaned.

'We can't take Humphrey to the library,' Mrs Brisbane insisted. 'What would he do?'

Miranda – dear Golden Miranda – raised her hand and the teacher invited her to speak.

'He wouldn't hurt anything,' she said. 'He could stay in his hamster ball.'

Wait-for-the-Bell-Garth Tugwell spoke up, too. 'He's never been to the library before.'

'Very well,' said Mrs Brisbane. 'Just keep an eye on him.'

And that was it! As Garth picked up my hamster ball, I realized that Og would be left behind. Since he spends a lot of time in water, he'd probably enjoy meeting someone called Mr Fish, too.

'See you later, Og!' I squeaked. 'Sorry!'

I wasn't sure if he could hear me through the hamster ball. Also, Og doesn't have any ears that I can see, although he seems to hear just fine.

My friends lined up and marched down the hall towards the library.

'You have to be quiet in the library, Humphrey Dumpty,' A.J. bellowed. 'And you can't check out books without a card.'

I was too busy trying to stay upright to figure out what kind of card I needed. I know Garth tried to hold the ball steady, but it was a bumpy trip. Even if I felt a little queasy and uneasy, it was well worth the trouble because the library was a HUGE-HUGE-HUGE room lined with colourful shelves.

I love books, especially the ones that Mrs Brisbane reads to us. Although she can be serious as a teacher, when she reads, she becomes a new person with all kinds of different voices that make my whiskers wiggle and my fur stand on end!

'Sorry we're late, Mr Fish,' she said. At least I think that's what she said. 'We brought along another member of our class,' she added. 'Humphrey.'

Suddenly, I saw a large pair of round eyes surrounded by a large pair of round glasses peering down at me. 'So this is the famous Humphrey!' Mr Fish exclaimed. 'Welcome to the library.'

'THANKS-THANKS-THANKS,' I replied politely, although I know all he heard was SQUEAK-SQUEAK-SQUEAK.

'I'm Mr Fitch, the librarian,' he continued.

So it was *Fitch*, not Fish. But he looked a little bit like a fish with his big round eyes and his large round mouth. Then there was that shirt with the black-and-white stripes and all that blue water behind him. What was all that blue water doing in the library? Was this the ocean after all?

'Humphrey, look at all the fishies!' Lower-Your-Voice-A.J. shouted in his loudest voice. Garth held my hamster ball up, and when I stopped swaying from side to side, I saw lots and lots of blue water filled with lots and lots of fish!

'It's a, uh, naquarium,' A.J. explained.

'An *a*quarium,' Mr Fitch corrected him in a kind voice. 'A home for fish.'

Oh, yes, it was quite a home for fish. There were orange fish, silvery fish, fish with black-and-white stripes like Mr Fitch's shirt, big fish, little fish and more! There was even a tiny boat lying at the bottom of the aquarium, which started me wondering just whose boat it was and what had happened to the owner. The ship was small – about the right size for a hamster – but it didn't look very seaworthy. What had happened to make it sink? Was it an accident, bad weather (not too likely in the library) or . . . pirates?

'What do you think, Humphrey?' Mr Fitch asked.

'Eek!' I squeaked. It just slipped out.

Actually, I was thinking that I'd like to be out of the hamster ball so I could see better. But I was lucky to be in the library at all, so it wouldn't be polite to complain.

'Hey, Humphrey!' Kirk leaned down close to the ball. 'Why did the fish go to the library?'

I knew it was one of Kirk's jokes, but I didn't have an answer, so I just squeaked politely.

'To find some bookworms!' Kirk gleefully answered.

'Oh,' I squeaked, even though I wasn't sure that

books had worms in them unless they were books *about* worms.

'Okay, folks, gather round,' Mr Fitch told my classmates. 'We have a lot to do today.'

As my friends sat on the floor, Garth gently set me down near him so I could start rolling my way around the room.

That's when I got a better look at something even more amazing than the fish. Books! Red, blue, green, yellow, pink and purple books. Big, thick books and tall, thin books. Shelves of books all the way to the ceiling. Racks and stacks of books everywhere else. I didn't know there were so many books in the whole wide world, yet here they all were in one big room in Longfellow School. I tried to make a sudden stop as one book caught my attention because of the pirate on the cover. And the pirate flag. It was hard to make out the title from behind the yellow plastic. *Jolly Roger's Guide* . . .

'Attention, please!' Mrs Brisbane said in her most attention-getting teacher's voice.

I rolled a little closer so I could hear what she was saying.

'A test,' she said.

Oh my, we were going to take a test and I didn't have my little notebook and pencil with me. No one had even mentioned a test before we came to the library.

I still couldn't hear very well, but I did hear Mr Fitch say, 'What floats?'

That's why everyone was staring at the aquarium. With its deep blue waters, all those fish and the sunken ship, it looked a lot like the ocean, which is what Mrs Brisbane said we'd be studying.

'Yes, Mandy?' Mr Fitch said. I couldn't see her, but she must have raised her hand.

'Mr Fitch, I think we should take Humphrey out of the hamster ball so he can have some fresh air.'

My, what a nice girl Mandy was! I used to think her name was Don't-Complain-Mandy Payne, but she hardly ever complained any more.

'That's a good idea,' Mrs Brisbane said.

'I was thinking about what my hamster would like,' Mandy replied with pride in her voice. She did have a very fine hamster, thanks to me. And if I was let out of my ball, I could roam freely and get a closer look at all those beautiful books.

'Here,' Mr Fitch said as Kirk released me from the ball. 'Put him in this.'

'This' turned out to be a little square on his desk surrounded by books. Because the desk was lower than the aquarium, I had a good view of what Mr Fitch was doing.

'Class, Mr Fitch is going to let us use his tank to do some tests to figure out what floats and what doesn't – and why,' Mrs Brisbane explained.

I stood up on my hind legs to get a better look. Although the world wasn't yellow any more, I had absolutely no idea what floats. But I knew something that didn't: that little hamster-sized boat at the bottom of the tank.

> If ye be seeking adventure, mateys, the only place to look be the high seas!
>
> from *Jolly Roger's Guide to Life*, by I. C. Waters

2

Sink or Swim

Here is what I learned:

* A wood block is heavier than a plastic bottle-cap. Which one floats? The plastic bottle-cap.

* A piece of aluminium foil isn't nearly as heavy as a block of wood. But when you roll it up into a ball, it drops to the bottom of the water like a small sunken ship.

* A ball of clay sinks like a great big ship-wreck.

* When you spread the foil out in the shape of a little boat, it floats! (Though I'm not sure I'd try sailing in it.)

* By golly, when you spread the clay out into
   a little boat, it floats, too!

I saw it all with my own little hamster eyes, but
when Mrs Brisbane asked why the foil and clay
boats floated when the balls didn't, I was squeak-
less. So were my friends.

'Come on, try a guess, then,' Mr Fitch said in an
encouraging voice.

'What was the question again?' Pay-Attention-
Art Patel asked.

'Why did the foil and clay boats float, but the
balls didn't?' Mrs Brisbane patiently repeated.

Art shrugged.

'You look like you have an idea,' Mr Fitch said to
Speak-Up-Sayeh.

I stood up extra high on my tiptoes to see my shy
friend.

'Well,' she said in a soft voice, 'I think it's
because it's spread out and there's more water
underneath it to hold the weight.'

Leave it to Sayeh to say something clever. I was
so glad she wasn't too shy to speak up any more.

'Bingo!' Mr Fitch said. Even though I thought
Bingo was a dog in a song, I knew he was telling
her it was the right answer. It just had to be. There
was more to whether something floats or not than
just how much it weighs. Once again, I'd learned

something new, which is the amazing thing about school.

'Let's try some more stuff,' said Heidi, without raising her hand again.

I thought it was a GREAT-GREAT-GREAT idea, but suddenly a loud voice that did not belong to A.J. said, 'Excuse me for interrupting. I need to check the temperature.'

I recognized that voice right away. It was big. It was bossy. It was, of course, the voice of Mrs Wright. Who else but Mrs Wright would be checking the temperature of the library? It wasn't even sick!

'Is something wrong, Mrs Wright?' the librarian asked.

'I believe the temperature control is not working properly,' she said. 'And as the new chairperson of the Committee for School Property, I need to keep track.'

Mrs Wright taught physical education at Longfellow School. Thank goodness she didn't teach Room 26. In physical education, they play all kinds of games and sports, which have rules.

Mrs Wright loved rules.

Mrs Wright loved her whistle.

Mrs Wright didn't love me.

'Come on in,' Mr Fitch said.

Mrs Wright scurried across the room in her

puffy white shoes. She headed for the temperature control on the wall. But before she reached it, her puffy white shoes stopped right in their tracks next to the edge of my table.

'What is *it* doing in here?' she asked huffily.

'It?' asked Mr Fitch. 'What's an *it*?'

It was pretty clear what 'it' Mrs Wright was talking about. She was staring right at me.

'The rat,' she said.

Mrs Brisbane quickly corrected her. 'Hamster.'

'Whatever,' Mrs Wright replied. 'He doesn't belong in the library.'

Mr Fitch smiled. 'Because he's not a book?'

'Because he's out of his cage. It's insanitary! What about his *waste*? Where will that go?'

It was very quiet in the library until suddenly Kirk laughed. 'She means his *poo*!' he said.

The word *poo* started the rest of the class laughing out loud. Heidi and Gail giggled. Kirk and Richie rolled their eyes and elbowed each other. Even Miranda and Sayeh chuckled. Mr Fitch bit his lip, while Mrs Brisbane shook her head.

My poo is just a part of life, but for some reason, it makes children giggle. And it sometimes makes grown-ups nervous. I don't know why, because I keep my poo FAR-FAR-FAR away from my food and everything else in my cage. In my view, you won't find a cleaner animal than a hamster.

Mrs Brisbane took two steps towards Mrs Wright. 'What waste?' she asked. 'I don't see any waste.'

'*You know*,' said Mrs Wright.

'Weren't you here to check the temperature?' asked Mrs Brisbane, looking Mrs Wright right in the eyes. 'It does feel a little *chilly* in here.'

That caught Mrs Wright off guard. 'Really? I thought it was a little warm,' she said, hurrying towards the temperature control.

While Mrs Wright fiddled with the control, Mrs Brisbane continued talking to us. 'Class, we'll be returning to Room 26 now. But we'll be coming back soon, because Mr Fitch will be helping us with the new unit we're beginning,' she said. 'I'll tell you about it a little later today.'

Surprisingly, Sayeh raised her hand. Mrs Brisbane invited her to speak right away.

'Could we please check out some books?' she asked in her sweet, soft voice.

Mrs Brisbane and Mr Fitch exchanged looks. Then they both nodded.

'Okay,' said Mr Fitch. 'You've got ten minutes.'

Did you ever cross your fingers and HOPE-HOPE-HOPE for something special? I don't actually have fingers, so I closed my eyes, crossed my toes (both sets) and made my wish.

Wishes are funny. Most of the time, they don't come true. Sometimes they come true and later you wish they hadn't! But once in a while, you make a wish and it happens and it's a good thing. That's what happened in the library. I wished that Mrs Brisbane would pick the pirate book about Jolly Roger. I couldn't check it out because I don't have a library card.

And what do you know – she did!

'YES-YES-YES!' I exclaimed as Garth carried me out in my hamster ball. I was so happy that when I saw Mrs Wright leaning in over the temperature control as I left, she didn't even worry me.

Not very much, anyway.

⋅ŏ⋅

My next wish came true after lunch when Mrs Brisbane began reading that book to us. The full title was *Jolly Roger's Guide to Life,* and it was about a boy and a girl named Violet and Victor who are sent to spend the summer with their mysterious uncle J.R. You can imagine their surprise – and mine – when he turns out to be a pirate called Jolly Roger and he decides to teach them to be pirates, too! Then they set sail to find lost pirate treasure. My fur tingled and I was hanging on every word when the teacher suddenly closed the book.

The other students groaned and I was unsqueakably disappointed until Mrs Brisbane said she wanted to tell us exciting news.

'Og, did you hear?' I squeaked with delight. 'Exciting news.'

'BOING!' my neighbour answered in his odd, twangy voice that green frogs like him have, but he didn't sound particularly excited.

'The reason we talked about what floats is that tomorrow, we'll start a project about sailing,' she said. 'We'll be doing sailing problems in maths and science, and then you'll start building your own model sailing boats.'

My friends murmured excitedly while Mrs Brisbane paused and then cleared her throat.

'Three weeks from tomorrow, if the weather is good, we'll go to Potter's Pond for a contest to see which of your sailing boats can get across the water first. We'll have a picnic and prizes and maybe . . .' Mrs Brisbane paused again. 'Hidden treasure!'

Potter's Pond. Picnic. Prizes. Treasure! My heart pounded at the possibilities, and my classmates' cheers were almost deafening.

'What are the prizes?' Heidi asked.

'Raise-Your-Hand-Heidi,' Mrs Brisbane said. 'The prizes will be a surprise.'

My friends groaned again, and I let out a bit of a squeak myself.

By the afternoon, Mrs Brisbane had written the rules for the sailing boat contest on the blackboard:

1. Each student will work with a partner.

2. The boat must be powered by the wind; no batteries or remote controls can be used.

3. All students will be given the same materials for their boats, but they will be allowed to add one item of their choosing (except batteries).

4. Materials will include wood, cardboard, cloth, paint, glue, markers and other art supplies.

5. The first boat to make it from the starting point to the opposite shore of Potter's Pond will win the grand prize for Most Seaworthy.

6. There will be a prize for Most Beautiful Boat.

At the end of the day, my friends were still chattering away about sailing boats as they rushed out of class.

Once the coast was clear, I shouted to my neighbour. 'Og? Did you hear all that? She said *all students*. I wonder if . . .' I didn't dare finish that thought. Most of the time, I did everything my friends in Room 26 did, like taking tests and learning new things. Sometimes we even had games or parties, and I was right there with the rest of them.

But sometimes, I was left out. Break, lunch, PE, field trips. Still, I could hope.

I was so busy hoping, I didn't realize that it was night time until the door flew open, the lights came on and a familiar voice said, 'Give a cheer, 'cause Aldo's here!'

'Greetings, Aldo!' I answered as he wheeled in his cleaning trolley. 'Did you hear about our wonderful contest?' As usual, all that came out was SQUEAK-SQUEAK-SQUEAK.

I'm not sure if he understood me, but as he cleaned the room, he noticed the vocabulary words on one blackboard and the rules for the contest on the other.

'So that's what you're worked up about, Humphrey!' he said with a hearty laugh. 'I'd like to be part of that!'

'Me too!' I answered, and Og splashed wildly.

'That gives me a great idea!' Aldo announced.

I waited breathlessly for him to say more. Instead, he started sweeping up the aisles of the classroom. Occasionally, I'd hear him chuckle, but I had no idea what he was thinking.

'Squeak up!' I finally insisted.

'You'll see,' Aldo answered. 'All in good time.'

'What was all that about?' I asked Og after Aldo was gone.

'BOING-BOING!' Og replied. Then he leapt into the water side of his tank. While he was splishing and splashing, I daydreamed about life on the open sea, riding the waves, going up and down and up and down. (I stopped thinking about that when my tummy got a little queasy.) If I had a boat, I could sail the seven seas! I could sail anywhere in the world. I could even sail to far-off Brazil, where Ms Mac lived.

Ms Mac! She was my first human friend, and what a friend she was. She was full of life with her bouncy black curls, her big happy smile, her large dark eyes. She was also adventurous. She even took me on a bike ride once, and at night, she liked to play bongo drums. Life with Ms Mac was THE BEST.

Then it broke my heart when Mrs Brisbane came back to Room 26 and Ms Mac left for Brazil. A broken heart hurts a lot. Sure, she sent us letters and pictures, but it wasn't like seeing her every day. At first, I didn't think I'd ever squeak to her again. But by now, my heart wasn't exactly broken. It was just sprained. And I'd be GLAD-GLAD-GLAD if I could see her again.

I don't think Ms Mac meant to break my heart.

I do think Ms Mac would be glad to see me again, too.

Funny how a book about pirates gets you thinking about all kinds of crazy things. Even love.

There be treasures aplenty just for the asking, if ye dare look!

from *Jolly Roger's Guide to Life*, by I. C. Waters

Portrait of a Hamster

BOATS-BOATS-BOATS! Just about all we talked about in Room 26 had to do with boats. There was a maths problem about a boat race, and a history lesson about the Vikings, who were great sailors and wore impressive hats with horns on them. There were also those lovely vocabulary words.

And there was the story. Every day, Mrs Brisbane read another exciting chapter from the book. Uncle Jolly Roger, who did seem unusually jolly for a pirate, taught Vic and Vi (that's what he called Victor and Violet) all kinds of wonderful things about sailing. They even had a run-in with a huge whale!

That part of the story gave I-Heard-That-Kirk the chance to tell this joke: 'What do you call a baby whale? A little squirt!' We all chuckled at that.

So, in just a few short days, I went from never

thinking about boats to thinking about them all the time. There were so many kinds of wonderful boats, from rowing boats you move with oars and muscles to sailing boats and tall ships powered by the wind. Then there were motorboats, yachts, tugboats and ferries, which all have engines. And there were the great ships powered by steam. Mrs Brisbane brought in more books about boats and put up huge posters on the wall.

It would be hard to choose a favourite, but the Chinese junk did catch my eye. That boat isn't junk at all, but a beautiful craft with colourful sails. I could almost feel the sea breeze tickle my whiskers whenever I looked at the picture.

In the evenings, I tried to talk to Og about boats and pirates and treasure, but as soon as I'd bring up the subject, he'd dive into his tank and swim around. Maybe he was trying to tell me that he didn't need a boat to make his way through the water.

I was a little jealous, although I still wouldn't want to be a frog. As nice as Og is, he has goggle eyes, green skin and no nice soft fur at all!

I occupied my spare time by drawing pictures of boats in my little notebook. I must admit, my drawing of the SS *Golden Hamster*, complete with a hamster flag, was quite impressive.

On Friday, it was time to find out which of my friends would take me home for the weekend. 'Do you have the permission slip, Gail?' Mrs Brisbane asked.

Gail pulled a slightly crumpled paper out of her pocket. 'Here it is!' she said with a giggle.

So, I was going home with Gail. Since Gail loved to laugh so much, I was bound to have a fun weekend. Yippee! I was happy to see that she was also taking home a stack of books about boats.

Gail's mum, Mrs Morgenstern, came to pick us up. She was a colourful human who wore blue jeans, an orange sweater with red flowers on it, a yellow cap and high red boots. Her hair was in a long braid half-way down her back.

'You know what, Humphrey? I think I'm going to paint you this weekend,' she said.

Oh, dear! Mrs Morgenstern seemed like a nice person, but the thought of being all covered in wet and messy paint didn't sound fun to me.

'It won't be easy,' Gail warned her. 'He won't stand still.'

Mrs Morgenstern just smiled. 'I'll find a way.'

As she carried me out of the classroom, I squeaked to Og, 'Wish me luck, Oggy boy! I don't know what colour I'll be when I come back! Maybe green, like you!'

'BOING-BOING-BOING-BOING!' Og sounded a little upset. Maybe he liked being the only green creature in Room 26.

When we got to the house, instead of painting me, Gail's mum gave me some carrots and gently set my cage on the night stand in Gail's room.

When we were alone, Gail curled up on her bed with her stack of books.

Suddenly, there was a thundering sound, like a herd of wild horses coming into the room.

'Humphrey!'

It was Gail's brother, Simon. I'd met him once before when I'd stayed at the house. He was just about as tall as Gail, but she still called him her 'little brother'.

'How's it going, Humphrey? What's new? What's happening? Look at your wheel! Can I feed you? Want to come out of your cage?'

That was how Simon talked. Fast.

'Simon! Humphrey's *my* class hamster. I'll feed him and take care of him,' Gail scolded him.

'Ah, I just wanted to say hi. Hiya, Humphrey!' Then Simon made a funny face, sticking his teeth out and holding his hands up in front of him. 'See, I'm a hamster, too.'

'You're an idiot,' said Gail. 'Go away.'

'Okay,' said Simon. 'But I'll be back!'

As he hurried out of the room, Gail let out a big sigh. 'My *brother*,' she groaned.

She made a brother sound like a very bad thing. And yet, to a hamster who lives alone in a cage with a frog who doesn't even squeak for a neighbour, having a brother seemed like a very nice thing.

Once Gail and I were alone, I decided to entertain her with a new trick I'd taught myself. Instead of getting on my wheel and spinning it, I lay down on my back underneath it, then reached my paws up and made the wheel spin with my feet.

Stop-Giggling-Gail just couldn't stop giggling at that, until there was a knock at the door and Gail's mum peeped into the room. 'May I come in?'

Mrs Morgenstern entered, carrying a stack of boxes, with a lot of colourful bags hanging from her arms.

'Guess who went shopping today?' she asked.

I guessed Gail's mum did . . . and I was right. She dumped the boxes and bags on Gail's bed.

'Wait till you see,' she said, excitedly opening the boxes. 'I got you the cutest outfits! Look at this darling skirt!'

She held up a skirt with blue, pink, yellow and green stripes on it. 'It will look great on you.'

Gail wrinkled her nose. 'But Mum, I like trousers for school. I mean, at break . . .'

'Well, these tights go underneath.' Mrs Morgenstern held up a bright pink pair. She rummaged around in a bag. 'I bought three skirts – one with stripes, one with stars and one with flowers.'

'But, Mum . . . I don't like skirts,' Gail repeated.

'Try something new, dear.' Mrs Morgenstern pulled out a fuzzy-looking sweater. 'Like this!'

Personally, I like fuzzy things – like hamsters – but Gail ran her hand over the sweater and said it looked itchy.

'Just try it.' Gail's mum then reached over and opened a box. 'I had another *brilliant* idea today,' she announced. 'We're going to redo your room!'

Gail blinked hard. 'Again?'

'In with the new, out with the old,' her mum said with a smile.

'But we only painted it last year,' Gail reminded her. 'And I like the blue-and-white stripes.'

'*Two* years ago,' said her mum. 'It's something we can do together. It will be fun! We'll give it a whole new look. You and I could paint a mural. We could make the whole room like the universe with all the planets. Or the whole room could look like the ocean. Or . . .'

Gail sighed. 'I've just got used to my room the way it is.'

Mrs Morgenstern reached out and patted Gail's face. 'Honey, try to open up to new things. Change is good!'

Gail didn't answer. She just stared down at her blue bedspread.

Her mum frowned. 'Tell you what. I'll leave these samples here and you look at them. And think about a mural, okay? Just think about it.'

'Sure, Mum,' Gail replied.

Gail didn't seem very excited about painting her room. But I thought it was a much better idea than painting *me*.

After Mrs Morgenstern left, Gail stared at her striped walls for a while. She pushed the paint samples aside and picked up one of her books. She turned a lot of pages, then suddenly held up her book to my cage.

'Look at this ship, Humphrey,' she said.

It was a picture of a lovely sailing boat with a billowing white sail.

'I like it!' I squeaked. I know that all Gail heard was SQUEAK-SQUEAK-SQUEAK, but she seemed to understand.

'It's beautiful, isn't it?' she asked.

'YES-YES-YES!' I agreed.

Gail sighed again. 'Sometimes, I'd like to sail off on a ship and go far, far away,' she said.

'To Brazil!' I said with a squeak. Maybe it was more like a shriek.

'You could come with me,' said Gail. Then she went back to her bed and her stack of books.

·ö·

Really, Gail's family couldn't have been nicer to me. Great snacks, a great cage-clean, no jokes about my poo. Still, I was nervous about being painted.

You see, I'm a Golden Hamster, which means I have very beautiful, glossy golden fur. I never really wanted to be another colour. Not red. Not blue. Not green. (I'm not sure there *are* any hamsters in those colours.)

'Humphrey, you didn't eat your carrots,' Mrs Morgenstern said later that night.

I didn't have the heart to tell her that every time I saw the carrots, I thought about being painted orange.

Orange is a very nice colour for a sweater or a book or a hat. Even for a pair of socks.

It's not a good colour for a hamster, at least not in my opinion.

'Hi, Humphrey! Want to spin on your wheel? Go on, spin it! Want to climb your tree branch? Come on, climb!'

It was morning and Simon was back. As much as I liked Simon, it was hard to keep up with him. Still, he was so excited about everything, I wanted to make him happy, so I hopped on my wheel.

This time, Gail didn't even seem to notice. She just sat on her bed, staring at the pictures of boats in books.

'Out, out,' Mrs Morgenstern said as she came

into Gail's room. 'I'm here to paint him.'

'Oh, Mum,' Gail groaned. 'Can't we just take a picture?'

'Anyone can do that,' her mum answered. 'This is more original.'

'Can I paint him, too?' Simon asked. 'Please?'

Mrs Morgenstern smiled. 'Of course! We'll *all* paint him.'

Eek! If they all painted me, I'd end up looking like a rainbow and I'd probably be a soggy mess. Og wouldn't even recognize me when I got back.

'Okay,' said Gail, but she didn't sound all that happy about it.

Soon, my cage was on the Morgensterns' kitchen table. Simon, Gail and their mum all sat around with paper and paints and stared at me. Mr Morgenstern, who seemed like a kind and sensible man, said he had errands to do and hurried out of the house before the painting even began.

'Okay, artists,' Mrs Morgenstern said. 'Feel free to paint Humphrey any way you like. He doesn't even have to look like a hamster.'

'But I'd prefer to look like a hamster,' I squeaked. 'A nice golden hamster with lovely fur and no paint at all, thank you very much.'

'What's he squeaking about?' Simon asked.

'I don't know, but please hold still, Humphrey,' his mum told me.

I tried to hold still, but my whiskers were quivering and my legs were shaking. I closed my eyes, waiting to feel the wet, gloppy paint on my fur. But my fur felt just fine, so after a while I opened my eyes and saw the three Morgensterns putting lots of lovely paint on paper. They weren't painting me at all! They were painting *pictures* of me.

WHEW-WHEW-WHEW! I was so relieved, I hopped on my wheel for a lovely spin.

'Humphrey, hold still!' Gail told me.

'Oops, sorry,' I squeaked. I jumped off the wheel and kept as still as a lively hamster can. After a few minutes, though, my back leg started itching and my nose started twitching and I had a little cramp in my front paw.

Luckily, Mrs Morgenstern said, 'Well, I think I've captured our little friend. How about you two?'

She held up her painting to show Gail and Simon. I couldn't get a good look at it, but I could see that there wasn't anything golden about her hamster. There was yellow and blue and maybe some purple. 'I think this shows the true spirit of Humphrey.'

I didn't have time to think about why my true spirit was yellow, blue and purple because Simon waved his picture right in my face. 'Here you are, Humphrey!'

Simon's painting showed an orange blob with all kinds of swirly lines but no hamster that I could see.

Mrs Morgenstern leaned in to examine the picture closely. 'That's very interesting, Simon. Tell me about it.'

'It's all squiggly because he was spinning on his wheel. Like this!' Simon jumped out of his chair and began twirling in a circle.

'Perfectly wonderful. I see his eye in the centre,' said his mother. 'You can stop spinning now.'

Then she turned to Gail. 'Let's see your Humphrey.'

Gail held up her paper, which showed a perfectly wonderful picture of *me*! I had two ears, two eyes, two front legs and paws, two back legs and paws, some whiskers and lovely golden fur.

'Oh,' said Gail's mother.

'It looks like him, doesn't it?' asked Gail.

Mrs Morgenstern nodded. 'Yes, it looks a lot like him. It's just . . .'

Gail seemed upset and not at all giggly. 'What's wrong with it?'

'It's fine, honey,' her mum said. 'I'd just like you to paint what you *feel*, not just what you see. Like Simon's picture – you can feel Humphrey's energy, can't you?'

Actually, Simon's picture made me feel a little

queasy, while Gail's picture made me feel very handsome.

Mrs Morgenstern patted Gail's hand. 'It's a very good picture, Gail.'

After her mum and brother left, Gail sat and stared at her picture for a while. 'You're such a pretty colour, Humphrey. Why would I make you blue?' she asked.

I didn't have an answer, but it was time for me to squeak up! 'I LOVE-LOVE-LOVE your picture!' I told her.

I'll never know if she understood me, because the phone rang and Gail ran off to answer it.

> The life of a pirate – ah, there be a work of art, me buckos!
>
> from *Jolly Roger's Guide to Life*, by I. C. Waters

A Golden Moment

Later, Gail's best friend Heidi came over and the two girls went outside to play with a skipping rope. Even in the house, I could hear them chanting:

> Teddy bear, teddy bear, turn around,
> Teddy bear, teddy bear, touch the ground,
> Teddy bear, teddy bear, touch your shoe.
> Teddy bear, teddy bear, that will do!

Gail was giggling again, which made me feel GOOD-GOOD-GOOD.

Then I heard Mrs Morgenstern go outside. 'Gail, maybe Heidi can help you decide how to decorate your room,' she said.

The giggling stopped. 'Later, Mum,' Gail answered.

'That sounds like fun,' Heidi said. 'Paint it pink,' she said. 'Pink with purple curtains and bedspread.'

Heidi always had very definite ideas.

'I don't like pink,' said Gail. 'I like it the way it is.'

'We'll talk about it later,' Mrs Morgenstern told them. 'Just think about a mural.'

Soon the girls were skipping again.

I hopped on my wheel and started spinning. Spinning always helps me think. I could tell that Gail was unhappy about changing her room. I hate to see my friends feeling unhappy, so I needed to come up with a Plan.

On the one paw, Gail didn't like change.

On the other paw, her mum wanted to encourage Gail to try something new.

So far, neither of them wanted to give in.

I don't know much about decorating girls' rooms. Personally, I like to be surrounded by soft bedding and tree branches with my wheel and my sleeping hut near by, but I didn't think Mrs Morgenstern would go for that.

And I didn't see anything wrong with Gail's room.

Still, I'd been happy when Mr Brisbane took the cage I liked and added all kinds of fun things. Maybe Gail would be happy with some changes in her room, too.

As I whirled and twirled my wheel, I stared at the paint samples lying on Gail's bed. Maybe there was something Gail would like if she'd only look at them.

The sounds of Heidi and Gail skipping drifted in through the open window.

> Mabel, Mabel, set the table,
> Just as fast as you are able,
> Don't forget the salt, vinegar, mustard . . .
>   hot pepper!

Then they counted very fast as I heard the SNAP-SNAP-SNAP of the rope hitting the ground.

From the sound of things, they'd be skipping for a while, so I decided to take an unsqueakably big chance and check out those paint colours for myself.

It was easy to swing open the door of my cage. My lock-that-doesn't-lock has never let me down. The hard part of my job was getting from place to place.

Leaping from the bedside table to the bed looked too dangerous, even for me. I'm adventurous, but I like to be safe. I also needed to get to the samples and back to my cage as fast as possible in case someone decided to check up on me. While I was thinking how hard it is for a very small hamster to get around in a human-sized world, I noticed the electrical cord leading from a lamp on the bedside table to – well, I couldn't see exactly where, but it was probably plugged in behind the bed.

I am smart enough to know not to fool around

with electricity – nibbling on that cord could be a BAD-BAD-BAD mistake – but I figured I could *gently* slide down the cord and leap onto the bed at just the right moment.

I took a deep breath and grabbed the cord. It was smoother than I expected, which meant the ride down was also much faster than I expected.

'Wheee!' I squeaked as I slid down towards the bed, and I let go. Plop!

I hadn't expected my slide down the cord to pull the lamp over on its side with a loud THUMP! Thank goodness, it didn't break.

I also hadn't planned to land right *on* the stack of paint samples, but it was lucky that I did, because they all spread out like a beautiful rainbow before me. I never knew there were so many colours, but where to start?

I pulled out sky blue, which was a nice colour. The clouds and the sun and the trees all look pretty against the sky. Grass green was nice, too. Flowers look GREAT-GREAT-GREAT against a green backdrop. I wasn't too fond of pink, and neither was Gail. Oh, dear, I wasn't making much progress.

> Engine, engine number nine,
> Coming down Chicago line,
> If the train jumps off the track,
> Do you want your money back?

At least Gail and Heidi were still busy.

I pulled out the next sample, which was a golden-brownish-tan. Golden. I held my paw against it, and the paint exactly matched my golden fur! My fur was a beautiful colour; everybody said so.

I pulled the sample away from the others so it stood alone right in the middle of the bed.

Just then I heard thundering footsteps and a familiar 'Hiya, Humphrey!'

Simon was coming, and there was no way to get back to the cage before he arrived. I dived under Gail's pillow and crossed my paws, hoping he wouldn't find me there.

It was dark and scary and awfully stuffy under that pillow. I could hear Simon's muffled voice say, 'Want to ride in your hamster ball? Humphrey? Hey! Humphrey!

Oh, no! Humphrey!' Simon must have noticed that I wasn't in my cage.

Next, I heard the distant sound of footsteps leaving the room. Gasping for air, I crawled out from under the pillow and scurried across the bedspread. Oh joy, this was my lucky day! The lamp was still lying on its side with the shade on the bed and the base on the bedside table, forming a perfect bridge. I pulled myself up on the shade, scampered across the lamp and gently dropped down on the bedside table. I made sure to close the cage door behind me before taking a dive under the bedding.

'He's gone, Mum. He's not in his cage!' Simon shouted as he dragged his mother into Gail's room. I could hear Gail and Heidi coming up behind them, making worried noises about me.

'Calm down, everybody,' Mrs Morgenstern said. 'Let's check out his cage.'

Just as they were approaching, I crawled out from under my bedding, trying to look a little sleepy.

'See, Mum, he's gone! He's really gone!' Simon exclaimed.

I yawned, making sure to let out a little squeak.

'There he is, honey,' I heard Mrs Morgenstern saying. 'He was just hiding!'

Simon shook his head. 'No, Mum. He was *gone*!'

Mrs Morgenstern noticed the lamp and picked it up. 'I suppose Humphrey also knocked over the lamp. Is that right, Simon?'

Simon looked truly puzzled. 'I don't know. It wasn't me.'

I felt a little guilty about tricking Simon, but a hamster's got to do what a hamster's got to do.

Mrs Morgenstern set the lamp back in place.

'At least it isn't broken.' She smiled and turned towards Heidi and Gail. 'Let's look at those paint colours now,' she said. 'Then we can head down to the paint shop.'

Gail sighed. 'Oh, Mum!'

'How cool!' said Heidi, walking towards the bed. 'Look at all these great colours.'

'But I like blue and white.' Gail suddenly stopped and stared. 'Oh, but I like *that*!'

I had to strain to see Gail walk to the middle of her bed and pick up one of the paint samples. 'It's golden!' she said.

'Yep!' I agreed. It just slipped out because I was thrilled to see Gail smile.

'It's golden like Humphrey,' she added.

'It is pretty,' said Heidi. 'Almost as pretty as pink.'

'Fabulous!' said Mrs Morgenstern. 'I never would have thought of gold, but it's brilliant! We could paint a hamster mural on the wall.'

'Not a mural, Mum.' Gail sounded very definite.

Mrs Morgenstern sighed. 'How about a picture of Humphrey?'

'My picture of Humphrey?' Gail asked.

Gail's mum smiled and nodded. 'Your picture.'

'Yay, Humphrey!' Simon shrieked.

'Great idea!' I agreed.

When I squeaked, Gail giggled. That was a wonderful sound.

'Let's do it,' she said.

I was feeling pretty proud of myself. Gail and her mum both seemed happy. And that made me feel HAPPY-HAPPY-HAPPY, too.

Late that evening, after Heidi had left, I rolled through the kitchen in my hamster ball while Gail and her dad made popcorn, which smelt unsqueakably delicious.

The telephone rang in the next room, and I heard Gail's mum answer it. 'Mrs Brisbane!' she said. 'So nice to hear from you!'

I rolled towards the living room to hear what Mrs Morgenstern was saying.

'Sensational,' she said. 'Fabulous! I love it!'

Then she listened some more and said, 'Yes. Yes. Of course!' She didn't say anything else except 'Okay, goodbye.'

Once she was off the phone, I rolled back to the kitchen alongside Gail's mum.

'What did Mrs Brisbane want?' asked Gail.

'It's a surprise,' said Mrs Morgenstern. 'A very nice surprise.'

No matter how much Gail and I protested, she wouldn't say any more.

As you can imagine, I was anxious to get back to Room 26 on Monday morning to see just what the nice surprise would be!

'Og, I thought I was going to be orange and purple when I came back today, but I'm glad that I'm still golden. It's a very good colour for a hamster,' I told Og when I arrived back on Monday morning.

'BOING!' he answered. 'BOING-BOING!'

'Of course, green is the best colour for a frog,' I quickly added. I didn't want to hurt my friend's feelings.

'BOING-BOING-BOING!'

He hopped up and down in his tank, twanging away.

'Keep it down over there,' Mrs Brisbane told us. 'We've got to start building our boats for the contest.' She turned to the class. 'I hope you all spent some time thinking about what kind of boat you'd like to make.'

My friends all started talking at once, which is not something Mrs Brisbane likes to hear.

'Silence!' she said in a firm voice. 'Now, I need to know which students are pairing up so I can make a list. Then I'm going to give you some time to get together and plan your boat.'

There was a lot of hubbub, but it wasn't long before the students were sitting in pairs, jabbering away and looking at pictures.

When I was sure no one was looking, I slid my notebook out from my hiding place behind my mirror. I took it into my sleeping hut and stared at my boat drawing. Yep, the SS *Golden Hamster* was the boat for me! Of course, it was only a dream because I didn't have a partner, much less the materials to build a boat. Not only that, my friends kept going to the library to learn more about boats, but I wasn't invited back. (I wonder if Mrs Wright had something to do with that?)

Once, my friends were in the library a LONG-LONG-LONG time, and when they came back, they were all talking about some fellow named Long John Silver. I could picture someone named John who was very tall, but I'd never seen a silver human – or hamster, for that matter. Oh, and Lower-Your-Voice-A.J. kept shouting out, 'Pieces of eight! Pieces of eight!' in a screechy voice. And everyone else would giggle as if he'd said the funniest thing.

I wonder if I'll ever understand humans.

> Silver and gold be my favourite colours, me hearties! Bright, shiny silver and gold!
>
> from *Jolly Roger's Guide to Life*, by I. C. Waters

The Trip to Treasure Island

My classmates weren't the only humans acting strangely. One night, instead of saying his usual 'Never fear 'cause Aldo's here', our caretaker threw open the door and shouted, 'Ahoy there, me hearties!'

I peeped out of my sleeping hut, half-expecting to see a real pirate with a patch over his eye and a sack full of doubloons (though I wasn't quite sure what those were). Instead, I saw my old pal Aldo staring into my cage.

'Are ye in there, matey?' he asked.

'YES-YES-YES, and you certainly fooled me,' I squeaked.

When he threw back his head and laughed, his moustache shook so hard, I thought it might fall off. Luckily, Aldo's moustache is *firmly* attached. 'Ye be all right, Jack,' he replied, even though he knows perfectly well my name is Humphrey. 'I be here to swab the decks. And don't ye be worrying – I'm not a real pirate,' he added with a wink. '*Not yet*, anyway.'

That comment got my whiskers wiggling, I can tell you! Did he mean he might become a pirate some day?

He didn't explain what he meant, just whistled a merry tune I'd never heard before. After he cleaned the floor and emptied the wastepaper baskets, he stood in front of my cage and said, 'Check this out.'

He danced a very happy, bouncy kind of dance as he whistled his tune. When he was finished, he bowed and said, 'That's a hornpipe dance. It's named after a musical instrument sailors play. What do you think, Humphrey?'

I was happy he remembered my name again and even happier to be able to squeak the truth. 'It was GREAT-GREAT-GREAT!'

'Thanks, matey. Gotta set sail now.' With that, he pushed his cleaning trolley out of Room 26.

It was very quiet once he was gone. So quiet that I couldn't help remembering the thing he'd said about not being a pirate *yet*. Since Aldo was one of the nicest people I'd ever met, it was hard to think of him as a person who would steal people's treasure, which is what real pirates do. Still, with his fine moustache and excellent hornpipe dancing, I could almost believe he was a pirate.

I couldn't sleep a wink that night, not just because I'm nocturnal, but also because of all the strange goings-on.

'Og, if I could go to the library, maybe I'd understand what everyone is talking about,' I told my neighbour.

Og floated in the water side of his tank as if he didn't have a care in the world. I flung open the door to my cage and came a little closer.

'Wouldn't *you* like to know what's going on?' I squeaked loudly, just in case he hadn't heard me before.

He didn't answer at all. He just floated around. Maybe he was sleeping, but who can tell with a frog?

'I was thinking, maybe I should go down there and check things out,' I said, raising my voice even more.

Still nothing from Og.

Since I was already out of my cage, I decided to have a little adventure. Aldo would have gone home by now so the coast would be clear. I slid down the leg of the table and scurried across the floor. The door was closed, sure, but I was able to squeeze under the bottom. After all, I'd done this before!

The corridors of Longfellow School are always a

little eerie at night. There are low lights on, and the street lights shine through some of the windows. But it's odd to be in a school with no children, no teachers and no head.

It doesn't feel quite right.

I hurried to the library, squeezed under that door – oops, a little tight – and there was that marvellous room filled with books. At first, it was SCARY-SCARY-SCARY because the fish tanks had their lights blazing, so they glowed in a way that was pretty, but kind of ghostly. The colourful fish swam around in the bright blue water, and luckily, they didn't look scary at all.

It was cool in the library (maybe Mrs Wright was right about the temperature being off). I walked up the big aisle between the shelves and the tables and stared up at the tanks.

The sunken ship was still there, and I have to admit, it fascinated me. Whose ship was it? A tiny pirate? A hamsterish fish? Or some creature of the deep I'd never heard of? I crept a little closer to get a better look. There was a series of shelves next to the desk. I found that if I reached up and pulled hard with all my might, I could raise myself from shelf to shelf until I reached the top of the desk.

The light blazing from the fish tank blinded me for a second, and as I stumbled across the desktop, I stepped on something hard and lumpy.

Like magic, a big screen in the front of the room lit up. I scrambled over the bumpy object and – whoa! – pictures came up on the screen and music blared. I looked down and realized that I had been standing on a remote control with all kinds of buttons, one of which had turned on a television. But I forgot all about the remote when exciting music began to play. I looked up at the TV screen, and what I saw there amazed me.

The words on the screen spelled out *Treasure Island.* (I am so glad I learned to read!) There was the sea and a ship and a boy named Jim Hawkins. Before I knew it, I was watching an amazing adventure starring a pirate known as Long John Silver.

Oh, and there was a parrot that squawked, 'Pieces of eight! Pieces of eight!' even louder than A.J. had. The bird had a sharp, pointy beak that I would NEVER-NEVER-NEVER want to come into contact with. And there were great big waves rolling up and down, up and down. As I settled down to watch, I accidentally hit another button and the movie started all over again. The words, the music, the parrot. And those waves rolling up and down, up and down, until my tummy felt funny.

This time, I didn't wiggle a whisker. I sat quietly and watched the whole movie from beginning to end.

It was one of the best nights I could remember, at least at Longfellow School.

When it was over, I carefully tapped the remote control until the picture went off. Then I dashed back to Room 26, grabbed the cord for the blinds that hangs down next to my table and swung myself back up like I was swinging my way up to the crow's nest of a ship.

A crow's nest is a lookout on the topsail of a ship. I learned that watching *Treasure Island*.

Soon, I was back in my cage, safe and secure.

'Ahoy, Og! Would you like to hear about *Treasure Island*?' I asked my friend.

'BOING-BOING!' he answered.

I took that to be a very big *yes*.

·ö·

It took me most of the night to tell Og the whole story of the movie I'd seen. If I do say so myself, I did a great job, especially when I screeched, 'Pieces of eight! Pieces of eight!'

Whenever I did that, Og responded with an enthusiastic 'BOING-BOING!'

The next morning, once class was under way again, I was dozing away, dreaming about a desert island.

This wasn't just any desert island, because in addition to the swaying palms and the ocean breezes, Ms Mac was there with me. Oh, and we had such fun, eating dates and nuts and playing in the sand (which I must admit, I like better than water).

In my dream, I heard roaring waves, screeching seagulls, the singing of an ocean breeze. Then there was the sound of Mrs Brisbane. Maybe I wasn't dreaming any more. I poked my head out of my sleeping hut.

'Class, I have a big surprise for you,' Mrs Brisbane announced. 'I've brought in some helpers to advise you about your boats.'

'Whoo-hoo!' A.J. hooted loudly. Garth joined him.

Mrs Brisbane went to the door and when she opened it, in came her husband Bert and – surprise – Gail's mum!

'Remember, there's a prize for Most Beautiful Boat and a prize for Most Seaworthy,' said our teacher. 'Mr Brisbane can advise you on building your boats, and Mrs Morgenstern is an artist who can help you make them look good.'

That news created quite a stir in class. Personally, if I were sailing, I'd want a solid, seaworthy boat. But I also liked the idea of a good-looking craft. Having these two helpers was just the kind of idea a very clever hamster might have come up with!

All my classmates were buzzing with excitement, except for Gail, who stared down at her desk. I was puzzled. Wasn't she glad her mum was there? I decided to think about it for a while, but I guess I dozed off.

The next time I woke up, Mr Brisbane was talking. 'A boat that floats is a success,' he said. 'A boat that sinks is not.'

I nodded in agreement and then drifted back to sleep. I was awakened again by the sound of Mrs Morgenstern's voice. 'A thing of beauty is a joy for ever,' she said. 'Your job is to make your boat a joyful reflection of who you are!'

Suddenly, I was wide awake. The SS *Golden Hamster* was definitely a joyful reflection of who I was. But would a boat like that actually float?

My friends were already busy drawing and discussing their boats. If only I had a partner to help me build my boat! I stuck my head outside the hut.

'Og, would you like to build a boat with me?' I asked.

'BOING!' he answered, followed by loud splashing.

I guess the idea of a boat is pretty silly to a creature that can swim like Og.

So I watched my classmates make their plans. Mr Brisbane provided each group with a light wooden hull (the body of the boat), which he had hollowed out because Mrs Brisbane said it was too dangerous for her students to be carving with knives. He wheeled his chair from table to table, encouraging my friends about their ideas. Mr Brisbane moves around in a wheelchair after an accident last year, but it hasn't slowed him down one bit.

Mrs Morgenstern also moved around to each group. She was wearing a green and gold flowered tunic with gold trousers tucked into her red boots.

'Colour is the key!' she told Seth and Tabitha. 'Choose your colours carefully.'

'The sail's the thing,' Mr Brisbane told Art and Mandy. 'Remember, that's what powers your boat. The Vikings were great sailors. Good choice.'

Vikings! My whiskers wiggled with excitement and I strained my neck, hoping for a glimpse of their drawing.

Mrs Morgenstern moved to the table where Gail was working with Heidi.

'Come on, Gail,' she said. 'You can be more creative than that! Think colour!'

Gail wasn't giggling. She wasn't even smiling.

Kirk, who was almost always joking, was also very serious as he worked on his boat with his friend Richie.

'I've got a great idea,' Kirk said as he quickly sketched a drawing. 'I know all about boats. We'll make it a tall ship . . . like this!'

My heart thumped a little faster. Tall ships were amazing with MANY-MANY-MANY sails billowing in the wind!

'That's cool.' Richie picked up his pencil. 'What if we put a thing on the front, a whatdyoumacallit?'

He started to draw on the paper, but Kirk reached out and stopped Richie's hand. 'A figurehead? I don't want to take the chance. It might throw the ship off balance and sink it.' Richie stopped drawing, but he didn't look very happy.

'It would look good,' he complained.

'Yep,' Kirk agreed. 'But you want to *win*, right?'

'Sure,' Richie said, although he didn't sound completely convinced.

'Hey, Richie, what did the ocean say to the boat?' Kirk asked.

'What?' Richie asked.

'It didn't say anything. It just waved!' Kirk joked, and Richie laughed. Just then, Mr Brisbane came to their table. 'This is a happy group,' he said.

He studied the sketch of the tall ship. 'It's a fine-looking craft, boys,' he praised them. 'Good work.'

Kirk and Richie beamed with pride.

'Mr Brisbane, want to hear a joke?' asked Kirk.

Mr Brisbane smiled. 'Always.'

This time, Richie started. 'What did the ocean say to the boat?'

'It didn't say anything. It just waved!' Kirk responded. Then he and Richie exploded into laughter.

They were a good team. Or so I thought.

·ᴼ·

Mrs Morgenstern's voice rang out. 'Now that's what I call original!' She was standing by the table where Sayeh and Miranda were working.

'Gail? Heidi?' she said. 'Look at this! Simply beautiful.'

Heidi and Gail came over to look at the drawing.

'It's a swan boat,' Miranda explained. 'I saw one once in a park.' She sounded very proud. Speak-Up-Sayeh didn't say anything, but she looked proud, too.

'Okay,' said Heidi. 'We'll make ours really pretty. Right, Gail?'

Gail didn't answer. She just followed her friend back to the table and stared down at her drawing. I wished I could see it from my cage, but I couldn't.

After Mr Brisbane and Mrs Morgenstern left, Mrs Brisbane pulled her chair to the front of the room, took out my new favourite book and began to read. Uncle Jolly Roger and Vic and Vi finally reached the tropical island where there was supposed to be buried treasure. But when they arrived, they discovered that a band of pirates had got there before them. The very thought of meeting a real pirate gave me the shivers. But it was the good kind of shivers, where you feel happy and scared all at the same time.

When Mrs Brisbane stopped reading, my friends all begged for more. 'I'd like to read another chapter,' she said. 'But I don't think there's time.'

Just then, the bell rang, announcing the end of school. The day had gone so quickly, none of us had noticed. Not even Wait-for-the-Bell-Garth, who was always the first one heading out of the door.

Usually, after school was finished for the day, I looked forward to Aldo's arrival. It was the high point of my evenings. But that night, I was anxious for Aldo's visit to be over as fast as possible.

For one thing, I liked normal Aldo better than pirate Aldo, despite his hornpipe dance. For another thing, I was still thinking about *Treasure Island* and Long John Silver and Jim Hawkins, the boy who went to sea. I stared out of the window until I saw Aldo's car pull out of the car park. Then I threw open the door to my cage, slid down the table leg and zoomed across the floor. I was so excited, I almost forgot to tell Og what I was doing. I felt a little guilty about having so much fun without him, but I couldn't resist the chance to see that movie again.

I squeezed under the library door and headed straight for the remote control. I punched it and – boom – the monitor lit up. I was all ready to set sail on the open sea.

I was SO-SO-SO surprised when instead of a pirate movie, there was some kind of programme about how the human eye works! I guess Mr Fitch had showed it to some other class. I must admit, I learned a lot about the cornea and the iris and cones and rods.

But believe me, it was nothing – *nothing* – like sailing to Treasure Island.

> Keep your eyes open, mateys. There
> may be rough seas ahead!
>
> from *Jolly Roger's Guide to Life*, by I. C. Waters

Wright Is Wrong

By the time class started the next morning, my mind was spinning as fast as my hamster wheel, thinking about pirates, sailing boats and the sailing contest.

Once class began, however, there was too much going on to think about any of those things. The vocabulary test came first. I'd had boats on my mind all week but *not* spelling. I took the test with my friends (sneaking into my sleeping hut to write in my notebook) but I managed to miss three words, including *squall*. For some reason, I thought there was a *w* in there. Like *sprawl*. Or *bawl*.

I must admit, I had a little doze during the maths period. As soon as that was finished, Mr Brisbane and Mrs Morgenstern returned and the sailing-boat building was in full swing again. I perched near the top of my cage and watched my friends at work.

Oh, what lovely boats they were! The boat Miranda and Sayeh were working on really looked like a graceful swan. It was a sailing boat that curved up high at each end. The front part looked like the head of a swan. The back part looked like the tail feathers. The girls were carefully gluing colourful feathers to the sides of the boat. It was quite a sight!

A.J. and Garth designed an impressive sailing boat that had a skull-and-crossbones pirate flag (which is called the Jolly Roger, like the uncle in the book Mrs Brisbane was reading to us).

Tabitha and Seth were building a Chinese junk. It had several sails. The biggest one was red, with a dragon painted on it. And the Viking ship designed by Art and Mandy was beginning to take shape. It was long and low with a square sail with blue and white stripes.

But the sailing boat to end all sailing boats was the one Kirk and Richie were building. It was still early, but I was already thinking they had a good chance of winning the race.

Richie was sanding the hull, and Kirk was work-ing on the sail.

SCRITCH-SCRITCH-SCRITCH! went the sandpaper. Richie was really throwing himself into his work when suddenly Kirk pulled the boat out of his hand.

'Hold it, Richie. You have to sand it evenly. You're taking way too much off this side, see?' Kirk pointed to one side of the boat.

'Okay, okay. You don't have to grab it like that.' Richie, who was usually a happy-go-lucky guy, looked grumpier than I'd ever seen him before. 'Give it back.'

'I'll sand it,' said Kirk. 'I know how to do it.'

He started sanding while Richie glared at him. 'I know how to do it, too,' he told Kirk.

'Look, Richie, just let me do this. I can practically promise we'll win because I know just what to do,' Kirk assured his partner. 'My dad and I built one of these last year.'

'I can at least *sand* it,' Richie protested, but Kirk didn't give in.

'I'll do it,' Kirk said. 'And we'll get the prize.'

Kirk kept sanding. He didn't even seem to notice how upset Richie was.

After a while, Kirk said, 'Hey, where do you take a sick boat?'

'Who cares?' Richie muttered.

'To the dock!' Kirk replied with a big laugh. 'Get it? To the doc!'

Richie didn't answer, and he certainly didn't laugh.

Gail didn't seem to be enjoying the assignment any more than Richie. Heidi painted the hull while Gail was supposed to design the sail. Mrs Morgenstern loved all of Heidi's ideas.

'Oh, those squiggles look like waves! That's a wonderful theme for the boat,' she exclaimed. Then she turned to her daughter. 'Gail, why don't you do something like that for the sails?'

Gail didn't smile, and she didn't answer.

Mrs Morgenstern didn't seem to notice. 'Let your mind go wild. Think mermaids! Think seagulls! Think lighthouses!'

I don't believe Gail was thinking about any of those things. Luckily, Mandy had a question for Mrs Morgenstern, who moved away from the table.

'Why don't you listen to your mum?' Heidi asked Gail. 'If you do what she says, maybe we'll win the prize for Most Beautiful Boat.'

Gail stared at the big poster of a sailing boat for a very long time.

'See that picture on the wall?' she asked Heidi at last.

'Sure,' Heidi answered.

'What does it look like?'

Heidi thought for a moment. 'Well, it's a wooden boat with big white sails.'

Gail nodded. 'And doesn't it look beautiful sailing across the water with those white sails against the blue sky?'

'I guess so,' Heidi said.

'I don't think there's anything more peaceful than a sailing boat with white sails,' Gail explained. 'I hate to mess it up with mermaids and seagulls.'

'But the contest . . .' Heidi protested.

Gail sighed. 'Okay,' she said. 'I'll try.'

She didn't sound as if she meant it.

·ö·

I was GLAD-GLAD-GLAD when Mrs Brisbane told my friends to put their boats away until school was over. After the students left, Mrs Brisbane stayed to tidy up her desk. It was quiet for the first time all day, so I guess I dozed off. I wasn't asleep for long, though, because I was awakened by a familiar voice, loudly saying, 'I think we need to talk about your field trip.'

The voice, which belonged to Mrs Wright, said 'field trip' in the same way she might say 'bad smell' or 'chicken pox'.

'Oh, you mean the trip to Potter's Pond?' Mrs Brisbane asked. Her voice was friendly, but I knew our teacher well enough to know that she was on her guard. With Mrs Wright, it's a good idea to be on your guard.

'Yes, I see you filed the proper form, but I did

have some questions,' Mrs Wright explained. 'And some *concerns*.'

I was concerned that Mrs Wright was sticking her nose where it didn't belong.

'What concerns?' Mrs Brisbane asked.

Mrs Wright leafed through a stack of papers she had in her hand. '*Safety concerns*,' she said. 'I need to know that you will have the required number of parent volunteers.'

'Of course. That's never a problem with this class,' Mrs Brisbane assured her.

'And all students must have permission slips. No exceptions,' Mrs Wright said in an ominous tone of voice. 'Not one.'

'Of course,' Mrs Brisbane said.

'I am also concerned about *water safety*,' Mrs Wright continued. 'I'm not sure whether or not we'll need a lifeguard.'

'If we need one, we'll get one,' said Mrs Brisbane. 'But the students aren't swimming. They're just sailing boats.'

Mrs Wright shuffled her papers some more. 'Yes, well, these are *model* boats, I hope.'

I don't think Mrs Wright saw Mrs Brisbane roll her eyes, but I did.

'Very small model boats,' she answered.

'Yes, yes, I see,' said Mrs Wright. 'We'll also have to make sure the students are properly dressed.

They will need sweaters. Possibly boots.'

Mrs Brisbane sighed, but Mrs Wright kept on talking. 'Then there's the matter of food. All the snacks must be on the approved list.' She whipped out a piece of paper and handed it to Mrs Brisbane.

'Mrs Wright,' our teacher said, 'I have been taking students on field trips for many, many years and I've never had a problem so far.'

Mrs Wright smiled, but it wasn't a nice smile. '*Of course,*' she said. 'But regulations have changed over the years.'

I couldn't take it any more. I just had to squeak up. 'Leave her alone!' I shouted. Even if it sounded like SQUEAK-SQUEAK-SQUEAK to her, I figured she could tell I wasn't happy.

'BOING-BOING-BOING!' Og chimed in. I know I sometimes complain about him, but Og always comes through when you need him.

'Goodness, what's that noise?' Mrs Wright asked. 'Are you sure those animals are all right?'

Mrs Brisbane ignored that question. 'Just give me the forms. I'll make sure they're all filled in.'

'Thank you,' Mrs Wright icily replied. 'It's for the students' safety, you know.'

After Mrs Wright was gone, Mrs Brisbane paced around the room making huffing and puffing noises. I understood.

'She is WRONG-WRONG-WRONG!' I told her.

'BOING!' Og agreed.

Mrs Brisbane stopped pacing in front of my cage. 'I shouldn't let her upset me. I think I understand her problem.'

I wasn't sure I wanted to understand Mrs Wright, but I listened politely.

'She teaches games to her students all day long, but *she* never has any fun,' she said.

'Yes!' I squeaked. 'She's no fun at all!'

Mrs Brisbane chuckled. 'Poor woman. I have an idea of just how to handle her.'

She picked up her handbag and left the classroom, still smiling.

I was glad Mrs Brisbane had an idea. Her ideas are almost always good. I just wished she had told me what it was.

·ö·

For the rest of the week, my friends worked hard. The boats looked good, but Richie and Gail didn't look any happier.

Mr Morales, the head, stopped by Room 26 one afternoon. He was wearing a tie that had little sailing boats all over it.

'I've been hearing so much about these boats of yours, I had to come and see for myself,' he said.

Everyone always sat up straight and paid attention when Mr Morales came to visit. After all, he was the Most Important Person at Longfellow School. He was also a personal friend of mine.

He took the time to look at each and every boat, and he always had something nice to say.

'They all look seaworthy,' he announced when he was finished. 'And I should know. When I was your age, my friends and I spent half a summer building a raft. We couldn't wait to sail it on Potter's Pond. I guess I thought we'd be like Huckleberry Finn.'

I'm sorry to say I had no idea who Huckleberry Finn was, but I really wanted to hear what happened.

Mr Morales continued: 'That raft was heavy, and it took six of us to carry it. We slipped the raft into the water, hopped on board and guess what happened?'

None of my friends seemed to know, so he answered the question himself. 'It sank straight down. It's probably still lying at the bottom of the pond today.'

Amazingly, he chuckled.

'Oh, no!' Mrs Brisbane exclaimed.

'It was disappointing,' Mr Morales continued. 'But I can assure you, the water in Potter's Pond is very shallow.'

'Mrs Wright will be happy to hear that,' Mrs Brisbane said.

'It's also very muddy. My shoes got so stuck in the sludge, I had to pull my feet out and go back with a shovel to dig them out.' He chuckled. 'My mama and papa were not pleased.'

Mrs Brisbane and my classmates laughed, too.

'Just make sure you've got a boat that floats,' the principal continued.

On his way to the door, he passed by my cage. 'How's it going, Humphrey?' he asked. 'Where's your boat?'

'That's what I'd like to know,' I squeaked back.

He laughed, so I guess he didn't actually understand what I was saying.

But when I went into my sleeping hut for a nap, I kept picturing a raft lying at the bottom of Potter's Pond, just like the sunken boat in Mr Fitch's tank.

On Friday, after Mr Brisbane and Mrs Morgenstern left, Mrs Brisbane made a surprising and shocking announcement.

'Class, we were so busy with our boats this week, I forgot to arrange for anyone to take Humphrey home for the weekend.'

Whew – that statement took the wind out of my sails! For one thing, my classmates usually *begged* to take me home. For another thing, if nobody took me home, I'd get awfully hungry and thirsty because I can't go without food and water as long as Og can.

'I can't believe we all forgot,' Heidi said.

'Raise-Your-Hand-Heidi,' Mrs Brisbane said. 'But don't worry. I'll be taking him home with me.'

I felt a lot better hearing that. But I felt worse when she said, 'I'm afraid there's no time for me to read aloud today. We'll continue with our book on Monday.'

No time to read aloud! Just when Uncle Jolly Roger and Vic and Vi were in great danger! I was about to squeak up in protest when the bell rang. Class was over, the school day was over and as soon as Mrs Brisbane gathered up her jacket and books, we were on our way out of Room 26 for the weekend.

'Farewell, matey,' I called to Og.

'BOING-BOING!' he twanged in return. I wonder if that's how frogs say, 'Aye-aye.'

> Life at sea – it's either sink or swim, mateys. Sink or swim.
>
> from *Jolly Roger's Guide to Life*, by I. C. Waters

7

An Unpleasant Discovery

My friends in Room 26 had been thinking so much about boats, I was relieved to be at the Brisbanes' house, where they always paid a lot of attention to *me*. You can imagine my surprise when *they* continued to think of nothing but boats all weekend, too!

Mr Brisbane read about model sailing boats, sketched them and worked on them in his garage workshop. Meanwhile, Mrs Brisbane kept busy writing things on a piece of paper. Every once in a while, she'd stop and chuckle.

When I first met Mrs Brisbane, she never chuckled. In fact, she hardly ever smiled, because of Mr Brisbane's car accident. But slowly, over time, she regained her sense of humour. Maybe I helped just a little bit. Still, it was unusual for her to sit and chuckle in a room all by herself. People often say and do very strange things in front of me, almost as if I'm invisible.

Finally, Mr Brisbane came in from the garage. 'You're still working on your list?' he asked.

'Yes,' she said, chuckling again. 'I tell you, this is going to be one fun field trip.'

So that was it. She was planning the picnic at Potter's Pond. Oh, what I would give to get a peek at her list! Luckily, the Brisbanes started yawning early, and even though I would have liked them to have set up a nice obstacle course for me to run, I wasn't that sorry to see them go to bed.

You see, I had a Plan. And when a hamster has a Plan, nothing (well, almost nothing) can stand in his way.

I waited until the house was VERY-VERY-VERY quiet. Then I fiddled with my cage door, and as usual, it swung right open. Thank goodness for my lock-that-doesn't-lock!

I was feeling especially adventurous because the only peril I faced at the Brisbanes' house was the possibility of being caught outside my cage. I was willing to take the chance because I had a mission: to find out more about the picnic at Potter's Pond.

I could see that the list was sitting right on Mrs Brisbane's desk. Of course, before I set out I had to map my route, just like sailors – and even pirates – do.

I slid down the leg of the low table where my

cage sat and scurried across the carpet. It felt nice on my paws, but I couldn't move as fast on it as I can on Aldo's shiny, slippery floors. The desk looked like a mountain to a small hamster like me. However, I knew that where there's a will (and a Plan), there's a way.

Close to the desk, there was a nice cosy chair with a striped blanket draped over it. I grabbed onto the blanket and pulled myself up, paw over paw, then hopped onto the desk. There was Mrs Brisbane's list, right in front of me.

I was pretty excited until I looked more closely and saw that Mrs Brisbane had a rectangular paperweight angled on top of the list, blocking part of the writing. I could only make out parts of a few words:

> lun
> trea
> Captai
> red, blue
> secret g

My heart was pounding. *Lun.* Were we studying the lungs, was something going to lunge at us – or maybe it was lunch? (That's what I was hoping for!)

Trea made my heart pound a little. It surely meant treasure!

Captai just had to be a captain. Was a real ship captain coming along? Or was it the captain of a pirate ship? Eek!

What about those colours? Were red and blue the colours of the jewels in the treasure?

And what on earth was *secret g*? Secret guy? Secret girl? Secret gold? It could be so many things.

I tried moving the paper around so I could read the rest of the words, but it wouldn't budge. I pushed the paperweight with all my might, but I couldn't move it an inch. It must have been made of solid rock! I was still struggling with it when I heard Mr and Mrs Brisbane talking. Goodness, I thought they were asleep!

I quickly dived off the desk and slid down the chair cover, which was like a bumpy slide. I landed on the seat, paused to catch my breath, then continued to slide down the leg of the chair. Next, I scurried across the floor to the table. I was moving fast but I skidded to a stop when I realized I had no idea how to get back up. I certainly couldn't slide *up* the table leg. Still, I'm a clever hamster, so I stayed calm and checked out the area.

I breathed a sigh of relief when I discovered a big stack of magazines on the floor. I carefully climbed up them one by one. However, when I made the leap to the table, my back paws pushed the top magazine off and the whole stack collapsed with a loud thump. I dashed into my cage and pulled the door behind me.

A few seconds later, Mrs Brisbane came shuffling out of the bedroom, wearing her dressing gown and slippers. 'I'll check it out, Bert. I'm sure it's nothing.'

She turned on the light and looked around the living room. 'Sorry to wake you, Humphrey,' she said while I tried to look as innocent as possible. Then she saw the heap of magazines. 'Oh, that's what it was.' She shook her head. 'I hope they didn't scare you.'

'Just a little,' I squeaked, even though I knew she couldn't understand me.

'I'll straighten these up tomorrow,' she said, turning off the light. As she was close to the bedroom door, I heard her tell Bert, 'You're going to have to build me a magazine rack.'

'I'll be happy to,' he replied. 'After the boat race.'

It was quiet for the rest of the night, but I didn't sleep a wink because of what I'd seen on Mrs Brisbane's list. Especially the mysterious *secret g*.

The boat race at Potter's Pond, the maps and the colourful treasure certainly sounded exciting. With a pirate captain along, it could be scary and even dangerous. Still, the more I thought about it, the more I knew that scary or not, I didn't want to miss that boat race for anything in the world!

·ö·

I slept in late on Sunday and awoke revived and refreshed. The Brisbanes were in a happy mood, and so was I. After all, I was going on a treasure hunt soon – or so I hoped.

In the afternoon, Mr Brisbane brought a model sailing boat into the living room. It was a fine-looking craft with a crisp yellow sail and a bright red hull.

'I couldn't resist making a boat of my own,' he told Mrs Brisbane.

'It's great, but only a student can win the prize,' she replied.

'I know,' Bert said. He sat the boat on the table and opened my cage door. 'Let's see what kind of a sailor Humphrey would make,' he said.

Mrs Brisbane quickly stacked up books around the edge of the table so I couldn't escape. 'I don't think he'll like it one bit,' she said.

I couldn't believe that my teacher, who is SMART-SMART-SMART most of the time, could be so wrong! I'd make an incredible sailor – I just knew it.

Mr Brisbane gently set me in the boat. 'See, Humphrey? It's just your size.'

Yes, it was *exactly* my size. I felt as if I'd been born to sail in that boat. I stood at the bow (that's the front of the ship) and imagined myself setting sail for a far-off island in search of hidden treasure.

'Looks like he's a born sailor,' Mr Brisbane observed. Now there's a smart man!

'Don't be ridiculous,' his wife said. 'I wouldn't let Humphrey get within sight of the water.'

What an unsqueakable thing to say!

'Why?' Mr Brisbane asked.

'WHY-WHY-WHY?' I asked, too.

'Because hamsters must never get wet,' Mrs Brisbane explained. 'They catch chills easily and get sick or even die. Plus water removes the good oils in a hamster's fur. You really should read up on hamsters the way I have, Bert.'

My heart sank to the bottom of my paws. This was worse news than anything Mrs Wright ever said.

'Guess you're not going to Potter's Pond, my friend,' Mr Brisbane told me.

I felt like I was spinning without my wheel. I felt sick with disappointment. I felt just about as bad as I did when Ms Mac left and broke my hamster heart.

'No way,' Mrs Brisbane agreed. 'Besides, the poor thing would be terrified.'

A lot she knew! She had no idea of the fur-raising

adventures I'd had. And I'd hardly ever been terrified, except by large and unfriendly animals, like
Miranda's dog Clem.

Mr Brisbane put me back in my cage.

'Sorry, Humphrey,' he said.

'You think you're sorry,' I squeaked. 'I'm about
the sorriest creature in the world.'

They laughed at my squeaking, which hurt my
feelings, but I forgave them.

They're only humans, after all.

> A landlubber's life is a sorry one, me
> hearties. I pity the poor wretch who's
> never known life on the briny deep!
>
> from *Jolly Roger's Guide to Life*, by I. C. Waters

8

Batten Down the Hatches

Once I was back in Room 26, I spent a lot of time in my sleeping hut, trying hard not to think about boats. Every once in a while, though, I couldn't resist checking up on my friends' progress.

With Mr Brisbane's advice and help, holes were drilled, keels were attached, boats were sanded and painted and sails were raised. He seemed especially pleased with the progress Kirk and Richie were making with their tall ship. 'Just make sure that those sails don't weigh the boat down,' he told them.

'I'm going to test it at home tonight,' Kirk said.

After Mr Brisbane moved on, Richie turned to Kirk. 'Maybe *I* could test it at home.'

'Have you ever sailed a model boat before?' asked Kirk.

Richie admitted that he hadn't. 'But I can tell if it sails or sinks.'

'Look, I've done this before with my dad,' Kirk explained. 'He knows all about boats. He was in the navy!'

'But I haven't done anything,' Richie complained.

'Great!' said Kirk. 'You'll get a prize and you don't have to do the work. Trust me, we'll win.'

I guess Richie couldn't think of anything else to say, but he looked really miserable. Kirk didn't seem to notice.

'Hey, where do fish sleep?' he suddenly asked.

Richie just stared at Kirk.

'In a *water bed*!' Kirk chuckled. Richie didn't.

Gail didn't look any happier than Richie. Heidi was off sick with a bad cold, so Gail had to work alone. And her mother, who was so encouraging to the other students, continued to insist that she decorate the sail.

'Why can't it be white?' Gail asked.

'That's so unimaginative,' Mrs Morgenstern replied. 'Remember how you resisted changing your room? Now you love your golden walls, don't you?'

'Yes, but that's different,' Gail answered quietly.

So Gail continued to spend her time working on the hull of the boat. I think she was delaying the time when she had to decorate the sail (or upset her mum if she didn't).

I felt sorry for Richie and Gail, but at least they'd have the chance to sail on Potter's Pond and have a picnic with treasure, while I'd just sit in Room 26 with no one to talk to but a twangy old frog. I know, Og's a nice guy and I wasn't being fair to him, but I was feeling down in the dumps.

Even when Mrs Brisbane read from *Jolly Roger's Guide to Life*, I wasn't very cheered up.

·ŏ·

I thought I couldn't feel any lower, until school was over and Mrs Wright came in. She was carrying a clipboard and had her shiny whistle around her neck. It's hard to relax around a woman who always wears a whistle!

'Mrs Brisbane, here are a few more forms you'll need for the field trip,' she announced abruptly.

I was surprised to see that Mrs Brisbane just smiled and said, 'Fine. I'll make sure they're taken care of.'

'By the deadline,' Mrs Wright snapped back.

'Of course,' Mrs Brisbane replied. 'Now, Ruth, I have an idea. To make sure that our field trip is safe and orderly and everything goes smoothly, I was wondering if there was any chance you could come along and help supervise.'

I think if I'd been on my wheel, I would have fallen off.

Mrs Wright looked about as startled as I felt. 'Well, I don't know,' she said. 'I mean . . . yes, it would make sense. Perhaps I can rearrange my schedule that day.'

'You'd be a big help,' Mrs Brisbane said (although I didn't agree). 'And you'd have a lot of fun.'

Mrs Wright looked even more startled than before.

'Oh well, of course, that wouldn't be my purpose in being there,' she said.

Mrs Brisbane flashed her a big smile. 'Of course not. But it wouldn't hurt to have some fun, would it?'

So that was Mrs Brisbane's idea! She wanted to help Mrs Wright have some fun. I didn't think that even a wise teacher could make that happen. The only fun Mrs Wright had was when she blew her whistle, which wasn't fun for small creatures with sensitive ears like mine.

'Good luck,' I muttered as Mrs Brisbane left the room.

'Good night!' she answered cheerily.

'o'

That evening, I had to listen to the splishing and splashing coming from Og's tank, which only reminded me that he could swim as much as he liked, while I was forbidden to be in water. Ever.

I guess Aldo didn't know that I wouldn't be joining the class at Potter's Pond. He continued to whistle and dance the hornpipe and say things like 'Arrgh' and 'Me hearty'.

When he called me a 'salty dog', I felt SAD-SAD-SAD, because if there's one thing I'm *not*, it's an unreasonable creature like a dog.

On Thursday night, Aldo said a very strange thing. 'Maria has made me a pirate's outfit. She says I look handsome in it!'

Maria was Aldo's very nice wife, and I could hardly believe that she wanted him to be a pirate, too.

'I tell ye, me buckos, this pirate life agrees with me!' he added. Then he pushed his cleaning trolley out of Room 26, turned off the light and closed the door.

'Og?' I squeaked.

I could hear the faint splashing of water. 'Og? Do you think Aldo is going to be a pirate and sail away and we'll never see him again?'

'BOING-BOING-BOING-BOING!' Og responded in a very alarming way.

'I hope not, either,' I answered, although I'm usually only guessing what Og is trying to say.

Aldo had left the blinds open, so that the street

light outside lit up Room 26 and bathed it in a soft glow. The tables were pushed together so the boats were all in a row.

'I'm taking a little walk, Og,' I suddenly announced, flinging my cage door open.

I was able to drop down from the table where Og and I live directly onto the table with the boats. It was grand seeing them up close. There was the beautiful swan boat, with real feathers that Sayeh and Miranda brought in. The pirate flag looked wonderfully menacing on the boat Garth and A.J. built. I had nothing but admiration for the colourful Chinese junk that Tabitha and Seth designed. The Viking boat that Art and Mandy created tilted a bit too much to one side, but they still had time to fix it.

The tall ship was missing because Kirk had taken it home to test it.

Gail's boat (and it was practically hers alone, since Heidi had been sick all week) was plain and simple, just like the poster of the classic sailing boat on the wall.

My friends were doing a GREAT-GREAT-GREAT job, and in spite of my own disappointment, I was proud of them. But I suddenly remembered the boat I'd sketched in my notebook: the SS *Golden Hamster* with its impressive hamster flag. None of my friends had even thought of a flag (except the pirate flag on Garth and A.J.'s boat).

I looked around at the piles of art supplies in front of me and picked out a lovely triangle of aluminium foil and a toothpick. I carefully inserted the toothpick in the foil, and what do you know? It looked just like a silvery flag on a flagpole.

I planted it right in front of Gail's boat, sticking it in a mound of modelling clay. It was a way to make my mark and congratulate my friends on their good work, even though they'd never know whose flag it was.

After all, it wasn't their fault I'd be a landlubber for ever.

•ö•

There's always plenty of time to think after Aldo leaves, and that night, I couldn't help thinking about Kirk and how he was treating Richie. I'd never seen him act that way before. Everybody in Room 26 wanted to win the prize for the race, but my other friends weren't acting like Kirk. What had got into him?

Then I started to think about the weekend I'd spent not long ago at Kirk's house. It was a FUN-FUN-FUN place to visit because Kirk's family is nice to visiting hamsters and they all like to laugh, like Kirk does. He has a mum, a dad, an older sister Krissy and an older brother Kevin.

Kirk and Kevin shared a room. They had matching beds, matching lamps and matching desks. Over each desk was a shelf.

On Kirk's shelf, there was a dictionary, a globe, five joke books and a blue ribbon tacked to the edge.

On Kevin's shelf, there were three silver trophies, four gold trophies, four plaques and a row of red, blue and yellow ribbons. There must have been at least ten of them.

I didn't pay much attention to the difference between the shelves until Kirk pointed it out that Saturday afternoon. He and I were alone in his room. Kevin was out on the running track, which according to Kirk is a lot like spinning my wheel except you run in a circle on the ground.

'See all those trophies and ribbons, Humphrey?' Kirk asked me. 'Those are Kevin's awards for sport. He's great at all sports. Basketball, football, track, swimming. Look at them all,' he said. 'Pretty amazing, aren't they?'

'YES-YES-YES!' I squeaked. I must admit, I was impressed.

Kirk pointed to the lone ribbon on his shelf. 'That's the only award I ever got, for an honourable mention in the talent show last year. I did a comic routine. I should have got a red ribbon.'

Since I hadn't been around for the talent show

and wasn't even sure what it was, I didn't comment.

'You should see my sister's room,' Kirk continued. 'I'd show it to you, but she doesn't let me in there. Anyway, she has *two* shelves of awards for good grades and the debating team – that's where people get points for arguing – and drama competitions and speech contests and – I don't know, every time Krissy opens her mouth, she gets an award.'

I was still thinking about debating. I don't like arguments one bit, but humans get awards for them!

Kirk flopped down on the bed. 'Dad always says I'd better get busy if I'm going to fill up my shelf. Then he says he's just kidding, but I'm not sure. It's just, well, I'm good at being funny, but they don't give awards for that!'

I got an award once for my Hallowe'en costume, but Kirk seemed so upset, I didn't think it was a good time to mention it.

Suddenly, Kirk sat up. 'Hey, Humphrey, did you hear about the scarecrow who got the big award . . . for being *outstanding in his field!*' He laughed loudly. 'Get it? See, a scarecrow stands in a field. Outstanding in his field!'

'Unsqueakably funny,' I said, though I was exaggerating a little.

'I've got a million of them,' Kirk said. 'Did you hear the story about the spaceship? It was out of this world!'

He chuckled again, and so did I.

Kirk jumped up and stood close to my cage. 'Here's one for you, Humphrey. What did the hamster say when he broke his leg? 'Quick! Call a *hambulance*'!'

A hambulance! Now *that* was funny. I hopped on my wheel to show Kirk the joke made me happy.

If I'd had a red ribbon, I would have given it to him.

Like I said, it was quiet in Room 26. Og never squeaks up, much less tells a joke.

'Og, did you hear the one about the boy who wanted a prize so badly, he'd even hurt his best friend's feelings to win it?' I asked my neighbour.

Og didn't laugh, but that was okay. The situation wasn't one bit funny. And I didn't have any idea how to make things better between Kirk and Richie.

It didn't take long for Gail to notice the flag the next morning. Heidi was back, too, and she asked who had made it. When the girls asked around, no one knew anything about it. (Except me, but nobody asked.)

When Mrs Morgenstern came over to check on their progress, she asked Gail how she'd decided to decorate the sail.

'Mum, could I make a flag instead?' she asked.

'Fabulous idea!' Mrs Morgenstern replied. 'I love it!'

She seemed pleased, and so did Gail, who went right to work. First she studied nautical flags in one of Mrs Brisbane's books. It turns out there's a whole language for flags. Boats raise them to send messages to shore or to other boats. Then Gail designed her own series of flags with brightly coloured stripes and patterns. I was happy I'd been able to inspire her again.

Mr Brisbane helped her string them along the side of the mast. Mrs Morgenstern loved them, and best of all, Gail did, too.

It was a fine boat. They were all fine boats, especially after Mr Brisbane helped Art and Mandy get their Viking ship to stand up straight.

Kirk looked very pleased when Mr Brisbane checked out their tall ship.

'It floated perfectly last night,' Kirk said. 'I knew it would.'

Mr Brisbane was full of praise. After he moved on, Kirk turned to Richie and said, 'I think we've pretty much got first prize wrapped up.'

'*You've* got first prize wrapped up,' Richie snapped. 'I'm just a big nobody.'

Kirk looked surprised. 'Come on, Richie. No

one has to know I did all the work. You'll look like a winner.'

'But I won't feel like one.' Richie quickly got up and sharpened about a million pencils. After a while, Mrs Brisbane noticed and went over to talk to him.

'Is everything okay?' she asked.

'I guess,' he answered.

She tried to get more information out of him, but he just kept sharpening pencils. So she wandered over to Kirk and asked him if everything was all right.

'Yeah. The boat's fantastic – look!' he answered.

'I mean between you and Richie,' Mrs Brisbane said.

'Sure. We make a great team,' Kirk said. He sounded as if he meant it.

'Does Kirk really think Richie doesn't mind being left out?' I squeaked to Og.

'BOING,' Og answered. He didn't sound very enthusiastic.

> Keep an eye on thy enemies, me hearties. There may be mutiny a-brewing!
>
> from *Jolly Roger's Guide to Life*, by I. C. Waters

Secrets, Secrets Everywhere

Richie cheered up a little when Mrs Brisbane announced that I'd be going home with him for the weekend. I was happy, too. I thought maybe we could both get our minds off boats. But once I got to the Rinaldi home, I found out I was WRONG-WRONG-WRONG. In fact, boats were just about all that Richie thought about.

There's always a lot going on at Richie's house with his parents, brothers, sisters, aunts, uncles and cousins hanging out there. They were all there on Saturday – so many kids! Serena and Sarah, Anthony and Alex, George and Josie, Richie and Rita! Late in the afternoon, they all ended up in the bathroom – with me!

I was in my hamster ball, which Richie carefully set on top of a tissue box so I wouldn't roll off.

At first, I was happy that Richie brought me along.

A little later, I wasn't so sure.

'Watch this,' said Richie as he turned on the taps and the bathtub began to fill with water.

'What's going on?' asked Rita.

George backed away. 'I don't want to take a bath! I had one yesterday!'

'I doubt that. Maybe the day before,' his sister Josie snapped. 'Maybe.'

'We're not here to take a bath,' said Richie. 'We're here to see what floats!'

Aha! I realized that Richie was going to show his cousins what Mr Fitch and Mrs Brisbane had showed us in the library.

Richie started things off by holding up a penny.

'Float or won't float?' he asked.

'Won't!' his cousins shouted in unison.

The penny sank to the bottom of the tub.

Next, George took a pencil out of his pocket. 'Float or won't float?'

'Will!' Rita, Serena and Sarah agreed.

'Won't!' Alex, Anthony and Josie agreed.

The pencil floated beautifully. All it needed was a sail to look just like a sailing boat.

The cousins soon scattered all over the house and returned with more things to test. They tried a peppermint stick (sank), a flip-flop (floated), a leaf (floated until it got soggy and sank) and a seashell (sank). A plastic cup did something very surprising.

It floated on its side until it was three-quarters full of water, then it tipped up and floated upright.

Finally, a teddy bear floated on his back with a big happy smile on his face.

I guess it's okay for furry teddy bears to get wet, unlike furry hamsters.

Then George and Anthony got into a splashing fight. George's dad looked in to see what was going on.

'It's a science experiment,' Richie told him.

'Anything that can get George to the bathtub is fine with me,' he said. 'Just clean up the mess when you've finished.'

It was fun to watch all the splashing until Alex grabbed the hamster ball and said, 'What about this? Will it float?'

'NO-NO-NO!' I squeaked. I didn't know if the ball would float or not, but I knew that I didn't want to get wet! And even though the plastic would protect me from the water, those air holes were sure to let water in. When I'd wished for an adventure on the water, this wasn't what I had in mind!

Alex was carrying me towards the bathtub as I shrieked, 'Stop him! I shouldn't get wet!'

I wasn't sure if anyone could hear me with all that plastic around me.

He held the ball over the water. I took a deep breath and squeaked, 'Eeeeeeek!'

At that point, my friend Richie grabbed the ball out of Alex's hand. 'Not with Humphrey in it, you dodo.'

Richie opened the ball, took me out and handed the ball back to his cousin. 'Here,' he said.

Alex dropped my hamster ball into the tub, where it bobbed up and down on the water, floating along.

My heart was pounding, but I was GLAD-GLAD-GLAD I wasn't inside.

Richie put me back in my cage, where I burrowed into my sleeping hut for a long, dry nap.

On Sunday afternoon, Richie cleaned my cage. He did an excellent job. While he was changing my water, his mum brought in the phone and said he had a call.

'Hello?' Richie said. 'Oh . . . Kirk.'

He didn't seem too happy to hear from his partner.

'Okay. Okay. Okay.' That's all I heard. I couldn't hear what Kirk said, but Richie told me after he said goodbye.

'Stupid old Kirk. He took the boat home again and wanted to tell me it sailed really great,' Richie explained. 'What a jerk! Kirk the jerk.'

Then he unexpectedly slipped me into his

pocket. It was dark in there, but I could make out a couple of dried-up raisins and half a stick of gum stuck to the cloth. Luckily, I was only there for a few seconds.

Richie went into the bathroom, locked the door, took me out of his pocket and set me in an empty soap dish. I was a little nervous when he started filling the bathtub with water, especially after the experiments of the day before.

'Don't worry, Humphrey. You're not getting a bath,' Richie assured me. 'I just want to show you something. It's a secret.'

Once the tub was full, he showed me a strange-looking boat. 'This is my remote-controlled submarine. Pretty cool, isn't it?'

The submarine was a very sleek boat, nothing like the sailing boats we'd been studying. It was completely grey and had no sails at all – just a tower-like thing coming up out of the middle.

'Here's the periscope.' Richie pointed to a long, narrow tube coming out of the tower. 'When you're under water, you can use it to see what's on top of the water.'

Amazing.

'In real submarines, people can live under water for weeks. Even months. They can sneak up on enemies because no one even knows they're there,' Richie said.

After he put the submarine in the tub, he used a remote control – like the one for Mr Fitch's television – to make it move through the water.

'I can control when it goes up and when it goes down,' he explained. 'See?'

Using the controls in his hands, he made the submarine dive down until it was completely under water. It glided silently across the bottom of the tub.

'Now, watch this,' he said.

I watched carefully as he pushed some buttons, and suddenly the submarine glided up to the surface of the water.

'That's GREAT-GREAT-GREAT,' I squeaked happily.

My classmates are so clever!

But my little hamster heart sank almost to my stomach when Richie said, 'I'm going to take this submarine to Potter's Pond for the boat race.'

'That's against the rules,' I squeaked.

'Kirk thinks he's so smart,' Richie muttered. The submarine dived to the bottom of the tub. 'I'll hide it in my backpack. While the race is on, I'll sneak to the sidelines, slip the submarine into the water, then bring it up right next to his stupid tall ship. Just to show him I can handle a boat, too.'

'Something could go wrong! What if the submarine hits the boat?' I tried to warn him, but it was no use.

'I'll probably get into trouble,' Richie admitted. 'But I don't want the stupid prize, anyway.'

My mind was racing. If I could get my paws on that controller, maybe I could stop him. But Richie put the submarine and the device in a cabinet way up high. I could see there was no way a small hamster could reach it.

I've helped a lot of my friends on a lot of my weekend visits, but there was no way I could change Richie's mind.

'It'll be our little secret,' he told me.

It wasn't a secret I wanted to keep. At least I wouldn't be there to see it.

ö

'Good news, class,' Mrs Brisbane announced on Monday. 'The weather tomorrow should be picture-perfect, so the trip to Potter's Pond is on.'

My friends gave a cheer. Even though the picnic was *off* for me, I managed a celebratory squeak.

I felt terrible for Mrs Brisbane. She'd planned everything so well, but things weren't going to go according to her plan unless I came up with a bright idea to stop Richie.

Everyone was excited about the picnic the next day, but they were perfectly quiet when Mrs Brisbane read the final chapter to the Uncle Jolly Roger book. Vic and Vi helped their uncle scare off the pirates (with the help of a very loud whistle – can you believe it?). And then, to the children's surprise, they set sail with the treasure to return it to the real owners. It turns out that Uncle Jolly Roger was a *good* pirate!

Richie was a good guy, too. And good guys don't do bad things, do they? Well, maybe sometimes they do.

I needed a Plan. But in order to have a Plan, I needed research. Mrs Brisbane talked about research from time to time, and I figured out it meant learning more about a subject. When students had to do research, they usually went to the library. So I decided to undertake a little research project of my own.

First, I had to wait for Aldo to finish cleaning the room. He was very cheery that night, whistling the hornpipe song and dancing around with the broom.

'Well, me buckos, tomorrow I set sail,' he said. 'I hope your friends don't get attacked by pirates.'

The thought of pirates attacking anyone, especially my friends, made my whiskers twitch, but Aldo let out a jolly laugh.

·ö·

I waited a long time after Aldo had gone to make sure he'd left Longfellow School for the night.

Then I told Og about my mission, slipped out of my cage, slid under the door and headed towards the library. The corridors didn't seem so eerie any more. I guess I was getting used to my night-time journeys.

Once I had squeezed under the door of the library, I stopped to catch my breath and look around. The fish tanks were glowing, thank goodness, because I needed the light. I headed straight for the remote control. If I could figure out how it worked, maybe I could figure out how to make Richie's remote *not* work. I scrambled up the stair-like shelves and scampered across the desk to the remote control.

Research can be HARD-HARD-HARD, as I found out that night, but I learned a lot. First of all, remotes don't have cords that you can plug and unplug, like televisions and irons and other objects humans use.

Second of all, those buttons do some very strange things besides turning a television on and off. I found the On/Off button and up on the screen, I saw a group of children walking down a pavement. When I pushed the next button, the children started walking backwards, which was pretty funny. I hate to admit, I spent quite a bit of time making those kids walk forwards and then backwards.

Then it was time to get on with my research. One

button turned the sound on and off, and others made the picture do all kinds of strange things, like change colour and get squiggly lines. None of the buttons made the remote stop except the On/Off button.

There had to be something else that made the remote work. I checked more carefully and found a little compartment at the back. When I jiggled it open, two batteries rolled out. The batteries were the secret! Sure enough, when the batteries weren't in the remote, no matter how many times I pushed the On/Off button, nothing happened.

If I could take out the batteries, I could put Richie's remote out of action. So the next morning, all I had to do was (a) get into his backpack, (b) find his remote and (c) take out the batteries . . . (d) without anyone noticing!

That was a tall order for a small hamster, but I vowed to give it my best shot. I could only cross my paws and hope that my friends would leave for Potter's Pond after morning break and not first thing in the morning.

But before that, I needed to get Mr Fitch's batteries back in their little compartment. Let me tell you, taking batteries out is a lot easier than putting them in. It took me four – no, five – tries before the screen lit up and those children walked down the pavement again.

Whew! I couldn't resist hitting the button that took the movie back to the beginning, and I saw its title: *Safety First*. It explained how children should cross a street safely, and oh, it was a very frightening sight! The children learned how to look both ways before crossing a street, how to wait for a kindly lollipop lady to stop traffic with a sign and how to press a button on a pole and wait until a picture of a person walking lit up. Those kids were very good at being safe.

But I couldn't help thinking about how unsafe a little hamster would be out on the pavement. All those big feet clomping along and huge cars whizzing by! The kindly lollipop lady probably wouldn't be able to see me, and there was NO-NO-NO way a creature of my size could reach up that pole and press the button for the green man.

Not only were hamsters in danger around water, we were unsafe out on the pavement. I hit the On/Off button and dashed for the door. But as anxious as I was to get away, I was stopped in my tracks by the sight of something under Mr Fitch's desk.

Being a naturally curious creature, I looked more closely. I was amazed at what I saw. It was a genuine pirate hat: big and black with a broad brim, right there in the library!

Had a pirate been here and left it behind? Was Mr Fitch secretly a pirate?

'Shiver me timbers!' I squeaked, and I dashed out of the library and back to the safety of Room 26 as fast as my small legs could carry me.

Be careful, all ye treasure seekers. You might find more than ye bargained for!

from *Jolly Roger's Guide to Life*, by I. C. Waters

10

Anchors Aweigh

'BOING-BOING-BOING!'

That was Og's reaction when I told him about my experience in the library. Even though I didn't think he understood what a remote control is, he got the general idea, and when I told him about the pirate hat, he splashed so madly, I was in danger of getting soaked right there on our table.

After Og settled down a little, I knew I should get some sleep so I'd be alert and ready if I had a chance to get into Richie's backpack the next morning.

Still, I couldn't resist taking one more look at the beautiful boats my classmates had worked so hard on. They looked seaworthy enough, thanks to Mr Brisbane's advice. And they were beautiful, with Mrs Morgenstern's help. Gail's nautical flags were bright and colourful. So were the sails on the Chinese junk. But in the end, my favourite was the tall ship, because it looked as if it really could sail FAR-FAR-FAR away.

Standing in front of this wonderful boat was about as close as I was going to come to the adventure I'd been wishing for. I longed to be a little bit closer. It couldn't hurt if I just crawled into the boat and pretended to sail for a minute or two, could it?

I stood at the bow of the boat and tried to imagine what it would be like to be captain of such a fine vessel.

'Ready about!' I squeaked. 'Trim the sails! Swab the decks!'

I admit, I didn't know what all those things meant, but I'd heard them in books and movies.

'Lower the boom! Batten down the hatches!' It felt good to say those things.

'Heave-ho!' I shouted. I heard Og splashing in the background, but I was hardly aware that I was in Room 26.

I don't know how long I spent pretending to be sailing. I only know that after a while, I suddenly felt sleepy. Sleepier than I've ever been, in fact. It must have been the fresh sea air I was imagining.

I turned and noticed a nice piece of sailcloth in the bottom of the boat. I decided that a short doze was in order, so I burrowed under the cloth and closed my eyes. I guess I was dreaming because I could see the boat gliding across a silver sea, and then the dream turned SCARY-SCARY-SCARY because I saw a pirate ship approaching. And there were real live pirates on board, wearing shiny red jackets with gold buttons and big pirate hats.

'Turn back!' I yelled. 'Trim the sails! Flibber the gibbet!'

I wasn't making much sense, but the words sounded pretty good. Suddenly, in my dream, a huge wave came up and shook the boat. I was being violently tossed around by the waves (and feeling slightly sick, too). And I heard the ship's bell chiming an odd sound: 'BOING-BOING-SCREEE!'

That's when I woke up. I pulled back the sailcloth just enough for me to see that I was moving out of Room 26. Og had been trying to warn me, but I guess the cloth muffled the sound.

I heard voices.

'Can't I at least carry it?' Richie begged.

'Better if I do it,' Kirk replied. 'Trust me.'

It took me a few sleepy moments to realize that I was still in the tall ship, which the boys were carrying to the bus for the trip to Potter's Pond! I was about to squeak up in protest when I thought that at last, I had an opportunity for real adventure. I was going to Potter's Pond! And maybe, just maybe, I'd still have the chance to disable Richie's remote.

'Nice breezy day for sailing,' I heard Mr Brisbane say.

I burrowed back under the cloth as my friends chattered away. Soon I felt the vibration of the bus.

'Everybody, find a seat.' That, I knew, was the familiar voice of Miss Victoria, the bus driver.

SCREEEEEECH!

It's a good thing I was already lying down in the bottom of the boat or I would have surely been knocked over by the horrible sound of Mrs Wright's whistle. If that was her idea of fun, I was already sorry I'd stowed away.

'I am missing one permission slip,' she announced. 'This bus cannot leave the school without it. Is Richie Rinaldi on the bus?'

'What?' Repeat-It-Please-Richie's muffled voice replied.

'Richie, I must have your permission slip or you will have to leave the bus,' Mrs Wright told him.

It was mostly quiet – except for the shuffling of some paper. He must have been rummaging around in his backpack. Backpack! That's probably where he had the remote control, too.

'I've got it!' Richie said.

A few minutes later, the bus rumbled away from the school, on its way to Potter's Pond . . . with me on board!

My friends were very noisy – they always are on

the bus. Then I heard Mrs Brisbane say, 'Mrs Wright, I think it would be fun if you led us in some songs.'

Mrs Wright sounded surprised. 'Me? Well, I could, I suppose. If you'd like me to.'

'I'd like you to,' Mrs Brisbane replied.

I braced myself for the whistle. SCREEEECH!

'All right, class. Everybody sing!' Mrs Wright commanded my friends.

Everybody sang – probably to avoid hearing the whistle again – as Mrs Wright led them in a song that was VERY-VERY-VERY noisy!

> If you're happy and you know it
> Clap your hands.

And everyone clapped!

> If you're happy and you know it
> Clap your hands.

More loud clapping.

> If you're happy and you know it
> And you really want to show it,
> If you're happy and you know it
> Clap your hands.

Thunderous clapping!

I clapped my paws, too. Then I remembered Richie's backpack again. Was there any way for me to slip out of the boat and into the backpack without anyone noticing?

Mrs Wright blew her whistle loudly again. SCREEEECH!

'Keep it going, students!' she barked. And they did.

> If you're happy and you know it
> Stamp your feet.

The students stamped in a way that would have got them into trouble if they had been in class and not on the bus.

I decided this was *not* the time to escape from the boat.

> If you're happy and you know it
> Stamp your feet.

Even louder stamping.

I was surprised the floor of the bus didn't collapse with all that stamping, but my friends – and Mrs Wright – were having so much fun they kept on going. They added a verse where everyone shouted, 'We are!' and then another where everyone did all three things: clapping, stamping and shouting, 'We are!'

Much as everyone was having fun, I was feeling quite miserable. I wanted to get to that remote control and stop Richie from getting into trouble. And I wanted to warn my friends that they might meet up with some unfriendly pirates.

But I also knew that if Mrs Wright discovered a small, insanitary hamster on the bus, it would ruin *everything*. So I listened to the happy commotion and stayed put.

Suddenly, the rumbling of the bus stopped.

'Let's thank Mrs Wright for making this trip so much fun,' I heard Mrs Brisbane say.

My friends all cheered loudly, which must have made Mrs Wright feel good.

'All out for Potter's Pond,' Mrs Brisbane announced.

There was so much noise, so much bumping and thumping, so much confusion that all I could do was to lie low, hang on tightly and hope for the best.

It took a while to get everyone lined up. I heard the voices of some of the parents, like Heidi's mum, Miranda's dad, Gail's mum, Art's mum and Sayeh's dad. This was a big party!

At last Mrs Brisbane made the big announcement. 'Boys and girls, on the count of three, set your boats on the water,' she said.

'One . . . two . . . three!'

SCREEEECH. Somehow, I wasn't surprised that Mrs Wright blew her whistle to start the race.

There was a big bump, a bigger thump and then

– oh my – I felt myself floating for the first time in my life. It felt like I was riding on a cloud.

My classmates screamed, 'GO-GO-GO!' Once I was used to the feeling of drifting on water, I pushed the cloth back a little and peeped over the side of the boat.

What a sight! Ahead of me, rippling blue water. In the distance, a leafy green shoreline. On either side of me, my friends' boats, now afloat. Above me, sails gently rippling. I ventured up to the bow of the ship and felt the soft breeze against my fur. It was glorious!

On the shore, my classmates were lined up on both sides of the pond, cheering their boats on.

The ship was sailing so smoothly, I relaxed a little.

I glanced behind me just in time to see the delicate swan boat that Sayeh and Miranda had worked so hard on rapidly sink out of view. There were moans and groans from the shore, and I groaned a little, too.

The pirate ship was the next boat to go under. There were more groans, but others cheered for the remaining boats.

I was getting nervous. Was my boat going to sink, too? My tummy did a FLIP-FLOP-FLIP. But my tall ship seemed to glide effortlessly through the water. I guess Kirk really *did* know what he was doing.

The Chinese junk and the flag-filled sailing boat were still on the water but lagging far behind me. Even farther back was the tip of the Viking ship, which was sinking rapidly.

'Go!' my friends chanted. 'Go!'

Then suddenly, I heard Lower-Your-Voice-A.J.'s loud voice booming, 'Humphrey Dumpty's on that boat!'

There was a gasp, and Mrs Brisbane shouted, 'It *is* Humphrey! How did he get on that boat? Kirk? Richie?'

In the distance, I heard Kirk say, 'I don't know.' He sounded confused. 'I didn't see him.'

'Somebody's going to be in big trouble.' Mrs Brisbane didn't sound happy at all.

If Mrs Brisbane was right about hamsters getting wet, I was already in big trouble, but as the boat glided through the water, I felt freer than I've ever been. This was my greatest adventure yet, and I decided to enjoy it.

Pillaging and plundering can be a bit wearing, but there be no better place to live than on the open sea!

from *Jolly Roger's Guide to Life*, by I. C. Waters

11

All at Sea

'Ahoy, mateys!' I squeaked towards shore, even though I knew no one could hear me. Then in my best pirate voice, I added, 'Arggh!'

My friends were cheering wildly when suddenly, out of the corner of my eye, I saw something dark in the water. For an instant, I remembered a report on sharks that Art had read to the class. Eek! Then I recognized the shape of Richie's submarine gliding through the water, heading straight for me!

Suddenly, the submarine began to surface. Richie had said it was supposed to come up next to the boat, but it was heading directly for it. I wasn't the only one who noticed as I heard voices, voices, everywhere!

'It's a submarine!'

'Where'd that come from?'

'Richie's in the bushes and he has a remote control!'

'It's going to hit the boat!'

EEK-EEK-EEK!

That's when I heard Repeat-It-Please-Richie's voice. 'What?' he asked.

A.J.'s voice was loud and clear. 'It's going to hit the boat, and Humphrey's on it!'

'Humphrey?' Richie sounded shocked.

'Do something, Richie!' Mandy screamed.

'I'm trying!' he shouted back.

I could see people running around onshore, but I was hanging on for dear life and didn't have time to pay much attention to them. Just then, the submarine hit and the sailing boat tilted sharply to one side. Luckily, I managed to hang onto the bow of the boat or else I would have slid into the water to, well, certain disaster.

I'm sure Richie didn't mean to hit the ship. Maybe he wasn't as good at handling a submarine as he'd thought.

Onshore, my friends were in a panic. 'Save him! Save Humphrey!' they screamed.

'Save me!' I squeaked as the boat rocked and rolled.

'Whose sub is it?' Mrs Brisbane called. I'd never heard her voice so alarmed.

'Mine,' Richie answered. 'I'm backing it away.'

SCREEEEECH! I don't know what Mrs Wright thought the whistle would do to help me, but she blew it over and over again.

And then, the boat tipped all the way over onto its side, the sails floating next to it in the water.

My friends all shrieked, 'Humphrey!'

'Eeek!' I squeaked. I suddenly wished Og was around to help me out.

I hung onto the side for dear life, but the water was getting closer and, believe me, it was too close for comfort.

'We're going down!' I squeaked, although I was actually the only one going down.

I remembered Mr Morales saying the pond was shallow, but for a hamster it would surely be DEEP-DEEP-DEEP. I tried not to think about the little sunken ship at the bottom of Mr Fitch's fish tank.

I also recalled Mrs Brisbane's warning about hamsters getting wet. I wasn't sure whether I could swim or not, but I didn't want to find out.

Just then, I saw the long periscope of Richie's submarine right next to me. I took a deep breath and leapt across the water to grab hold of it. (All those hours of jumping on my wheel and spinning have certainly paid off.)

'Now he's hanging onto the periscope!' That was A.J. shouting. 'Look!'

There were cheers from the shore, but I wasn't

about to cheer until I reached dry land.

I was clinging to the periscope for dear life when the beautiful tall ship dropped down below the surface of the water.

Mrs Brisbane shouted at Richie. 'Can you bring him in safely?'

'I can do it,' he answered.

No hamster ever hung onto anything as tightly as I hung onto that periscope. The water was only centimetres below me. I wouldn't have minded being a goggle-eyed green frog with no fur at all, at least for a few minutes. But soon, the submarine glided towards shore.

Without hesitation, Richie and Kirk both waded out to rescue me. They didn't even worry about their clothes getting wet. Luckily, Mr Morales was right. The water in Potter's Pond was shallow – at least to humans.

'Hurry!' said Kirk. 'It's going to sink.'

'Okay, but watch it,' Richie replied as they approached the submarine. 'We don't want to splash water on Humphrey.'

Richie gently plucked me off the periscope and held me in his cupped hands.

'Sorry, Humphrey,' he said softly. 'I'm so sorry.'

I was shivering as he carefully carried me to shore and handed me to Mrs Brisbane.

'You're shaking,' she said, and she was right.

She opened the lid of a small woven basket and took out a pile of colourful ribbons. 'You'll be safe in here,' she told me. Golden Miranda brought me a little cup of water to drink. Nice.

'This is strictly against the rules,' Mrs Wright insisted. 'I demand an explanation!'

'Yes, please tell us what happened, Richie,' Mrs Brisbane said in a VERY-VERY-VERY angry voice.

'I can't believe Humphrey was on board,' he said. 'How'd he get there?'

That was a question only *I* could answer. 'We'll figure that out,' Mrs Brisbane said. 'But why did you sink your own ship?'

'I didn't mean to sink it!' Richie protested, and I believed him. 'I just wanted to show Kirk I know about boats, too.'

Mrs Brisbane turned to Kirk. 'Do you know what he means?'

Kirk shrugged. 'Um . . . I guess he didn't think I let him help enough.'

'You didn't let me help at all!' Richie said. What he said was true.

Mrs Brisbane turned to Kirk again. 'Why didn't you let Richie help?'

Kirk, who was always cracking jokes, looked very serious. 'I wanted to win. I thought we had a better chance if I did the work.'

'So whose fault was it that Humphrey almost

drowned?' the teacher asked.

Whoa! Hearing her say that made me shake and quake.

'Mine,' Richie answered. 'But I wouldn't want anything to happen to Humphrey.'

'It was your fault, Richie.' Mrs Brisbane nodded. 'Don't you agree, Kirk?'

Kirk stared at the ground and didn't answer right away. Finally he said, 'Yes, but I guess it was kind of my fault, too, because I made Richie angry. Winning wouldn't have been worth it if something had happened to Humphrey. I'm sorry.'

'Well, don't apologize to me!' Mrs Brisbane said. She sounded pretty upset.

Kirk looked at Richie. 'Sorry, Richie. I wasn't very nice to you.'

'I'm sorry, too.' Richie looked embarrassed. 'It was a stupid idea to bring the submarine. I was just so angry.'

'The next thing I want to know is who put Humphrey in the boat,' Mrs Brisbane said. 'But I'll deal with that later. Right now, it's time for our treasure hunt!'

My classmates and I squealed with delight when Mr Brisbane passed out treasure maps. (My guess about *trea* from the list was right.) He said, 'Boys and girls, it's said that the famous pirate Captain Kidd buried his treasure right here by Potter's Pond.'

So that's who the captain was: Captain Kidd!

'Follow these old maps to find the hidden treasure,' Mr Brisbane explained. 'Remember, *X* marks the spot.'

My friends set off among the paths and trees, looking for clues. I longed to join them, but I'd had enough adventures for one day, so I watched and listened.

It wasn't too long before I heard Mandy shout, 'I've found it! There's the *X* carved in the ground!'

There was a rush of footsteps. Mrs Brisbane picked up my basket and said, 'Come on, Humphrey. You might as well see this, too.'

She carried me to a little clearing where Mandy, Art and Tabitha stood by an old trunk that looked just a pirate's treasure chest. She pushed the lid of my basket back so I could see better.

'Should we open the chest?' Tabitha asked.

They all agreed they should, but just as they tipped the lid open, one-two-three pirates leapt out of the bushes!

My friends screamed at the sight of the strangers, who lunged at the crowd. My heart just about jumped out of my chest. I'd almost forgotten about the pirates!

'Arrgh!' growled the first pirate.

'Avast!' snarled the second pirate.

The third pirate was even more menacing. 'Stop

right there, mateys,' he roared. 'Don't even be thinking of touching Captain Kidd's treasure!'

The three pirates stood in front of the treasure chest, looking SCARY-SCARY-SCARY and MEAN-MEAN-MEAN.

The first pirate had on a bright red shirt and a bright blue sash. He had dark hair, a big gold earring and a patch over one eye.

The second pirate wore shiny black trousers, a long red coat with big gold buttons and a genuine pirate hat! (At least it looked genuine to me.) He also had big round glasses. Funny, I'd never seen a pirate with glasses before.

The third pirate had striped trousers tucked into black boots, a black tunic with a belt, a kerchief on his head and a big black moustache.

'Landlubbers!' he shouted in a familiar voice. 'Back off from me treasure or I'll introduce ye to Davy Jones!'

My friends screamed and backed off. But I could swear I'd seen that moustache before.

Suddenly Richie called out, 'It's Uncle Aldo!' and the other students started to laugh and shriek.

'It's Aldo!' they yelled.

Of course it was Aldo! He'd been practising being a pirate for weeks. He gave a jolly laugh when they recognized him.

But what about the others? The first pirate

pushed up his eye patch and we could see who he was: Mr Morales.

'Arrgh!' he repeated, but this time he was smiling.

My friends squealed with laughter.

The second pirate took off his hat and bowed before us. 'Greetings,' he said, and we all realized that it was Mr Fitch. That pirate hat in the library was his after all.

Suddenly, these pirates didn't seem scary at all!

'Be ye ready to unlock the secrets of the deep?' asked Aldo as he opened the lid. Inside were mounds of yummy sandwiches and juices and biscuits.

My friends acted as if they'd never seen food before. They screamed with delight as they hurried towards the chest.

Seth and Tabitha got there first, but as soon as they put their hands on the food, another voice rang out.

'How dare ye touch me treasure?' This was definitely a female voice. 'Stop or the lot of ye will end up asleep in the deep!'

Everyone gasped – including me – as out of the bushes stepped a *female* pirate. She had on tall boots, a red skirt, big gold hoop earrings and a white top with billowy sleeves.

Even with the pirate hat and the eye patch she wore, I could see her bouncy black curls. And I knew that voice!

'That treasure came all the way from Brazil . . .' she started. But my friends didn't let her finish.

'Ms Mac! Ms Mac!' they shouted with joy as they rushed forward to greet her.

There she was: Ms Mac, the teacher who rescued me from Pet-O-Rama, who gave me a notebook and pencil and first discovered what a handsome and smart hamster I am.

'Ms Mac is back!' I squeaked loudly, surprising even myself.

Ms Mac hurried over to my basket. 'Humphrey!' she cried. 'There's the real treasure.'

She gently scratched my back, and I had a FUNNY-FUNNY-FUNNY feeling from the wiggly tip of my nose to the squiggly tips of my toes.

I'd had that feeling before, way back when.

I think they call it love.

❛❜

All of my friends loved Ms Mac and wanted to be near her. They gave her sandwiches and juice and gathered around her.

'What do you think of our secret guest?' Mrs Brisbane asked us.

Ms Mac was our secret guest! So that's what the *secret g* on the list stood for!

'Do you have to go back to Brazil?' Miranda asked.

'No, I was just there to teach for one term,' Ms Mac explained. 'I'm back here for a while – if I can find a job.'

While everyone ate, Mr Fitch played the harmonica and Aldo and Mr Morales danced the sailor's hornpipe. (Aldo did a better job, but he'd had a lot of practice.)

'Well done, me hearties!' I squeaked, but no one could hear me over the applause.

Then Mrs Brisbane quietened everyone down. 'Don't you think it's time for the prizes?'

In her hand were the ribbons she'd taken out of the basket.

Everyone cheered when Sayeh and Miranda received yellow ribbons. Even though their swan boat didn't last, it definitely was the Most Beautiful boat.

But when it came to the Most Seaworthy boat, it wasn't so easy to decide who won.

'Undoubtedly, the tall ship would have won,' Mr Brisbane said. 'But because of what happened, I can only award it an honourable mention.' Richie and Kirk didn't seem disappointed to receive blue ribbons.

'As for first place, we were all so busy worrying about Humphrey, no one really noticed which boat came in first. Since Seth and Tabitha's Chinese junk and Heidi and Gail's sailing boat both made it to shore, we're calling it a tie. You'll all receive red ribbons.'

From the cheers and smiles, I could tell that no one was disappointed. Seth and Tabitha did a funny victory dance. Heidi and Gail joined in.

Then Mrs Morgenstern came over to congratulate the girls. 'You did a great job!' she said. 'I was so focused on you winning the Most Beautiful award, I didn't think of you actually winning the race. But you did it!'

Gail and Heidi beamed.

'And the sail was spectacular! That white sail on the blue water – it was a classic. Gail, you were right all along. I'm very proud of you.'

Gail and her mum hugged. Then Heidi and Gail's mum hugged. Then Heidi and Gail hugged. I wished there was someone for me to hug, although hugging might be a little dangerous for a small hamster.

It was almost time to get back to school. As everyone else was busy packing up, I spotted Kirk and Richie wading out into the water to retrieve their tall ship which was now half-submerged in the pond. Luckily, the water only came up to their knees. Sayeh and Miranda watched onshore as a few of their colourful feathers floated by. Garth and A.J. looked for their boat, too, but all they could find was the flag. Art and Mandy waded in the water, but the Viking ship was totally gone.

On the edge of the pond, Mr Morales cupped his hands around his mouth and yelled, 'If you see an old raft down there, let me know!'

When Kirk and Richie finally pulled the remains of the tall ship out of the water, it was muddy and mucky, but they cleaned it up, working together.

·ö·

I was happy to stay in my basket on the bus ride back. I sat between Mrs Brisbane and Ms Mac – the best seat in the house. If I grabbed onto the inside of the basket, I could lift the top with my head just enough to see them both.

'You certainly picked an interesting day to return,' Mrs Brisbane said.

'Every day is interesting for the kids in Room 26,' Ms Mac replied.

Mrs Brisbane reached into her jacket and pulled out a piece of paper. 'In all the excitement, I forgot to check my list.'

Ms Mac and I could both see it.

lunches and drinks (in chest)
treasure maps
Captain Kidd and his motley crew
red, blue, yellow ribbons for prizes
secret guest: Ms Mac

'You didn't forget anything,' Ms Mac said.

Mrs Brisbane folded up her paper. 'No, but a few things happened that weren't on the list. You know what they say: the best-laid plans of mice and men often go astray.'

The best-laid plans of hamsters go astray, too. But that's what makes life interesting.

Soon, Mrs Wright led us all in singing a boat song that was very interesting because different groups started it and ended it at different times. I squeaked up the loudest of all.

> Row, row, row your boat
> Gently down the stream.
> Merrily, merrily, merrily, merrily,
> Life is but a dream.

It was a fun song to sing, and I thought, maybe some day I'd like to row *gently* down a stream. Even though today's trip had almost turned into a nightmare, seeing Ms Mac again was definitely a dream come true.

A good heart, mateys: there be the only treasure worth having!

from *Jolly Roger's Guide to Life*, by I. C. Waters

12

Land Ho!

When we got back to Room 26, I was almost too tired to squeak, but I managed to tell Og I'd had a great adventure, almost drowned, but lived to tell the tale.

'BOING!' At least he sounded interested.

I didn't get to tell him more because the bell rang for break and my classmates streamed out of the room. The room wasn't empty for long, though, because Mrs Wright, Mr Morales and Ms Mac all joined Mrs Brisbane in the classroom.

'Do you have a minute, Sue?' the head asked. He was still wearing his red shirt with the bright blue sash. He'd taken off his earring and eye patch, though.

'Of course,' she said. 'Please sit down.'

It's always funny to see grown-ups sitting on the kid-sized chairs in the classroom. I tried to imagine them as students. Mr Morales would be a good student with a playful streak. Mrs Brisbane would be an excellent student, like Sayeh. Of course, Ms Mac would be an almost perfect human, like Miranda.

But try as I might, I couldn't imagine Mrs Wright as a child.

'Did any of the students admit to smuggling Humphrey onto the boat?' Mr Morales asked.

Mrs Brisbane shook her head. 'No. I think Kirk and Richie felt so terrible, they would have confessed to it. But they didn't.'

'Maybe someone was jealous of their boat and did it to get them into trouble?' Mrs Wright suggested.

'Maybe,' said Mrs Brisbane. 'But I just can't imagine any of my students doing that.'

Mrs Wright sniffed loudly. 'I know you think all your students are perfect,' she said. 'But someone had to have done it. He certainly couldn't have got there all by himself.'

Suddenly, everyone turned to look at me.

'I didn't plan on going along,' I squeaked in self-defence. 'It just happened.'

Ms Mac laughed her lovely, tinkling laugh.

'He's been known to get out of his cage before,' Mrs Brisbane said. 'But Bert fixed the door so he can't escape.'

Mrs Wright stood up and clomped over to my cage. 'Even if he could open the cage, you can't tell me this little rat or guinea pig or whatever he is could possibly get down from the table, run all across the room and get into the boat by himself. Impossible! Simply impossible!'

'I'm a hamster!' I squeaked back at her. 'And it's NOT-NOT-NOT impossible!'

'BOING-BOING-BOING!' Og chimed in.

This time everyone laughed, except Mrs Wright.

I guess Mr Morales was sorry he'd laughed. 'You have a point, Ruth.'

Mrs Wright sniffed again. Maybe she was allergic to hamsters. 'We can't have animals running willy-nilly around the school and the buses and on picnics.'

'It was only one animal,' Mrs Brisbane said softly.

The bell rang again, and Mr Morales stood up. 'Look, Mrs Brisbane has been handling her students and their problems for thirty years. I think she can handle this one. Let's move on.'

He left, along with Ms Mac and Mrs Wright. Just before my friends returned from break, Mrs Brisbane came over to my cage and jiggled the door. It was fastened tightly, of course.

'Humphrey, I must say life is never dull with you around.'

'Thanks,' I squeaked. 'That's what a classroom hamster is for.'

⚬

After school, when we were alone, I told Og the whole story. When I had finished, I remembered something else.

'I have to say, Og, that as I was about to sink, I thought of you.' It was strange to remember seeing his goofy face flash before me.

'I know if you'd been there, you would have saved me, because you can swim. And because you're my friend.'

I was surprised at how quickly Og responded with a 'BOING-BOING-BOING-BOING!'

'I'd do the same for you,' I continued. 'I can't swim, but I'd think of something. I guess we make a pretty good team after all. Maybe Kirk and Richie will, too.'

Og dived into the water with an impressive splash.

And with that, I crawled into my sleeping hut and slept soundly, dreaming about the high seas, pirates, best friends and yes, Ms Mac.

⚬

No more boat building. No more pirate talk. No more contests. The very next day, we were back to

· 290 ·

normal old school again, but after my close call with Davy Jones's locker, I didn't mind.

Not that the subject of the boat race didn't come up. Mrs Brisbane began the day with a very serious look on her face. 'Boys and girls, we still don't know who sneaked Humphrey into that boat and onto the bus. If the guilty party would like to confess now, it would make all our lives a little easier.'

There were some shuffling feet and a few cleared throats but no one confessed. There was no one *to* confess, except for me.

'I hate to punish the whole class . . .' Mrs Brisbane began.

I couldn't take it any longer. 'I did it! It was ME-ME-ME!' I squeaked as loudly as I could.

Everyone laughed. Even Mrs Brisbane.

'I guess Humphrey has the last word for now,' she said. 'If anyone would like to confess to me in private, I'd appreciate it. Meanwhile, we're moving on.'

Over the next few days, there were a few changes in Room 26.

First of all, Richie and Kirk had to write letters of apology to each other. Then each of them had to give a speech to the class, apologizing for almost ruining the boat race.

In his speech, Kirk said that teamwork was more important than winning and the team that works together always comes out ahead in the end. As usual, he ended with a joke. This time, it was one I'd already heard, about the scarecrow winning the award for being outstanding in his field.

Richie made the point that two wrongs don't make a *right*. At first I thought he was talking about *Mrs Wright,* and I shivered a little just thinking about her whistle, though she's a very good song leader.

But then I realized that he meant just because Kirk treated Richie the wrong way didn't make it right for Richie to break the rules and bring along the submarine.

I cheered loudly at both speeches.

Aldo changed back to his normal non-pirate ways of talking and cleaning, thank goodness. But every once in a while, he'd do a little hornpipe dance while he was dusting.

The other change in Room 26 was something – or someone – wonderful. Ms Mac came in to help Mrs Brisbane for two hours every day. Then she would go to the library and help Mr Fitch for another hour or two.

She smelt so good, and she always remembered to bring me yummy treats like apple slices and strawberries. Having her around was a dream come true.

One day, she asked Mrs Brisbane if she could

have lunch with her. They sat across from each other at Mrs Brisbane's desk and took out sandwiches and water and yummy-looking fruit as they talked.

'I'm so glad it worked out with Humphrey,' Ms Mac said. 'When I left here, I wasn't sure you'd like having a classroom hamster.'

'I wasn't sure myself,' Mrs Brisbane admitted. 'But he's added a lot to the class.'

'Good,' said Ms Mac. She chewed on her sandwich some more and then said, 'I'm a little worried about what I'm going to do now that I'm back. I need to make some money.'

'Funny, I've been worrying about that, too,' Mrs Brisbane replied. She didn't look worried, though. In fact, she was grinning. 'And I have some ideas.'

Ms Mac's big brown eyes got even bigger. 'What?'

'I don't want to say yet, but you are a very talented young teacher, and I know of several opportunities coming up.' Mrs Brisbane was being awfully mysterious. 'You'll find out soon.'

'WHAT-WHAT-WHAT?' I shouted.

The two women chuckled. 'It sounds like Humphrey has a few ideas, too,' Ms Mac said.

'He always does,' Mrs Brisbane agreed.

'Speaking of Humphrey, has anyone confessed to smuggling him into the boat?'

'Well, yes. You actually heard him confess.' So Mrs Brisbane had understood me!!

Ms Mac glanced over at my cage. 'Could Humphrey really do that?'

Mrs Brisbane looked my way, too. 'If there's one thing I've learned this year, when it comes to Humphrey, *anything* is possible.'

'BOING-BOING!' Og twanged, splashing in his tank.

The two teachers burst out laughing.

When they finished their lunches, they each gave me a treat. From Mrs Brisbane, it was a small and crunchy carrot. From Ms Mac, it was a sweet-smelling chunk of banana.

I crossed my paws and hoped they would have lunch in Room 26 more often!

And then something really wonderful happened. Ms Mac brought Mr Fitch to Room 26 one day. He said that due to my bravery during the boat race and my contributions to the class, he was presenting me with my very own library card!

And there it was: a lovely little rectangle that read, *This card grants full library privileges at Longfellow School to HUMPHREY*. He taped it to the outside of my cage.

Everyone applauded. Then Miranda Golden, my

special friend, raised her hand. 'But how is Humphrey going to take out books? He can't get to the library by himself!'

Oh, humans! There's so much they don't know. In fact, I was already planning to stroll down to the library later that night to see if there was a good movie I could watch.

'We'll just have to help him out,' Mrs Brisbane answered. 'Just like he's always helped us.'

'Hooray for Humphrey Dumpty!' A.J. suddenly shouted. My friends all joined in, and I even heard Og say, 'BOING!' in agreement.

'Thanks, mateys,' I squeaked back happily. 'HOORAY-HOORAY-HOORAY!'

> Even a pirate can say thank ye, mateys!
>
> from *Jolly Roger's Guide to Life*, by I. C. Waters

Humphrey's Ten Favourite Pirate Facts

1 Many pirates did wear earrings, not just for looks, but because they thought it made their eyesight better.

2 Going to Davy Jones's locker means losing your life at sea.

3 Although Long John Silver kept a parrot as a pet, most pirates probably didn't have parrots. Dogs and cats were often on sailing ships to help keep down the rodent population. (As a rodent, let me tell you that dogs and cats are VERY-VERY-VERY scary.)

4 Food on pirate ships wasn't very good. Pirates lived mostly on hard biscuits and a little meat. Sometimes they brought fruit like limes on board to prevent a disease called scurvy.

5 There were some famous female pirates, like Anne Bonny and Mary Read. (Ms Mac was not one of them. She's much too nice to be a pirate.)

6 A piece of eight was a silver coin that was worth eight of the Spanish coin called the *Real*. Really! A doubloon was a gold coin.

7 A 'landlubber' is someone who doesn't know how to sail. I used to be a landlubber, but not any more!

8 A pirate says, 'Thar she blows,' when a whale is spotted.

9 The poop deck of a ship is the part farthest at the back, above the captain's quarters. It does not have anything to do with poo!

10 While it's fun to talk and dress and pretend to be a pirate, they are not nice humans. Yes, there are still pirates today, so beware, me hearties!

Oh, and yes, there really is a book called *Treasure Island* with Long John Silver and Jim Hawkins in it. It's by Robert Louis Stevenson, and you can find it in your library. If you don't have a card, get one!

Holidays According to Humphrey

Contents

The End (of School)

It was a warm afternoon and there was a lovely ray of sunlight beaming into my cage, as golden as my fur. It made me feel so cosy and dozy, I guess I nodded off during science class. The last thing I remembered Mrs Brisbane saying was 'cumulus clouds'. Then I was floating away on my own fluffy little cloud, as peaceful as a hamster can be. *Until* I was awakened by a LOUD-LOUD-LOUD voice that could only belong to my classmate Lower-Your-Voice-A.J.

'How many more days are there?' he boomed.

'Four,' Mrs Brisbane answered.

I opened one eye and listened carefully.

'Just four days until the end of school,' she continued.

I opened both eyes, jumped up and let out a loud 'Eeek!'

'Sounds like Humphrey Dumpty is anxious for school to be out,' A.J. said. 'Like me!'

The end of school? Did she mean that there wouldn't be school EVER-EVER-EVER again? Or was it just another holiday?

'I will miss you,' the teacher said. 'But it's time to move on.'

Move on? Can a school move?

'Og,' I squeaked to my neighbour, 'did you hear that?'

Og splashed in his tank a little, then let out a loud 'BOING!' That's the twangy way green frogs like him talk.

Stop-Giggling-Gail giggled. 'I guess Og is ready for summer, too!'

'Hands up before speaking, please, class,' Mrs Brisbane reminded her students. She wouldn't be able to remind them much longer. 'Yes, Kirk?'

'May I tell a summer joke please?' he asked. At least I-Heard-That-Kirk Chen had learned not to blurt out his jokes without asking.

'Yes, if it's short,' Mrs Brisbane told him.

'What did the pig say on the beach on a hot summer day?' he asked.

'I don't know,' the teacher admitted.

'I'm *bakin'*! Get it? Like, I'm *bacon*!' Kirk proudly explained.

'I get it,' Mrs Brisbane said.

Gail giggled again, of course, along with her best friend, Heidi.

There was a shuffle of feet as the clock moved towards the end of the school day.

'Wait-for–the-Bell-Garth,' Mrs Brisbane told Garth Tugwell. He was always the first one out of his chair.

As soon as he sat down, the bell rang and, with plenty of clattering and chattering, my friends hurried out of Room 26. While they hurried, I worried.

Was it the end of Longfellow School for ever?

What would everyone *do*?

And, most importantly, where would Og and I go?

What does a classroom pet do when his job is over?

Mrs Brisbane tidied up her desk, the way she usually did when school was over for the day. She didn't seem bothered about the end of school. In fact, she was humming a happy tune.

I didn't feel like humming.

Maybe Og and I would go to live with Mrs Brisbane and her husband, Bert. I enjoyed staying at their house, but I didn't want to be there all the time without my friends around. How I'd miss Sayeh and Art and Seth and Tabitha and Miranda. Miranda! I could hardly imagine not seeing Golden Miranda again.

'Eeek!' I squeaked. Again. It just slipped out.

Mrs Brisbane heard me and walked over to the table by the window where Og and I lived.

'I guess you fellows are wondering what you'll be doing when school is over,' she said.

'RIGHT-RIGHT-RIGHT!' I replied, although all that came out was SQUEAK-SQUEAK-SQUEAK as usual.

'Well, I can't tell you because it's a surprise,' she said.

And then, humming her little tune, Mrs Brisbane left Room 26 for the day, and left me with a lot to think about.

While my mind raced, I suddenly noticed that it was warm in Room 26. Even a little bit hot. I almost wished I could take off my fur coat. Or that I could swim around in nice cool water like Og. (Not that I ever would, since hamsters should never – and I mean *never* – get wet.)

Also, I'd been noticing for a while that the sky was staying light longer, which makes life a bit difficult for a nocturnal creature like me, who looks forward to night-time.

One reason I look forward to night-time is that Aldo comes in to clean.

'Greetings, friends! You are looking at a happy

fellow,' he announced as he pushed his cleaning trolley into the classroom.

Aldo had always seemed like a happy fellow, but that night he was even happier than usual.

'Hi, Aldo! What's new?' I squeaked.

Og added a friendly 'BOING!'

'School's out for me! It's over!' Aldo was beaming happily. 'And my grades were very good. Even in Spanish!'

'Way to go, Aldo!' I squeaked.

Aldo cleans at night but goes to school during the day so he can be a teacher some day. He had a little trouble with his Spanish class earlier in the year, so I was happy for him.

I thought for a moment, trying to remember the Spanish word for 'good'.

'*!Bueno!*' I added.

'School's out, school's out. Teacher let the mules out,' he said with a laugh.

I had no idea there were mules at Aldo's college!

Mrs Brisbane had been humming earlier in the day and now Aldo whistled as he briskly swept the floors and dusted the furniture. The end of school certainly seemed to make people musical.

When he had finished, he pulled a chair up close to my cage and Og's tank. Then he took out his dinner.

'No more eating from paper bags for a while,' he said, biting into his sandwich.

I liked to watch Aldo eat. His big black moustache made it difficult to see his mouth, so when he ate the food just seemed to disappear.

'No, my friends,' he said. 'When Longfellow School closes next week, I'm leaving town! I'm out of here.'

I shivered even though it was hot. That meant there would be no more school *and* no more Aldo!

'Here, buddy, have a carrot,' Aldo said, slipping me a crunchy treat as he did every night.

No more treats either, I thought.

It wasn't just the end of school. It was the end of life as I'd known it.

ᵒ

'Can you believe it, Sue?' our head teacher, Mr Morales, asked the next morning before class began. 'Three days until it's all over.' Mr Morales had a collection of special ties and today he was wearing a blue one with bright yellow suns on it.

He seemed happy about the end of school, too. But what does a head teacher do if he doesn't have a school to go to every day?

'The whole family will be hitting the road,' he said. 'What about you and Bert?'

'We're leaving, too,' she said. 'Jason's getting married in Tokyo and we're going for the wedding.'

Mrs Brisbane was positively beaming with joy. Jason was her son and he lived in Tokyo, which is FAR-FAR-FAR away.

So I guess she was going FAR-FAR-FAR away, too. Was that her surprise – *everybody* was leaving?

'What about us?' I squeaked to Og.

He splashed loudly in his tank.

'I guess we'll have to hit the road, too,' I said. But it didn't sound like much fun.

That night, I dreamed about Og and me on the open road. It was a scary dream because we had to dodge huge cars and lorries that were whizzing by. Once, I saw Mr Morales and his family speed right past us. Then I heard a loud engine buzzing. I looked up and saw Mr and Mrs Brisbane waving to us from an aeroplane. Later, a big bus passed us and a lot of my friends from Room 26 shouted and waved: Golden Miranda and Repeat-It-Please-Richie and Don't-Complain-Mandy Payne.

Og and I walked and hopped for hours and hours, but we didn't get very far. I was glad to wake up, I can tell you that. And I was tired from all the walking.

But I was happier than ever to see my friends the next morning. I looked around at them smiling, fidgeting, whispering. They seemed unsqueakably happy. Why was I the only one who was upset that Longfellow School was closing down?

Nobody seemed to mind the End of School . . . except me and possibly Og.

The next night, after Aldo's visit, I opened my cage's lock-that-doesn't-lock (it just looks locked, which allows me to get out and have adventures without anyone knowing) and wandered over to Og's tank.

'Whatever happens, Og, let's stick together, okay?' I suggested.

It's always a little hard to tell if Og is listening, because he just stares with those googly eyes and a huge frozen smile on his face.

'BOING-BOING,' he said, jumping up and down.

I can't understand everything Og says, but it sounded as if he agreed with me.

At least I wouldn't be alone. That was the good news.

But hamsters and frogs have very different likes and needs. That was the bad news.

I decided it was time to take a final walk through the halls of my beloved Longfellow School. Such a fine building – why on earth would humans close it down?

I felt a little sorry for Og as I started my journey. After all, he isn't able to get out of his tank and roam freely, the way I do. Even if he could, he'd probably start to dry out after a while, which wouldn't be comfortable for a frog.

After bidding Og farewell, I slid down the leg of the table and scampered across the floor. I took a deep breath, then slipped through the narrow space under the classroom door.

It was DARK-DARK-DARK in the hallway, though there were some low lights around the building. There was a time when Longfellow School at night seemed mysterious and even scary, but not any more.

I visited the library first, sliding under the door. Even in the semi-darkness, I could see the big aquarium, glowing and alive with brightly coloured fish. I scurried forward to take a peek at the little sunken ship lying at the bottom of the tank. It always gave me a thrill – and a chill.

I wondered what would happen to the fish when Longfellow School was no more.

Then I hopped up a series of shelves next to the desk until I reached the top. I pulled hard with all my might and raised myself on to the desktop. It was a few quick steps to the remote control that was always there. I hit the 'on' button and was thrilled to see pictures appear before me on a big screen as music played.

I never knew what I'd see on my trips into the library at night.

Tonight it was a thrilling but frightening film about a dense jungle full of beautiful, dangerous creatures such as lions and tigers. I was gripped by the growls and roars, the teeth and claws that I saw and heard!

When the show was over, I tapped the 'off' button, a little reluctantly since I didn't know when – if ever – I'd have the chance to see a film like that again. I hurried back down the shelves to the floor of the library. Without bothering to glance back at the aquarium and the sunken ship, I scurried out into the hallway to have one last look around.

I strolled along the darkened corridors, past other classrooms, down to Mr Morales's office. I stood there, looking up at the sign that said 'Head Teacher', the glass window and the suggestions box hanging high up on the big door.

I couldn't reach the box, but if I had been able to, I know what my suggestion would be: 'Don't close the school!'

On my way back, I passed the big double doors to the cafeteria. That's where my friends have lunch every single day. I'd always wanted to see it and this was my last chance. I slid under the door but was disappointed to find that it was a large empty room with tables folded against the wall and not a crumb of food left on the floor!

By the time I got back to my table in Room 26, I was pretty tired, because that's the hardest part of my adventures. I can slide DOWN-DOWN-DOWN my table leg, but I can't slide UP-UP-UP. Instead, I have to grab on to the cord of the blinds, which is very long, then swing it back and forth until I'm up to the table level. Then I cross my paws, close my eyes and leap on to the table. Whew!

Still, as tired as I was, I had a lot of thinking to do. So I took out the little notebook I keep hidden behind my mirror, and the little pencil that goes with it, and I began to write.

NOTE TO SELF: Unlike hamsters, humans love to make big changes. Unfortunately, they almost always forget to tell their pets what's going on.

The Beginning (of Summer)

The last few days passed quickly.

Mr Fitch, the librarian, came to Room 26 and collected all the library books. Every last one of them. This was unsqueakably sad to me, because I love the library and I love to hear Mrs Brisbane read to us. But now that was over.

Then Mrs Wright, the PE teacher with the loud, shiny whistle, came in with a list of games and equipment that my friends had borrowed. (I guessed I wouldn't miss *her* too much.)

At the end of the day, Mrs Brisbane told all of us about her forthcoming trip to Tokyo and showed pictures of the wonderful places she would visit – without me.

The next day would be the last day of school. That night, when the door swung open and Aldo said, 'Give a cheer, 'cause Aldo's here,' I felt happy and sad and all mixed up inside. I was happy because I was always glad to see Aldo, but I was sad because I didn't know when – or if – I'd *ever* see him again.

'This is it, pals,' said Aldo. 'Tomorrow school is over.'

'Don't remind me,' I squeaked.

'I'll be here tomorrow night,' Aldo continued. 'I'll be waxing the floors. But you guys will be gone . . . somewhere.'

He suddenly stopped twirling his broom.

'Where *will* you be?'

My heart skipped a beat. Aldo didn't know where we'd be and I certainly didn't know where we'd be. So who *did* know?

Aldo chuckled and started sweeping again. 'I'll bet Mrs Brisbane has cooked up something special for you. She's one nice lady.'

Aldo finished his work early and hurried through his dinner, but he remembered to give me a bit of lettuce. I wasn't very hungry, though, so I hid it at the bottom of my cage. I'd been saving food all week – just in case Mrs Brisbane *hadn't* cooked up something special for us the way Aldo said.

•ö•

All that time ago, back in September, when a beautiful woman named Ms Mac brought me from

Pet-O-Rama to Room 26, I was excited and amazed to find myself surrounded by so many bright and bouncy students (no frogs yet). Learning about humans was FUN-FUN-FUN and I also learned to read and write.

The world looked pretty wonderful from my cage until the day Ms Mac left to go to Brazil and Mrs Brisbane – who was the real teacher – came back.

It turned out that Ms Mac was just a substitute.

It turned out that Mrs Brisbane didn't like me.

It turned out that I didn't like her back!

But over time I learned that Mrs Brisbane was a very good teacher who cared about her students.

And over time she learned that I was a very good hamster who cared about her students as much as she did.

A wonderful thing happened. We grew to like each other. In fact, Mrs Brisbane became one of my favorite humans in the whole wide world.

Until now. The Mrs Brisbane I had grown to like – even love – wouldn't just head off for a faraway land without making sure I was well taken care of. So maybe I had been right not to like her in the very beginning. But that couldn't be! She'd taken good care of me for a long time now.

I was just going to have to trust her and believe that whatever surprise she had in store for Og and me would be something good. Even though I knew from experience that surprises can also be bad things, like meeting Clem the dog or Sweetums the cat!

Just in case I was wrong, I stayed up late writing in my notebook that night.

My last night at school.

Things I Could Do without School — a List

1 *Go back to Pet-O-Rama. (The pet shop I came from — not a good idea!)*

2 Teach other hamsters to read and write. (Where? Pet-O-Rama? What about Og?)

3 Find a school that doesn't end. (How would I find one? In my hamster ball?)

4 Work at Maycrest Manor. (I've already been there to help people who are sick or injured. Maybe they'd like Og, too.)

5 Hit the road with Og and roam free. (But not after seeing those scary creatures in the film in the library!)

My list didn't look too promising.

The sun came up the next morning, like any ordinary day.

The bell rang and my friends rushed in, like any ordinary day.

But that BAD-BAD-BAD feeling in the pit of my stomach told me that this was not an ordinary day.

'Og?' I squeaked loudly so he could hear me. 'I hope we'll stay together, but if we don't, you've been an unsqueakably nice neighbour and I'll miss you.'

'BOING-BOING-BOING!' Og twanged and splashed so loudly, I thought he'd pop the top right off his tank. He's done that one or two times before.

I felt a bit better knowing he agreed with me, but I was still worried. I hopped on my wheel for a fast and furious spin, just to let off some steam.

It was a very busy day in Room 26. Mrs Brisbane collected all of my friends' textbooks, though *not* my little notebook. (I keep it well hidden.)

Instead of reading and writing and taking tests, Mrs Brisbane and my fellow students were busy emptying their desks and tidying up. Room 26 had never been so neat before!

At the very end of the day, Mrs Brisbane said

that we were the most wonderful students she'd ever had and she knew that we'd all go on to great futures.

That would have been nice, if only I'd known what my future was!

Then she made a Very Important Announcement.

'Reports will be posted out this week,' she said.

Some students groaned.

'Now, now,' Mrs Brisbane continued, 'none of you have anything to worry about.'

That seemed to please my friends a lot.

'But there are two students getting their reports today,' she said. 'They are very special students who have helped to make this the best class I've ever had.'

Then, to my surprise, she picked up two small pieces of paper from her desk and walked over to the table where Og and I live – at least for the moment. She read the first one.

'Og, you have got top grades in Water Skills, Loud Noise Making, Splashing and Being Very Green. Straight As,' she announced.

My classmates clapped and cheered as she placed the report up against Og's tank.

'BOING-BOING-BOING!' Og twanged.

Then Mrs Brisbane turned to me.

'Humphrey, you have also got top grades in

Wheel Spinning, Hamster Ball Rolling and Squeaking. Straight As.' Mrs Brisbane hesitated. 'But you have got an A+ in one other subject: Helping Your Friends. You are truly the most helpful hamster I have ever known.'

Oh, how my friends clapped and cheered. They whistled and stomped. Then they stood up and applauded some more.

'Hum-phree! Hum-phree! Hum-phree!' they chanted.

I was just about the proudest hamster in the whole wide world.

'THANK YOU-THANK YOU-THANK YOU,' I squeaked as loudly as I could.

Everything was perfect. Except that little part about *not knowing what I was going to do for the rest of my life* . . .

'Mrs Brisbane?' a voice called out.

Someone was speaking out of turn, but for once it wasn't Raise-Your-Hand-Heidi.

It was Sayeh, the shyest girl in Room 26. Or at least she used to be the shyest girl in the class.

'Yes, Sayeh,' Mrs Brisbane said.

Sayeh stood up next to her desk. 'I'd like to thank Humphrey for helping me to learn to speak up,' she said in a strong voice. 'I will never forget him. Not for my whole life.'

'You're welcome, Sayeh!' I squeaked.

Suddenly, Sit-Still-Seth Stevenson stood up. 'And I'd like to thank Humphrey for helping me to settle down. At least a little bit.'

Then, one by one, they all stood up. Don't-Complain-Mandy thanked me for helping her to meet her hamster, Winky. Pay-Attention-Art said I'd helped him with his maths. (And it's not even my best subject!) And Golden Miranda thanked me for being her best friend.

'And I want to thank Og for being a great frog,' Heidi Hopper said. And she even raised her hand before saying it.

Later, Mr Morales came into the classroom. He was wearing a tie that had tiny cars all over it.

'Students in Room 26, I want to congratulate you on a great year,' he said. 'And I wish you a wonderful summer ahead.'

He was in and out of the room quickly, but as he left I didn't know if I would ever see the Most Important Person at Longfellow School again.

·ö·

I was happy. I was tired. I was nervous. As the clock went TICK-TICK-TICK, I wondered what my future – and Og's – would be. I hopped on my wheel again and spun.

Then something surprising and wonderful happened. Ms Mac entered Room 26.

Ms Mac! With bouncy black curls tumbling around her lovely, happy face. With her big dark eyes and that slight smell of yummy apples. My friends all cheered when they saw her. Like me, they had started off with her as their teacher.

She'd broken my heart when she went to Brazil. But I forgave her when she came back. That's what happens when you love somebody.

'Am I too early?' Ms Mac asked.

Mrs Brisbane smiled. 'No, your timing is perfect. Please, go ahead.'

Ms Mac was wearing a pink blouse and a bright red skirt and TALL-TALL-TALL red shoes.

'Students,' she said, in a way that made the word sound wonderful, 'I know you all have exciting plans for the summer. And Mrs Brisbane has exciting plans, too. But I just want you to know that your friends Humphrey and Og are going to have a fantastic summer as well. Because they are coming with *me*!'

'Eeek!' I actually tumbled off my wheel. Of all the wonderful, fabulous, remarkable and amazing things Og and I could do for the summer, being with Ms Mac would be the most wonderful, fabulous, remarkable and amazing of all!

'BOING-BOING-BOING-BOING-BOING!' Og obviously agreed with me.

'I'm glad you're pleased,' said Ms Mac, 'because we are going to have a *great* adventure.'

I was overjoyed. Og and I didn't have to go to Pet-O-Rama or search for unending schools or hit the open road. We were going to have a great adventure!

I had a big lump in my throat just thinking of leaving my friends. But my heart went pitter-patter at the thought of being with Ms Mac again.

And then it happened. The bell rang and my friends all raced out of Room 26, out of Long-fellow School.

'BYE-BYE-BYE!' I squeaked, but I don't think anyone could hear me.

Og dived into his tank and made a huge splash.

'Well, boys, here comes summer,' Ms Mac told us, with a big smile on her face.

Summer! What a wonderful word, I thought.

> NOTE TO SELF: Any time you start to think humans know what they're doing, they'll usually prove you WRONG-WRONG-WRONG.

The Mysterious Journey

After my friends left, Ms Mac and Mrs Brisbane stayed and talked. They chatted about Mrs Brisbane's trip and her son's wedding. They spoke about the nice weather. They discussed what a good class it had been.

They talked about just about everything except the great adventure Og and I were going to have.

I thought they'd never stop talking, but finally Mr Morales came in to say goodbye. Then he helped Ms Mac carry our supply of Nutri-Nibbles and Mighty Mealworms and Og's unsqueakably yucky crickets out to her car.

While they were gone, Mrs Brisbane stopped and looked first at Og, then at me.

'It's been a pleasure having you in Room 26, fellows, but I hate goodbyes,' she said. 'So I'll just say good luck.'

'Goodbye and thanks for everything!' I squeaked, clinging to the side of my cage as Mr Morales and Ms Mac returned and carried Og and me out of the door, down the hallway and out to the car.

SLAM! The door was shut. Ms Mac tooted her horn and waved goodbye to Mr Morales, then off she drove.

I glanced back at Longfellow School. Would I ever see it again? Would I ever see Mrs Brisbane or Mr Morales again?

I was just about to ask Og when Ms Mac turned up the radio and music began to blare. The windows were open, the music was jazzy and we were on our way – somewhere.

At least I knew that life with Ms Mac was never ever boring.

I was a little disappointed over the next two weeks because, although it was nice to be with Ms Mac again, our lives weren't really that exciting.

Ms Mac liked to cook and the apartment always smelled of YUMMY-YUMMY-YUMMY things. She had a lot of friends over and they ate the yummy food, listened to loud music and sometimes Ms Mac played the bongo drums.

To my surprise, Og like to BOING-BOING along with the bongos!

Still, I have to admit I missed Mrs Brisbane and my friends in Room 26. Nobody called me 'Humphrey Dumpty' the way A.J. did. No one spoke as softly and sweetly to me as Sayeh. And no one giggled like good old Gail!

I was beginning to think my life was going to be an endless round of bongos and BOING-BOINGS, when one day Ms Mac got out a large suitcase.

'Og?' I called to my neighbour, whose tank was next to my cage on Ms Mac's coffee table. 'I think she's leaving again! I hope she's not going back to Brazil!'

Like I said, Brazil is where Ms Mac went when she left Room 26 and I remembered well how she told me she couldn't take me with her.

Og splashed madly. 'BOING-BOING!'

I could tell that he had come to love Ms Mac as much as I did.

'Calm down, guys,' Ms Mac said. 'This summer, you're going wherever I'm going. And I think you'll like the place we're going – a lot!'

'Did you hear that, Og?' I was almost crazy with delight. I started my wheel spinning at warp speed. 'We're going with her!'

'BOING-BOING-BOING-BOING-BOING!' Og twanged.

Even though I had no idea where we were going,

I was unsqueakably happy that Og and I were included.

'Of course, we'll have to drive a long way,' Ms Mac continued. 'And you'll be in very unfamiliar territory. In fact, it will be just a little bit *wild*.'

As soon as she said 'wild' I stopped spinning, which is never a good idea because I tumbled off the wheel and landed in a soft pile of bedding, a little closer to my poo corner than I like.

I thought about what I'd seen in the library just a few weeks earlier. Fierce animals with sharp teeth and sharp claws. They were marvellous beasts, but somehow I knew they wouldn't be friendly to small furry creatures like me. Or small green fur-less creatures like Og.

Especially at dinner time, if you get my drift.

Ms Mac didn't seem worried, though. She was too busy washing clothes and sewing little labels into them.

She packed her clothes and got more food and supplies for Og and me. 'We won't be near a town,' she explained. 'I'll bet you guys will like getting out in nature as much as I will.'

'Wait!' I squeaked. 'Exactly what do you mean by "getting out in nature"?' I asked. Because about the only time I'd been out in nature (in A.J.'s back garden), I was inside my hamster ball. And even so something BAD-BAD-BAD almost happened to me.

'The call of the wild must be answered!' Ms Mac laughed. Then she closed her suitcase and zipped it. 'We leave first thing in the morning.'

I had to spin on my wheel for a long time that night, trying to get the thought of lions and tigers out of my head. And I tried to tell myself that Ms Mac was a wonderful human who loved me.

I could trust her. Couldn't I?

·ö·

When Ms Mac said early, she meant early. The sun was barely up when Og and I were in the car, cage and tank nestled among boxes and bags and pillows and bongo drums.

BUMP-BUMP-BUMP went the little car as it chugged down the road.

THUMP-THUMP-THUMP went my heart (and tummy) with every bump we hit.

We drove and drove and drove some more. I couldn't see out of the window, so I didn't know if there were any lions or tigers around. I believe lions can make a lot of noise, but even if they'd been roaring right next to the car, I wouldn't have heard them because Ms Mac had loud music playing.

After several hours, the tummy-thumping BUMP-BUMP-BUMPS became slower BUM-PETY-BUMP-BUMPS and I knew that we had turned off the main road.

Ms Mac switched off her music. 'Ah, there's the sign,' she said. 'We're almost there.'

I crossed my paws and hoped that was good news.

'ö'

When you're a small creature who can't see out of the car windows, you learn to listen for clues. Here's what I heard as the car slowed down:

A crunching sound beneath the wheels, which meant we weren't on a paved road any more . . .

More and more bumps . . .

Birds chirping . . .

Buzzy sounds . . .

And here's what I didn't hear:

Other cars whizzing by . . .

City noises . . .

People . . .

Then I heard Ms Mac say, 'Oh, wow.'

The car stopped. She opened the door and told Og and me that she'd be right back.

The windows were open and a nice breeze drifted in. I didn't smell chalk and rubbers and marker pens and packed lunches, like I had in Room 26. I smelled grass and trees and things I couldn't even name.

'Can you see anything, Og?' I asked my friend.

No answer. Maybe the car ride had upset his tummy. He looked a little greener than usual.

I tried to concentrate on the sounds of the birds singing and the buzzy things. Then I heard other sounds, too.

SKITTER-SKITTER-SKITTER.

SCRITCH-SCRITCH-SCRITCH.

These were the soft sounds of small creatures scurrying about. I wondered if there were other hamsters around.

Then I heard footsteps. Not Ms Mac's footsteps, though. These were CLOMPITY-CLOMPITY-CLOMP footsteps. Ms Mac would never clompity-clomp.

Suddenly, a man's big red face with bright red hair under a red and white baseball cap popped right in through the open door!

'Well, who do we have here?' Goodness, his voice was almost as loud as Lower-Your-Voice-A.J.'s.

'I'm Humphrey!' I squeaked back. 'Who are you?'

'Yoo-hoo!' Ms Mac was calling in the distance.

The man's face disappeared. 'Hello!' his voice boomed out again.

'Hi, Mr Holloway!' I heard Ms Mac say. 'I was just up at the office looking for you. I'm Morgan McNamara.'

Oops! I'd almost forgotten that Ms Mac had a longer name.

'I remember from your interview. Call me Hap,' the man replied. 'And welcome to Happy Hollow.'

'Did you hear that, Og? We're in a place called Happy Hollow!' I squeaked to my friend. 'That's a nice name. It must be a nice place.'

'BOING!' Og replied.

Then I heard Hap Holloway say, 'I see you brought your friends along.'

'Yes, the hamster and the frog, as we discussed,' Ms Mac answered.

'That's us!' I told Og.

'Great! Why don't you get unpacked and then come on up and we'll get organised? You'll be in Robins' Nest tonight. Just up the hill on the right. It's all clean and aired out.'

Ms Mac hopped back in the car and drove up the hill. I was unsqueakably excited. Were we really sleeping in a birds' nest? Would it be up in a tree? Would the robins actually be there? And would a small furry hamster be welcome?

Room 26 suddenly seemed FAR-FAR-FAR away.

> NOTE TO SELF: No matter what you think humans have planned, they'll always surprise you (like it or not).

Camp Happy Hollow

I wasn't too disappointed to discover that Robins' Nest was not a nest at all. It was a little wooden house surrounded by trees and grass and more trees and more grass.

'Here's our cabin,' Ms Mac said as she gently lifted my cage out of the car.

'Looks nice!' I said.

My, the air smelled fresh, and I smelled something I'd never smelled before. It was the scent of something *wild*.

Outside, the cabin looked like a normal little house with a covered veranda. Inside, it was a room with four beds – actually, eight beds stacked on top of each other in pairs. Ms Mac called them bunk beds.

Everything was made of bare wood, except for the red plaid curtains on the windows and the white sheets on the beds.

'Enjoy the quiet,' Ms Mac said after she had Og and me settled on a table by the window (she's thoughtful that way) and had given us both fresh water. 'It won't last long.'

Then she had a quick wash and left us alone.

There we were: one frog, one hamster, one bare wood cabin. No desks, no ringing bells, no shouting children. I missed them all: Kirk's corny jokes, Seth and his sports scores, Aldo's sweeping, Mrs Brisbane's stories. I was even starting to miss Mrs Wright (though *not* her whistle).

'What do you think of this place?' I asked Og.

Og splashed around in the water but said nothing.

I hopped on my wheel and began to spin. There was really nothing else to do. I tried looking out of the window but it was unsqueakably frustrating. All I could see was green wherever I looked. Green tree branches when I looked up. Green grass when I looked down. Green bushes straight ahead.

Finally, I couldn't stand it any longer. 'There must be something else to see,' I told Og.

He splashed agreeably. So I jiggled the lock-that-doesn't-lock and the door swung open. I knew it would be difficult (and dangerous) to get down to the floor and go outside. So for the first time ever, I climbed up the *outside* of my cage to get a little higher.

I guess I surprised Og with this new behaviour, because he let out an alarmingly loud 'BOING!'

Standing on top of my cage, I could look above some of the bushes blocking my view and see a teeny-tiny bit more. There were several other cabins in sight – all of them just like the one I was in.

And there were many paths that criss-crossed through the grass.

Mostly, though, there were trees. And more trees.

I was pretty sure there had to be something else out there other than trees. I knew there were birds, because I could hear them singing. (Thank goodness Ms Mac had left the windows open.)

Then I heard people singing, way off in the distance. I'm pretty sure I heard bongo drums playing, too.

·ö·

Ms Mac came in at night, but she went right to bed and got up very early in the morning. She did this a few days in a row. Eight beds. One human. Nothing much to do.

Sometimes – night or day – I would hear SKITTER-SKITTER-SKITTER and SCRITCH-SCRITCH-SCRITCH.

'Who's making that noise?' I asked Og one day

when my curiosity got the better of me. 'Is it inside or outside?'

'BOING-BOING!' said Og, leaping around his tank.

'I should probably check it out,' I said, but I was almost wishing Og would talk me out of it.

A skittering or a scritch could be made by a number of different creatures and some of them might not be too friendly. Still, I am a very curious hamster. Perhaps just a peek would ease my mind.

With a lump in my throat, I jiggled the lock-that-doesn't-lock. I was about to swing the door open when I heard footsteps approaching. I pulled the door back just as Ms Mac came into the cabin. She was wearing shorts and a shirt that had the words 'Camp Happy Hollow' printed on the front.

'You must have thought I'd abandoned you,' she said.

The thought had crossed my mind, especially with that skittering sound, but I was too polite to mention it. Though I was glad to have a reason to stay in my cage.

'I've been in training,' she said. 'Things are about to start popping.'

My mind raced, thinking about what kinds of things popped. Popcorn did and sometimes balloons, which are a little scary for a small furry creature.

Ms Mac lifted up my cage ever so gently.

'I need to get you guys up to the hall to meet the rest of the crew,' she said. 'I think you already know a couple of them.'

I was relieved to get out of the quiet cabin. Ms Mac carried first me and then Og down a winding path. We passed other cabins like the Robins' Nest before we entered a much bigger wooden building with an even bigger veranda and a large sign that said 'Happy Hollow Hall'.

Inside was an unsqueakably big dining room with long tables and benches. There was even a stage at the front with heavy curtains on either side of it. We went through the dining hall, past the kitchen and into a large room behind it.

Ms Mac put Og and me on a table in front of huge windows that looked out on even more trees and grass.

'Sorry you've been cooped up in that lonely cabin.' Sometimes Ms Mac seemed to read my mind. 'You'll like it better here in the rec room. And you'll be busy from now on.'

'Doing what?' I squeaked. But she had moved to the door, where she was talking to someone.

'Busy doing *what*, Og?' I asked my neighbour.

He wasn't paying attention. He was enjoying the waves in his tank created by our move. They made me feel a little seasick.

I looked around the wreck room. It didn't look like a wreck at all. There were couches and tables and chairs and a fireplace and bookshelves and cabinets – oh, it was a cosy place.

'Meet our first campers,' Ms Mac told whoever was at the door.

I scampered up the tree branch in my cage to see who was coming in. And I almost fell right off again when I saw – well, I couldn't believe my eyes. It was Aldo! He was wearing shorts and a shirt with 'Camp Happy Hollow' written on it just like Ms Mac.

'Never fear 'cause Aldo's here,' he said as he rushed over to see Og and me.

'Aldo! What are you doing here?' I squeaked in disbelief.

'I told you I was leaving town,' he said. 'I didn't tell you I was coming here to be a counsellor. And guess who else is here?' He turned and gestured towards the doorway. 'Come here, honey!'

Suddenly, Aldo's wife, Maria, was standing in front of me, smiling happily.

'Maria's taking a break from the bakery to cook here for the summer,' Aldo said.

Maria worked nights in a bakery while Aldo worked nights at Longfellow School. And I'm happy to say I helped them get together in the first place.

'It will be the best camp food ever,' Aldo assured us. 'You guys are lucky this recreation room is so close to the kitchen.'

Oh, so the 'wreck' room was really a 'rec' room! A place for games and fun.

'And I'm lucky that Humphrey and Og are close to me,' Maria said with a twinkle in her eye. 'I have to do something with the extra fruit and veg.' Yum. I do love fruit and veg. Og, on the other paw, likes ickier things, like crickets.

•ö•

More people came in. Ms Mac called them counsellors. Some were grown-ups like Aldo. Some were college students and there were junior counsellors, who were high school age. Ms Mac brought some of them over to meet me. It was hard to tell them apart because they all had on shorts and identical shirts.

One of the college students, a young woman with short blonde hair called Katie, rushed over to see me. 'Oh, Morgan, he's so cute! He's the cutest thing I've ever seen!'

I liked Katie a lot.

And there was Hap Holloway. He leaned down and put his big red face right next to my cage.

'Glad to have you aboard at my camp,' he said in his loud voice.

His camp?

'Just try not to get eaten by a bear,' he added, roaring with laughter.

I didn't dare tell him that this wasn't a bit funny. After all, it was *his* camp.

It was VERY-VERY-VERY noisy in the room with everyone laughing and talking.

Then suddenly it got VERY-VERY-VERY quiet. The quiet was broken by footsteps, heading towards my cage.

'Do you think it's a good idea to have *him* here?' a voice boomed.

The way the voice said 'him' was very familiar.

I raced to the side of my cage to get a closer look. I knew it. It was Mrs Wright, the PE teacher who liked rules more than hamsters. (Let's face it, she *loved* rules and she didn't like hamsters at all. I don't think she was very fond of frogs either.)

'The kids will love them,' Ms Mac said.

I was proud of how brave she was, standing up to Mrs Wright.

I braced myself, waiting for Mrs Wright to blow her loud whistle. But she didn't.

'There are health issues. *Allergies*. Disease,' she said.

'We're in the woods,' Ms Mac said. 'There's lots of stuff to be allergic to.'

Then, to my surprise, Hap Holloway stepped forward. 'We've got medical histories and consent forms,' he said firmly. 'We've got a nurse, too. She arrives tomorrow.'

'She'll sort things out,' Hap Holloway continued. 'You can concentrate on being Activities Director.'

Mrs Wright was speechless, which was a first.

I knew I was going to like Hap Holloway.

'Now it's time for pizza and singing,' Hap told the group. 'And in the morning, the fun begins!'

Actually, I had a lot of fun that evening. Aldo and Ms Mac slipped me bits of lettuce and carrot from the salad and I even got a teeny piece of mushroom from the pizza.

Katie played the guitar while Ms Mac pounded the bongos, and all the other counsellors sang amazing songs I'd never heard before. There was a song about a peanut on a railway line and another one about an alligator. There was something about ears hanging low which Og probably didn't understand because he doesn't have ears (that I've seen so far).

And my very favourite song was about a bucket with a hole in it. It got sillier and sillier and faster and faster, and silly old me, I was spinning on my wheel and almost fell off, the song was so funny.

If the real fun was beginning tomorrow, I knew that I was going to like Camp Happy Hollow a lot.

Even if I didn't know who would be sleeping in all those beds.

> NOTE TO SELF: Humans tend to pop up where you least expect them — and some of them have *whistles*.

5

Happy Campers

After breakfast the next morning (Maria kindly slipped me some yummy strawberries), Og and I watched through the sunny open windows of the rec room as Ms Mac and the other counsellors headed outside and began to set up tables and put up banners reading 'Welcome to Camp Happy Hollow'. Believe me, they were BUSY-BUSY-BUSY.

'The fun's beginning soon,' I said to Og, although what I was watching looked more like work than play.

And then a line of cars came up the bumpy road, parking near the hall. The car doors opened and out poured mums and dads and kids of all shapes and sizes. Suitcases, boxes, backpacks and duffel bags came out of car boots and started piling up near the tables.

'Og, look at all the people! Mums and dads and whole families coming to camp!' I told my neighbour.

Og leaped up. 'BOING-BOING-BOING!' he twanged.

Then it came. I should have expected it, knowing Mrs Wright was around. But the piercing blast from a whistle that is very painful to the small, sensitive ears of a hamster surprised me so much I squeaked 'Eeek!' rather loudly. Not that anyone could hear me, since Mrs Wright blew the whistle again.

'Line up at the tables and get your information packs,' Mrs Wright ordered the families. 'Line up, *please*!'

I crossed my paws and hoped the families would line up before she could blow her whistle again. She did it anyway.

'In an orderly fashion, *please*,' she insisted.

Once the families were in a queue, I noticed something. While many of the faces were new to me, I recognised some of the people.

'Look, Og! There's Repeat-It-Please-Richie!' I squeaked. 'From Room 26!'

Og splashed wildly. 'BOING-BOING! BOING-BOING!'

I climbed higher up in my cage to see what Og was so excited about.

'It's Stop-Giggling-Gail!' I squeaked. There was a flash of blue next to her. 'And her brother, Simon.' Simon was always on the move.

'BOING-BOING!' Og said, before diving to the bottom of his tank.

As I peered out of the window at the growing crowd of kids and parents, I saw another familiar face. It was Sayeh. She and her father looked a little bit lost among the bustle of excited families.

'Hi, Sayeh! It's me – Humphrey!' I squeaked at the top of my lungs. Unfortunately, my small voice didn't carry above the hubbub of the crowd.

Luckily, her friend, Golden Miranda, appeared behind her. The girls hugged and Sayeh's dad shook hands with Miranda's dad. There were two other familiar faces with Miranda. I was glad to see Abby, Miranda's stepsister. She didn't go to Longfellow School but I'd met her at Miranda's house.

I was not glad to see the other familiar face.

My heart skipped a beat when Miranda's dog, Clem, hopped out of the car. After all, Clem is bent on my total destruction! I've always managed to outwit him – *so far*. Luckily, Miranda's dad quickly put him back in the car, much to my relief.

'Richie! Hey, Richie!' That booming voice could

only belong to Lower-Your-Voice-A.J., who had arrived with his friend Garth and Garth's parents.

'A.J.! It's me – Humphrey Dumpty!' I shouted, using A.J.'s favourite name for me. Again, he couldn't hear me above the noise. Neither could his brother, Ty, who was standing next to him.

Mrs Wright gave her whistle another mighty blast and Aldo helped her get the people to line up at the tables. Then, one by one, the families hurried off on paths going in many directions and disappeared. They headed towards the cabins and I figured that each cabin would house a different family.

I figured wrong, because to my amazement, after a while, the parents all returned to their cars and drove away, leaving their children behind at Camp Happy Hollow!

'Og, they can't leave their children here all alone,' I told my neighbour.

'BOING-BOING,' Og twanged in agreement.

But they had. I thought for a while and realised they weren't actually all alone. Aldo and Ms Mac were at camp, and Mrs Wright and the other counsellors. They could help the kids.

And so could I. Maybe – just maybe – a camp needed a pet hamster as much as a classroom did.

It was so peaceful and quiet after the ruckus at the tables that I had a nice little nap. But I was rudely awakened by the ding-donging of the loudest bell I have ever heard. It was even louder than Mrs Wright's whistle.

Og must have heard it (even if I can't see his ears) because he leaped up so high, he almost hit the top that covered his tank.

Suddenly, the paths were filled with kids wearing shorts and T-shirts, all heading straight for Happy Hollow Hall. Some were laughing and joking, and some looked as if they had been crying. My friend Gail *definitely* wasn't giggling any more.

There were yummy smells coming from Maria's kitchen, so I didn't think anyone would be crying for long.

Once they were in the hall, I couldn't see the campers but I could certainly hear them. My friends in Room 26 got pretty noisy sometimes, but there were MANY-MANY-MANY more kids at camp and they were all talking at once.

'Goodness, Og,' I squeaked over the racket. 'If Mrs Brisbane were here, she'd quieten them down.'

Og splashed around agreeably until there was a loud, shrill blast. Things settled down then and, for once, I was almost glad Mrs Wright was there with her whistle.

I couldn't make out everything that was being said, but I heard Hap Holloway welcoming the campers. Then Ms Mac taught the kids a song about chewing – I am not kidding! Since hamsters are excellent chewers, I enjoyed the words a lot.

> *Chew, chew, chew your food,*
> *Gently through the meal.*
> *The more you chew, the less you eat,*
> *The better you will feel.*

Then the hall got noisy again with talking and the clinking and clanking of forks and spoons. I was getting unsqueakably curious about what was happening in the hall, but I didn't think it was a good idea to slip out of my cage while it was still light outside.

After a while, the whistle blew and things quietened down again. Hap Holloway said something about 'campfire' and 'games'. And then he said, 'You'll be getting to know your new friends over the next few days, but I want you to meet two more Happy Hollow Campers.'

Just as I was wondering who they might be, Aldo came into our room and picked up Og's tank while Ms Mac picked up my cage.

Things were really buzzing when we came into the room!

'Humphrey Dumpty!' A.J. shouted, and some of my friends cheered.

'Og the frog!' Garth shouted, and other friends cheered.

Mrs Wright had to blast her whistle several more times until things were quiet again.

I looked around and oh, my! The tables were filled with enthusiastic boys and girls. Even the ones like Gail who'd looked weepy before had perked up quite a bit.

Hap Holloway introduced us and explained that we'd be staying in different cabins every night and that each cabin would have a chance to earn us for the night by keeping their cabins neat and obeying the rules.

The kids clapped and stomped their feet, as I did, too.

Then Hap told them that for the first night, while they were at the campfire, the counsellors would be checking out the cabins to see how well everyone had unpacked and made their beds.

There were a few groans, which probably meant there were some unmade beds.

But I wasn't groaning. I was squeaking with joy, because Og and I weren't going to be stuck in some wreck of a room from now on.

Og and I were REALLY-REALLY-REALLY going to camp!

NOTE TO SELF: Nothing can cheer a
person or hamster up faster than
seeing an old friend.

Cabin Fever

The dining hall emptied as quickly as it had filled up. Some of my old friends, like A.J. and Miranda, tried to come up to say hi to Og and me, but a few shrill blasts of you-know-who's whistle kept them moving.

I looked around at the empty tables, the over-flowing rubbish bins, the stacks of dirty trays and dishes which a teenage boy and girl were collecting.

'What next?' I asked Og.

Og was silent. I guess he was a little confused about what had just happened and what was going to happen next. So was I.

I hopped on my wheel for a little spin and I started thinking of that song that went 'Chew, chew, chew your food'. That got me thinking about food, so I hopped off the wheel and rummaged around the bedding of my cage to see what I'd stored there. I found a bit of crunchy carrot, which kept me busy for a while.

Once the teenagers had got all the dishes out of the dining hall, it was quiet again. In the far-off distance, I could hear voices singing. I couldn't catch all the words but 'Happy Hollow' kept coming up.

Then things weren't so quiet any more. I heard the patter of soft footsteps running, which soon became the clamour of loud footsteps coming closer and closer. The door to the dining hall slammed open and A.J. rushed over to my cage.

'We won!' A.J. bellowed. Even though he was slightly out of breath, that boy still had an amazingly loud voice. 'You get to stay with the Blue Jays tonight!'

He didn't have a chance to explain, because the door slammed again. Miranda rushed over to Og's cage.

'Og, you're going to be a Robin tonight!' she said. 'Our cabin was the neatest girls' cabin.'

'Well, ours was the neatest boys' cabin,' A.J. said. He grabbed my cage and whisked me out of the dining hall.

'See you soon, Og,' I squeaked back to my friend. 'I hope!'

The Blue Jays' cabin was just like the Robins' Nest, except the curtains were blue plaid. Each bed had a pillow and blanket on it and at the end of the beds were large trunks. Clothes were hung on hooks around the room and it was extremely neat.

There were boys sitting on the beds and trunks. Some of them I recognised, like Richie and Stop-Giggling-Gail's brother, Simon. Others I didn't, but they jumped up when I came in and gathered around as A.J. set my cage on his trunk.

'Listen up, guys, this is Humphrey. He was our class pet and he's amazing. So we've got to take good care of him. And we've got to keep this place neat,' he said. 'We want the Blue Jays to rule, right?'

They all agreed.

'I'll go get him some fresh water,' said Richie.

'Me too! Me too!' Simon shouted, following Richie outside.

I soon found out the bathrooms, the showers and the water fountain were outside the cabin instead of inside. (I was lucky to have my water and poo corner inside my cage.)

The other boys in the cabin seemed nice and welcoming.

Then a face appeared close to my cage. 'Why's it such a big deal to have a hamster in your cabin?' he asked. 'I have a dog. A gigantic dog.'

'Wow,' said Richie, who was putting the fresh water in my cage.

I was thinking that I NEVER-NEVER-NEVER want to go to this kid's house. *Ever.*

'My dog can do tricks,' the boy continued.

'Oh, so can Humphrey,' A.J. assured him.

'Yeah, I saw him. He stayed at my house,' Simon said.

'My dog is really smart,' the boy added. '*And* he's got papers.'

'He can *read*?' Richie was clearly impressed, but the thought of a dog reading made Simon giggle just like his sister, Gail.

The boy frowned and shook his head. 'I mean he's *pedigreed*. He's like dog royalty. He has papers to prove it.'

'His *pet has peed*!' A.J. burst out laughing and the other Blue Jays started hooting and hollering. I chuckled, too, even though I knew the boy had said 'pedigreed'.

The laughing annoyed the boy with the dog. He flung himself on his bed and sighed. 'How did I end up here?' he asked no one in particular.

I was beginning to wonder the same thing. I was even beginning to think this Blue Jay was not a very nice kind of person.

'Blue Jays rule!' I squeaked without even thinking.

'You tell him, Humphrey,' A.J. said.

'He's just making meaningless noises,' the unpleasant boy said.

A.J. and Richie exchanged looks.

'What's your name again?' A.J. asked.

'Brad,' the boy answered.

Things got quieter in the cabin. A.J. came over to my cage and whispered, 'Show him what you can do, Humphrey.'

He didn't have to ask me twice. I climbed up my ladder and leaped on to my tree branch. I landed pretty hard, so I had to hang on tightly as it swayed back and forth, back and forth. Once I had my bearings, I climbed to the highest branch and reached up to grab the top bars of my cage. Very carefully, paw over paw, I made my way across the top of my cage while the Blue Jays watched. All except Brad, who was reading a magazine.

'Look at him go,' A.J. said.

'Are you watching, Brad?' Richie asked.

'Hmm?' Brad pretended to be too busy to notice.

I took a deep breath, dropped down from my ladder and jumped on to my wheel, where I immediately began to spin.

The cabin mates all clapped and whistled.

'Hold it down, guys,' Brad said. 'I'm trying to read here.'

'Admit it, Brad. He knows a lot of tricks,' A.J. told him.

'Lots and lots and lots,' said Simon, jumping around my cage.

Brad glanced up from his magazine. '*That's* a *trick*?'

I could almost feel A.J. getting hot over Brad's bad attitude. He strolled over to Brad's bed and said, 'You know we're going to have to compete in the Clash of the Cabins. So what's your sport?'

Clash of the Cabins? He had my attention.

'I don't know.' Brad looked a little worried. 'I guess I'm okay at all of them.'

'Good!' A.J. smiled. 'We'll need your help.' He swivelled around. 'How about you, Simon?'

Simon wrinkled his nose while he thought. 'I'm the best burper in our class,' he said proudly, and then let out an ear-splitting but impressive burp.

Everybody giggled, even me. Though I know it's really not polite to burp, it can be funny.

'What else?' A.J. asked, still laughing.

Simon thought for a second. 'I've never done archery or canoeing before. I'm a good swimmer, though. And I can dive.'

'Great!' A.J. and Simon exchanged high-fives. 'And Richie likes volleyball, right?'

'I've got a pretty good serve,' Richie agreed.

'Well, then it looks as if Blue Jays rule!' A.J. shouted.

He said it again and everybody joined in . . . except Brad.

'My old camp had a high dive. *Really* high,' he said. 'This place is dinky.'

I saw A.J. clench his fists and I have to admit I felt my paws tightening up.

Luckily, just then the door swung open.

'Never fear, 'cause Aldo's here!' a voice called out.

I thought Aldo had probably come in to clean the Blue Jays' cabin, just as he'd cleaned Room 26 every night. But I was wrong.

He wore his Happy Hollow shirt and shorts and carried a clipboard. 'Listen up, guys. It's almost time for lights out. That means no more talking, okay? Before you go wash up, I just want to run over tomorrow's schedule.'

I kept spinning while he talked about canoeing and swimming and archery. Then the boys got ready for bed.

Just before Aldo turned off the lights he said, 'No more talking until wake-up call tomorrow morning. Sleep well.' He reached for the light switch. 'You too, Humphrey.'

Then it was dark in the cabin and quiet. Before long I could hear the boys breathing quietly the way humans do when they're asleep.

I was just about to doze off myself when I heard that sound I'd heard before.

SKITTER-SKITTER-SKITTER.
SCRITCH-SCRITCH-SCRITCH.

The same sound I'd heard back in the Robins'
Nest. It wasn't a human type of sound. It was a different noise from the ones I'd heard in Room 26
and at all the houses I visited. It was a *wild* sound.
And maybe, just maybe, it was following me!

I was awake for a LONG-LONG-LONG time.

NOTE TO SELF: Humans who brag are
not pleasant to be around (especially
one human named Brad).

Ghosts, Humans and Other Scary Creatures

That was some wake-up call the next morning, let me tell you. Even from inside my little sleeping hut, the music from a loudspeaker outside made my ears tingle and my whiskers twitch.

I was still twitching when Aldo stuck his head in the door and said, 'Rise and shine, guys. Breakfast in half an hour.'

Slowly, the Blue Jays rose. I didn't see them shine but they got dressed and, when the bell rang, they headed out for breakfast.

And there I was, all alone and wishing Og was still my neighbour. One thing about camp, people were certainly coming and going all the time. I was considering leaving my cage for a little exploration when I heard the bell, followed by the pounding of footsteps like a herd of elephants coming up the path. The door swung open and the Blue Jays raced into the room.

'Humphrey! We had pancakes-sausage-juice-milk-bananas-strawberries,' Simon announced in one breath. Then he let out a tremendous burp, which made all the other Blue Jays laugh, except Brad.

'Food was better at my old camp,' Brad said, slumping on his bed again.

No one paid much attention to him.

'Up and at 'em, Brad,' A.J. said. 'We've got to clean the cabin. Maybe we can earn Humphrey for another night.'

Brad rolled his eyes. 'Big deal.'

'It's a big deal if we can collect enough points over the next two weeks to spend a night in Haunted Hollow,' Richie told him. 'That's the prize for winning the Clash of the Cabins.'

Haunted Hollow? It sounded unsqueakably scary. I was wondering why anyone would want to spend the night in a place with ghosts.

'We all collect points, see?' A.J. explained. 'It's cabin versus cabin and boys versus girls. You don't want the girls to get a sleepover in Haunted Hollow, do you? And the chance to see the Howler?'

Howler? Did he say *Howler*?

Just as I was trying to picture what on earth the

Howler was, all the Blue Jays except Brad opened their mouths and let out a horrendous howl!

'Owoooo!!!'

My fur stood on end, but the boys just burst out laughing.

'Who cares about some dumb ghost?' Brad said. 'My old camp had a ghost. We saw him every night.'

The other Blue Jays just glared at him. So did I.

'My cousin saw the Howler last year,' Richie continued. 'He said he was scarier than Frankenstein, Dracula and the werewolf all put together.'

Just then Aldo popped his head round the door. 'Get those beds made, clothes folded, shoes under bed. Come on, Blue Jays – hustle!'

Soon the cabin looked exceptionally neat again. When the bell rang next time, the Blue Jays raced out, leaving me all alone.

But almost immediately the door burst open again and A.J. raced back in. 'I couldn't forget you, Humphrey Dumpty!' he said, and he carried my cage down to Happy Hollow Hall.

A.J. was in a hurry. I grabbed hold of the side of my cage and hung on tightly as he told me that he was going horse riding for the very first time. From my bumpy point of view, I got a glimpse of large round things with bullseye targets painted on them. And a whiff of something that just might have been a horse. A.J. dashed through the dining hall, past the kitchen (yum, what was Maria cooking for lunch?) and into the recreation room.

Whew! I wasn't sorry to be back in front of those big sunny windows. And guess who was already waiting there for me? Og, of course.

'Oggy, old boy! How were things in the Robins' Nest?' I asked. I didn't expect much of an answer but he surprised me by doing a watery somersault. If only he would squeak up! (But I did envy his swimming skills.)

I quickly filled Og in on what I'd learned about Haunted Hollow and the Howler, though I'm afraid my 'Owoooo' was a little too squeaky to be scary. But I'm sure Og got the idea.

We didn't have a chance to discuss it any more because Ms Mac came in with her friend, Katie.

'I hope you two don't think you're going to sit around and do nothing all day,' Ms Mac told us. 'We're putting you to work!'

I was unsqueakably excited as she picked up my cage and Katie picked up Og's tank, even though I didn't know where I was going or what I would be doing.

We headed towards a cluster of small buildings at the top of a hill. But unlike the other cabins, we went into one with big doors that opened all the way, so the front of the cabin was completely open.

Down the hill, I saw something blue and glistening, like water.

Inside there were tables and chairs and leafy plants and big charts showing leaves and trees and animal tracks and oh-so-many interesting things. Ms Mac and Katie set Og and me down on a table near the front of the room.

'Welcome to the Nature Centre,' Ms Mac said. 'You're the nature part. As well as your new friends.' She gestured to a tank and a crate further down the table. 'Meet Jake.'

I saw a tree branch on the bottom of the tank. Just when I was thinking that Jake was a strange name for a tree branch, it moved!

'He's a garter snake. Very harmless,' Kate said.

'Eek!' I squeaked without thinking first. Sorry, but I don't think hamsters and snakes should get too close together. And I didn't like the way his tongue darted about, not one bit.

'Don't worry, Humphrey,' Katie said. 'We'll keep him away from you.'

Ms Mac pointed to the crate, which was really a large box with openings on the side. 'And this is Lovey Dovey. She's a mourning dove we found in the woods with a broken wing. She's almost healed now.'

Lovey made a low sound in her throat: 'Woo-oo-oo-oo.' I think she was saying 'thank you' for helping her to get better.

'Every day, all the campers have horse riding and swimming,' Ms Mac continued. 'Then they get to choose their other activities, including classes here.'

So I was back in a real classroom again!

'Bring on the students!' I squeaked. Then I jumped on my wheel and began to spin, HAPPY-HAPPY-HAPPY to be going to work again.

In some ways, camp was like school. A bell rang several times a day. At school, I learned those bells meant the start of school, break, lunch period, another break and the end of the day. At camp, the bell was even busier. It announced breakfast, cabin cleaning, first activity, second activity, lunch, rest hour, third activity, fourth activity, free time, dinner and the evening programme. Whew!

Twice a day, groups of campers came in to take care of the animals (that's us) and learn all kinds of interesting facts about nature. They had a whole class on rodents (that includes me)! A whole class on frogs! Of course, they studied snakes and birds, too, just so Jake and Lovey wouldn't feel left out. I had to hide in my sleeping hut when I heard some of the things snakes eat. Og and I weren't safe at all. Harmless, indeed!

Sometimes the campers went out for a hike, but they always came back laughing and happy.

There were differences between camp and school, too. For one thing, I didn't see the same kids all day every day. Since the kids could pick their favourite activities, certain nature-loving ones showed up time and time again. Sayeh came every single day and so did Garth. A.J.'s brother, Ty, was a regular, too, and Miranda was usually around (but she was also very interested in drama classes).

Another difference: there were no tests! I thought this was an excellent idea.

Just like the campers, Og and I got a lot of fresh air and lovely outside sounds and smells. Plus Katie and Ms Mac made everybody – including me – excited about the wonders of nature.

Yes, I loved the Nature Centre very much. I would have loved it more without the snake. I guess it wasn't his fault, but he made me very nervous.

At least during the day I didn't have time to think about the SKITTER-SKITTER-SKITTER, SCRITCH-SCRITCH-SCRITCH sounds.

And I tried HARD-HARD-HARD not to think about the Howler. But I was always listening for that 'Owoooooo!!!'

NOTE TO SELF: Humans are unsqueakably smart but they have an odd habit
of liking scary things like dogs, cats
and Howlers.

Night Owls

'Humphrey, we worked our fingers to the bone to win you for the night.' That's what Miranda told me as she carried my cage to the Robins' Nest the next night.

Her golden hair glistened in the moonlight, but I couldn't see her bony fingers, because it was dark outside. I was also distracted by someone asking, 'Who-who? Who-who?' over and over.

'It's me – Humphrey!' I finally squeaked back.

Then the someone asked, 'Who-who?' again.

'We dusted and swept. Lindsey wanted to wash the windows but we didn't have a bucket,' Miranda continued. 'We were determined to have you here tonight.'

Inside, the Robins' Nest was clean as could be. Stop-Giggling-Gail was there, along with Miranda and some girls I didn't know. They all crowded around my cage, squealing with delight.

'He's *so cute*!' said a girl called Lindsey.

The Robins weren't there long, though. Ms Mac came in and said, 'Time for our first campfire, ladies.'

The girls seemed very excited, but Miranda had a question. 'Shouldn't we take Humphrey?'

Ms Mac thought for a few seconds. 'Maybe not, Miranda. It might be a little hot and scary for him.'

Miranda seemed to understand and the girls raced out of the cabin, leaving me to wonder why anyone would go *to* a fire. Weren't fires hot and dangerous things that humans (and hamsters) should avoid?

Yet I knew that Ms Mac wouldn't let my friends do anything truly dangerous.

I could smell the faint aroma of smoke in the distance. I jiggled my lock-that-doesn't-lock to make sure I'd be able to get out in case of danger. And I remembered when a firefighter came to Room 26 and told us if our clothes (even fur coats) caught on fire, we should 'Stop, Drop and Roll'.

But soon the girls were back, smelling just a little smoky. Whatever the campfire had been about, they'd certainly enjoyed it.

'Poor Humphrey,' Miranda said. 'I'm sorry you couldn't go. You need to get out sometimes.'

She picked up my hamster ball. 'Watch this,' she told her friends. She carefully placed me inside, gently set the ball on the floor and there I was, free to roll around the cabin. I hadn't been in my hamster ball in a while, so it took time to get used to everything being yellow again (from the yellow plastic). And it took a little longer for me to remember how to spin around corners and change directions. Every turn I took seemed to amuse the girls.

'Oh, if only Heidi could see you!' Gail said at one point. She plopped down on her bunk and pulled out a notebook from under her pillow. 'I'm going to write to her about everything you did.'

Raise-Your-Hand-Heidi Hopper was Gail's best friend in Room 26. She wasn't here at camp, but I noticed that Gail certainly brought up her name a lot.

A little later, while the other Robins followed me around, I glanced up and saw Gail staring down at her notebook with tears in her eyes. Was she sad because Heidi wasn't here at camp? I managed to roll the ball right up to her bunk, hoping to take her mind off home.

'Oh, Humphrey! You're so funny!' Gail reached

down to pick up the ball. 'When I finish writing to Heidi, I'll write to my mum and dad to tell them you're here.'

Okay. So my idea didn't work.

Later, after Ms Mac checked in to make sure the lights were out, it was finally quiet in the Robins' Nest. But it wasn't dark for long. There was an eerie light coming from Gail's bottom bunk.

'Hey, what're you doing down there?' Miranda asked in a sleepy voice.

'Just finishing my letter home,' Gail answered.

I could see that the light was coming from a teeny-tiny torch.

'Lights out,' Miranda said in a very firm voice. 'We can't afford to get into trouble. We want to spend the night in Haunted Hollow.'

'Okay,' Gail answered. I thought I heard a little sniffling but the light went out.

After the sniffling stopped, it was quiet again and I relaxed in my sleeping hut. A bit later, I heard an even more disturbing sound. Again.

'Who-who? Who-who?'

It was coming from outside the cabin and the voice was strange and mysterious.

'Who-who? Who-who?'

I was tempted to say, 'Me-me! Me-me!' but I managed to keep quiet.

I heard one of the girls roll over on her bed.

'Who-who? Who-who?' the voice called again.

The girl got up and went to the open window. 'For Pete's sake, be quiet, you old hootie owl!' She clapped her hands loudly and it was quiet again.

'Thanks, Kayla,' Miranda said.

'No problem,' Kayla answered.

Even though I didn't hear 'Who-who?' again, I heard other words rolling around in my brain.

Hootie owl! That morning in the Nature Centre, Katie had talked about owls. They were strange creatures of the night who like to prey on very small furry creatures – gulp – like me!

Slithering snakes, skittering, scratching sounds, haunting, howling and now hooting.

The wonders of nature were starting to get on my nerves.

·ö·

When I lived in Room 26, I spent week nights in the classroom and each weekend I went home with a different student. But at Camp Happy Hollow, I slept in a different cabin every night of the week – and so did Og. But the two of us never ended up in the same cabin.

The night after I slept in the Robins' Nest, I stayed with the Bobwhites. They had taken to imitating the bird they were named after and liked to get in a group and shout, 'Bob-*white*! Bob-*white*!'

My old friend Garth was in this cabin, as well as A.J.'s brother, Ty, who was only a year younger. It was funny, but A.J. and Garth were best friends and now Ty and Garth were hanging out together.

Then there was Noah. It was a good name for him because he seemed to Know-a-Lot, at least about nature.

'I wish they let us sleep outside,' he said, looking out of the window.

'Ouch! Mosquitoes.' Garth swatted an imaginary insect. 'I'll take the cabin.'

'I'll bet there are caves out there,' Noah said. 'I'd love to see some vampire bats.'

I'd learned a little bit about bats in school and I'd seen a vampire film at Kirk's house once. So I knew that a vampire bat was something I NEVER-EVER-EVER wanted to see.

'The only bat I want to see is a baseball bat,' a boy named Sam said.

'Me too!' I squeaked.

'I want to see the Howler,' Ty added. Of course, all the Bobwhites went, 'Owoooo.'

Like the Robins and the Blue Jays, the Bobwhites spent a lot of time talking about winning the Clash of the Cabins and spending the night in

Haunted Hollow. Unlike the other groups, though, the Bobwhites were pretty sure they'd win, because of Sam.

Super Sam was what they called him. As in, 'You should see him canoeing – super!' Or, 'Did you see him pitch today – wasn't he super?'

Apparently everything Sam did was super and he excelled in horse riding, swimming, diving, softball, volleyball and tennis.

I was happy for the Bobwhites to have such a super – I mean outstanding – camper in their group. But it got a little tiring after a while.

Especially when Garth said, 'Turn out the lights, Sam. Super!'

But the next morning, as Garth carried me to the Nature Centre, I understood why he was so glad to have Sam around.

'You know, I'm not very good at sports and things,' he said. 'No matter how hard I try, my legs just don't go as fast as the other boys'.'

'You're not so bad,' I squeaked, even though I knew he wasn't so good either.

'The only way I have a chance of spending the night in Haunted Hollow is if a guy like Sam is in our group. He's so good at everything, we can't lose a game.' He paused before saying, 'And I *really* want to spend the night in Haunted Hollow.'

I wanted Garth and all my friends to get to

spend the night in that scary-sounding place, if that's what they wanted.

I just wasn't sure I wanted to be there with them.

Who-who was afraid of meeting up with the Howler? Me-me!

NOTE TO SELF: Beware of things that hoot and howl — especially at night!

9

Knots to You

'Humphrey . . . ' Sayeh's soft, sweet voice woke me from a short afternoon doze as I waited in the Nature Centre for the next group to come in.

I dashed out of my sleeping hut and hurried to the side of my cage, where she was peering in at me.

'Sayeh!' I squeaked. 'Glad to see you!'

Sayeh smiled, but it was a sad smile. 'I wish you could talk to me.'

'What's wrong?' I asked. Because I could tell from her face that she needed a friend.

'You know how to get along with people so well,' she said. 'I'm never sure what to say.'

'Just speak up, Sayeh,' I advised her. But I know all she heard was SQUEAK-SQUEAK-SQUEAK, which is one of the most frustrating things about being a hamster.

Sayeh didn't like to speak up. When I first came to Room 26, Mrs Brisbane was always telling her, 'Speak-Up-Sayeh.' And over time, with Mrs Brisbane's help (and mine), she gained the courage to squeak up in class and became friends with many students, especially Miranda.

But she was still what humans would call *quiet*.

'Tell me, Sayeh,' I said. 'What's wrong?'

Sayeh pulled up a chair so she could be close to my cage.

'You probably don't even know about the Clash of the Cabins,' she said.

'I do!' I squeaked back.

'I was helping Miranda with her backstroke – that's a swimming stroke. But she's a Robin and I'm a Chickadee. Now the other Chickadees say I shouldn't help her.' Sayeh sighed. 'We were just having fun, like in the Happy Hollow song they taught us.'

Then Sayeh began to sing softly in her beautiful, sweet voice.

Happy Hollow – a place close to my heart.
Happy Hollow – we loved it from the start.
Where we work hard, play hard and have lots
*   of fun,*
Where it's one for all and it's all for fun.
We'll remember for ever these happy magic days.

We'll remember for ever our sharing, caring
ways.
And for all the days and weeks and years that
follow,
We'll remember happy days at Happy Hollow.

Sayeh's big dark eyes turned on me. 'You hear that, Humphrey? "One for all and all for fun?" Wouldn't it be more fun if we could *all* do things together no matter what cabin we're in?'

'It's only a song,' I squeaked weakly, but I knew she was right.

'Well, thanks, Humphrey.' Sayeh pushed her chair back and stood up. 'It's nice to know *somebody* will listen.'

I hopped on my wheel for a good, hard spin. While I was spinning, I talked to Og.

'I *like* to help humans. You know that, Og. But I don't see how one small hamster can make a whole big camp more fun,' I said. I was huffing and puffing a bit, partly because I was spinning hard, but partly because I was getting a little worked up.

'BOING-BOING-BOING!' Og splashed wildly in his tank.

'Okay, okay, I'll think of something,' I told him.

Suddenly, the next group of campers streamed into the Nature Centre, along with Counsellor Katie and Ms Mac.

'Okay, kids. Who's ready to learn some more about the wonders of nature?' Katie asked.

A hand shot up and Ms Mac called on Noah. He was the boy from the Bobwhites' cabin who liked bats and knew a lot about nature.

'Why are these animals in cages?' he asked, pointing to our table.

Ms Mac explained that Lovey and Jake had been rescued and that Og and I were pets.

Noah wrinkled his nose. 'Garter snakes live outside and they can get along almost anywhere.' My, Noah did know a lot.

'And hamsters are related to mice and rats. He'd probably be happier out in the woods,' he said.

'Not necessarily!' I squeaked. As much as Noah knew, he didn't understand everything about hamsters.

'I'm impressed with how much you know about animals,' Katie said. 'But I'm not sure Humphrey would be safe outside. What do garter snakes eat?'

Noah looked up, thinking. 'Bugs, worms, frogs, small rodents . . . ' he began.

'Hide!' I yelled to Og as I darted into my sleeping hut.

But Noah wasn't finished. 'I think we should let them out.'

'No!' a chorus of voices called out.

'Not if Jake's going to eat Humphrey and Og!' Ty shouted in a voice almost as loud as his brother A.J.'s.

'Calm down, now,' Ms Mac said gently. 'We hope to get Lovey back outside this summer, if she's ready. But Humphrey and Og are classroom pets. And Jake is kind of the camp mascot.'

'Animals aren't meant to live in cages,' Noah argued. 'They should roam free.'

The thought of roaming free at Camp Happy Hollow made me feel all shivery and quivery. Without a cage, what chance did a classroom hamster have when there were hootie owls, vampire bats and Howlers around? And when I thought of Jake out there, the shivers and quivers turned to shakes and quakes.

'We'll talk more about it when we take our nature hike,' Ms Mac said. 'Thanks for all the information, Noah.'

Noah seemed satisfied . . . for now.

That night, I ended up in the Chickadees' Nest. Sayeh carried me there and on the way she said, 'You'll make it more fun, won't you, Humphrey?'

She knew I'd at least try.

I must say, the girls in the Chickadees' cabin were very welcoming. Miranda's stepsister, Abby, was one of them. Once upon a time, I thought Abby was mean and crabby, but it turned out that I was wrong. (Sometimes it's good to be wrong!)

I didn't know any of the other girls except Sayeh, but they seemed quite nice. They all watched me climb my tree branch and 'oohed' and 'ahhed' and said how cute I was – perfectly normal behaviour for humans.

I think I made the cabin more fun. But then, as on the other nights, the girls left me alone while they went to the campfire. I was unsqueakably surprised that Aldo and Ms Mac and the other counsellors would take my friends to a dangerous fire. I will NEVER-NEVER-NEVER understand humans (but I'll never stop trying).

Once they were back (smelling a little smoky) Abby clapped her hands and said, 'Listen up, Chickadees.'

She sat on a large trunk and the other girls gathered around.

'Do you know that a girls' group hasn't gone to camp out at Haunted Hollow for five years?' she asked.

A girl named Val groaned. 'No way!'

'Not fair – right?' asked Abby. 'But this year, *we're* going to win. I'm sure of it.'

'But how can you be sure?' Val asked.

'Because,' Abby began, leaning in close to the

circle of girls gathered around her, 'I figured it out last year. And I've worked all year to make sure we win.'

Abby had my attention, too. 'How? What? Huh?' I squeaked.

'Knots.' Abby gave the word great emphasis. 'Nobody thinks about knots.'

The other Chickadees looked as puzzled as I was.

'There are seven areas where cabins get points: Camp Spirit – which means stuff like good sportsmanship, cleanliness, being on time – swimming, canoeing, volleyball, softball, archery and outdoor skills,' Abby explained. 'We're okay in volleyball but probably can't win against the Bobwhites in swimming or canoeing.'

'Not with Sam on their team,' Val said.

'Yeah, but softball and volleyball are team sports, so he might not be able to carry the whole team. Then there's archery,' Abby continued. 'A.J.'s good, too. And his brother, Ty.'

The other Chickadees all nodded.

'But we could wipe them out in outdoor skills.' Abby spun around so she was face to face with Sayeh.

'There's a quiz on all that stuff like animal tracks and habits,' she said. 'Sayeh, you can ace any test, so my money's on you to win that.'

Sayeh looked startled. But after a few seconds she nodded and said, 'I will try.'

So, there were tests at camp after all!

'Trail reading is part of outdoor skills, too. We've got to work on that. But since this is my third year here, I think I can train a winning team there.'

Abby sounded very confident.

'And then we come to knots. Like I said, nobody pays much attention to the knot-tying competition, so I've been practising all year on my knots. I can tie knots blindfolded and behind my back. If I ace the knot-tying, we've won outdoor skills,' she concluded triumphantly. 'We just need to hold our own in the other events. Anybody good at archery?'

Val pointed to a tall girl with long plaits. 'Marissa got a bullseye today.'

Abby walked over to Marissa. 'Fantastic!' she said. 'Then we're counting on you. Any questions?'

I raised my paw. I guess I forgot I wasn't in Room 26. But Marissa asked Abby the question I was thinking.

'Can we see you tie some knots?'

Abby reached into her trunk and pulled out a handful of rope pieces of different lengths and widths. 'Anybody got a watch with a second hand?' she asked.

Sayeh did.

'Time me, Sayeh,' Abby said. 'First, a square knot.'

I scampered up to the top of my tree branch to get a good look as Abby took two pieces of rope and began tying.

According to Sayeh, it took her four seconds.

The sheepshank was next. It took a second or two longer. The bowline looped around and around. Abby went so fast, I could hardly see how she did it. The sheet bend was a very fancy knot and the alpine butterfly was most impressive.

'Go, Abby!' I squeaked in encouragement.

It was quite a sight to watch her and no knot took more than about ten seconds.

The other girls clapped and cheered when Abby finished.

'You are amazing!' Val exclaimed. 'Even Sam couldn't top that!'

'Thanks,' Abby replied. 'But let's keep quiet about this. What goes on in the Chickadees' Nest stays in Chickadees' Nest. And that means you, Sayeh.'

Sayeh looked completely surprised. 'Me?'

'Yeah. I don't want you blabbing to Miranda about this,' Abby said. 'I made sure she never saw me practising.'

Miranda's dad was married to Abby's mum, so

Miranda split her time between her dad's house and her mum's flat.

'I won't blab,' said Sayeh, but I must say, she looked miserable.

The door swung open and Katie poked her head round the door.

'Lights out in ten minutes, ladies,' she said. 'You too, Humphrey.'

After the door closed, Abby made everybody raise a hand and promise to keep their plans secret.

I raised my paw, too. Amazing Abby just might show Super Sam a thing or two, which would be good.

But Sayeh looked unhappy, which was definitely bad.

> NOTE TO SELF: Humans aren't so good at climbing, squeaking or spinning, but they have some VERY-VERY-VERY unusual talents.

10

Lovey Dovey

It was raining lightly the next morning. *Sprinkles*, humans call them. Thankfully, not enough to get me wet on my way to the Nature Centre.

'I don't like keeping secrets. Especially not from Miranda,' Sayeh said, as she carried my cage.

I clung tightly to the bars and watched the trees along the path bob up and down.

'I can understand that,' I managed to squeak back, though my throat was as wobbly as my tummy.

'I'd love to tie knots with Miranda. We're always plaiting each other's hair. It'd be fun if we all got good at knots, but I don't want to let the other Chickadees down,' she continued.

'Eek!' I said as Sayeh turned a corner abruptly. 'I mean, of course not.'

Sayeh sighed. 'I guess I'll concentrate on doing

well in that test.'

'You can do it!' I said, and I believed it, too.

When we reached the Nature Centre, Sayeh placed me next to an empty spot on the table. The spot where Og's tank usually sat. I'd been all set to tell him about Sayeh's dilemma and he wasn't there! Besides, his tank was usually between my cage and Jake the Snake, and not having him there made me just a little jittery. I hoped he'd been fed that morning.

Sayeh moved on and found a place to sit. Counsellor Katie was already in the room, setting up a small projector.

'I think you'll be interested in what I've got for today, Sayeh,' Katie said.

I thought I'd be interested, too, as long as it didn't involve snakes.

A few more campers trickled in. I climbed up to the top of my cage to see if Og was coming. Just as I was feeling quite worried, Brad, from the Blue Jays' cabin, entered, carrying Og's tank.

'HI-HI-HI!' I squeaked as Brad plunked the tank down on the table.

'BOING!' Og replied.

'Dumb frog,' Brad muttered.

I was stunned. Og . . . a *dumb frog*? He clearly didn't know what he was talking about.

'He doesn't even say *ribbit* like a normal frog,' he complained.

I scampered down to the bottom of my cage and looked up at Brad. 'Now see here,' I squeaked. 'That's because he's not an ordinary frog. He's a very special frog with a very special sound!'

I wished he could have heard more than just SQUEAK-SQUEAK-SQUEAK.

Brad wasn't paying any attention to me. He was checking out the Nature Centre.

'Welcome, Brad,' Katie greeted him. 'You picked a great day to come.'

'Is this the whole thing?' he asked. 'A frog, a bird, a hamster and a plain old snake? My other camp had practically a whole zoo in theirs,' he said. 'They had a hawk and . . . a raccoon and a boa constrictor!'

Katie kept smiling.

'We try to keep the animals in the wild as much as possible,' she explained. 'Of course, Humphrey and Og are pets. Some of the workers found Jake under some boards. And Lovey here was a rescue. You'll learn more about her today. Just take a seat.'

Brad sat down next to Gail, who was busily writing a letter. She might as well have been at her desk at Longfellow School. I guess she would have been happier in Room 26.

When the session began, Katie explained that while she was hiking one day, she found Lovey lying out in the woods. It was obvious that her wing was broken.

Then she dimmed the lights and started showing slides. I must say, seeing the lovely Lovey on the ground with one wing just hanging limply was a sad, sad sight. There were even a few drops of – gulp – blood.

'Look at this, Og!' I rushed to get a better view of the screen.

Katie said that it's not a good idea to try and approach a wild bird who might be injured. But in this case, it was obvious that the dove was in trouble. When she approached and the bird didn't fight her, she scooped it up with a net and put it in a box. She'd read that mourning doves panic in a cage with bars, which is a little strange to me, since I think the bars on my cage give me wonderful protection from dogs and cats and other scary things.

The next slide showed Katie examining the broken wing with her friend, Dr Singleton, at the local wildlife refuge. He was a vet who specialises in birds. It made me think of Dr Drew, who helped me and helped my hamster friend Winky find a new home with one of my friends from Room 26.

The two of them washed the wing and put medicine on it. Then they VERY-VERY-VERY carefully taped the wing back into its original position.

'Og, isn't Lovey very brave?' I squeaked to my neighbour, who took a long, noisy dive into the water of his tank. I could tell he was as impressed as I was.

They gave Lovey food and water, then let her rest.

Katie turned off the projector and turned the lights up again. The rain was heavier now, pounding on the roof of the Nature Centre.

'Lovey's wing is just about healed now,' she told the campers. 'If things go well, before you leave for home, we'll be able to free her back into the wild. Anyone who'd like to be part of Lovey's release, let me know.'

'ME-ME-ME!' I squeaked. But there was so much talking, no one could hear my hamsterish cries. In fact, all the campers gathered around Katie, begging to be part of the release.

I looked over at Lovey in her crate. Nothing appeared to be broken any more. She seemed strong and proud.

'Did you hear that, Lovey?' I squeaked at the top of my lungs.

I know birds can't smile, but the look on Lovey's

face was as close as a bird could come to a big, fat grin. I think I was smiling a little bit, too, as the other campers left the Nature Centre, chattering away.

Brad stayed seated with his arms folded. How could he not think that would be exciting? Ooh, he made my whiskers twitch!

And Gail was still writing non-stop. She didn't even look up.

Ms Mac went over to talk to her. 'You certainly are taking a lot of notes,' she said.

Gail looked up then. 'Oh, I'm finishing a letter to Heidi. I write to her and to my parents every day so they know everything that's going on at camp.'

Ms Mac's face became kind of serious. Then she said, 'Why not put away the pen and paper for a little while? Since it's raining, Arts and Crafts would be a good choice for your next session. You like that, don't you?'

Gail hesitated before folding up her paper. 'Yes,' she said.

Ms Mac smiled. 'I'll walk you there.'

Is there any wonder I LOVE-LOVE-LOVE Ms Mac?

Then I saw Brad standing and staring at Lovey. Katie came over to him.

'Would you like to help with her release?' she asked Brad.

The boy shrugged his shoulders. 'It doesn't seem like such a big deal,' he said. 'At my other camp, we had a ropes course. Now *that* was cool.'

Katie gave him a curious look. 'It sounds great. But this is something different. We could use your help. What was the name of that other camp you went to?'

'White Pines,' Brad said in a husky voice. 'It was a lot bigger than this.'

'Why did you come here?' Katie asked, which was exactly what I was wondering.

'My parents thought this would be a good change,' Brad muttered.

Katie kept on smiling. 'Sometimes at a smaller camp you can make more friends. I'll be sure to let you know when we're going to release Lovey,' she said.

Brad didn't say anything for a while. He just stared at Lovey.

'Whatever,' he said.

> NOTE TO SELF: Humans can be very kind and caring to birds, hamsters and other small creatures.
> *Most* humans.

11

The Thing Beneath the Floor

'Whatever! He said *whatever*!' I screeched to Og when all the campers and counsellors had left the Nature Centre and gone to lunch. I had to talk extra-loud because of the rain.

'BOING-BOING,' Og responded.

'What's so great about a ropes course?' I added, though I wouldn't mind some ropes to climb on in my cage.

Og splashed briskly, agreeing with me, I think.

I hopped on my wheel to calm myself down.

'He's always bragging about that other camp,' I complained out loud. 'His name should be Bragging Brad. And bragging is *bad*.'

'BOING!' Og twanged, so I knew he was listening. Maybe Lovey was listening, too, because she made a little noise in her throat: 'Woo-oo-oo-oo.' Jake stuck his tongue out, which is what I wanted to do to Bragging Brad. However, I am a very polite hamster.

I was still trying to cool off when the next group of campers began to gather. They were dripping wet, but they didn't seem to mind.

Gail and Brad and Sayeh weren't having as much fun as they should have been, but most of the other campers were. I don't think I've ever seen Garth so happy before. While the campers from the other cabins worked hard on their camping skills and athletic contests, Garth and his fellow Bobwhites seemed to have no worries at all.

Later that evening, Aldo brought Og and me into the dining hall. It was still raining, but the showers were gentler now and Aldo threw a sweatshirt over my cage to keep me dry.

'The kids are pretty unhappy about the rain,' he told us. 'They hate to miss the evening campfire. But they're in for a big surprise.'

'WHAT-WHAT-WHAT?' I asked, hoping it was the good kind of surprise.

'Welcome to the Happy Hollow Comedy Club,' he said, gesturing towards the tables.

It looked like the regular dining room to me, without the food. He set my cage and Og's tank on a table near the stage.

'I know you like to be in the middle of the action, so enjoy yourself.'

It was noisy inside while the campers roamed around, laughing, joking, dancing and talking in unsqueakably loud voices. A.J. stopped to say hello to me. At least his voice was loud enough to hear over the commotion.

'How's it going, Humphrey Dumpty?' he asked.

'FINE!' I squeaked at the top of my lungs.

Suddenly, Garth appeared with A.J.'s brother, Ty, at his side.

'Hey, Humphrey!' Garth said, leaning in close to see me.

'I saw you canoeing today,' A.J. told Ty. 'You're going to have to work a lot harder if you want to beat the Blue Jays.'

Ty shrugged his shoulders, but Garth turned to face his best friend from Room 26.

'Whoa,' Garth said. 'We've *already* beaten the Blue Jays. You just don't know it yet.'

A.J. looked puzzled. 'You're crazy!'

'Not.' Garth smiled mysteriously. 'In fact, we can't lose. Can we, Ty?'

Ty grinned. 'No way can you beat us.'

Just then Super Sam strolled by.

'Yo, Garth. Yo, Ty. Bobwhites rule!' He high-fived Garth and Ty and moved on.

A.J. shook his head. 'Sam's good but he's not perfect,' he said.

'Okay,' Garth replied. 'Just remember that when you're in your bunk and *we're* sleeping out at Haunted Hollow.'

Garth and Ty turned to one another and let out a huge 'Owoooo', which truthfully set my fur on edge a little.

And then it happened. Without warning, Mrs Wright gave an ear-splitting blast on her whistle. I'd be unsqueakably happy if she lost that thing, but I have to admit it worked. Soon the campers were sitting down and were even fairly quiet as everyone's attention was directed to the stage.

'Welcome to the Happy Hollow Comedy Club,' Hap announced. 'Let the show begin!'

As I said, I had a good view of the stage and what I saw was quite unexpected. All of the counsellors, from Ms Mac and Katie to Aldo and even Maria, put on a series of little plays – they called them 'skits' – that were extremely silly and VERY-VERY-VERY funny! One was about chasing a bear in the woods and one was about putting up a tent.

I especially remember the point where they all put on rabbit ears and sang 'Little Bunny Foo Foo'. I'm not sure whether it was the song or the sight of Aldo with his big moustache and floppy bunny ears that made me laugh most, but I almost fell off my tree branch!

Og splashed around, which almost always means he's having a good time.

At the end of the show, Mrs Wright took the stage. I braced myself for the whistle, but instead she led us all in singing that song about finding a peanut, which made me wish I had a yummy peanut hidden in my bedding. But I didn't.

When it was all over, Ms Mac said that next time all of *us* (she pointed to us campers in the audience) would put on the show, so we'd better get thinking!

Goodness, I couldn't think of any funny songs or skits, but I was going to try.

·ö·

I spent that night in the Robins' Nest again. It was pretty quiet, even before lights out. Gail was busily trying to finish a long letter to Heidi. Miranda and the other girls were sharing a magazine and talking about hairstyles.

'Come on, Gail. Let's try this hairstyle on you,' Miranda said in a very encouraging voice.

'In a minute,' Gail said, still writing. 'I made this friendship bracelet in Arts and Crafts and I want to send it to Heidi.'

I saw the other Robins roll their eyes and I didn't blame them.

The rain had finally stopped and once the lights

were out for the night I had a lot to think about. For one thing, I was trying to figure out what was wrong with Brad. Camp Happy Hollow seemed like a wonderful place to me, but to him the pool was too small, the dining room was too big and the cabins were too far. He spent so much time thinking about his old camp, I'm not sure he even noticed what was going on at his new one.

Of course, this was my first time at camp, so I didn't have anything to compare it with.

Then there was Gail. Her friends were getting a little tired of hearing that 'I'll bet Heidi would love archery' or 'I'm going to show Heidi how to tie a lanyard.' She must have had a sore paw from writing letters all the time. If she'd just stop writing for a day, she'd see what a fun place camp could be.

I must admit, every time she mentioned Heidi I had a kind of flip-flop feeling inside, because it made me think of all the kids in Room 26 whom I missed, as well as Mrs Brisbane, Mr Brisbane and Mr Morales. I missed the library, the bell for break and even the vocabulary quizzes.

But there were so many new things to see and do at Camp Happy Hollow, I tried to think about them instead. I wished Brad and Gail could, too.

It was clear I wasn't going to get a lot of sleep

that night. Besides trying to come up with a plan to help Brad and Gail, there was that noise again.

SKITTER-SKITTER-SKITTER.

SCRITCH-SCRITCH-SCRITCH.

In the past, those scratching noises had been somewhere in the background. But that night, they were much louder, which meant that whoever or whatever was making them was CLOSE-CLOSE-CLOSE.

They sounded like they were coming from directly under my cage!

In a way, I was glad the girls didn't hear them. They were deep in sleep.

At least the sounds were coming from *under* the cabin and not *inside* the cabin. I paced back and forth in my cage until my curiosity got the best of me. I reminded myself that I'd gone on dangerous explorations before. So, taking a deep breath, I carefully opened the lock-that-doesn't-lock, tip-toed out to the edge of the table and looked down. Most creatures, especially nocturnal ones like me, can see quite well in the dark and what I saw were wide gaps in between the wooden floorboards.

SKITTER-SKITTER-SKITTER.

SCRITCH-SCRITCH-SCRITCH.

The sounds continued. Since none of the girls stirred when I got out of the cage, I took the plunge. I slid down the leg of the table to the floor.

Then I found the widest possible gap and bent down to see what was under the cabin.

There was earth down there – nice dry earth. There was a little beam from the outdoor lights that helped me see the skitterer: a small furry creature digging in the earth. It was a hamster! No, its ears were bigger than mine and its fur was not nearly as golden and fluffy. It wasn't a hamster, but something very hamsterish. Something that reminded me of my days at Pet-O-Rama, where I had lived until the day Ms Mac found me.

It was a mouse! A brown mouse, digging furiously.

I was afraid of waking the Robins up, but I managed to venture the tiniest possible 'Squeak!' to get the mouse's attention.

Its head jerked up so we were looking eye to eye. It froze for a moment and then answered with an 'Eeek!'

'Quiet, Humphrey,' Kayla mumbled sleepily.

Startled, the mouse skittered away and was quickly out of sight.

I was sorry I had frightened it away. It looked like a friendly mouse – a lot livelier than some of my former neighbours at Pet-O-Rama. They mostly napped in their cages and didn't bother to skitter or scritch.

I was even sorrier when I was ready to get back

to my cage and I realised that there was no way to reach the top of the table!

Here there were no blinds. There was no cord.

I was stuck.

It was like standing in a canyon, looking up at a mountain top with no way to get there.

I thought and thought and thought some more, but there was nothing around that would help me climb that mountain.

In desperation, I crawled into Miranda's baseball cap, which she'd left on the floor near her bunk.

It was a LONG-LONG-LONG wait until morning.

The problem was, whenever I was found outside my cage, some human got into trouble for leaving the door open. That bothered me, because the only creature responsible for my being out of the cage was – well – me.

The next morning, I braced myself for the deafening wake-up music that would soon blare away. I knew somebody was going to be blamed and I only wished it could be me.

So no one was more surprised than I was when the girls rolled out of their beds and Lindsey scooped up the hat I was in.

'Miranda, you'd better be more careful about leaving things around,' she cautioned.

Then she set the cap on the table right next to my cage and hurried off to the bathrooms (which for some reason they called 'latrines').

I was stunned when I saw the girls all hurrying outside.

Without another thought, I scampered out of the hat, raced to the door of my cage, flung it open and hurried inside. I quickly pulled the door behind me and that was that. My entire night of paw-biting worry was a complete waste of time because no one even noticed I was out of my cage.

NOTE TO SELF: Don't worry so much over things that might NEVER-NEVER-NEVER happen.

12

A Sticker-y Situation

It was a sunny day and, as usual, the Robins dropped me off in the rec room, where I met up with Og. We waited there until Katie and Ms Mac took us to the Nature Centre.

While the campers and counsellors ate the yummy breakfast Maria and her assistants prepared (*oh, the smells!*), I told Og about seeing the mouse under the floorboards.

'BOING! BOING-BOING-BOING!' he repeated excitedly.

I guess he hadn't seen a mouse before.

Or had he heard a skittering noise in his cabin, too?

Our conversation was interrupted when Katie and Ms Mac came into the room, even though breakfast was still loudly going on in the dining hall.

'I know I saw a stack of blank notebooks in here the other day,' said Ms Mac, looking through some boxes on a shelf. 'Maybe it was in this box.'

She set the box on the table right next to my cage and began to check what was inside.

'Oh, these are fun,' she said, holding up some papers.

'What are they?' Katie asked.

'Stickers. Fun, cheery thoughts to encourage kids. Here's one with a frog on it.' Ms Mac read it aloud. '"I'd be hoppy to be your friend."'

'It looks like you!' I squeaked to Og, who cheerily BOINGed.

'Maybe we can find a use for these,' Ms Mac said.

Katie rummaged through another box. 'Here they are. They'll be perfect for our nature notebooks.'

Then it came: a shrill blast from the whistle.

Katie and Ms Mac got up quickly.

'Oh-oh! It's Rhonda Wright. Better go,' Ms Mac said, putting the stickers down on my table.

'Yes,' Katie answered with a giggle. 'Because everyone is wrong except Rhonda Wright!'

The two counsellors hurried into the dining hall, carrying the notebooks with them.

So Mrs Wright not only had a whistle, she had a

first name: Rhonda. Maybe she annoyed the humans a little bit, too.

I knew what would come next. Morning announcements from Hap Holloway, followed by the camp song and team cheers from each cabin group.

I could hear all that happening in the background, but I was thinking about something else. *Fun, cheery thoughts to encourage kids.* I knew some kids who needed encouragement. And now I had a Plan.

Despite the previous night's bad experience outside my cage, I pushed on the old lock-that-doesn't-lock, threw open the door and grabbed as many stickers as my paws could handle. Then I raced back to my cage and pulled the door behind me. Whew!

However, I had a new problem. Where was I going to hide the stickers? I knew I had just minutes – maybe seconds – until the counsellors came to get me.

Then it dawned on me that I had the perfect place: behind the mirror in my cage, where I keep my little notebook.

I slid the notebook out of its hiding place and stuffed the stickers inside, then pushed the notebook back in place.

At that exact moment, Ms Mac and Katie returned.

'We'd better put those boxes away before Rhonda Wright sees we've done something wrong,' Ms Mac said.

She reached for the box and caught a glimpse of me out of the corner of her eye.

I was still pushing on the notebook behind the mirror. Had I been caught in the act?

'Look at Humphrey!' Ms Mac chuckled. 'He's staring at his good-looking self in the mirror!'

Katie laughed, too. Then the two of them returned the boxes to the shelf.

It was the second time that morning that I said 'Whew!' (But I said it very softly.)

Katie picked up my cage. 'Time to go to work,' she said cheerily. 'And don't worry, Humphrey. You look as handsome as ever. You too, Og.'

(I think she was just being nice about Og.)

Once I was settled into the Nature Centre, I saw Brad sitting there. He had a sour expression on his face – as usual – and no one talked to him. He was definitely hard to like, I thought. Yet I'd never met a kid who deep down didn't *want* to be liked.

I guess it didn't help that Gail was sitting next to him. She was too busy scribbling a letter to notice he was even there. I suddenly wished that Mrs

Brisbane was around. The teacher would know how to get Gail's mind off Heidi.

Thinking of Mrs Brisbane made me feel a little guilty, too. After all, I'd just stolen a bunch of stickers that most certainly didn't belong to me. I'd hidden the stolen goods in my own cage. Now I realised that I had no idea how to get them to the person who needed them, even though he was sitting in the same room as me.

I was a thief *and* a dimwit. But at least I was handsome. (I'm just quoting Ms Mac and Katie on that.)

While I was thinking about my new life of crime, suddenly all the campers got up and left the room.

'Where are they going?' I asked Og, even though I knew the answer that was coming.

'BOING-BOING.'

Og meant well, but I sometimes wish he could be more helpful.

Then I had the good sense to look up at the board and see what Katie had written there: NATURE HIKE TODAY.

I guess I wasn't such a dimwit after all. I wasn't sure how long this hike would take, so there was no time to waste.

'Og, there's something I need to do, but I don't have time to explain it to you now,' I squeaked to my friend. 'Wish me luck!'

'BOING-BOING-BOING!' he twanged in a way that sounded more like a warning than a luck-wishing thing.

But there was no turning back. This time, unlike the night before, I figured out my route before I left my cage. It was actually an easy course to get to my goal: Brad's new nature notebook, which was on the floor next to his chair.

I reached behind my mirror, pulled out my notebook and opened it. I didn't have a lot of time to study the stickers so I grabbed the frog one and carefully held it between my teeth.

I jiggled the lock-that-doesn't-lock, slid down the table leg and scurried across the floor, straight to Brad's notebook. I carefully removed the sticker from my mouth – the tooth marks were hardly noticeable – and slipped it under the cover.

That's when I made an interesting discovery. Stuck to the bottom of the frog sticker was another sticker with a big smiley face. It read, 'Smile! Somebody likes you!'

There was no time to waste, so I pushed that sticker under the cover of Gail's notebook, which was beneath her chair.

Then I made a dash back to the table for the more difficult part of my journey.

Next to the table (at Jake the snake's end, I'm sorry to say) was a basket with a TALL-TALL-

TALL stalky plant growing out of it. It took strength to climb up the basket, but the woven straw was easy for my paws to grab on to.

When I got to the top of the basket, it took even more strength to leap on to the plant. I then climbed up the stem, just as if I were climbing up the tree branch in my cage. When I was level with the table, I held my breath and took a giant leap. I hadn't even thought about how slippery that table top might be, but I immediately slid right into the side of Jake's tank. I bounced off and was slightly stunned . . . until I saw Jake.

I'd never had such a close look at a snake before (and hope I never will again). He twisted and thrashed about, sticking his tongue out at me. Heart pounding, I scurried past him and back to my cage, where I made sure the door was tightly closed.

I checked it three times.

Og splashed around wildly in his water. It took me a while to catch my breath, so I could explain what my mission had been.

I'd barely got my story out when the hikers returned to the Nature Centre. They were chattering happily, except for Brad. And Gail.

Katie instructed the campers to open their notebooks and write a list of everything they'd observed on their hike. 'Don't worry about the writing – just jot things down as you remember them.'

Brad rolled his eyes but he reached for his notebook and opened it up.

Gail also grabbed her notebook, her pen poised to write. But the pen stayed in mid-air as she saw the smiley-face sticker in her notebook.

'Watch carefully, Og!' I squeaked as I watched her every move.

Gail studied the sticker carefully. She even turned it over to see if there was anything written on the back.

Then Brad saw his sticker. He picked it up and he read it. He puzzled over it for a few seconds, then he began looking around the room.

'That's it, Og! He's trying to figure out who put it there!' I was unsqueakably happy.

Brad looked all around. Gail looked all around.

At one point, they actually looked at each other, but they were embarrassed and quickly looked away.

Soon the session was over and the kids left their notebooks with Katie.

Gail put her sticker in her pocket. She wasn't smiling, but she did look interested in knowing who liked her.

Brad put his sticker in his pocket. He was still watching the other campers closely. I was pretty sure he was wondering who'd be hoppy to be his friend.

Maybe I was a thief and even a dimwit. But at least I'd helped a couple of humans, or so I hoped.

NOTE TO SELF: Usually it's not a good idea to be sneaky. But sometimes *it is*.

Goldenrod

That afternoon, Know-a-Lot Noah showed up in the Nature Centre, as he always did. Just before the session started, he stopped by our table.

'I'm going to try to get you out of that cage, Humphrey. You too, Og.'

'Don't do us any favours!' I squeaked to him. I guess he meant well, but I had owls and vampire bats and many scary creatures on my mind.

'I know, I know.' Noah acted as if he understood me, though he clearly had not. 'You want to be free! I'll get you out of here.'

I had that shivery, quivery feeling again, but Ms Mac was talking and I tried to forget what Noah said. It wasn't long, though, before he was waving his hand.

'Yes, Noah?' Ms Mac said.

'If we can't free the animals, couldn't we at least let Humphrey get some fresh air?' he asked.

Ms Mac looked puzzled. 'This classroom is in the open air. The front wall is completely open.'

'He could walk around in his hamster ball,' he suggested.

Everyone, including Katie and Ms Mac, seemed to think this was a good idea and soon I was lazily spinning my way through the rows of chairs. Ms Mac switched off the lights so she could show some slides of flowers. As I rolled down the aisle, I passed by Garth's chair just as he was stretching his leg and I bounced off his foot. I then rolled to someone else's chair leg, bounced again and picked up speed. Everyone was watching the slides – except me – as my hamster ball rolled through the open wall of the Nature Centre on to a small veranda.

I stopped moving my paws and let the ball coast slowly across the veranda. It was bright outside and the air was very fresh. The rough boards made my ride a little bumpy, but it was lovely being out of my cage and experiencing freedom, like Noah had said. (As long as I had the sturdy plastic hamster ball to protect me.)

Then I hit an especially big bump, took a sharp turn and bounced down three little steps. BUMPITY-BUMP-BUMP!

The ball picked up speed and whirled and twirled its way down a path, veering off to the side into thick underbrush. THUMPITY-THUMP-THUMP!

I was feeling pretty anxious when the ball came to a sudden stop against the trunk of a tree, hitting it with such force that the lid popped open! If I'd wanted to, I could have hopped out of the ball and disappeared into the wild.

I was pretty sure I didn't want to.

While I was trying to figure out my next move, I heard that sound again.

SKITTER-SKITTER-SKITTER.
SCRITCH-SCRITCH-SCRITCH.

'Hello?' I squeaked.

'Eeek!' a familiar voice squeaked.

'Eeek yourself,' I squeaked back. 'Can you help me?'

That's when I saw the little brown mouse with big dark eyes peek out at me from behind a tree trunk.

'Oh, it's you,' the mouse said. 'What are you doing in that . . . thing?'

'It's not a thing. It's a hamster ball.' I was a little annoyed with it for even asking. But then I had an amazing revelation. Unlike Og, or Lovey or Jake (who actually didn't make any sounds at all), I could understand this creature, just as I'd been able to understand Winky, the hamster I'd met a while back. Maybe we *were* related.

'Would you happen to be a hamster?' I asked.

'A *what*?' it replied. 'Don't be silly. I'm a mouse! A girl mouse.'

'I knew that,' I admitted. 'I've seen mice before. But they were in cages at Pet-O-Rama.'

'Eeek!' she squeaked again, her big eyes blinking. 'Cages?'

'Never mind,' I said. 'Can you help push me back towards the Nature Centre? I think I've rolled off course,' I explained. 'If you could push down the lid of this thing it would help.'

The mouse came a few steps closer, but she was definitely on her guard.

'Who are you?' she asked.

'I'm Humphrey. I'm a hamster. A classroom hamster,' I added proudly.

'Oh,' she said. 'I'm not sure what that is, but you look a lot like a mouse. Why don't you come out of that thing?'

It was an interesting question.

'Don't you want to come out into the wild?' she asked.

Out in the wild – me?

'Well . . .' I stalled for time. 'Um, I live in a school, in a classroom.'

She was clearly horrified. 'With *humans*? *Inside*?'

'What's wrong with humans?' I asked.

She shuddered. 'They don't like mice, for one thing. Besides, you're not meant to live inside. You should live outside, like me.'

I didn't agree with her, any more than I agreed with Noah.

'By the way, who are you?' I asked, only because she'd asked me the same question earlier.

'I'm Goldenrod,' she said in a friendlier voice. 'I mean, that's what everybody calls me.'

'Nice name,' I said, and I meant it. 'Isn't it very dangerous to live outside? With owls and bats and Howlers?'

Goldenrod looked puzzled. 'Howlers? What are they?'

'Oh,' I answered. 'They're horrible, terrible things. They're . . . well, I'm not sure what they are. I've only heard about them. They go "Owoooo!"'

Goldenrod's nose twitched as she thought about it. 'I've never seen them or heard them. Owls are very scary, of course, but bats aren't a worry. Yes, there are dangers out here, but it's better than a life in prison. Isn't it?'

'Prison?' I asked. 'Who's in prison?'

'I've seen them carry you around in that prison,' she said.

I couldn't help chuckling. 'That's my cage! It protects me from dangerous things, like dogs and cats.'

'What are they?' Goldenrod asked.

'DANGEROUS-DANGEROUS-DANGER-OUS creatures!' I said. 'You're lucky you've never met them.'

'Goodness, I guess I am,' Goldenrod replied. 'I've seen foxes, of course, and coyotes. But never dogs and cats.'

Foxes and coyotes sounded every bit as dangerous as dogs and cats, but I didn't say so.

'Besides, I can get in and out of my cage whenever I want,' I explained. 'I have a lock-that-doesn't-lock.'

Goldenrod tilted her head to one side. 'Lock?'

I could see it wasn't going to be easy to explain the role of a pet to her. 'Anyway, it's not a prison. In fact, humans love me.'

Goldenrod gasped. 'Humans *love*?'

I gasped in return. 'Of course! They love each other and they love their pets.'

'Wow. I had no idea,' Goldenrod said. 'I thought they just made noise and tore down trees and lit fires.'

'No,' I told her. 'They like to feed animals and play games and burp and sing silly songs about Little Bunny Foo Foo.'

Goldenrod's eyes opened wide. 'Bunny Foo Foo? Does he live around here?'

'No,' I chuckled. 'Never mind.' Then I changed

the subject. 'Can you help me, Goldenrod?' I asked. 'Could you close this lid and give me a push?'

Luckily the ball had stopped with the lid on the side, right at Goldenrod's level.

'Yes, if that's what you want,' she said. 'It's been interesting to meet you, Humphrey.' She reached up with her front paws and pushed the lid closed.

'Oh, and I'll never forget you, Goldenrod. We have a lot in common, you know,' I told her.

'I won't forget you either, Humphrey,' she said. 'If you ever decide to be wild, come and see me.'

And with that, she gave the ball a big push and I rolled back towards the Nature Centre. I was impressed by her strength.

'THANKS-THANKS-THANKS!' I squeaked to her.

'Bye, Humphrey!' she squeaked back.

I had to run as hard as I could to roll the ball to the bottom of the steps. As I caught my breath, I heard noise coming from the cabin. There seemed to be quite a commotion going on there.

'Humphrey? *Humphrey!*' That was Ms Mac's voice but I'd never heard her quite so excited before.

'Maybe he rolled under the desk,' Katie said.

'Or outside,' another voice suggested.

There were footsteps as Ms Mac and some of the kids ran out on to the veranda.

'I hope he didn't roll out here.' Ms Mac sounded worried.

'Wait a second! I see him!' I recognised Simon's voice.

More footsteps, then Ms Mac reached down and gently picked up my hamster ball.

'Oh, Humphrey, you had us so worried,' she said softly. 'I guess you had yourself a little adventure.'

'You have no idea,' I squeaked weakly.

Noah was out on the veranda, too. Ms Mac turned to him. 'Noah, you can see how dangerous it can be for a pet to be out of his cage.'

'He was in his hamster ball,' he said. 'But I bet he wishes he could have just kept going.'

'That's not for you to decide,' Ms Mac said firmly.

'Right!' I agreed.

In a few seconds, I was safe and secure in my cage. I was glad to be back. And when I'd rested a little, I'd tell Og what had happened.

For the moment, I crawled into my sleeping hut to have a nice doze. In the background, Ms Mac was talking about how everybody – even she – was responsible for what had happened.

When I closed my eyes, all I could see was Gold-enrod's face. As I drifted off to sleep, the words 'I won't forget you, Humphrey' repeated themselves over and over in my mind.

NOTE TO SELF: Even a creature who is a lot like you can have very different opinions!

Problems, Problems and More Problems

That night, I was back with the Chickadees again. The boys were annoyed because it meant I'd been with the girls more than with the boys. But, I had to admit, lately the girls' cabins were a lot neater than the boys'.

While the girls were doing well in winning me for sleepovers, the boys – particularly the Bobwhites – were ahead in everything else. Wherever I went, I heard kids buzzing about the activities outside the Nature Centre.

'Sam hit a home run, bases loaded – he's awesome!' I heard Garth say that morning.

Later, I heard that Sam broke the camp record for swimming lengths. *And* that he'd scored the highest number of points in the volleyball game.

Wow, it was true. Sam really *was* super, which

made Garth and the other Bobwhites unsqueakably happy.

Still, the Chickadees were far from giving up.
Instead of chatting and relaxing before bed the way
most of the campers did, Abby had the girls study
their trail skills right there in the cabin.

I have to say, Abby certainly wasn't lazy. She'd
made a big chart showing the signs they'd have to
read out on the trail. The counsellors would mark
the trail and, to score points, the campers would
have to follow the markings correctly and reach the
end. Whichever group made the best time won.

It was actually quite interesting. There were
arrows and warning signs and even left- and right-
turn signs, all made out of rocks, sticks and leaves.
I secretly thought that I would be good at following
a trail.

The Chickadees seemed tired from a day of
swimming-canoeing-hiking-volleyball but they
tried hard to pay attention. Even so, could anyone
beat Super Sam?

Just before lights out, I overheard Abby take
Sayeh aside.

'Listen,' she said. 'Listen.'

I was sure Sayeh was listening, but Abby wanted
to make her point.

'I saw you hanging out with Miranda in Arts
and Crafts. If you spill the beans about any of

our plans, you'll be betraying the Chickadees and all the work we've put in. Are you with us?' she asked.

'Of course,' Sayeh said. 'But that doesn't mean I'm not Miranda's friend.'

'Fine,' Abby added. 'But right now, being a Chickadee comes first.'

'Did you hear that, Humphrey?' Sayeh asked me the next morning as she took me back to the rec room. 'Abby would probably even be cross with me for talking to you.'

'I'm sorry, Sayeh,' I answered. 'I won't tell a soul.'

Sayeh sighed a huge sigh. 'I am *not* a telltale,' she said.

'Of course not,' I agreed.

'I'd love to be Miranda's canoeing partner. I'd love to practise volleyball with her.'

She looked very sad. Which made me feel VERY-VERY-VERY sad indeed.

But I had more than Sayeh on my mind, because I'd just seen Brad come into the Nature Centre. In the past, Brad looked down at his feet most of the time. But today, he was looking at people. He wasn't exactly smiling, but he acted more like he was part of the group.

Gail came in a little later and luckily took the seat next to his, although she didn't seem to notice he was there.

I was staring at the two of them and didn't even notice Noah standing by Og's tank. Goodness, he startled me.

'Og, I've found your true home,' he said softly. 'You need water – lots of it. And other frogs to be friends with. I'll help you, don't worry.'

I couldn't tell if Og was worried, but *I* sure was. Og *had* a friend – me! Did he really need more frogs and water? He did quite a lot of splashing in the water he had. If Og's true home wasn't his lovely tank, what was?

I didn't have time to think about Og any more, because Ms Mac started the session. I crossed my paws, hoping that this would be the day for a hike.

'Okay, campers, who's up for a nature hike?' she asked.

'ME-ME-ME!' I squeaked. I was sorry right away, because if Noah was around, he might think I wanted to go on a hike into the wild. Alone.

No one heard me anyway, since everyone was getting up and heading for the door.

It wasn't long before the humans had all left the room, leaving just us animals on the table. Luckily, their notebooks were on the floor.

'Okay, Og,' I told my friend. 'A hamster's gotta do what a hamster's gotta do.'

I grabbed a couple of stickers from my notebook, jiggled open the lock-that-doesn't-lock and slid down to the floor.

I chose a sticker with the outline of a hand on it. 'A new friend is close at hand!' it read. That went into Brad's notebook.

'A smile can work magic,' said the other sticker. It had a magic wand with a star on it. I tucked that into Gail's notebook.

Luckily, that nice tall plant made it easy for me to get back to my table. Now my goal was crossing that oh-so-slippery table without sliding into Jake's tank.

I'd thought about it beforehand, so I leaned my weight to my left and sailed across the table, narrowly missing the tank and coming to a smooth stop next to Og.

'I've never been so glad to see you in my life!' I told him.

'BOING-BOING!' Og replied. He'd obviously been impressed with my moves.

I scurried back to the safety of my cage and took a nice spin on my wheel. When I'd calmed down a bit, I glanced towards Jake's tank.

I thought about what Noah had said and wondered if Jake liked living in a tank. I also wondered if he had a way to get out of it, like my lock-that-doesn't-lock.

I didn't like what I was wondering. Luckily, it wasn't long before the campers were back.

Brad and Gail weren't exactly smiling, but I crossed my toes and hoped my efforts would pay off.

'Okay, nature-lovers,' Ms Mac said. 'Write your observations in your notebooks.'

Brad grabbed his notebook and quickly saw the sticker there. He stared at it for a while.

When Gail opened her notebook, she saw her sticker right away. After she read it, I saw her sneak a quick glance in Brad's direction.

He must have noticed, because he looked back at her. 'What?' he asked.

'I didn't say anything,' she responded. 'I thought you said something.'

Brad shook his head. 'Nope. I'm just writing in my notebook.'

'Oh,' Gail said. She started making notes, too, then turned to Brad. 'Is ladybug one word or two?'

'One word, I think,' he said. 'You saw them, too?'

Gail nodded. 'Red ones and kind of orange ones.'

'Did you see that purple bird? What was that called?' Brad asked.

Gail wrinkled her nose. 'A purple martin, I think.'

'I have a cousin named Martin,' Brad said, which set Gail off giggling. It was good to hear that sound again.

'Is he purple?' she asked.

'Nope. He doesn't have wings either,' Brad replied. 'But he is short.'

Gail giggled again.

'*Because* he's only three years old,' Brad added, and they both laughed.

And so it went. Brad never mentioned his old camp. And Gail was having a conversation without bringing up Heidi or her parents once.

When the session was over, they were still talking as they walked out.

'Did you see that, Og?' I asked my neighbour.

'BOING-BOING!' Og answered.

Even I was amazed at what we'd just seen. And I still had some stickers left.

ᵒ

Stickers couldn't solve every problem, though. Certainly not the problem the Robins were having, which I learned about that night when they returned to the cabin after campfire.

'Listen up,' said Miranda. 'All the other cabins have skits planned for the Comedy Club but we still don't have a clue.'

'Yeah,' Kayla said. 'And it counts for a huge part of our Camp Spirit score.'

The Robins looked very, very gloomy as they slumped on their bunks. (Although, as sad as they looked, I was happy to see that Gail wasn't writing any letters.)

I knew a little bit about the skit planning. I'd seen the Blue Jays outside practising a funny little play about looking for bear tracks. That part was a surprise – I couldn't even tell Og about it.

And the Chickadees talked about sitting on an invisible bench, which would be impossible, I think. But every time they talked about it, they burst into laughter. Abby was sure it would be a winner.

But the Robins still had no skit.

'What about the invisible bench skit?' Lindsey asked. 'They did that in Scouts last year.'

'Ms Mac said another group was already doing it,' Kayla explained.

'That's what we get for being last,' Lindsey said.

Miranda began to pace. 'I wish Humphrey could talk. Maybe he'd have some ideas.'

'Better than ours,' Kayla agreed.

I hopped on my wheel for a spin, which is a hamster's way of pacing. Actually, I didn't have any ideas, because I hadn't seen many skits.

The girls were silent for a LONG-LONG-

LONG time. In fact, the only sound in the room was the squeaking of my wheel going round and round.

'Hey, Humphrey, could you hold it down?' Miranda got off her bed and came over to my cage.

'Maybe he wants to help,' Lindsey said.

Kayla jumped up and came over to my cage. 'Yeah! We should put Humphrey in a skit.'

Me, in a skit? I'd never been on a stage before. And the stage in the hall was very big.

'Eeek!' I squealed, and dashed into my sleeping hut.

Then all the girls gathered around my cage and giggled.

'Come out, Humphrey,' Miranda said in her friendly voice. 'We need you.'

When someone says they need me, it's hard for me to say no. I crawled back out and looked up at the smiling faces of the Robins.

'He's so cute,' Lindsey said. 'Who could ever be afraid of a little hamster?'

Miranda wrinkled her nose. 'No one's afraid of a hamster.'

'Oh, yeah?' Lindsey replied. 'My mum is. We had a hamster named Chip and when he got out of his cage my mum started screaming and got up on a *chair*! Like he was a monster or something. My brother and I laughed so hard we cried.' Lindsey wasn't crying now. She was laughing and so were her friends.

'That'd be funny,' Miranda said. 'If someone was afraid of Humphrey.'

Then the most amazing thing happened. The girls started chattering and then they started acting things out. Sometimes they agreed and sometimes they disagreed, but they began to work out a skit that looked pretty interesting. Until they got to the last part.

'And that's where Humphrey comes in,' Gail said. She was giggling again and I was glad.

'You'll help us, Humphrey, won't you?' Miranda asked.

I could never say no to Golden Miranda.

By the time Ms Mac came in for lights out, we'd rehearsed the skit several times. The Robins begged her to stay so we could act it out for her. She loved it, but suggested they needed a few more people.

'Counsellor Katie and I would love to help out,' she said.

The girls all cheered.

'So where'd you come up with the idea?' Ms Mac asked.

The Robins all pointed to my cage. 'Humphrey!' they said.

Ms Mac smiled. 'Who else?'

·ö·

Later that night, I looked up at the moon through an open spot in the curtains. It reminded me of a big spotlight. Like a spotlight shining on a stage.

A BIG-BIG-BIG stage for a SMALL-SMALL-SMALL hamster. I spun on my wheel for a long time.

> NOTE TO SELF: When you offer to give someone a helping paw, you'd better mean it — because you might end up a lot more involved than you ever imagined.

15

A Taste of Freedom

'Guys, it's not going to be easy,' A.J. announced that night in the Blue Jays' cabin. They'd worked extra hard to win me for the night. 'We're getting massacred by the Bobwhites, all because of that stupid Sam. Why'd he have to come to camp?'

'Yeah,' Richie agreed. 'Why didn't he go to that camp Brad's always bragging about? The one that's so much better than Happy Hollow?'

I glanced over at Brad, who was sitting on his bunk.

'It wasn't that great,' he said.

That got everybody's attention – especially mine!

'This camp isn't so bad,' he admitted. 'The pool is smaller but White Pines didn't have a lake. I like canoeing. In fact, I tied with Sam today in the race across the lake.'

A.J.'s jaw dropped. 'You did?'

'I was thinking,' Brad continued. 'I've been spending a lot of time at the Nature Centre and I might do pretty well on the nature quiz. And the canoeing would help our score. And what about that knot-tying thing – I mean, doesn't that just take practice?'

'I forgot about that,' A.J. admitted. 'Has anybody been working on that?'

The other Blue Jays shook their heads.

'I could practise that,' Simon volunteered. 'I practised burping for months and look how well that turned out.' He let out another thunderous burp, which made everybody laugh.

Simon was always moving . . . but maybe if he put all that energy into one thing – like knot-tying – it just might work.

'The Bobwhites are depending on Sam,' A.J. said. 'But that's no reason for us to give up. Blue Jays rule!'

They all cheered and high-fived, including Brad. At least for that night, I thought, even Super Sam couldn't defeat the Blue Jays.

By the next afternoon, I was not so convinced. Sam scored a bullseye in archery and was pitcher for the winning softball team. He was amazing, all right. So where did that leave everybody else?

That night, I heard the noises under the cabin.

SKITTER-SKITTER-SKITTER.

SCRITCH-SCRITCH-SCRITCH.

'Hi, Goldenrod!' I squeaked softly.

'Hi, Humphrey,' she answered. 'Won't you join me? Someone dropped some lovely peanuts under the floorboards.'

'Thanks a lot, but I've already had dinner,' I said.

She went back to scratching in the earth. I still wondered what it would be like to live her life. But I had too many things to worry about to wonder for long.

°ö°

The next morning, Miranda and Kayla stopped by the rec room after breakfast. Ms Mac was already there, getting her supplies for the day.

'Ms Mac,' Miranda said, 'can we ask you something?'

'Anything at all.' Ms Mac's hands were full of marker pens and glue sticks.

'We were just thinking, maybe Noah is right,' Miranda continued nervously. 'About Humphrey.'

Ms Mac looked amazed. 'You don't think we should set him free?' she asked.

'Eeek!' I had to squeak up before things went too far.

'No,' Miranda said. 'But he hasn't seen very much of camp. He's just been cooped up in the Nature Centre.'

It was true. I'd heard my friends talk about canoeing and swimming and archery, but I hadn't seen any of that. And where were those horses they mentioned? I wanted to see more of camp – but from inside my cage. The girls asked Ms Mac if they could take me out of the Nature Centre that afternoon and give me a tour.

Ms Mac thought for a while before answering. 'You girls are very responsible. Yes, I suppose so,' she said. 'As long as you absolutely *promise* not to let him out of his cage.'

The girls promised and soon Miranda and Kayla had enlisted Sayeh and Abby to help them show me around Camp Happy Hollow.

And oh, what a place it was! So much bigger than I had imagined from just travelling between the cabins and the Nature Centre and Happy Hollow Hall.

There was the softball diamond, the volleyball court, the archery range. (I was glad no one was around, as I wasn't interested in dodging sharp arrows!)

There were horses, too – the biggest creatures I'd ever seen, or hoped to see! Their hooves were gigantic and they must weigh a million kilos!

And sitting right on top of one huge beast was A.J.

'Hi, Humphrey Dumpty!' he shouted.

I closed my eyes, hoping his loud voice wouldn't scare the horse. (It didn't.)

Then we moved on, passing by a deep-blue swimming pool. And who was diving off the diving board? Super Sam, of course.

Then the girls took me out to the lake.

'We've saved the best for last,' Miranda said. 'Welcome to Lake Lavender.'

Though I'd been sailing once before (quite unexpectedly), I'd never seen such a large and thrilling stretch of water. There was a dock where canoes were lined up and, just for one teeny-tiny second, I almost wished I could be a human! But then I realised that being a hamster gave me the chance to see and do things humans never could. And humans seem to have so many problems – I'm only glad to be around to lend a helping paw from time to time.

'What do you think, Humphrey?' Miranda asked as we gazed out at the rippling water.

'It's breathtaking!' I exclaimed.

And it was. With the blue of the lake and the blue of the sky and the – what was that circling in the blue sky? I squinted to get a better view of a very large bird.

'Oh, look! A hawk!' said Abby.

Oh, no! A hawk! Katie had talked about them, too. They were not friends to small furry creatures.

'Eeek!' I squeaked, and the girls all giggled.

But the lake was lovely. How Og would like it! It was hard to see water without thinking of my friend, whom I was beginning to miss.

Next the girls carried my cage to the top of a hill. From way up there, I could see the camp nestled in its low spot.

'There it is, Humphrey. That valley there – that's Happy Hollow,' Kayla said.

So that's where the camp got its name!

Miranda swung my cage around to another hollow right next to the camp. 'And that's Haunted Hollow,' she said in an ominous tone of voice. 'Where one group will get to spend the night.'

'Yeah, the Chickadees!' said Abby.

Miranda looked a little surprised. 'Or the Robins,' she countered.

Abby folded her arms and shook her head. 'Sorry, Miranda. We've got it nailed. Right, Sayeh?'

I swivelled round in my cage to see Sayeh's face. She looked surprised and upset at the question.

'May the best team win,' Miranda said. Then she added, 'And that will be us!'

I wasn't sure who the best team was. And I wasn't at all sure who would win.

When we got back down to camp, something had changed. There was a group of campers gathered around a tree. And another group gathered around the next tree.

'I wonder what's going on,' Miranda said.

Once we got closer, I could see another clump of kids staring up at the side of the Nature Centre.

'Come on,' Kayla said, and we picked up our pace (which made it a tummy-wobbling trip).

When we reached the first tree, Miranda elbowed her way through the small crowd.

'What's up?' she said.

'This is up.' Richie pointed at a hand-made sign tacked to the tree trunk.

It read: FREE THE ANIMALS! RELEASE OUR WILD ANIMALS!

(Okay, on the poster it actually said 'Aminals' but I think we all knew what it meant.)

Smaller letters underneath the sign said: FREE LOVEY, JAKE, OG, HUMFRY.

(The sign-maker was definitely not a good speller.)

'Eeek!' I said without even thinking.

'Free Humphrey?' Miranda sounded truly puzzled.

'That's not right,' Sayeh added.

'I am not a wild animal!' I protested. 'Or aminal!'

'He is not a wild animal,' Sayeh repeated, even though she probably didn't understand what I'd said. We just thought alike.

Just then Counsellor Katie approached. When she saw all the kids gathered, she came up to check things out. 'What's going on?' she asked.

'This.' Miranda pointed to the sign.

Katie studied the sign and said, 'Oh.' She stuffed her hands into the pockets of her shorts and asked, 'Who put this up?'

'Duh,' Richie said. 'It must be Noah. All he talks about is animals.'

Now, talking about animals is not a bad thing. In fact, I usually think it's a very good thing.

But even though Noah cared a lot about animals – and he did – I was almost as frightened of him as I was of the hootie owl, the vampire bat (if there was such a thing), the hawk and the Howler (which obviously was real, because Richie said his cousin had seen him).

'I'll talk to him,' Katie said.

She left and the campers scattered. Miranda took me back to the Nature Centre and set me down on the table next to Og.

We were alone then, except for Lovey and Jake, who were at the other end of the table.

I was still thinking about that hawk.

'Listen, Og,' I said. 'Noah wants to free us. But I've been out there and I just want to say, you might not *want* to be free.'

'BOING.' It was a quiet response. 'BOING-BOING.'

'I'm just saying there are some dangerous creatures out there who are our enemies. They don't like hamsters and frogs at all, except maybe for dinner.' I realised I was getting slightly hysterical. 'Like owls and hawks and snakes!'

I was sorry as soon as I said it. I craned my neck to try and see Jake in his cage, but Lovey's crate blocked him.

'Maybe you don't feel that way, Jake,' I said. My voice was a little weak. 'I'm sure you're a friendly snake, like I'm a friendly hamster and Og's a friendly frog,' I added, hoping it would help.

I'm afraid I didn't sound very convincing.

I crossed my paws and HOPED-HOPED-HOPED that I would not be with the Bobwhites – and Noah – that particular night.

> NOTE TO SELF: It's great to be free –
> but only when you want to be!

16

On Stage at the Comedy Club

Despite the disturbing signs, my day out had done me a world of good and I was planning on a long, dozy evening in somebody's cabin.

But I had forgotten something: it was Happy Hollow Comedy Club night. As much as I would have liked a nap, I knew I wouldn't get one.

After dinner, Aldo brought Og and me into the dining hall and gave us a ringside seat near the stage. It looked a lot bigger than it ever had before.

I was concentrating on remembering my part when Hap Holloway came out on stage with a very serious look on his face.

'Before we start, we need to do a little talking,' he said. 'There were some signs that went up today about freeing our animals. First of all, if you want to talk about a problem, just come to me. No need to put up signs anonymously.'

'Anonymous' was the funny name people called themselves when they didn't want to give out their real names.

'It's a good issue to discuss,' he said, 'so let me say this. We're hoping to release Lovey, but only when she's completely healed. Jake has been our camp mascot for a while, but I'd be happy to see how you all feel about releasing him.'

I gulped hard. It sounded like Hap Holloway was in favour of letting us all go wild. My whiskers twitched as I listened intently.

'As for Og and Humphrey, they are pets. They are not to be released into the wild. They are only on loan to us. Understand?'

He waited and there was an uproar from the crowd.

Half of them were chanting, 'Hum-phree! Hum-phree! Hum-phree!'

The other half chanted, 'Og-Og-Og-Og-Og!'

All except Noah, who wasn't chanting at all. He was just watching the other campers, looking surprised.

The noise was deafening – until Mrs Wright gave a mighty blow on her whistle.

'There *will be order*!' she cried.

And there was, because the skits began.

The Blue Jays got the show off to a great start. A.J. came out on stage, looking intently down at the floor. Aldo appeared and asked him what he was doing.

'I'm trying to figure out what kind of tracks these are,' A.J. answered loudly, pointing at the ground.

Aldo said, 'They look like wolf tracks to me.'

Then Simon came out and asked Aldo and A.J. what they were doing. When they explained, Simon said, 'They look like bear tracks to me.'

Brad came out next and asked what they were doing, then said, 'They look like badger tracks to me.'

This went on a few times with the other Blue Jays, until A.J. rushed on again and said, 'You guys! Those are *train tracks*!'

Suddenly Richie appeared, leading Ms Mac, Aldo and Maria and even Mrs Wright directly towards the rest of the boys. They were hanging on to each other's waists, huffing and puffing, tooting and chugging – yes, Mrs Wright blew her whistle like a real train, while the Blue Jays ran off screaming.

The skit was a hit! I laughed and cheered and so did the others.

I was so HAPPY-HAPPY-HAPPY for the Blue Jays, I almost forgot that I would have to be out there soon.

॰०॰

The Chickadees came next. One by one, they

joined Abby, who was standing but with her legs bent, just as if she was sitting on a bench.

Once all the girls were sitting on the 'bench' (there was no bench, but they did a good job of pretending to sit on one), Maria came strolling by and asked them what they were doing.

'We're sitting on this invisible bench,' Marissa answered.

'Oh,' Maria said. Then she pointed to the other side of the stage. 'But I moved it over there yesterday.'

With that, the Chickadees all tumbled to the floor, while the crowd laughed and clapped. I clapped, too.

Next up were the Bobwhites. They all appeared on stage holding balloons. Super Sam came out and directed them like an orchestra conductor. All together, they let out the air from their balloons a little at a time and – you won't believe it – it sounded just like the song 'Jingle Bells'. It was such a silly sound, the crowd laughed so loud you could hardly hear the end of it! When it was finished, they all took deep bows.

I was cheering, too, until Miranda came and whisked my cage off the table – a little roughly, I must say.

'Bye, Og! Enjoy the show!' I squeaked to my friend.

Ms Mac and the other Robins were setting up a stand-alone door on the stage, with the curtains on either side of it, while Miranda put my cage directly behind it.

'Okay, Humphrey,' Miranda said in a calming voice. 'It's showtime. You know what to do.' And the she was gone.

I was all alone in the middle of the stage (although no one could see me – yet).

The skit began as Kayla came up to the door and opened it part-way. Then she slammed it shut and immediately began running around the stage, screaming, 'Help! Help!'

Lindsey ran on stage and asked her what was wrong.

'There's a monster behind the door! A big scary monster!' she yelled.

'No way,' said Lindsey. Then she opened the door, shut it again and began running around the stage, shouting, 'Help! Help!'

When Miranda came out and asked what was wrong, Lindsey described the monster's glowing eyes, red fangs and ugly face. Then she asked if anybody was brave enough to take a look at it.

Gail was next. She took one look, screamed and ran away. Oh, she was a good screamer, too.

The rest of the Robins did the same.

My ears were twitching from all that screaming

and I was feeling a little itchy and twitchy.

Finally, Kayla addressed the audience. 'Is there anyone out there brave enough to look behind the door?' she asked.

Ms Mac stood up. (This was all arranged ahead of time, I have to admit.)

'I will,' she said. Then she came up on stage, opened the door wide and jumped back, screaming.

At the same time, Miranda came from behind me and pushed my cage out on to the stage so everyone could see me.

'A monster! A monster!' she screamed, running around the stage. She acted really scared.

There I was, on the big stage with all the campers watching. As soon as everyone saw me, they smiled and started laughing, because they knew *I* was no monster.

'Eek!' I said, though I'm not sure how well my voice carried, especially over all the applause.

'Hum-phree! Hum-phree! Hum-phree!' they shouted.

The Robins all came out on stage and took a bow. They looked so proud. Gail had the biggest smile of all. She hadn't sniffled in a long time.

My heart was still pounding when Miranda put me back on the table.

'Thanks for saving us, Humphrey,' she said. Her

eyes were sparkling and her cheeks were pink.

'Any time,' I answered. And I meant it.

When she was gone, I turned to my neighbour.

'How'd I do, Og?' I asked.

Og made an impressive dive to the bottom of his cage, then came out of the water, up on his rock and twanged, 'BOING-BOING-BOING!'

It was better than any applause.

Then the older campers put on their skits and sang some funny songs, too.

It was hilarious . . . and it lasted well over an hour!

ö

That night, I stayed with the Bobwhites. They were still playing crazy songs with their balloons.

Once lights were out for the night, they talked a little bit in the dark about Haunted Hollow.

'Do you really think we'll get to see the Howler?' Richie asked.

'It's a cinch,' said Sam. 'I've got you covered in volleyball, canoeing, swimming and archery.'

'You can handle the outdoor skills, can't you, Noah?' Garth asked.

Noah's mind seemed to be far, far away. 'Huh? Oh, sure. I know a lot about that stuff.'

'Bobwhites for ever!' said Garth.

'Bobwhites for ever!' the other boys chimed in.

I squeaked along with them, but by now I really didn't know who to root for.

·ö·

The next morning, right before breakfast, Sayeh slipped into the rec room to visit Og and me.

'I am very tired today,' she told us. 'Last night Abby marked up the whole cabin with twigs and rocks so we could practise reading trail markings. We even got in trouble for keeping our lights on too late.' Sayeh sighed. 'That won't help our Camp Spirit score.'

'MY-MY-MY.' I couldn't think of anything else to say. Here I'd been, listening to funny balloon music, while Sayeh had had to work late!

'I tell you, Humphrey, I like Camp Happy Hollow very much, but I'll be glad when the Clash of the Cabins is over so we can relax and have fun,' she said.

Suddenly, a deep voice spoke. 'What's this? An unhappy camper?'

It was Hap Holloway. He'd been standing at the door, listening.

Sayeh jumped as soon as she heard his voice, but when she turned to look at him, he had a friendly smile on his face.

'I'm always looking for ways to make Camp Happy Hollow a happier place,' he said. 'It sounds like you might have some good ideas, Sayeh. Why don't you come to my office and we'll talk for a few minutes?'

Sayeh looked down at the floor. I was hoping for her sake that she didn't cry.

'You'll be doing me a favour,' Hap said in a softer voice.

'Okay,' Sayeh said. 'If it will help you.'

Then she followed Hap out of the rec room. I watched her through the window, following him up to a cabin where he and the counsellors had an office.

She glanced back at me once and I gave her a wave of my paw.

'Good luck, Sayeh,' I said, wishing with all my heart she could hear me.

> Note to self: An hour of comedy is FUN-FUN-FUN, but laughs don't always last.

17

The Case of the Missing Frog

I kept my eyes fixed on the office building but it was a long time before I saw Sayeh leave again. Even from a distance, I could see that she was smiling. And she gave a happy wave to Hap Holloway as she skipped back down the path.

How I wished I could have heard their conversation.

At last, it was a peaceful day. Sayeh was still smiling the next time I saw her, and Brad and Gail both seemed more relaxed. Brad talked to lots of people now and so did Gail. Who would have thought a couple of stickers could do that much good?

Garth and the Bobwhites were brimming with confidence that they would be spending the night at Haunted Hollow, and who could doubt it, with Super Sam on their team. But Abby and the

Chickadees stood strong and tall and still thought they had a chance.

Miranda and the other Robins were more relaxed as well, since their skit had gone over well.

I thought maybe it was time for me to lie back and just enjoy camp. I was so relaxed, I took a nice long doze while my friends were off on their hike.

But I was wide awake when Ms Mac made an announcement at the end of the session. 'Tomorrow we start two days of competitions to round off the Clash of the Cabins. The nature quizzes will be tomorrow, for anyone who wants to take them,' she said. 'Good luck, campers, and have a great time!'

I felt a little shiver of excitement but also some uneasiness. So soon? I thought. Were my friends ready? Was I ready?

I hopped on to my wheel to relieve my anxiety. It didn't work.

I spent that night with the Blue Jays, but they left for a while to go to the evening campfire. I wasn't sure what was special about campfire nights, but my friends were always keyed up when they came back.

'I've just got to see that Howler,' A.J said. 'It would be awful if my little brother Ty got to see him and I didn't.'

'We've got a good chance,' Richie said.

'Yeah. Blue Jays rule!' That was Brad, and

whether or not the Blue Jays got to spend the night in Haunted Hollow, he was still a winner in my book.

·ö·

Richie took me down to the rec room the next morning. I was there before Og, but I didn't think anything of it at first. I was busy watching my friends streaming into Happy Hollow Hall, chattering away.

Og still wasn't there by the time breakfast began. I was puzzled, but I was also interested in how the whole atmosphere of camp had changed. While the kids from different cabins often hung out together during their free time, I noticed that today the campers who shared cabins stuck together.

The place just *sounded* different.

'Bob-whites! Bob-whites!' came the call from one table.

'Chick-a-chick-a-chickadees!' rang out from another.

A.J. led his cabin's 'Blue Jays rule!' chant.

'Robins! Robins! Rah-rah-rah!' was followed by a lot of giggling.

I heard it all, but Og didn't. Because Og had never arrived.

'Maybe somebody already took him over to the Nature Centre,' Ms Mac said as she carried my cage down the path after breakfast. Of course, somebody must have taken him over to the Nature Centre, I thought. But who?

As soon as we entered, I knew something was VERY-VERY-VERY wrong. Og's tank was there all right . . . but Og wasn't in it. I could see right away that he hadn't popped the top himself, because it was firmly in place.

Lovey, who was usually calm and quiet, was flapping her wings and making excited sounds. Even Jake wiggled more than usual.

Ms Mac set my cage down and checked the tank to make sure Og wasn't hiding behind a plant.

Some of the campers were gathering to take their nature quizzes. Ms Mac asked them if they'd seen Og, but no one had.

Katie came in and she was pretty upset at the news. She organised the kids and they searched every inch of the room, under chairs and in potted plants.

'Og! Where are you?' I squeaked at the top of my lungs. 'Og! Come out! We're worried!'

I waited to hear a friendly 'BOING-BOING', but it didn't come.

The rest of the morning was a blur. The very loud bell rang to call all the campers to the dining hall. Thank goodness, Ms Mac took me, too.

Once everyone was gathered, Hap Holloway got

up on stage and explained that Og was missing. That caused quite a stir. I thought Miranda was going to cry!

Hap asked if anyone knew what had happened to him.

There was a lot of shuffling and whispering. Finally, Noah stood up.

'I know,' he said.

You can bet that all eyes were on Noah. He didn't seem very happy about it.

'Where *is* he?' I screeched.

Hap motioned for him to come up to the stage. 'Come on up here, Noah, and tell me.'

Noah slowly made his way to the stage.

'Well,' he said, 'sometimes I get up early and go down to the lake. I guess that's against the rules, but it's beautiful at that time of day. The birds sing more then and I even saw some deer one morning.'

Hap nodded. 'We'll discuss that later. So what happened?'

'I was sitting on the shore and watching these frogs swimming and hopping in the shallow water. They looked so happy, I thought Og might like to meet some other frogs and play in a real lake,' he explained. 'So I came back to our cabin and I borrowed him. Everybody was sleeping.'

'And you let him go at the lake?' Hap asked.

Noah looked a little frightened. 'No, I didn't

mean to! I just thought I'd let him play there for a while. But as soon as I put him down, he hopped off into some tall grass and disappeared. I looked and looked, but I couldn't find him.'

There was a lot of commotion among the unhappy campers. No one was as unhappy as me.

'So I just took his tank over to the Nature Centre,' Noah continued. 'I didn't know what to do.'

'You should have told us,' Hap said. 'It's not easy for pets who are used to being fed to find their own food.' He sounded firm but kind.

Noah hung his head. 'I'm really sorry. I looked for him, honest.'

The noise in the dining hall had grown to an uproar.

Then it came, that ear-piercing blast of a whistle. Mrs Wright joined Hap on the stage.

'Do you know where you left him, young man?' she asked Noah in a voice that wasn't as kind as Hap's.

Noah nodded.

'We should organise a search party,' she announced. 'You can take us down to the spot where you last saw him. All right with you, Holloway?'

'It's all right with me!' I squeaked. 'Great idea!'

And I thought Mrs Wright didn't like Og! I guess I'd judged another book by its cover.

There wasn't much Hap could do except agree with her. He nodded and soon the counsellors were organising the campers into groups. They gathered up nets and buckets, sunscreen and caps, and Noah and Mrs Wright led them out of the hall.

'Sam will find him,' I heard Garth tell Simon. 'He can do anything.'

I hoped he was right.

Just as I feared, they left me behind. Ms Mac took me to the rec room and told me not to worry. She didn't tell me *how*.

I nervously peered out of the window for hours and hours and hours. Maria came in from the kitchen once and gave me some lovely bits of lettuce, but I couldn't think of eating until my old friend was safely back in his tank.

·ö·

When they returned from lunch, I could tell by the faces of the searchers that they hadn't found Og. The dining hall was a lot quieter than usual.

After lunch, Hap Holloway had the kids vote to decide if they wanted to go back and look some more. Apparently, they all did.

Before they left, they sang the Camp Happy Hollow song.

I tried to sing along, but a big lump in my throat made it unsqueakably difficult.

The afternoon seemed to go on for ever and when the campers returned they still weren't smiling.

Ms Mac came in the rec room and pulled up a chair next to my cage.

'Humphrey, we didn't find him. I'm sure he'll be fine there in the lake with the other frogs,' she said. Her eyes looked all wet. 'But I know he misses you as much as you miss him.'

Sayeh and Miranda came in, arm in arm.

'May we see Humphrey, please?' Miranda asked.

'Sure,' Ms Mac said.

'I'm sorry, Humphrey,' Miranda finally said. 'We really tried. I looked so hard, my eyeballs hurt.'

'We're going back tomorrow,' Sayeh said. 'I'm never giving up. Never.'

'Thank you,' I squeaked weakly.

For the first time in my short life, my cage felt like a prison.

'I'm never giving up,' Sayeh had said.

I heard those words in my head all evening. And after I was safely in the Robins' Nest that night, I kept hearing them. My friends had given their all looking for Og and I hadn't done a single thing!

I was cross with myself and sorry for myself all at

once. I was cross with Noah and sorry for him, too. And then I heard it.

SKITTER-SKITTER-SKITTER.

SCRITCH-SCRITCH-SCRITCH.

Goldenrod was under the cabin again. I didn't think twice about what I had to do. I slid down the table leg and found an opening between the floor-boards.

'Goldenrod? It's Humphrey,' I squeaked.

'Hi, Humphrey! What are you doing out of your cage?' she squeaked back.

'I need your help,' I said. 'I'll meet you outside.'

I scampered to the door. There was a nice wide opening between the bottom and the floor and I slid through it easily. When I got out on to the veranda, I saw Goldenrod waiting in a clump of bushes.

I was so excited, I probably didn't make sense, but I told her about Og and what had happened.

'Maybe he wants to be wild,' Goldenrod said.

'Maybe,' I agreed. 'But I have to know for myself.'

Goldenrod thought for a moment. 'I'll help you, but it's a long way to the lake. Oh, wait – I know a short cut.'

Soon, I found myself following Goldenrod down the path in the moonlight. Then she veered off into thick undergrowth – almost like the jungle I'd seen in that film back in the library all those weeks ago. Longfellow School seemed a million, zillion miles away now.

I was out in the wild, like the lions and tigers and hootie owls.

It was SCARY-SCARY-SCARY. But it was also *thrilling*.

> NOTE TO SELF: Always help a friend in trouble . . . or at least try.

Moonlight Rescue

Goldenrod moved quickly through the under-growth. I was right behind her but oh, the grass and branches and tiny rocks tickled my whiskers, scraped my paws and made me itchy all over.

SKITTER-SKATTER-SKIT.

There was someone else here. Could it be the Howler?

SKITTER-SKATTER-SQUEAK.

I was pretty sure the Howler didn't squeak.

'Come on, Lucky,' Goldenrod said. 'We have to help our friend, Humphrey.'

Then I heard SQUEAK-SKITTER-SKAT.

'You can help, too, Go-Go,' she said.

Soon, there were about a dozen mice accom-panying us, Goldenrod's brothers, sisters and cousins. They scampered along through the under-growth as I desperately tried to keep up.

Then I heard HOOT-HOOT. HOOT-HOOT.

'Excuse me,' I said, gasping a bit for air. 'But did I just hear an *owl*?'

'Sure,' said Goldenrod. 'That's why we try not to go out in the open.'

'Good idea,' I agreed.

And then I saw the most wonderful sight I'd ever seen. The moonlight shimmered and glimmered across the surface of the lake. The water was silvery-purple. I guess that's why it was called Lake Lavender. It was beautiful.

Oh, but I also felt a bad feeling deep in my tummy. Maybe Og would prefer this beautiful lake to his tabletop tank. Maybe Og was happier with the frogs in Lake Lavender than he was living next door to a hamster.

Goldenrod led us to the very edge of the water, where there were tall plants and soft grasses.

'Here we are,' she squeaked. At least I think that's what she squeaked. I could barely hear her over the deafening chorus of frogs!

I never knew there were so many kinds of frogs and so many different sounds.

QUANK-QUANK-QUANK!

RUMM-RUMM-RUMM!

TUCK-A-TUCK-A-TUCK!

CHIRP-CHIRP-CHIRP!

But I didn't hear a single BOING.

'How can I find him?' I asked Goldenrod.

'Call him,' she said. 'Maybe he'll hear you.'

There was a nice flat rock nearby. I climbed up to the top, cleared my throat and squeaked with all my might.

'Og? This is your friend, Humphrey! Og? Og!'

The quanking and chirping continued. If only those big bullfrogs would stop RUMM-RUMM-RUMMING for a second.

'OG!' I shrieked. 'OG, IT'S HUMPHREY!'

Strangely enough, the chorus suddenly became quiet, quiet enough for me to hear a clear and distinct 'BOING!'

I'd know that BOING anywhere.

'Og, if you'd rather stay here at the lake where it's beautiful in the moonlight, I'll understand,' I told him. 'But if you'd like to come back and be my neighbour again, we can lead you.'

'BOING-BOING!' was the response.

'My friends know the way,' I continued. 'And the kids miss you a lot.'

'BOING-BOING-BOING!'

Did that sound a little bit closer?

'I'm here, on a rock on the shore,' I told him.

I was afraid my small hamster voice might not hold up much longer.

'BOING-BOING,' Og answered.

I waited and waited until I heard a familiar

splashing. And then I saw him: his bright green skin shining in the moonlight, his big googly eyes gleaming and that big old goofy grin. He was on shore, hopping towards me.

'Og! I missed you!' I shouted.

'BOING-BOING!' he replied, so I knew he'd missed me, too.

HOOT-HOOT. HOOT-HOOT.

'Hurry, let's get back into the grass,' Goldenrod said.

Quietly, without another squeak, Goldenrod, Lucky, Go-Go and others led Og and me skittering and hopping through the undergrowth on the long trek back to the Robins' Nest cabin.

'I can't thank you all enough,' I told my wild friends.

They squeaked 'Good luck' and scampered off, disappearing into the scrub.

Only Goldenrod lingered for a few seconds.

'You are a wonderful friend to Og,' she told me.

'*You* are a wonderful friend to *me*,' I replied. 'And Goldenrod? You'll be careful with that owl, won't you?' I asked.

'Of course,' she said. 'But Lucky can tell you more about that owl than I can. He was just a baby when an owl swooped down and picked him up.'

I gasped, 'Oh, no!'

Goldenrod nodded. 'But for some reason, he

dropped him right away. That's how he got his name – Lucky.'

I shuddered a little and she turned to leave.

'If I EVER-EVER-EVER can help you, please let me know,' I called after her.

'Thanks,' she said shyly. Then, in a flash, she was gone.

·ᵒ·

I looked over at my old pal, who seemed tired and pale. Of course – he needed water! Luckily, there was a lovely puddle at the bottom of the steps. After sitting in it for a while, he looked like his old self again.

I sat there with Og for the rest of the night. Neither of us said a thing. We didn't need to.

When it started to get light, I told Og to stay right where he was and what to do. Then I slid back under the door.

I knew from experience that there was no way to get back on the table, so I waited. When the loud-speaker played that awful wake-up song, the girls began to stir.

As soon as I saw Miranda sit up, I began to SQUEAK-SQUEAK-SQUEAK at the top of my lungs. She heard me and jumped out of bed.

'Humphrey! You're out of your cage!' she said, dashing towards me.

I was way ahead of her. I raced to the door and slid under.

'Come back!' Miranda ran after me and opened the door.

I hurried down to Og's puddle. He was still there, thank goodness.

Miranda stopped short and stared. 'Og! That's Og!' she screamed.

The other Robins were outside now, screaming with happiness. Gail picked up my cage first and then Og.

'I'll go and tell Ms Mac.' Miranda took off running, still in her PJs!

🐾

'Tell me again,' Ms Mac said, after Og was back in his tank and I was back in my cage.

So Miranda told her the story again.

'I'm afraid with all the fuss about Og, one of you forgot to lock Humphrey's cage,' she said.

'Sorry,' the Robins said in unison.

I felt a little guilty, because they didn't have anything to be sorry about.

Ms Mac pointed a finger in my direction. 'And you, Humphrey, were naughty to get out of your cage.'

Naughty, yes. But it was well worth it to have my friend back.

'I guess somehow Og found his way back, though I can't imagine how,' Ms Mac continued. 'But here he is and that's all that counts.'

I couldn't have agreed more.

ö

Og and I put in a special appearance in the dining hall at breakfast that morning to loud cheers and applause.

Noah got up and apologised to Og and to the other campers. I could tell he was REALLY-REALLY-REALLY sorry.

'I thought I knew a lot about animals,' he said. 'I thought that frogs belonged with frogs,' he said. 'But now I know some frogs belong with people.'

Then Hap prepared everyone for the final day of competitions.

'Play hard, play fair, have fun,' he said. 'And now, let the games begin!'

I glanced over at Sayeh. This was the moment she'd been dreading.

Surprise – she had a big smile on her face! Humans are hard to figure out. But that's what makes them so interesting.

> NOTE TO SELF: You can know a lot.
> But nobody knows everything.

19

The Winners After Dinner

'Wait, Garth!' Sam was standing right in front of my cage.

Garth hurried over 'What's the matter? Your pitching arm's okay, isn't it?'

At that moment, Sam was using his pitching arm to scratch his other arm. And then his neck. And then his leg.

'I'm itching like crazy,' he said. 'I can hardly stand it.'

Garth's jaw dropped open as he stared at Super Sam, who could now be called Scratching Sam. His skin was red and bumpy and blistery, and just watching Sam scratch made me itch.

A small crowd gathered around Sam.

'I'll get the nurse,' Richie said, and he took off running.

Nurse Rose took one look at Sam. 'Poison ivy,' she said. 'Come with me.'

Still scratching and looking completely miserable, Sam followed her to the infirmary, where the sick kids stayed.

'We're toast!' Garth told Ty. 'The Bobwhites are toast!'

• • •

I spent my day with Og (and Lovey and Jake) in the Nature Centre, where kids came and went all day to take the Nature Test. Katie stayed in the Centre, while Ms Mac was out on the trail, timing the groups for the trail-reading event.

It wasn't an easy day.

Part of me wished I could be there, out of my cage, watching the events and seeing how my friends were doing.

But the other part of me remembered that it was dangerous for a small creature to be out in the big woods. In fact, I worried about Goldenrod and her friends every night.

Still, I was anxious to know what was going on. I kept my eyes and ears open for any little titbits to tell me how the competitions were going.

The first thing I heard was from Garth, when he came in to take the quiz. He looked miserable.

• 466 •

'Nurse Rose gave Sam some lotion, but she says he can't swim,' Garth told me. 'He can try canoeing or softball, but I don't see how he can hit a home run when he's scratching all the time. The other teams say he shouldn't play volleyball because they don't want to touch the ball after he does.' Garth sighed. 'I don't think he can do anything but scratch.'

'I'm SORRY-SORRY-SORRY,' I told him, knowing that he and the Bobwhites had all counted on Sam to win for them. Maybe Sam's cabin mates should have put in a little more effort, but I was too polite to say so, especially when Garth was upset.

Sayeh was a lot more chipper than Garth when she stopped by after taking the nature quiz.

'Oh, Humphrey,' she said. 'No one can tie knots like Abby, though Simon did a good job. Marissa's ahead in archery. We're going trail-reading now. But even if the Chickadees don't win, we'll still have a great time tomorrow night.'

I was GLAD-GLAD-GLAD she felt that way!

The next night was when the winning group would sleep over in Haunted Hollow. But how would the Chickadees have a great time if they didn't get to go?

Sayeh walked away, but quickly returned.

'Oh, I forgot,' she said. 'Miranda was awesome

in volleyball, so the Robins are still in the game. I'm so happy for her.'

I was happy for Miranda *and* Sayeh.

Brad took the nature quiz and I could tell he worked really hard at it. He practically chewed right through his pencil, which would be easy for a hamster, but not so easy for a human. When the quiz was over, he called for Gail to wait.

'A.J. hit a home run,' he said. 'Even if we don't win, it will be close.'

'I'm sure you did well on the nature quiz,' Gail said. 'And my goofy brother was pretty good at tying knots. Who knew?'

'Did you hear that hammering noise?' he asked.

Then they wandered off, talking about woodpeckers, which are interesting birds but they make way too much noise for the sensitive ears of a small furry creature like me!

'Og, have you been keeping track?' I asked. 'Because I've been listening all day and I can't tell who's going to win. Can you?'

Og just sat there. I guess he was still trying to figure it out, too.

••

When they are nervous, humans bite their fingernails or pace the floor. When I am nervous, I hop on my wheel. (By the way, I don't think biting your fingers or paws is a good idea.)

So I gave my old wheel a good spin later in the day, when we were back in the rec room. The counsellors had gathered there with clipboards and all kinds of papers. They were going to decide who would spend the night in Haunted Hollow – and they were deciding it right in front of me.

'No doubt about it. The Bobwhites would have won if Sam didn't have poison ivy,' Aldo said, staring at his clipboard.

'I feel for them,' Hap Holloway agreed. 'It was a bad piece of luck.'

'Still, the others had been slacking off,' Mrs Wright observed. 'I think they relied too much on Sam. And their scores just don't add up.'

The others agreed with Mrs Wright and, amazingly, so did I! Really, she wasn't so bad, if she'd just lose that whistle!

Katie rummaged through her papers and chuckled. 'I've never seen anyone tie knots like Abby. She racked up points for the Chickadees on that one. And on trail-reading. And Marissa won archery.'

Ms Mac nodded. 'But the Robins had a lot of heart. Miranda and Gail came second in canoeing. And Lindsey was a big surprise with her volleyball serves.'

Aldo studied his clipboard some more. 'A.J. and Simon took the top spots in swimming. And Brad won the canoeing and scored very close to Sayeh on the nature quiz. I think the Blue Jays' scores are the highest.'

Hap Holloway was busily adding up scores. 'Yep,' he said. 'It's the Blue Jays.'

Katie shook her head. 'I guess there'll be a lot of disappointed kids, especially when they don't get to go to Haunted Hollow.'

'Not necessarily,' Hap said. 'No, I don't think they'll be disappointed tomorrow night, thanks to Sayeh.'

I had no idea what Hap was talking about.

I was worried about my friends being disappointed when Aldo brought Og and me into the dining hall that night so we could hear the results.

First, Hap congratulated everyone on being great campers.

Then he announced the rankings.

'The Blue Jays came in first,' he said.

He couldn't say anything else for a while, because the Blue Jays were chanting, 'Blue Jays rule!' over and over.

When the noise settled down, he announced that the Chickadees were number two, followed by the Robins and the Bobwhites.

Cheering followed that, just not as much.

'I have to single out one camper as being one of the most outstanding athletes I've ever seen at this camp,' Hap continued. 'That's Sam Gorman. Today's scores may have been quite different if it weren't for that poison ivy. So let's give Sam a big Happy Hollow cheer.'

Everybody cheered – even Og and me. Sam stood up and waved, but I still felt itchy just looking at him.

And wonder of wonders, afterwards the campers all mingled and were friendly again. A few looked disappointed, but Abby, Miranda and Sayeh chatted away as if nothing had ever happened. And I was happy to see that Brad and Richie were hanging out with Noah.

Humans are pretty amazing. I was sorry Goldenrod didn't know how VERY-VERY-VERY nice they can be.

·ö·

That night, I slept in the cabin shared by Ms Mac, Katie and Mrs Wright. (Believe it or not, she took off her whistle before she went to bed – but she placed it right under her pillow.)

Still, it was a quiet night and everyone slept well.

Everyone except me.

Because all I could think of was what would happen the next night.

The night the Blue Jays got to go to Haunted Hollow.

NOTE TO SELF: Winning is good, but not winning isn't as bad as most humans imagine.

20

Happy Day, Haunted Night

The next day, it was difficult for the Blue Jays to think of anything except their night with the Howler.

Even if they forgot about it for a few minutes, the other campers would come up to them and go, 'Owoooo! Owoooo!'

In fact, they did it so often, I think the Blue Jays were beginning to have second thoughts about spending the night in Haunted Hollow.

In the Nature Centre, however, there was a lot going on. During the first session of the morning, Katie and Ms Mac brought in a stranger – a very nice stranger as it turned out. He was Dr Singleton, the vet from the wildlife refuge who had helped Katie with Lovey's wing when she was first rescued.

'Dr Singleton's here to see if Lovey's healed enough to be released,' Ms Mac explained.

The vet was a big, tall man with a full black beard. But he was as gentle as he was big and was a real expert on birds.

While the kids in the first session watched, he examined Lovey carefully.

'She looks completely healed,' he said. 'And I imagine she's getting a little tired of her crate.'

Her crate was rather plain compared to my cage. She didn't have any fun things to play with, like I do.

'I think we could try her out today,' he said.

Katie looked at her watch. 'It's almost time for a break between sessions. I'll make an announcement.'

Dr Singleton stayed and answered questions while she went down to the office.

Then Ms Mac introduced him to Og and me.

'You're a fine specimen,' he said to me. 'I don't think you need my help at all.'

I hopped on my wheel to show him he was right.

'Ah, *Rana clamitans*,' he said to Og.

'No, his name is Og!' I squeaked, but he didn't understand me.

'I guess you kids are used to his interesting twang,' he said.

After living next to Og for months, I was very used to it.

Then Dr Singleton turned his attention to Jake

the snake. 'How did you end up in a tank?' he asked Jake.

Jake stuck his tongue out, as usual. How rude!

Then we heard Katie on the LOUD-LOUD-LOUDSPEAKER.

'Attention, campers,' her voice boomed. 'We are going to try to release Lovey into the wild after this session. Anyone who wants to participate, come directly to the Nature Centre.'

Within minutes, there was a rush, a dash, no – a *stampede* – to the Nature Centre as every single camper showed up. Ms Mac made them form a half-circle in front of the building.

Then she asked Sayeh, Brad and Noah to be her assistants. (They had scored the highest marks in the quiz.)

Miranda picked up my cage so I could watch – what a thoughtful girl!

Brad and Noah carried out Lovey Dovey's crate. Her head poked up out of the top as she watched everyone and everything.

Then Dr Singleton carefully lifted Lovey out of the crate and showed Sayeh how to hold her.

Sayeh held Lovey just the right way and looked completely confident.

'First, put her down on the veranda and let her try her wings,' the vet told her.

When Dovey touched the ground, the first thing she did was to spread her wings. I couldn't even tell which one had been injured.

Then she flapped her wings and hopped, as if ready for take-off.

The kids in the crowd stayed pretty quiet, as they'd been instructed, but they couldn't help 'oohing' and 'ahhing' a little. Neither could I.

'That's great,' Dr. Singleton said. 'That hopping means she's ready to fly. But we need a big open space. Pick her up again, Sayeh, if you can.'

Then he had her take Lovey up the hill to the spot from where I'd viewed the two hollows. It was a high open meadow surrounded by trees. The other campers – and Miranda carrying my cage – followed quietly.

It was time for Sayeh to put Lovey on the ground and see if she flew. But at the last minute, Sayeh didn't do it.

Instead, she turned to Noah and handed Lovey over. 'Here, Noah, I think you should do this,' she said.

That was just about the nicest thing I'd ever seen a human do.

I held my breath as Noah set her on the ground. And then, with no further encouragement, she flapped her wings and took off, flying up to a very high treetop in the distance.

The crowd couldn't stay quiet any longer. They let out a cheer.

Dr Singleton looked as pleased as Katie and Ms Mac.

'She knew just what to do,' he said. 'You all did a great job with her. Keep an eye out for her for a while, but I don't think there'll be a problem.'

Just then, Lovey flew away from the tree and circled right over the Nature Centre. We watched her until she flew out of sight.

'Any questions?' Katie asked while we were still in the meadow.

Noah slowly raised his hand. 'I was just wondering . . . what about the snake?'

Dr Singleton nodded. 'I was thinking about him, too. He looked a little confined to me. How would you feel about releasing him?'

Katie and Ms Mac looked at the campers.

'Should we take a vote?' Ms Mac asked.

They hardly needed a vote at all. Just about everybody thought Jake would be happier outside his tank.

This time, Brad was the one who got to let him out. He tipped the tank on its side and Jake slithered away and disappeared into the grass.

Again, the crowd cheered.

'Boy,' I heard Brad say. 'Nothing like this ever happened at my old camp.'

It was a thrilling sight, seeing Lovey and Jake go free. I only hoped I wouldn't be next!

But I had nothing to fear. The session was over and I was returned to the Nature Centre. It was a little lonely there without Lovey and I even missed Jake (a bit). But at least I had my friend *Rana clamitans* to keep me company. Who would have guessed that a little frog had such a fancy name!

ᐟᵒ̇

All the excitement at the Nature Centre had taken my mind off Haunted Hollow – at least for a little while.

In fact, I was so relaxed, I settled in for a long doze in the rec room.

Ms Mac came in to check on Og and me. She told me that she was taking all the campers except the Blue Jays to the nearest town to watch a film. 'See you later,' she said. Then she winked at me. I had no idea why.

I managed to doze off again, but I was awakened abruptly when I heard pounding footsteps racing towards me.

'Humphrey Dumpty!' A.J. shouted excitedly. 'You're coming with us to Haunted Hollow!'

'Who, me?' I was astounded.

'Yep, Hap Holloway said it was okay as long as we make sure your cage is locked at all times and keep you in our tent,' he explained. 'We didn't want you to miss out.'

There are some things I wouldn't mind missing out on and the Howler was one of them. But A.J. was already holding my cage and hurrying back to the dining hall.

'It's been nice knowing you, Og!' I called to my friend. There was not even time to say goodbye.

·ö·

It was dark outside. Instead of hiking in the dark, Hap drove us in a small bus what seemed like a LONG-LONG-LONG way from Camp Happy Hollow. Even though Haunted Hollow was next to our camp, to get there we had to drive on a road that wound round and round a hill.

'Blue Jays,' he said as he drove. 'You are about to join a small but special group of campers. Few have earned the right to go to Haunted Hollow. But none will ever forget . . . the Howler!'

He opened his mouth wide and let out the most spine-tingling 'Owoooo!' I'd heard yet. I dived under my bedding, just in case Hap really *was* the Howler.

At last, the bus stopped and Hap let us out. It was still quite a hike to the camping ground, where Aldo was waiting. Several tents had been set up and a fire was blazing in a big stone pit. The flames cast orange and yellow shadows, like huge fingers, on the nearby trees.

'Welcome to Haunted Hollow,' Aldo said. Somehow, he didn't seem as jolly and carefree as usual. 'Take a seat.'

The Blue Jays sat on big rocks around the campfire. A.J. put my cage next to his feet and I could feel the heat from the fire. As far as I was concerned, I was a little too close for comfort. And even though my friends had waited a long time for this night, they were suddenly unusually quiet.

When I glanced over at the dense undergrowth nearby, I thought I saw the friendly eyes of Goldenrod and her friends watching these strange humans. I hoped they were the *only* wild creatures hanging around.

Hap stood near the fire and addressed the campers. Like Aldo, he was acting very serious.

'Boys, you are about to share in the secret of Haunted Hollow,' he began. 'Twenty years ago, I bought this camp. The man I bought it from didn't want to sell it, but he ran out of money and had no choice.'

The strange shadows made Hap's face and hair even redder than usual.

'He was a crazy kind of fellow, with white hair to his shoulders and a white beard to his waist. On the day he signed the papers to hand the land over to me, he said, "It will never truly be yours, Holloway. For I will haunt this land as long as I live . . . and even after!"'

The boys gasped and I accidentally let out an 'Eeek!'

'I tore down his small cabin, which was on this spot. But once a year, the best campers are chosen to come here to show him that even if the place is haunted, *we are not afraid*,' he continued.

'My cousin saw him last year,' Richie said, his eyes wide.

Hap nodded. 'So far, the Howler has shown up every year. But this year, who knows? So I want you all to shout with me, "We are not afraid! We are not afraid!"'

The Blue Jays didn't exactly shout at first but they joined in.

'We are not afraid! We are not afraid!'

I joined in too, as the voices got louder and louder.

'We are not afraid! We are not afraid!'

Then they got more confident . . . and the volume increased.

'*We are not afraid! We are not afraid!*'

And then it happened. A howl so loud, so hideous, so unsqueakably scary, I think my heart stopped beating.

'OWOOOO! OWOOO!'

No one human could possibly make a noise that loud.

The noise grew closer and there was a rustling in the grass.

'OWOOOO! OWOOO!'

The Blue Jays all jumped up, screaming, and started running around in circles.

'OWOOOO! OWOOO!'

There I was, alone on the ground, with the Howler approaching. I closed my eyes.

Then *I felt my cage move*! It had grabbed me!

'Don't worry, Humphrey. I've got you. You're safe,' a familiar voice assured me.

It was Aldo.

'OWOOOO! OWOOO!' It was so close now, I thought I heard it breathing. 'OWOOOO-OWOOOO . . . *WE FOOLED YOU!*'

Then there were peals of laughter as out from behind the trees and the bushes came all the other campers: Sayeh, Miranda, Garth, Abby, even itchy Sam! They were pointing and laughing as the Blue Jays stood staring in total confusion.

'What are you doing here?' A.J. said when he saw his brother, Ty, in the crowd.

Hap was laughing harder than anyone. 'You want to tell them, Sayeh?' he asked.

Sayeh smiled, but shook her head. 'You do it, please.'

Hap gathered the whole group around the campfire.

'One of the counsellors usually comes out here and howls,' he explained. 'But when Sayeh explained that she didn't like the idea of so many campers being left out, we cooked up this idea. We figured this was a way for everyone to be part of the legend of the Howler and to have a little fun. What do you think?'

'I was scared to death,' Simon said. He looked a little pale.

'I thought I *had* died of fright,' Brad added. 'But then I saw you guys – pretty funny. You fooled us all right.'

'Listen up, folks, this is our secret,' Hap explained. 'What happened here tonight doesn't get out. We don't want to ruin the surprise for next year's campers, okay?'

Everyone agreed.

I was glad to see that the Blue Jays were good sports about the trick, and the evening continued with lots of songs and toasted marshmallows (which are a little too messy for hamsters), and Aldo even entertained us by balancing a broom on one finger for a LONG-LONG-LONG time – my favourite trick!

When it was bedtime, the Blue Jays went to their tents but the other campers returned to Camp Happy Hollow – and I went with them.

Og and I both slept in Ms Mac's cabin that night and, even though I'm nocturnal, I slept the whole night through!

NOTE TO SELF: I guess it's okay to fib a little (about something like a Howler) as long as it's for FUN!

21

The End and the Beginning

The next day was blissful and relaxing. I missed Lovey (and maybe even Jake) in the Nature Centre, but when my friends returned from their nature hike, they were very excited because they'd seen Lovey in a tree!

I was quite happy and content and managed to doze all through dinner that night.

Right after dinner, the counsellors came into the rec room and woke me up with all their chatter. They behaved in a very peculiar way that night!

First of all, they all put on strange costumes: crazy wigs, false noses, funny hats – they looked SILLY-SILLY-SILLY. Mrs Wright seemed completely ridiculous, wearing a pink and blue wig and a clown suit! (She kept her whistle, though.)

Nurse Rose was dressed like a little girl with a lollipop.

Ms Mac and Counsellor Katie were dressed like old ladies – which they were not!

They laughed and joked and generally acted more like kids than counsellors.

Aldo – wearing an out-of-control white wig, fake nose, huge glasses and a white coat like the ones doctors wear – carried Og and me into the dining hall.

'You guys won't want to miss this,' he said.

The campers roared with laughter when they saw the ridiculous-looking counsellors. And they went wild when Hap Holloway came out dressed like the Howler, wearing ragged clothes with a white beard hanging to his waist and long white hair that reached his shoulders.

'It's time for the Counsellor's Choice Awards,' Hap announced.

Then, one by one, they presented the goofiest awards you ever heard of.

Gail, who still loved to giggle, was named the Funniest Camper and A.J. was the Loudest Camper.

'THANKS!' he bellowed when he came on stage to accept his prize: a whoopee cushion which makes very rude noises.

Miranda received the prize for Most Likely to Become a Counsellor. (I'd like to go to her camp some day.)

Sayeh had the Best Smile and Kayla was the Best Sleeper. Abby got a prize for 'Knottiest' Camper and everybody cheered.

Naturally, Sam got an award for Itchiest Camper.

Noah got the Nature Lover's award.

Brad was very proud to be Most Improved Camper (which was true) and Simon was happy to be named the Loudest Burper (an award he deserved)!

The awards went on and on until I think everybody had received something.

Then Hap said there was just one award left: Most Popular. And this year the counsellors couldn't decide, so it was a tie.

I was waiting to hear who the lucky campers were, when Ms Mac picked up my cage and Katie picked up Og's tank and they carried us to the stage.

'The winners are Humphrey . . . and Og!' Hap announced.

We received special treats (the best kind – the kind you can eat) and again the crowd went wild.

The noise got so out of control, Mrs Wright had to use her whistle to quieten things down again.

Suddenly, Hap seemed a lot more serious.

'I have to say, this has been one of the best sessions ever at Camp Happy Hollow,' he said. 'I have learned a lot from all of you. And now that it's about to end, I just hope you'll all be back again next year!'

Camp was about to end? Just the way school had?

I wasn't just surprised. I wasn't just sad. I was SICK-SICK-SICK. It was bad enough that school had ended and I wasn't in Room 26 any more. Now camp was ending, too. Isn't there anything a hamster can count on to last?

When they all sang the Camp Happy Hollow song, I felt so miserable, I just crawled into my sleeping hut, even though I knew I'd never sleep.

•ö•

I spent that night with the Blue Jays, since they had won the competition for Best All-Round Team.

They exchanged addresses and phone numbers and emails and were a little quieter than on the other nights I'd stayed there.

Just before lights out, A.J. came over to my cage. 'Humphrey Dumpty, don't worry. I'm sure we'll see each other again.'

I crossed my paws and hoped so. I hoped so all night long.

•ö•

In the morning, Og and I watched from the rec room window as a line of cars drove up to the camp. Car doors opened and out came mums and dads and little brothers and sisters. Parents and campers carried suitcases, boxes, backpacks and duffel bags from the cabins to the cars.

Some of my friends came in to say goodbye: Miranda and Abby, Ty and A.J. and, surprisingly, even Brad. Gail came in by herself and she had gifts for Og and me.

'I made these friendship bracelets in Arts and Crafts,' she said, holding up two colourful woven bands. 'I was going to give one to mum and one to Heidi, but I changed my mind. I'll make new ones for them. I want you to have these.'

'THANKS-THANKS-THANKS!' I said, and Og splashed happily.

'I made a lot of new friends here,' Gail said as she taped one bracelet to the front of Og's tank and wove the other one in and out of the bars of my cage. 'But you'll always be my special friends.' As she turned to leave she told us, 'I'll tell Heidi hello from you!' then she hurried back outside.

After much hugging and many farewells, doors slammed and the cars pulled away, leaving the camp almost unbearably quiet.

'Was it just a dream, Og?' I asked my neighbour, who was floating lazily in the watery part of his tank. 'It went so fast.'

He didn't answer. He didn't have to. A camp

alive with fun-loving kids wasn't a dream, but now it was a memory.

Later, Ms Mac came in to check on us.

'Why are you two looking so gloomy?' she asked. 'Your work isn't finished yet! Tomorrow a new group of campers arrives for the *next* session of camp.'

'What?' I squeaked.

'BOING-BOING!' Og twanged.

Ms Mac laughed. 'Summer's not over yet,' she said. 'And neither is camp.'

That was the BEST-BEST-BEST news I'd heard since the end of school!

The counsellors had a quiet dinner in the dining hall. When Og and I were alone again, I looked out at the moonlit camp. If I went to the very top of my cage, I could even see a silvery sliver of Lake Lavender.

'You know what, Og?' I said. 'Camp is great because we get to help our friends and have lots of fun.'

He splashed gently in response.

'But the best part is, we get to be together,' I continued.

Og leaped out of the water and, goodness, I thought he'd pop the top of his tank!

'BOING-BOING-BOING-BOING!'

We stayed alone in the rec room that night but I really couldn't sleep, because the words of the camp song kept running through my head. And as I sang them softly to myself, I changed the words just a little.

Happy Hollow – a place close to my heart.
Happy Hollow – I loved it from the start.
Every day I wake up with so much to do,
Having fun with Og and that Bunny Foo Foo.
I'll remember for ever my new friend Golden-
*   rod,*
Lovey, too, and Jake, but he is rather odd.
Though I don't know where I'll be in days that
*   follow,*
I'll remember happy days at Happy Hollow.

NOTE TO SELF: Good things, unfortunately, end. But then you have good memories for ever and ever!

Humphrey's Top Ten Things to Pack for Camp

ö

1 Ear plugs – just in case somebody has a whistle.

2 Stickers – because you never know when you'll need one or more.

3 A good book, some cards or a game for a rainy day.

4 A cage – for protection – but preferably a cage with a lock-that-doesn't-lock so you can get out.

5 Lotion – for poison ivy (which I HOPE-HOPE-HOPE hamsters don't get).

6 An interest in learning new things, like horse riding, swimming and canoeing.

7 A good cook – like Maria – who is generous with treats.

8 Rope for tying knots, because it looks like fun.

9 A spirit of adventure – you'll need it.

10 A friendly attitude – you'll make new friends, which is what camp is all about!

Bonus item: bongo drums if your camp allows them.

Turn the page for puzzles and games from everybody's favourite hamster: ME!!

Pet Shop Wordsnake

Thank goodness there weren't any snakes at Pet-O-Rama, but here's a very different kind of snake – a wordsnake. (Believe me, this kind is much easier to deal with!)

Take a pencil (you might need to rub out) and begin at **START**. Find the first word **HAMSTER** and trace a continuous line through all the words that follow, in the same order as the list below. The line will snake up and down, backwards and forwards, but *never* diagonally.

HAMSTER   PUPPY

GERBIL   KITTEN

MOUSE   PARROT

GUINEA PIG   RABBIT

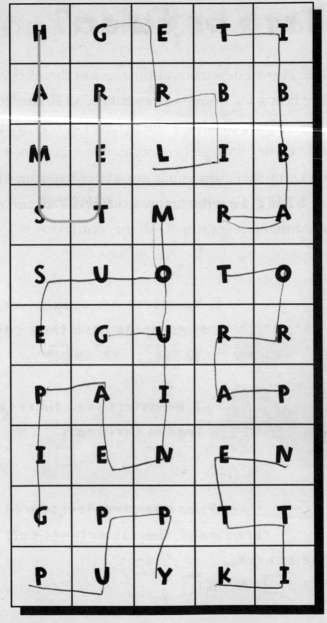

H	G	E	T	I
A	R	R	B	B
M	E	L	I	B
S	T	M	R	A
S	U	O	T	O
E	G	U	R	R
P	A	I	A	P
I	E	N	E	N
G	P	P	T	T
P	U	Y	K	I

True or False?

I've learned a lot about humans and their behaviour by visiting the homes of my friends in Room 26. And they've learned a lot about me and how I live. In fact, I'd say they have all become hamster experts! How much do you think you know about hamsters? Find out by reading the ten sentences below and deciding if they are true or false.

1. **Hamsters are usually very good at escaping from their cages.**
   TRUE ☐   FALSE ☐

2. **Hamsters sometimes store food in their ears.**
   TRUE ☐   FALSE ☐

3. **When hamsters feel scared or threatened, they sometimes puff up their cheeks.**
   TRUE ☐   FALSE ☐

4. Hamsters are not very good at climbing.
TRUE ☐ FALSE ☐

5. Hamsters have long tails.
TRUE ☐ FALSE ☐

6. Other animals such as cats and dogs could harm a hamster.
TRUE ☐ FALSE ☐

7. The dwarf hamster is the smallest type of hamster.
TRUE ☐ FALSE ☐

8. In the wild, hamsters usually live in trees.
TRUE ☐ FALSE ☐

9. Hamsters are able to carry up to half their body weight in their cheek pouches.
TRUE ☐ FALSE ☐

10. The hamster gets its name from a German word for storing food: 'hamstern'.
TRUE ☐ FALSE ☐

For the answers, and for more
puzzles, check out my book of
Fun-Fun-Fun!

Betty G. Birney   ff

Dear Friends,

When I first arrived at Longfellow School, I was unsqueakably happy! After all, the life of a classroom pet is FUN-FUN-FUN!

However, going home each weekend with a different student turned out to be quite a challenge, because humans need a lot of help! Along the way, I learned to shoot rubber bands at a nosy dog, teach a shy girl to squeak up for herself, help the caretaker find true love and star in the Halloween party. I really had my paws full . . . especially since the teacher, Mrs. Brisbane, was definitely out to get me! (It makes my whiskers quiver just to think about it!)

Your friend always,

Humphrey

Out Now!

Friendship According to Humphrey

Betty G. Birney ff

Dear Friends,

I was green with envy when Og the Frog moved
into Room 26. He had no fur at all and wasn't a
bit friendly. My fellow students were all having
problems with their friends, too. It took a clever
hamster (me) to set things straight and a lumpy
green frog to teach me the true meaning of
friendship.

Your friend to the end,

Humphrey

Out Now!

Betty G. Birney

Dear Friends,

Trouble was brewing all over Room 26. I was GLAD-GLAD-GLAD that my friends named their model town after me. But I was SAD-SAD-SAD that Golden-Miranda was in big trouble and it was all my fault! I just had to help her, even if it meant I'd be locked up forever.

Your funny, furry friend,

Humphrey

Out Now!

What's more fun than a computer mouse? A computer hamster — that's me! You can have FUN-FUN-FUN with me online at my website:

www.funwithhumphrey.com